Gillian White, a former journalist who comes from Liverpool, lives in Totnes, Devon, with her journalist husband and their two dogs. Their four grown-up children and two grandsons live near by. Three of her novels, *Rich Deceiver*, *The Beggar Bride* and *Mothertime*, have been successfully adapted for BBC television. Her latest novels, *The Sleeper*, *Unhallowed Ground* and *Veil of Darkness*, are available in Corgi, and *The Sleeper* is also to be a major drama production for BBC television. Her new novel, *Night Visitor*, is now available from Bantam Press.

'Gillian White is a skilled manipulator of the normal and ordinary into a chilling, nightmarish experience. Knowing that, it's clear that the heroine of *Unhallowed Ground* is not going to find an idyllic escape from her problems in her newly-inherited cottage in the depths of Dartmoor. The gradual increase in tension is cleverly handled, leading to an atmosphere of real menace and a shocking climax'
Sunday Telegraph

Veil of Darkness

'Compelling novel of suspense'
Good Housekeeping

'Simply spine-tingling'
Woman & Home

The Witch's Cradle

'Ten out of ten for topicality . . . strong narrative keeps the pages turning to the end where the reader is left guiltily wondering about TV intrusion and the viewer's complicity in it'
Home and Country

'This fast-paced tale explores the lengths to which people go to be loved, as well as the ruthlessness of the media when transforming real life into drama'
Good Housekeeping

'A gripping read which will make you think twice about the influence and motives of TV media'
Shine

Also by Gillian White

RICH DECEIVER
THE PLAGUE STONE
THE CROW BIDDY
NASTY HABITS
MOTHERTIME
GRANDFATHER'S FOOTSTEPS
DOG BOY
THE BEGGAR BRIDE
CHAIN REACTION
THE SLEEPER
UNHALLOWED GROUND
VEIL OF DARKNESS
NIGHT VISITOR

THE WITCH'S CRADLE

Gillian White

CORGI BOOKS

THE WITCH'S CRADLE
A CORGI BOOK : 0 552 14765 6

Originally published in Great Britain by Bantam Press,
a division of Transworld Publishers

PRINTING HISTORY
Bantam Press edition published 2000
Corgi edition published 2001

1 3 5 7 9 10 8 6 4 2

Set in 11/12 pt Times by
Hewer Text Ltd, Edinburgh.

Corgi Books are published by Transworld Publishers,
61–63 Uxbridge Road, London W5 5SA,
a division of The Random House Group Ltd,
in Australia by Random House Australia (Pty) Ltd,
20 Alfred Street, Milsons Point, Sydney, NSW 2061, Australia,
in New Zealand by Random House New Zealand Ltd,
18 Poland Road, Glenfield, Auckland 10, New Zealand
and in South Africa by Random House (Pty) Ltd,
Endulini, 5a Jubilee Road, Parktown 2193, South Africa.

Printed and bound in Great Britain by
Cox & Wyman Ltd, Reading, Berkshire.

*For Linda Evans, my editor,
with lots and lots of love.*

ONE

The collective hairs of the people of Britain stood up as one when the Higgins kids went missing.

One vast primordial horn.

It was chilling.

Skins crawled all the way from John O'Groats to Land's End, and the Post Office employed extra staff to deal with the load of sympathy mail. The phone lines of police stations throughout the land were jammed by 'sightings' and helpful 'information' and, as Detective Chief Inspector Jonathan Rowe observed dourly to his team, 'What else can anyone expect . . . it's like you're dealing with the royals. Everyone imagines they know them, poor things.'

Dammit, not just one little kid, but all three.

A publicity stunt, everyone reckoned, by some fanatical faction.

The stars of a documentary series that finished in the spring, the troubled Higginses had, in twelve episodes, typified penury at its most dire.

Therefore, and obviously, there would be no point at all in the abductors demanding a ransom from them, because the whole reason for choosing the Higginses for the series was that they were desperate, on their uppers, postage-stamp close to down and out.

But nice with it.

Attractively poor, not fecklessly.

A Cathy-Come-Home sort of fondness had briefly warmed the nation. But these were real people, not actors, as Griffin Productions were so frequently and distractedly forced to point out (a) when they returned kind donations or directed them to suitable charities like Shelter or Save The Children, and (b) when they took out injunctions to ban the press from outside the Higginses' grim fifth-floor flat, and (c) when the Higginses themselves began to demand artistes' wages.

Who would have dreamed that this would happen?

With a phlegmy intake of national breath the country waited for news. With puce noses and man-sized Kleenex, Britain's mothers watched Cheryl and Barry Higgins' desperate appeal on TV on a tidal wave of feeling that foamed with a spindrift of sadness and pity.

'Don't hurt them, *please* don't hurt them, they are very little . . .' Cheryl, pale and in sorrow, managed these three heart-rending phrases before collapsing on Barry's left shoulder. *Budweiser* his T-shirt said and he, unemployed and unshaven and very, very young, attempted to carry on bravely like a man. 'We'll do anything, *anything*, we're not after vengeance, you have your reasons whoever you are. All we want are our kids back safe.'

Cheryl Higgins had been at the clinic at the time of the baby snatch, two months after episode twelve of

10

The Dark End went on air. She had a ramshackle push-along box on wheels, constructed by Barry with odds and ends he had dug out of various skips. To make the box-pram comfortable it was lined with scraps of old blanket and a faded hammock cushion. It would not have passed a safety test conducted by any responsible body. There were no straps, no springs and nothing to protect the kids from the rain.

She was at the clinic with Cara, her third and most contentious child who, in half-inch-long embryonic form, had divided the nation on the righteousness of her existence and helped to turn opinion against them, bearing in mind the couple's precarious financial straits. Cara had a chest infection, which was why they were there, said Cheryl, attending a paediatric session set up primarily to clear GPs' waiting rooms of the usual clutter of sad-eyed moaners and cheerily chatting neurotics.

The trouble was that after the incident, nobody could actually remember seeing Cheryl arrive at the clinic in the first place. So that was fishy for a start.

The clinic was a square of unambitious modern brick. It dealt with post- and antenatal appointments, small, non-life-threatening emergencies and housed a chiropody practice and an ophthalmic surgery. Upstairs was a small geriatric ward funded entirely by charity, which existed to give local carers well-needed respite.

Suffering from cystitis again, Cheryl paid a hasty visit to the lavatory before her appointment with the nurse.

She described how the three kids, all under three,

11

were parked outside the door, the pram contraption being far too cumbersome to fit inside the ladies'.

When Cheryl came out they were gone.

She set up an immediate keening, and a kind of wringing of hands, the sort associated with black-clad crones at riverside funeral pyres in the East. This immediate reaction was sensible and activated a quick response from those in her close vicinity: two ambulance men outside, one high-heeled receptionist, three mothers with toddlers in tow and, finally, the police.

The immediate conclusion was that the abductors could not have gone very far, not with such a primitive and eye-catching mode of child conveyance. They must have been seen by many.

It could have been a joke.

Maybe some kids had been pratting about and fancied the box on wheels. It would have made an excellent go-cart. Police with loudspeakers toured the area within one hour of the disappearance, imploring witnesses to come forward, issuing descriptions, assuring any likely suspects that there would be no punishing consequences.

'Just bring the children back.'

But nothing.

Time passed.

Still nothing.

It was as if the three had gone up in a genie's puff of purple smoke.

Griffin Productions copped the blame. One way or another, that invasive documentary, which had turned the Higgins family into household names, had to lie at the heart of this dastardly crime.

12

The shareholders were beside themselves.

'Using ordinary folk for their own greedy purposes! This sort of thing's gone far enough,' exclaimed one Scouse radio listener, deranged with self-righteous Liverpool anger.

'Innocent and naive! If they'd had more advice, they'd never have agreed to let that damn film crew into their house, poking their noses into their business. And what for? They never got a penny is what I heard.'

'Patronizing bastards.'

It was suddenly as if fifteen million people had somehow been forced to tune in every week, much against their own better judgement. After a shaky start, *The Dark End of the Street* had, quite unexpectedly, turned into a broadcasting phenomenon. At one point the viewing figures overtook the soaps, and the ambitious creator of the series, Alan Beam, had seen his credibility and his career rocket overnight to unprecedented heights.

Families that had auditioned and failed came out in furious condemnation of Griffin, and made reasonable sums from tabloid features.

'This could have been us,' said the Carter family from Skegness, describing how they were forced to put up with cameras for a week, even in their bathroom. 'And then they just sodded off, if you please. We were so much cattle fodder.'

'Thank God we were spared,' came from the Duffys of York, who had pestered the director for months after their rejection, and still sent the odd threatening letter.

'Fame – you can keep it,' said the Cloons from Maidenhead. 'We'd rather keep our kids, thank you

13

very much.' In fact their kids were in care by then, on the At Risk register.

There were several obvious reasons why the Higginses were chosen above all others. For a start, they were the most charismatic, camera-friendly and, most importantly, they were triers. Their hapless struggles to wrench themselves free from the tangling chains of poverty were marvellous to behold. Also, to be honest, their dire circumstances were even more ghastly than those of their competitors, and that was saying something. Another point in their favour was that they were about to get hitched – a hopeless yet brave statement of responsible commitment, when you took their situation into account, and one which would appeal to the viewers. And, to the director's delight, the wedding itself promised to be a hopeless yet brave occasion, with its grim and utilitarian register office and its sordid reception venue, via the heavily graffitied and dustbinned back entrance to the Bunch of Grapes.

Anyway. Back to the abduction.

'The Higginses might have done it themselves. That's what the police are saying; it's one line of enquiry they're following, but they are keeping that under their hats for fear of exciting the public.' This is what Alan, creator and director, informed the meeting at Griffin's headquarters in Ealing Broadway. Alan, a flamboyant fellow who enjoyed his good looks and built his designer wardrobe around them, had never been in the closet; that dark place would be far too constricting for him.

His co-director, Jennie, gasped. 'No. That's un-

14

believable. They're just two ordinary, silly kids. They'd never have taken such risks. Anyway, where would they hide them?'

'There's loads of empty flats and derelict places around where the Higginses live,' said Alan. 'I know where I'd put them if it was me. There's been no ransom demanded yet, which is odd, but I've got Sir Art's agreement that Griffin must pay up if that can't be avoided.' Both Alan and Jennie knew well that Sir Art had had grave doubts about the programme right from its conception. 'Dangerous waters, poverty,' he had declared, in his privileged, well-connected voice, as if by rubbing shoulders with it he might succumb to infection. He had been persuaded eventually, but now it seemed he was being proved right. 'Damage limitation. If we don't play ball we'll be crucified, the way we've landed in the shit, the way this company is perceived by the public just now.'

'You wouldn't think those two had it in them,' suggested Alan, whose far-reaching dreams he fully intended to fulfil. 'Initiative was never Barry's forte.'

'Surely the cops are not suggesting that Cheryl and Barry could have done this alone?' And Jennie, skinny and clever and rising fast, with carefully highlighted hair suggesting a touch of purple, poured the coffee, very black, that had been left on the boardroom table. 'They should be looking for someone more sophisticated. Some fly cove who could have influenced them . . .'

'Not hard,' said Alan, knowingly. 'The Higginses are a gullible pair. Tell them to run and they'll run. Jump and they'll jump.'

'I don't see how they could carry it off. They're basically just too dim. Both of them.'

'Not dim, Jennie, just unworldly. Uneducated. Easily influenced. Anyway, there's been no demand for a ransom yet. But it's early days . . .'

'They probably can't spell it,' said Jennie.

Then the professional production team moved on to the more pressing matters of the moment. They were editing a brand new project ready for transmission that autumn.

Cheryl and Barry were old news.

They had known them fairly intimately for a while; some of the team had even grown fond of them. They had played with their kids and drunk their coffee; they had seen them getting up in the mornings and watched them going to bed at night. But *The Dark End of the Street* had finished in early spring, as do all worthwhile programmes, because the media people reckon folks will be out having barbecues in their gardens right the way through from then till September.

The filming for *The Dark End of the Street* had begun the year before and had gone on for four solid months and in that time Cheryl got herself pregnant again. The Christmas baby, too late to be filmed, was nevertheless conceived in time to do maximum damage.

A nosy nation was immediately divided, some clamouring for an immediate abortion, others for sterilization, and, for most viewers, this wilful breeding went way beyond the pale.

For goodness' sake. The Higginses could not

16

cope as it was – Victor was two, Scarlett was one and here was another one on the way.

Rabbits.

Rats.

Mink.

No wonder Cheryl's cystitis was a semi-permanent condition. Too much rumpy-pumpy. Their dingy flat was tiny, Barry was still jobless, despite his magnificent efforts, and Cheryl was more gaunt than ever.

The thought of abortion made Cheryl go cold. She could hardly discuss it rationally. She wanted this baby, she wanted it badly. But to Barry, exhausted, with headaches, an ear infection and at his wits' end, it seemed like the only sensible option, broken-hearted though he might be. This hard-faced demonstration of the fecklessness of the masses goaded the country to fiendish fury. The Higginses' popularity dropped overnight like a barometer in a hurricane – how could anyone be so short-sighted, no matter how gormless they were?

And what of the morning-after pill?

Had the daft cow never heard of the coil?

Hadn't the people of Britain supported, encouraged, laughed with them, cried with them – and then to be let down like this? Not on. Their behaviour was unforgivable, their ignorance unacceptable. Their feeble dependence on others was disgraceful.

The silent majority stayed silent as usual, curious, amused, disinterested, or quietly sympathetic.

But the vociferous self-righteous minority included everyone else in their ravings. Some called her a witch. 'Witch, witch', they shouted, some dark collective memory in resurgence of centuries gone by when women were fair targets. The ratings soared with the fierce emotions. The viewers were invited to stop spectating and participate instead. They jumped at the chance like they always do, egged on by an excited press, and Griffin rubbed gleeful hands.

Cheryl and Barry, in their Paddington home, moved mostly among the outraged. They were ostracized, spat at in the street; their neighbours cursed them or ignored them, and the programme-makers went through the letters and kept most back from the despised pair. The letters were vicious, threatening, demented. Most viewers seemed to feel deliberately slighted by the couple; 'let down' was a phrase often used, 'smacked in the face' was another.

The nation cried shame with what seemed to be one voice, and turned into one hellish, unforgiving, fifties' mother.

Dismayed by this change of fortune (they had both been basking in film-star acclaim), Cheryl and Barry pleaded with the Griffin bosses to pull the series for the sake of their sanity. Cheryl's voice cracked and her eyes filled with tears. They were alarmed that matters might escalate after their final decision was screened. And how right they were.

The Dark End of the Street

The birth of Cheryl's second child, Scarlett, to the curious background music of The Waterboys' 'Strange World' opened the documentary with a bloody Caesarean drama in a stark delivery room, or 'suite', as St Mary's preferred to call it. Much play was made of close-up shots of the still boyish Barry's defensive scowl, his round blue eyes full of love and concern for the loudly labouring Cheryl, his sharp white teeth gnawing painfully at his bloodless bottom lip.

A daddy again at twenty years old, yet with all the care and commitment of a proper, less hopeless parent. And then, afterwards, appalled viewers in the comfort of their own homes could follow him from the hospital through the dark and rainy streets of his world, between the broken, skeletal cars, over the rubble and mounds of smashed bottles, up the five flights of concrete steps to his chill and miserable flat where, as the director had anticipated, the electricity meter had run out.

And in his arms, gently and protectively, Barry had cradled the twelve-month-old Victor. The sense of despair and fading hope as he closed his mean front door was tangible.

Back in the hospital ward, the cameras waited for Cheryl to wake.

She slept like a baby.

The real baby looked more like a doll, a Cabbage Patch doll with its little squashed face and its rubbery, impossibly tiny fingers.

This was the first helpless image of Cheryl the viewers took to their hearts. In fact, the first of many. Her sharp, urchin face with its shy grin and its snub nose suggested a much younger eighteen-year-old. A tomboy on a wall with Kickers, jeans and bunches. A puppy would suit her more than a baby. A cheeky two-inch tuft of hair which sprung from an elastic band stood up like an exclamation mark, as if she was saying here I am! Look at me! Purple, green, red. The colour of this strange tuft varied according to what her mum could pick up, scrapings of dye from the salon where her sister, Sharon, worked. She could have been anyone's little girl, and the blue and white nightshirt which suggested denim had been cunningly provided by the costume department for the first pictures after the birth.

Eager to get herself into the frame, Sister Melanie Wilson stroked Cheryl's face. Well, the film crew couldn't hang around all night. Cheryl woke like a small animal, sweetly, not with slobber round her mouth, eyes stuck closed and puffy-cheeked.

Expertly Sister Wilson placed little Scarlett on Cheryl's small, childlike breast – and Scarlett was wrapped in a lacy shawl.

There were no flowers around Cheryl's bed as the panning camera made clear. There were no cards, no grapes, nothing special; just a sterile hospital cabinet with a sick bowl made out of some kind of grey cardboard. This and the glass of tepid-looking water made a violent contrast to the flowery surroundings of her fellow patients. The fact that none of Cheryl's ward companions had flowers arrive so soon after the birth event was missed by the vast majority of viewers, as was intended.

'Barry?' called Cheryl feebly, struggling to sit up.

'Barry has had to leave,' explained Sister Wilson, speaking up for the camera. 'Baby Victor was tired out.'

'He's gone home?' Cheryl's impish face fell. The automatic response was to pat her better.

'He said he was coming again tomorrow.'

Lonely and abandoned after her labour, after her noble struggle.

Again the camera panned round the ward where whole families – grannies, sons and daughters, aunts – vied with husbands to get close to the newly delivered as if, in the life-giving process, these mothers had been endowed with some earthy, potent magic which might shower on these tainted worldly visitors still in their hats and coats. Laughter and conversation filled the air along with the pink disinfectant and freesias. One patient hobbled past painfully with an obviously new and exquisite sponge bag hoisted over one arm – cue for the shot of the Tesco carrier into which Cheryl's humble toiletries were stuffed.

'She's dark, like me,' said Cheryl, enchanted, a mother again at eighteen years old, staring down at her newly born child. 'Just right for the name of Scarlett.'

'That's an unusual name,' said Sister Wilson. She had to say something, the camera was on her.

'Is it?' Cheryl directed her question to the film crew, who must have shaken their heads at her, because she held up her hand to her mouth, aware of her first silly blunder. She would get used to them in the end. Eventually she would manage to forget that they were even present, so quickly and foolishly do human beings adjust to unfamiliar situations.

Initially the director, Alan, tangled with The Mother. An unforeseen snag, assuming that members of such a family would unanimously rejoice in getting themselves on telly much as game-show participants do, no matter how ga-ga they are made to appear.

Not so.

'Believe you me, I've seen what happens,' said Annie Watts, Cheryl's massive mother, one day when he arrived at the flat to set up the cameras. As in the style of many large women she wore a short, skimpy top which hardly reached the elasticated waist of her black nylon leggings. 'And I've told Cheryl not to do it, I told her, I said, "on your head be it". And what about signing something, what about her and Barry's rights? I mean, they must have some bleeding rights in all this.'

They did have rights. But they signed them away quite happily. The film crew were granted unlimited access to every department of their lives, from bedroom to gynaecological couch. Even to their friends and relations.

Repelled as he was by anything ugly, animal, vegetable or mineral, despite his initial instinctive recoil, secretly Alan was delighted with The Mother he had heard so much about from his researchers, the character that would definitely bring an added frisson to the show. But was she too much of a cliché? She was every bit as grim as he'd hoped. How could such a brute of a woman have brought up a child as cute as Cheryl? That was a question he hoped would be on everyone's lips, once she was introduced and started to play her important role.

He set out to reassure her immediately, sitting beside her on the greasy slick of a sofa, she plunged down heavily at one end and he balanced high on the springs at the other.

'I wasn't born yesterday, matey,' said Cheryl's irate mother with a history of violence and a gravelly voice, fag hanging out of her mouth and chins resting on one another, twenty stone and rising. 'What d'you bleeders get out of this, that's what I want to know?'

'We get to make the sort of informative documentary which might actually help young people like Cheryl and Barry get some sympathy and understanding from an apathetic public.'

'Why them?' Annie insisted. 'They've got enough on their bleeding plates as it is. This is the last thing they need right now. So why them, I want to know?'

'They volunteered, Mrs Watts. We didn't set out to find them, or force them into doing anything they weren't perfectly happy to do.'

Annie Watts turned indelicately towards him, legs wide apart, the contents of her leggings bulging and grinning between. 'They'll end up the laughing stock, or in trouble, like that Australian family. They had to move. They got bleeding hate mail. They were set up from start to finish, that's what I read.'

'I can assure you that is not our intention,' said Alan, still overwhelmed by this perfect casting, imagining how the viewers at home would react to her coarse and uncouth persona. You always need a villain of the piece, and this woman hit the nail on the head.

Ash tumbled volcanically down Annie's formidable frontage. 'Just watch it, matey,' she said, 'that's all. I know your type,' and her eyes rolled menacingly over the engineers at work in her daughter's front room. 'I've had your type for breakfast.'

'Leave it out, Mum,' Cheryl piped up. 'We know what we're doing.'

'You've never known what you were doing, Cher, and that's half your problem,' said Annie.

*   *   *

23

Pride comes before a fall. And as Annie had predicted, the tide turned.

By episode eight the crowd turned ugly.

Cheryl wished she could disappear, but became more visible than ever. Naked. She felt she was being buried alive and suffered a dazed, suffocating panic.

Now, according to everyone, Cheryl was a bad mother, not worthy of two such endearing children. Her best was no longer good enough; her daily struggles were self-induced.

And as for Barry, what sort of a man was he anyway? Castration. Imprisonment. Hanging and quartering were too good for him. It was high time the lad grew up.

Why wasn't he working?

How conveniently they forgot how hard he had tried. It wasn't as if there weren't enough jobs. He could sweep the streets, clean lavatories – or was the loser too damn uppity?

So it remained a distinct possibility that some deranged member of the public, some sicko still affected by a programme that finished a good six months ago, had taken it upon himself to remove the Higgins children therewith, for their own protection. Very worrying. So DCI Rowe and his team were certainly not limited to one line of enquiry. At this stage in the proceedings anything could have happened. Nothing could be ruled out yet.

Although, in his heart of hearts, Rowe believed that the two young parents were somehow involved. An experienced officer with more than twenty years in the force, he recognized the importance of instinct – and there was something about this distraught young couple that gave him grave cause for concern.

So the questioning of the bereft pair went relentlessly on and on.

A police psychiatrist was employed to interview poor Cheryl.

But the wonderful letters that arrived at the Harold Wilson Building in a post-office bag every morning were full of love and sympathy. Some dark crime had been committed against them. They were in anguish, so the public was prepared to forgive.

Just as Cheryl had hoped that they would.

The answer to all her prayers.

TWO

'They think we did it.' Cheryl's tuft of hair is dayglo pink this morning. Freshly washed, the shape has changed from rude exclamation to soft question mark, and her nails are bitten to the quick.

'I know they do,' says Barry, sullen, his baggy sleeves pulled over his hands as if he would like to disappear with them into somewhere as soft as old wool.

How long can this farce go on?

How long before poor little Cheryl Higgins cracks up completely?

The flat is so empty, so neat, so quiet. You can hear the world outside. You can hear the shush of the trains. The sweet smell of babies is everywhere.

Cheryl twists her fingers together and stares at Barry with red-rimmed eyes while Barry, quite unable to cope, watches the football sightlessly.

'Come away from the window, for God's sake,' he tells her. 'That won't help.'

Back then, at the very beginning . . . And it seems like a whole world ago . . .

. . . The advert was in the back of *The Mirror*, a

26

small, square box, requesting anyone interested to contact a box number in Slough.

'Researchers for well-known television company are looking for young families living below the poverty line who would be interested in taking part in a serious documentary programme featuring the struggles of everyday life.'

Cheryl, breastfeeding Victor at the time and seven months pregnant with Scarlett, wiped the marmalade off the paper and read the ad aloud to Barry from their fifth-floor flat with a slummy balcony in the Harold Wilson Building, overlooking the graffitied approaches of Paddington station.

How she loved these mornings, when Barry went out early to fetch the milk and sometimes brought a paper back. The sun shone lightly through the window. They had the radio on. It felt like they were a proper family, with a garden outside the door and pedal tractors, broken cars and a dirty sandpit with spades in

'What does it pay?' he asked her, scouring a pan in a mottled sink. They'd had bacon, Smash and tinned tomatoes   that was special.

Cheryl checked. She badly wanted Barry to take this idea seriously. 'Nothing. But you must get expenses, or something.'

'No point then,' said Barry, sleeves rolled up high now and shaggy curls in the way of his eyes as he worked on the burned-out saucepan. He tried to puff them away, and a mass of bubbles flew out of the bowl. He turned to show her his foaming nose. He was always playing the prat like that. Normally it would make her laugh, but this morning she wanted to stay serious.

27

'They wouldn't choose us. Why would they?' he said, a man among the many who have been conditioned to walk side by side with rejection.

'You sad sod. We could try.'

'Anyway,' said Barry, his sense of fun subsiding like the click of a light switching off and chucking the useless scourer away, 'maybe I wouldn't want them to know my personal business.'

'Your personal business. Don't make me laugh. What's that?'

'Everyone would know we were skint.' And there was that scowl which he wore like a shield whenever they talked about money. When Barry got really, seriously defensive, he would pick up his football and chuck it hard from hand to hand without stopping. Cheryl hated to see him do this. It was too much like watching him mock his own dreams. He would have made it by now, he knew, he would probably have made the first division. He had the talent, it was up to him how he used it. That's what they used to tell him at school and when he played for the town's junior league. But it hadn't worked out like that, had it? And whose fault was that?

'Everyone knows we're skint anyway. And it might be a laugh,' Cheryl persisted. Anything, anything to escape for one day the remorseless grind of life stuck indoors, watching daytime telly, watching women in M&S clothes discussing life on new sofas, cooking in kitchens beyond Cheryl's dreams with saucepans with perfect bottoms, contestants winning the sort of money that Cheryl could hardly imagine, and that relentless news on the hour, as if Cheryl and Barry were part of it.

But where would they be without the telly?

Was this just a tragic patch in Cheryl's life, or was this condition permanent? What had happened to life's rich tapestry? The texture of her own life was sacking. Oh, where were those rich embroidered silks they showed in all the adverts? A flowered print would do.

OK, Barry might have made it, if he hadn't been so desperate to escape his mother's clutches, if he hadn't used his one marvellous chance as a self-defeating weapon against her. He'd been offered a trial for Spurs and he had turned it down. Can you believe that? Can you? To this day Cheryl cannot understand how anyone with his talent could have done that, to pick up so obstinately the precious jewel and lob it at the enemy. The only one he'd destroyed was himself. She likes to believe her talent is acting, and if she had been given the slightest encouragement she would have killed to succeed. She might have made it if things had been different, but everyone thinks that, don't they? She might have been an actress if she'd stayed at Parkwood School for longer and not had to move on again.

But what is the good of hanging on to all those might-have-beens?

Sometimes, when it was fine, they might take Victor out in his pushchair for a stroll round the park or down by the river. They might stop if it was warm enough and share a bench with Donny, who once lived next door to Cheryl's mum on the estate which had always been home. Marge Smith lives in Donny's house now. But Donny fell victim to circumstances which nobody was quite sure about, and now she wanders the streets of London with black rubbish bags on her feet. Mum said she drank herself soft, gin, she said, rolling her eyes, but there's no sign of that now. Victor adores smelly old Donny, who sometimes feeds him chips. She might be strange, she might be dirty, she might wear three coats but she's great with kids. Liza Donnolly, she once was. Her house used to be spotless. She once had a whole tribe of her own, according to Mum. 'Don't you remember? You ought to. You were always over at Donny's house, scrounging.'

The jobcentre was part of their route, part of the treasure trail, but it seemed more like snakes and ladders – they never managed to reach their goal without slithering down with a bump. The best they ever seemed to achieve was a lager outside The Castle, that's if they could scrape up enough, and sometimes a couple of bags of crisps. Barry desperately wanted to work, but it was worse when he was working. Most of his dead-end jobs were at night, and Cheryl got scared in the flat alone. Stacking shelves, office cleaning, kitchen work at a West End hotel, motorway maintenance.

Cheryl tried hard not to moan.

For God's sake, they needed the money.

They called her and Barry a drain on the state.

She watched herself on chat shows, she read about her type in cheap magazines.

Parasites, that's what they were.

Motorway maintenance was the worst. Barry was gone for days on end, leaving her stuck with Victor, and now she was pregnant again, feeling sick, worried sick. OK, they should have been more careful, but when she was pregnant something was happening, something important came into her life, she was a mother-to-be with appointments at clinics, other mums she could talk to and nurses who made out they cared.

When Cheryl was pregnant she was special.

Oh, Barry had been on all the schemes, government schemes that led nowhere. The only reason he still went on them was because they'd refuse his dole if he didn't. And when Barry was laid off, which seemed to happen every time, getting back on the social again was such an effort it didn't seem worth it. Forms, forms, forms, and interviews, and worsening debt.

In spite of Barry's initial scorn, Cheryl replied to the advert.

At least it didn't demand any money.

There had been so many wasted hopes in the past, replying to the spivs who promised – guaranteed or money back – income from home making silk flowers, addressing envelopes, filling crackers. You sent your postal order off, you got your kit and, Christ, you worked. You worked till your fingers nearly fell off and your eyes were like slits in your head. Barry sometimes worked all night and went without any sleep.

The money-back part was a real con. First you had to repay them for the stuff you had messed up. But still, it was hard to fight the next temptation when they made out it was so simple.

Cheryl posted off her reply to the box-office number in Slough.

But she didn't forget all about it, oh, no. She didn't forget all about things with so few diversions in her life. Instead they assumed enormous proportions, and if she wasn't careful she'd find herself dreaming.

31

She dreamed about Victor all the time. How Victor's life would be. They'd find a good school, he'd make friends, not hang about with the dope-heads round here. He'd be brighter than them, like his mum. He'd have much wider horizons. Cheryl and Barry would make him work, help him with his homework. They'd take him to galleries and museums, and, who knows, by then life might be different. They could get out into the country, show him something beautiful.

Maybe go and live in Ireland, where she'd heard you could pick up something cheap. Maybe a house of wattles and clay . . .

If she'd believed she'd have prayed for him.

Say what you like, Cheryl was a good mother. And no matter what happened later, nobody could take that away.

She'd done parent classes at school.

You could choose to do that instead of art.

They painted faces to personalize an egg and took it with them everywhere they went, 'and I mean everywhere, for one whole week', said Mrs Taylor firmly. 'And that will give you some inkling of the responsibilities involved in taking care of your very own baby.'

Some kids broke theirs, some wrapped them only in a tissue, but Cheryl kept hers in cotton wool inside a proper egg box. She knitted a red bobble hat and a scarf, she kept it alive till it stank and Mrs Taylor said, 'What's the matter with you? I hope you haven't got some sort of fetish.'

Throwing away that egg was hard.

That's love.

And Cheryl did know how to love, in spite of the massive scar that circled the top of her left arm like a pale amulet with rivets.

When Cheryl was little . . .

'Quick, quick, get out of the bath, Jack Frost is coming down the road and he'll bite your little tummy button, oh, yes he will . . .'

Cuddled in a pink dressing gown with a felt white rabbit on the pocket for stories Cheryl would never forget.

'Night-night, sleep tight, mind the bugs don't bite.'

And then came Fred.

'A man about the house,' cooed Mum.

Red-haired Fred with the earring.

'He's a right laugh. What a clown,' roared Mum.

Red, speckled-nosed Fred.

'I feel like a real woman again,' Mum flirted.

Red-armed Fred with the rose tattoo and his belief in UFOs, aliens and crop circles.

And Cheryl's mum, Annie, fluffed up, began to wear make-up and started crying when Fred was late home, or when he bought that dilapidated van, or stayed in bed watching *Alien* instead of going to his building job. Fred made holes in the doors because he refused to take down his dartboard, and his mates made dull, stabbing sounds which kept Cheryl awake and left her tired for school the next morning.

Fred moved the dogs in, which upset the neighbours and brought the council down on their backs.

The doctor gave Mum pills.

She would slap them in her mouth like a smack.

Mum's face, which was once country-round and happy, started crumbling in.

The garden became too shitty to play in and the swing chains rusted and rotted. It stank out there. No more rugs and lemonade in the sun. Even inside with the windows closed you could smell the dog-shit.

Friday and Saturday nights, when Cheryl was seven, Fred took Annie out to the club while Cheryl stayed home alone with a video. Mum used to worry. 'You'll be OK on your own now, won't you? Don't touch the dogs. They're fine in the yard. Don't let them out now, will you?'

One Friday night the coppers came round after a complaint from a neighbour.

'All on your own?' asked the woman PC.

'And how old are you?' asked the man.

They said Cheryl had to go with them while somebody else went to find Mum. They put the siren on the car specially for her. She waited in the police canteen – hurry up, Mum, hurry up. She couldn't eat more chips, she felt sick. But they said Mum was in no fit state, rat-arsed they called her, and they took Cheryl to Mrs Donnolly's and Mum went to court and was fined.

It was all Cheryl's fault.

After that, Dill came to babysit, the woman across the road.

Dill was so old that parts of her were already dead or dropping off, like her hair, her hands and her nails. Her poor skin was shredding in places. But Dill was prepared for death, she enjoyed considering it. She was having a simple cardboard coffin and no funeral service. 'Mumbo-jumbo.'

Dill worried too much about the dogs. 'It's all wrong to keep them out there in all weathers, poor buggers.'

'They never come in the house,' said Cheryl.

'Some folks dunno the first thing about kindness to animals. And it's time you were in bed. I promised your mum you'd be in by eight . . .'

'Fred does,' said Cheryl. 'Fred's an expert.'

'That Fred knows nothing. And he's driving your mother into her grave. I keep telling her. But will she listen?'

Dithering and doddering around in the kitchen, muttering daftly to herself with the sound on the telly so loud it was deafening, suddenly, on some mad impulse, Dill must have lifted the latch to the yard. The first thing Cheryl knew was when Gorgon came tearing in, tangling himself in Dill's lime-green knitting and knocking over the coffee tray in an effort to reach the custard creams.

Oh, no, no. '*Gorgon*,' shrieked Cheryl, mimicking Fred at his most severe. 'Back! Outside! Right now!'

The Dobermann cross whirled round, curled his lip and issued a menacing, warning growl.

Dill wobbled in with her walking stick, wielding it feebly in the air. A fatal manoeuvre. Gorgon slathered; his hackles were as spiked as a porcupine's. He sprang and brought Dill down in one. The other three dogs, uncertain, pausing red-eyed at the door, needed no further encouragement. They followed their leader. They fell upon Dill like lions at the kill, leaving the shrieking Cheryl to kick and boot the mass of wet fur.

Dill's injuries were massive.

She was 'unrecognizable'.

This time, things were serious.

Dill's heart gave up the ghost and Fred was up for possessing dangerous dogs and a whole list of manslaughter-type charges. They put him inside at the same time as Cheryl was let out of hospital with her left arm stitched back on her body.

She had gone to live with the Bradburys, because Mum was stuck in the mental ward, drugged up like a zombie.

When Mum left hospital she was as fat as hell.

'Unrecognizable', like poor dead Dill.

None of her own clothes would fit her, and Fred had long since departed, so it no longer mattered how she looked. But Cheryl clung on to the mother she'd known, closing her eyes to reality, hanging on so tight to the image that when it was dragged away from her, bit by bit over the years, it seemed to lacerate both her hands.

Barry and Cheryl went round to Mum's the week they replied to the advert. They walked all the way with Victor asleep in his pushchair.

They had just arrived when the shouting started.

'If you don't move your arse off my step by the count of three, I won't answer for your bleeding health,' shrieked big Annie dementedly at her neighbour, Marge, slapping the head of Cheryl's half-brother, Shane. 'And you, you sodding little shit, you can get indoors for a start before I commit bleeding murder.'

Marge sniffed and stiffened her hands on her hips. 'We're just sick and tired of you and your bloody lot round here. If it's not one it's the other; if it's not Shane it's that fucking Bobby . . .'

Inside the house, stiff on the sofa, Cheryl looked uneasily at Barry.

Here we go . . . Mum was never like this, never, before she went into St Hugh's. It was this violence that Cheryl detested, that made her so frightened. And the fat Mum came home with was full of it, like the gunge you can get sucked out by tube. To Mum this anger was a game, this constant war with her neighbours, but to Cheryl it was torment. When they showed violence on the TV you could control the sound and the shade of it; when it happened for real it was shatteringly loud, and surged in unpredictable waves of energy. She had seen Dill being torn apart. She had seen an eye ripped out of her head.

'Shuddup, you miserable bitch.' And Big Annie, as she was known since she came out of hospital, thrust her large face into Marge's space. This kind of thing left Cheryl raw. If only Donny still lived in that house. If only the Smiths had never moved in. 'I've never known a minute when you aren't complaining, you and your slut of a daughter. You'd think you'd find something better to do. Now, gerrout of here while I'm still in control of myself, or I can't answer —'

Marge turned on one slippered foot, shaking with excitement. 'And don't you think it's gonna rest here.'

'Oh, yeah? *Oh, yeah?*' And Cheryl's mum took a few steps forward, emboldened by Marge's retreat. 'Threaten me, would you, stuck-up cow?'

'It's no threat, love, not this bleeding time.'

For the first time Big Annie seemed to notice the little crowd that had gathered outside her broken gate, mostly kids. She was ashamed of her garden, full of rubbish, most of it dumped by the vermin round here.

She raised a fist.

She bared her teeth.

With her puffy face and her wobbling chins she ran at them like a maddened bull, two twisted curlers for horns. 'And you lot can fuck off for a start. Get a life, you sad arseholes.'

Cheryl watched solemnly from the window, behind the frayed net curtain. A small stone struck her mother's cheek. Her face looked brutal and congested.

Her large hand flew to the pain.

Something warm ran down her neck.

She wiped the skin and felt the wetness, brought it before her and saw the blood. Her eyes misted over with frantic rage. 'You buggers,' she screamed, 'you fucking buggers. I'll have you for this, every one of you.'

'Come in, Mum,' Cheryl urged, tugging her nervously from behind. 'Leave them. Don't waste your breath. Christ, they're never worth it.' But the touch of her hand on her mother's sleeve drove Annie to heightened fury.

'It's families like yours bring shame to this bloody estate,' called a youth, a ciggie drooping from the corner of his mouth, intent on prolonging the entertainment. 'The council should chuck you lot out on the street.'

'Don't worry,' said mean Marge loudly, stalking past him and feeling safe now there was distance between her and Annie. 'This time they'll sodding well have to.' And the bedroom window suddenly shattered, sprinkling glass on the path.

38

Somewhere in the distance a train slowed down, passing over a viaduct, a hopeless and lonely sound.

'Piss off, the lot of you,' Annie shouted, but fear, which showered down with the glass from upstairs, had pushed out most of the rage. Her mouth clamped shut. She shook herself down like a wet dog and crunched through the mess to her front door.

Tired, shivery and depressed, Annie lurched into her kitchen from where she could watch the dispersing crowd. Damn that bloody woman Marge Smith and Shane, the awkward bugger. How many times must she tell the lad to stay away from that viaduct and leave that weed Randall Smith alone?

'There they go, bloody animals,' muttered Annie.

Cheryl fetched a bowl and started to wash the blood off her mother's face. Tears, half of anger and half of nervous misery, came into her eyes. She bit her lip savagely in an effort to stop them running over. Her mother's large face hung in space, separated, unsupported and naked behind the haze of cigarette smoke, its great eyes burning through eyelids half closed with inexpressible weariness. With no mask over her eyes or lips, what Cheryl saw was sorrow. Why did Annie prolong this war, and what did she get out of it? If Cheryl was so completely despised by everyone around her she would never be able to handle it. She liked to be liked. She needed to be loved.

'I swear I'll put that cow's eye out next time she comes round here.'

Stop it Mum, please stop it. 'Come on, Mum, I'll get you a plaster. There's blood all over the place.'

'See if you can find my fags, love,' said Big Annie

in a throaty whisper, as Barry put a cup of tea in her hand.

'Half the time I wish they would move us,' said Mum, calming slowly. 'There's sod all for us here.'

Mum hadn't always been this way, not before the hospital, and that had been Cheryl's fault.

If she hadn't let Dill open that door, Mum would be different. But the only thing Mum went on about was that Cheryl ought to have been in bed. If she'd been in bed she wouldn't have been hurt . . .

After Fred there was Ely, the father of Shane and Bobby, Cheryl's two half-brothers. But Ely only lasted two years, leaving Annie bereft of passion, and malice, being a powerful force, had come to fill the hole in her life.

Eventually they sat down together, Annie, Barry, Cheryl and the two lads, Shane and Bobby. Bobby's T-shirt said, 'Have a shit day'. Annie buttered the bread but Shane snatched it off the plate before his mother could finish.

'You little bastard . . .'

'I'm hungry.' She slapped her son across the head. 'I'll give you bleeding hungry.'

Annie had already been warned by the council: control your kids or you're out. They were there on a wing and a prayer as it was, and Shane's behaviour only grew worse. They did tests to check that he was right in the head. He was already on probation. He had to see the school psychologist and was now in a special class.

And Bobby, one year younger, seemed to be gormlessly following suit.

'They'll put him away,' said Annie, 'that's the next thing they're threatening to do.'

Cheryl held Victor tightly to her. Nothing like this must happen to him. That was one reason why she loved Barry – there was no violence around him, just kindness.

In the comparative peace that followed, she described the advertisement.

'That's the last thing you want to do,' said Annie immediately, 'show yourself up, and in public. You'll be sorry.'

'That's what I told her,' said Barry, munching a fat chip butty, catching the sauce on his tongue. 'Anyway, they'll never have you.'

'You don't know that, Mum. We fit the bill. We're young and we're poor and we're struggling.'

'Daft. They don't use real people, Cheryl. Haven't you twigged that by now? Get real. All these so called documentaries, they're actors, aren't they, they're having you on. When the hell are you going to learn that they don't give a toss about people like us? Poverty, my arse.'

But Annie was never in the least bit resentful of her station in life. To the contrary, she had always regarded her circumstances – unmarried mother, resident of a soulless estate, never an extra penny to spend – as an upward, positive step from her childhood as a rude peasant in a pocket of rural deprivation deep in the Hertfordshire countryside. Brought up on hard work by her mother and her two sisters in a tied farm cottage with mouldering walls and a ramshackle privy at the gate, she firmly maintained that her own kids 'didn't know they were born', suggesting all kinds of unutterable discomforts which had darkened her peculiar past.

'Can you blame them for not caring?' said Barry.

41

'If I made the sort of dosh they do, I wouldn't give a damn either.'

Cheryl smiled to herself. All talk. Barry *would* give a damn. Barry cared. The only defence Barry ever used was to turn defiant and retreat into himself, a ploy he had learned from childhood to ward off his smothering mother. When he did this, you couldn't reach him. At those times, Cheryl could hit him. He was a like a naughty child with his fingers stuffed in his ears and humming so he couldn't hear you.

And that is how it all started.

THREE

'This is getting really hard.' Cheryl's whisper is damp and slippery; with luck, the hand at her mouth might catch it.

'Shh. We dunno if the flat might be bugged.'

'They wouldn't do that, would they?'

''Course they would. They do anything when it's kids.'

Cheryl and Barry lie silent in candlewick, each one trying to warm the other, in a bedroom where the wallpaper stretches but fails to reach the ceiling.

At the end of their divan is a rickety, empty cot.

In the room across the small, uncarpeted landing stands a second cot with a damp teddy bear where the baby ought to be. The fold-down bed along the wall is made up neatly, blankets tucked in tightly, topped by a faded counterpane depicting The Tele tubbies.

And on the sitting-room table, piled like a pyramid under snow, are the letters and cards from the caring public.

It seems incredible now, but it was only February last year. They had never dreamed they would be picked. Their heads were filled with preconceived notions about goodness and badness, loyalty and treachery, courage and cowardice, all the stiff bare things taught in school that don't fit life in the least. They believed that human beings were fundamentally kind. They were naive. They were young.

Luckily for them, Ealing Broadway was a short, cheap journey from Paddington, but far enough, thrilling enough for the Higginses, who rarely journeyed anywhere, and if they did, they used the bus.

At least they hadn't been traumatized by worries about what they ought to wear.

No choice.

Cheryl, her tuft of hair an intriguing silver and the lump that was Scarlett weighing her down, wore her black skirt with the patch in the front and a crochet top from Dorothy Perkins. Barry went in jeans and a T-shirt, with the Griffin letter in his back pocket along with his Swiss Army knife.

They fed Victor before they left and prayed he would sleep through it all.

The wide glass windows of the Griffin building looked like solid black marble from outside.

Porsches and jeeps and BMWs were parked in all the chained-off spaces.

The reception area was soft and quiet; they just about whispered their names to the girl and had to fill in the time in a book, who they were and who they were seeing. Cheryl did that because her writing was clearer than Barry's. Then they were given identity badges.

Nervously out of their depth, they rocked the pushchair backwards and forwards as they perched on the cold leather sofa, gawping at those who went by, impressed by the sense of urgency and chumminess, the casual but expensive clothes and the way everyone smiled so warmly. Cheryl wanted to put out a hand, find Barry's square, hard palm inside it, to be steadied and led by it as blind people are.

They were already well out of their depth.

They weren't married then, of course, but the wedding plans were in hand. Annie was in charge.

'Cheryl Watts and Barry Higgins?' asked a smiling girl with an outstretched hand. 'And this must be baby Victor. Isn't he just gorgeous?'

'You wouldn't have thought that at two o'clock this morning,' said Cheryl, but pleased.

'My knees are going,' she whispered to Barry as they followed the girl through a maze of passages and security doors with coded buttons.

'I told you not to wear those shoes . . .'

'It's not the shoes.'

'It's OK,' hissed Barry, 'just don't panic.' He noticed a stain on the back of her skirt.

'Huh, you're one to talk.'

Wouldn't Barry just have loved to work in a place like this? He supposed these were the top people, the ones in all the adverts, all fighting to get to the top but it was OK if they didn't. They could say they worked in the media. They were probably all hard, energetic, avaricious and intelligent, with nerves of iron, not like him. He vaguely remembered media studies . . . He'd liked to have been a cameraman. Imagine covering all the sport, travelling to the World Cup, seeing the Olympics, and the social life that must go with it . . . He had thrown away all his chances, he could be playing for Spurs by now. But God, this lot had it made.

There must be a catch somewhere, in spite of the sense of bonhomie. They were lolling about in the room, nothing formal, men and women with impressive watches and sleeves rolled up to a careful length, and even when they exhaled their vitality was different from Barry's. There was a camera there with wheels, the sort you see in studio discussions, and plastic cups on a trestle table, cold coffees with skin on, and charts and photographs stuck on the walls.

'Hi, Cheryl, hi, Barry, come and sit down. My name's Jennie St Hill and I'm the casting director, but that means nothing in this situation. Coffee? Tea? It's pretty disgusting, but it's wet. We're so glad you could come.'

Jennie St Hill stared from her violet, long-lashed eyes. Casually yet powerfully dressed in a trouser suit by Moschino, her lips fell into a charming smile. Alan was right when he told her these two were almost too perfect, especially her – Cheryl – who looked as if she ought to be in a freckled, dungareed advert for Cornflakes. This couple were cut out for the role, oh, yes. Unknown to the Higginses, the decision had already been taken. It was made when the researchers began the task of vetting the three front runners selected from the application forms. It was made with the amazing discovery that Cheryl Higgins had a skeleton in her cupboard.

Now they held this secret discovery up their sleeves like a dirty tissue.

The researcher had been remarkably lucky to stumble upon this nugget of gold. The photographs of Cheryl, well worn by old men's fingers (the photographs, she had been told, were not good

46

enough for a portfolio towards a modelling career), formed part of a collage in the back room of the newsagent's shop the researcher called into to check some local addresses, and he recognized the girl from the picture on the form in his hand. Sad little pictures of a sixteen-year-old who had posed in a seedy basement, legs apart, nipples erect, on a bar stool covered in mock zebra.

They were not particularly unscrupulous people, these two young directors. They were talented, they were ambitious. Needs must, if you aimed for the top of the tree in this most glamorous of professions. There were times when you had to swallow your scruples and go for the main chance.

Add to that the fact that dark stirrings and mutterings, which included the word downsizing, had been circulating the offices of Griffin Productions for a good six months, circulating as perniciously and surreptitiously as the state-of-the-art air-conditioning, inhaled by the most secure employees along with the most precarious, non-smokers and smokers alike, and you have the ingredients for a steamy stew.

These soft-porn pics could be used as a booster, should the production start flagging.

Four members of the production team were party to this distasteful secret. Director of Griffin, Sir Art Blennerhasset, as decent and upright a man as ever graced the industry, would have choked on his caviar had he realized what his employees were up to. He had started his prestigious career with Disney Productions, in the days when morality mattered. Heaven knows, in recent times there had been enough outraged scandal over rigged documentaries and hoaxers on talk shows to disgrace the best programme-makers, and just because competition was frenzied did not mean that standards must disappear.

Jennie and Alan were the first to know. It was only yesterday that they took the gamble and showed the photos to cameraman Leo Tarbuck. They had been surprised and gratified by his common-sense response.

For weeks Jennie and Alan had argued over the need to come clean with anyone. Why not keep this to themselves, Alan demanded; what was the point in risking the plan when there was no need to declare their intentions? At the appropriate time in the filming, Alan had only to instruct the crew to slap the photographs down on the table and film Cheryl's reactions.

It would, as he said, be interesting to find out if young Barry had seen them before, or if the mucky photo session had been a secret between Cheryl and some tacky models' agent.

'Why all this cloak-and-dagger stuff? You've told me, so Sebby should know.' Leo, quite unfazed by the plan, would not accept that the young guy he worked with should be kept in the dark until necessary. This bit of good luck should be exploited, they were all agreed on that. Knowledge of the photos' existence would influence the perspective with which they approached their subjects. It might, Leo insisted, make the difference between success and failure. If Barry and Cheryl were portrayed as two innocents fighting the slings and arrows of fate, then all the more impact the truth would make when all was revealed. Only clever work with the cameras could emphasize these extremes. Only by having the overall picture could the crew do the job properly.

Sebby, like his boss, Leo, was ambitious and clever. They both knew only too well the consequences of failure. Second chances were rare in this competitive field. Griffin was held in high regard for its popular docusoaps: there was every chance their programme would be looked at seriously by the commissioning editors. Backed by Sir Art, of course.

'So you intend to spring this lot on the Higginses if you think we need to breathe some extra life into the proceedings?' said Leo, blond, beautiful, flicking through the pictures with narrowed eyes like he was arranging a suit of cards. 'Not bad,' he commented. 'Not bad at all.'

'We'll assess the situation halfway through. It all depends how it's going,' said Alan, watching Leo with some fascination, despite his vow never to mix work with play. Leo's broad, easy shoulders slouched a little nonchalantly. His shining hair was parted in front and hung in curtains like a public schoolboy's.

'A pretty mean move,' said Sebby. More thoughtful, he was stuck in student mode, with owl glasses, thick cord pants, a sensitive, mobile face and dusty, desert-dry hair. Sebby was strictly decent and rigidly moral. Clearly uncomfortable with the idea, you could see he was tussling with himself, considering his options.

'Call it insurance,' said Jennie, more apprehensive than she sounded. 'And let's face it, a few tacky pictures in this day and age are not going to cause a hue and cry. Might even make them appear more interesting, who knows? And it's not as if the girl is having it off with a donkey.'

'But the Higginses. They're innocents.'

'They're fair game,' said Alan impatiently. 'Anyone who replies to an advert like this knows very well the risks they are running. And it's swings and roundabouts. Think of the publicity, the fame. Their pathetic lives could be changed beyond their wildest dreams.'

'Oh, yeah?' said Sebby. 'Since when?'

'It happens all the time,' said Jennie.

'A five-minute wonder,' said Sebby.

'Listen, sweetie,' Alan said petulantly, getting up from his swivel chair and crossing the room to pick up the pictures. He moved with the grace of a grazing animal, a giraffe, a gazelle with neck outstretched, unusual in a man, and his figure was slender. He kept himself fit. 'If you don't feel happy with this, then say so, and we can find someone else.' A naturally secretive man, he cursed Jennie's insistence to let these two in on the photos deal. There was never a need to do so. If Sebby blabbed, the game would be up and who could guess if the series would stand up without a little enlivening?

Leo spoke for his colleague. 'He's fine, ignore him. He goes through these spiritual crises as regularly as my wife. He sees himself as a visionary, a barer of the Word, the eyes of the common people wielding the sword of truth.'

'Balls,' said Sebby, his spectacles glinting.

But eventually, he had agreed.

*   *   *

Barry, exposed and ill at ease, had imagined it would be like an interview. Desks. Suits. Questions. But this was a reality he had not been prepared for. An interview he could have coped with. With this pretend equality he was lost. They were trying to be matey and ordinary, and yet it was nothing like that.

Oh, no, oh, no. This was a bad time for Victor to wake; he was always scratchy when he had been sleeping. Cheryl picked up her crumpled, red-faced baby and stuck his dummy in his mouth, slung him over her shoulder and patted his back as casually as she could. In the electric circumstances.

He hadn't imagined it would be like this. They just carried on chatting. Casual, like. Barry, feeling clumsy, gradually gathered who most of them were. There was a kind of deference here, but it took time to work it out. The guy called Alan asked the straightest questions, and everyone listened when he spoke. Someone said he was the director, the whole idea had been his

'You understand what we're trying to do here?' asked some bloke wearing Timberland boots, and Barry knew how much they cost. 'You know what *The Dark End of the Street*'s all about?' Was that inflection in his voice a warning? Did Barry detect some cynical amusement?

'Well, yeah, I think so,' said Cheryl, rocking the baby.

'And you do realize that the filming would involve four months of pretty invasive stuff? At your home. When you go out. Even your friends. Not just the good times, but rows, tears, mealtimes, bedtimes, sometimes we'll be around all night – and I hear you're getting married?'

Did they expect him and Cheryl to lead some sort of interesting life? Did they realize how boring they were? Had they any idea? By the way they were talking, you'd think their routine was one long, intensive happening.

'The thing is,' warned Barry, worried that Cheryl might be getting her hopes up, 'nothing much happens. The days are pretty much the same. Sometimes we don't go out.'

'It's not that we don't want to,' said Cheryl, shooting looks like daggers at him and twisting her tuft of hair round her finger, 'it's just that we can't afford it.'

And then they had to answer some questions, just general questions, not difficult ones, nothing to make you sweat. And while Barry just sat there struggling to digest it, Cheryl got chummy with the woman called Jennie, and it seemed that all her fear had gone and she revelled in being important.

Barry felt like a dumb lump beside her.

'Just carry on as you are while Sebastian gets some shots,' said Alan. 'Try to forget the camera's there. It's easy once you get used to it.'

They had had thousands of applicants, according to Jennie, who made Cheryl get up and play with Victor on the floor. She was laughing in a silly way. But they'd wanted somebody local for a start, of a certain age group, from a particular background, somebody charismatic . . . By then Cheryl was showing off, responding to the attention, looking quite red and excited. At least the day wouldn't be wasted.

'And this baby is due in April?'

'I can't wait', said Cheryl, 'to get it all over.'

'How would you feel about us filming the birth?'

'Wouldn't bother me,' said Cheryl without thinking.

Barry wasn't so sure about that, but it wasn't up to him.

He had to ask, no matter how angry it made Cheryl. 'Would there be any money in it?'

'I was going to come to that,' said Alan, and sensing Cheryl's annoyance, he added, 'I'm glad you asked. You see, Barry, we can't strut into people's lives and deliberately change them in some God-like way. We'd be accused of all sorts of things, social engineering, giving you false expectations, even ruining your lives if you went out of your depth and couldn't cope. But that's not to say there wouldn't be indirect spin-offs . . . Look at *Hotel* and *Driving School*, any number of docusoaps that have turned their subjects into stars overnight.'

'You'll find the publicity hard enough to deal with as it is,' Jennie said, 'if the show's a roaring success.'

'Which it's bound to be,' put in Alan.

'That wouldn't bother me,' said Cheryl, glowing. Now she was seriously showing off.

'How about you, Barry?'

'I dunno,' Barry said slowly, sitting there with his shoulders hunched. 'I've never had it happen before.' It was his job to take care of Cheryl, and it felt like he was failing.

They were in there for an hour. 'God, it flew, it seemed like ten minutes,' Cheryl told him on the train going home.

'You were great,' said Barry, impressed, 'like an old hand.'

'Well, there you are, shows what I could have been if I hadn't got shacked up with you.'

'But we still don't know.'

'A fortnight, they said, but I think they liked us.'

Cheryl was so easily conned. That lot would be nice to anyone. It was part of the job. They were good at it.

They still weren't sure if they had been chosen when the crew came round to the flat three weeks later.

They had tidied everything up, scrubbed out the kitchen, scraped off the mould, sprayed in an effort to conquer the damp and the washing basket was empty, thanks to a last-minute dash to the launderette.

They had never had any reason to make such an effort before. The feeling of doing it was so different, so purposeful, so positive. They had actually had the tape player on and sang as they went round with the bucket and cloth, as they took down the curtains and ironed them, as they sponged the old food off the sofa.

They hadn't realized the flat was so small until all those people were standing around. Barry and Cheryl might as well have gone out for all the notice they took of them. It was all to do with lighting, camera positions and microphones. In the car park below were two large white vans full of wiring and equipment.

At least all this looked hopeful.

At least it proved they were still in the running.

It grew into a life-and-death matter that this stunt

came off. From being just a casual idea, the whole enterprise seemed to become the main focus of Cheryl's existence.

It was her only subject.

Sometimes she forgot to feed Victor.

Barry would wake up at night and find her sitting up with the light on, thinking. Even when they watched TV Barry could see that her thoughts were elsewhere, her eyes way off in the distance. He didn't know what she expected from it . . . They had been told there was no money involved, but you'd think she had been offered the lead in a major Hollywood film.

She seemed to imagine her life would change.

There were differences in her already.

She began to take notice of her appearance. She washed her hair three times a week, she had cleaned her shoes the other day and he'd never seen her do that before.

Even their food took on a subtle change . . . 'There's garlic in this,' he had said. 'Is it garlic?'

'Yep,' said Cheryl, 'what's wrong with that?' Almost flirtatious, her voice soft and distant.

'Nothing, it's nice,' said Barry, tucking in.

And she bought tartare sauce for the fish fingers and sneered when he got out the ketchup.

She was getting ideas above her station, but when she came home with a pot plant from Tesco's he began to worry seriously. They had no money for plants that would shrivel and die within a week. They did without eggs for that sodding plant. She watered it to death. He chucked it down the rubbish chute, and wished he could shove her ideas down after it.

Because Barry, who loved her, dreaded what would happen if they were turned down. As they probably would be, bearing in mind the numbers of people who had applied to the Griffin advertisement. He had seen Cheryl depressed before. Oh, not just everyday, bedroom-slipper depression which affected everyone round about here, but serious, sleepless, red-eyed despair which left her thinner, and emptied her as if there was no more room left for hope.

She had stopped taking the antidepressants as soon as she found she was pregnant. Pregnancy seemed to have sorted her out; earlier on he had worried about a miscarriage and what that might do to her mental state.

Now it was Griffin's decision he feared.

The trouble was, if Griffin fell through, there was nothing on the horizon which he could use to cheer her up. Oh, yes, there was the birth, but in Cheryl's case it was being pregnant which seemed to give her the kick she needed. After Victor's birth she had sunk right down. Post-natal depression. All that crap. If only they could have a holiday, a dream holiday, in the sun. They watched the game shows together with envy, hardly able to cheer when some unknown contestant went home with the car, or the three weeks in the Maldives.

A job would be something to shout about.

If Griffin fell through he would have to try harder. He would run messages for Joe Trumper, if necessary . . . Although he had sworn not to touch drugs. He could always make out he was working, Cheryl need never find out.

Touchy-feely – shit – Barry hated all that, but Cheryl enjoyed being rubbed on the arm, kissed as if

56

the crew were intimate, spoken to as if she was part of it, not just a looker-on. These people made Cheryl laugh in a way Barry wished he could: they were witty, clever, casual, laid-back, they rolled their own fags and they drank Coca-Cola.

'Why must you wear white socks?' said Cheryl. 'And those trainers are so gross.'

They made plans to meet down the pub that evening, and you should have seen Cheryl's face, the new yearning in it, the wanting to join them as if she'd been hypnotized, stuck in a trance, and yet if he asked her she'd say, 'How can we?' Or, 'There's nowhere worth going to round here. Let's stop in and watch the box.' Making out he was boring.

They didn't hear and they didn't hear. Cheryl began to sink. Barry watched her.

'It's not the end of the world.'

'What do you know?'

'I know that six weeks back we'd never heard of the programme. We were OK then, weren't we?'

'OK?' She stared at him, made him uncomfortable. 'Is this OK?'

'It could be OK, if we had some luck.'

'Huh. Since when?'

'Your mum's dead against it.'

'Well, she would be.'

'Annie's not stupid.'

'She's a loser, Barry. She's sad, with her weird old ideas. She really believes that you lose something of your soul whenever you have a photograph taken.'

'I never heard you bad-mouth her before.'

'Maybe I never realized before. Maybe my eyes have been opened.'

57

'Oh, yeah?' said Barry. 'By a group of posers who don't give a shit? God, you're so gullible.'

Cheryl got up to warm Victor's bottle. She stood with her back to him, head drooped, wiping mindlessly round the sink. 'I just like them being around, that's all. It's something different, something happening.' She turned to face him, frowning, perplexed. 'Don't you feel it? Don't you sometimes like to feel special?'

'But you're not special . . .'

'Well I feel that I am,' she suddenly shouted, fists clenched, teeth tight together.

'You crave attention, that's what,' said Barry, turning to put on the telly and wishing he had dared to be kinder.

'I'm going to phone them up, I can't stand it,' said Cheryl one week later, staring out over the unkempt sidings of Paddington station.

'You'll scare them off,' warned Barry.

'You think I would?' And her voice was hesitant, like a child's asking for something from Woolies.

'I know it.'

'But I want this to happen so much – you don't understand,' and she fell, sobbing, into his arms.

'Cher, you're special to me,' he tried to remind her, yet fearing this was no longer enough. 'You are the most special person in my life, and always will be.'

He understood how it was for Cheryl. She found it hard to express her feelings. She preferred to joke and clown about, but for once she did not laugh. Or push him away.

The portentous news arrived by letter.

There were forms, solemn forms to read and sign.

They were advised to consult a solicitor. Cheryl laughed excitedly. 'We don't need to do that. Let's sign and get these off before they can change their minds.'

Barry felt such a lightness of spirit, he went along with her frenzied delight. He had ceased to care about anything except the pit of Cheryl's despair. If this was what she needed to pull back from that terrible brink, then he was as joyous as she, and he would do nothing to spoil her happiness.

Sometimes Barry wondered if she really understood the position they were being put in. OK, they might be a tiny bit famous, but not famous for being smart, for being gifted or brave. They would be famous for losing abysmally, for plumbing the depths of personal failure. Nobody would admire or envy them; pity would be the best they could hope for, and Barry couldn't get his head around this.

It must be worse for the man, he thought; maybe that was why Cheryl didn't care, because even in this age of equality, deep down it was still expected for the man to provide for his wife and children. He was the failure, she was 'the brick' and Victor, well, he was the victim. It was hard to think of himself in any positive role, home all day, watching telly, giving Victor the odd feed, shuffling off to the jobcentre to be told there was nothing worth having.

How would he come across to the viewers?

Hardly the hero of the day. Contempt was the only reaction that Barry could reasonably expect.

He tried to explain this to Cheryl – after they'd sent the forms back, of course; he didn't want to suggest that he was any less keen than she was.

'Don't be a jerk,' was her response. 'There's thousands of guys like you, it's not your fault, you didn't ask to be unemployed. You didn't ask to live in this dump, and you can't help being made to feel useless.'

'But it's easier for you . . .'

'Like hell it is.'

'I'll come across as a real loser.'

She shook her head despairingly. 'No you won't. Don't start that. They're not doing this programme to make anyone look like a failure. You are loving and caring, you do your best. The odds are against you, that's all. They're going to give you a positive image, that's what they said.'

'But how?'

'Oh, God, Barry, you're so bloody sad. Can't you, for once in your life, trust the experts to get it right?'

Huh. That was rich. A lower self-esteem than Cheryl's would be hard to imagine. He spread out his hands defensively. He wished they were calloused and soiled by work. He wished that his nails were broken, not smooth and symmetrical like a girl's. 'OK, OK, stay cool . . . I only meant that I don't—'

'I'm not listening. Stop it! Give over! Just be glad it's going ahead, and that something different's about to happen. Because of us, there could be changes. Because of us volunteering, people might look at poverty differently.'

'Oh, yeah, and I'm Richard Branson.'

'I wish. Get a life, bum,' said Cheryl, teasing, and pushed him back across the sofa.

Oh, yes. She was on top of the world.

Arrangements went ahead for the wedding. The baby was due on the fourth, so Annie reckoned the end of the month would be safe to pencil in. They could run to finger rolls, cheese and pineapple on sticks and a cake. But she was reluctant to share her plans with Alan or Bob, or Sebastian.

'That snotty mob. They'll take over, they'll spoil everything. For God's sake, you're having them at the birth. That's disgusting. If you feel happy with your danglies displayed for the world and his wife to see, that's your business. But I'm paying for this wedding. Just you remember that. And it's up to me who's invited.'

'Having them there will be better than Col with his old camcorder,' said Cheryl, sulking. 'He'll be rat-arsed anyway. Last time they had him he ran out of film.'

'That bunch of slapheads from Griffin, hah, you're out of your mind, Cher. You've lost it. They'll not be taking the sort of pictures you're going to want to see in the future. All they'll be doing is looking for trouble and taking the piss out of all of us.'

In the end, though, Annie capitulated. Alan's charms overwhelmed her. She had always had a soft spot for gay men, like the Queen Mother. It was probably the bottle of Gordon's which he thoughtfully bought to butter her up.

Barry had not been consulted about the media coverage of Scarlett's birth.

It was assumed that he approved, that he backed Cheryl in this delicate department. He wasn't quite sure what they intended. Some gory medical close-ups, all red and pink like porn magazines? Or something rather more timid and tasteful, featuring eyes and masks and hands? Nobody knew, not even Cheryl. 'I trust them', she said, 'to be respectful.'

Because of the film the birth was induced to fit in with the schedules. This gave the crew time to set up, and for the equipment to be sterilized.

When Barry and Cheryl arrived that morning for the first serious takes of the series, they were greeted with smiles and hugs and Barry was given a place to stand as if he was a superfluous vase. One of the girls took charge of Victor and the procedure began in earnest. Barry continued to feel uneasy with the male presence in the room. OK, there were only two, but you'd think they'd have chosen a woman for the job. All the midwives were women, after all.

The camera was 'down there', zooming in like the sleazy eye of a shameless peeping Tom. You couldn't tell what those guys were thinking. You couldn't imagine what they'd say after, to their mates, to their wives. As Cheryl groaned and thrashed, they encouraged her like this was a circus and she was a horse with bells on trying to stand on its hind legs. Barry didn't like to join in, in case his voice was being recorded and he sounded a real jerk in front of the world. But this was his child being born, not theirs.

He stayed beside Cheryl's head and stroked her hair, encouraging her with his eyes alone.

He knew he shouldn't be glad, but he was, when a Caesarean was suggested. At least they would cover her up, at least they'd get out from between her legs. But when little Scarlett finally arrived, after they'd laid her on Cheryl's breast, after they'd wiped Cheryl's face and kitted her out in her brand new nightshirt, she held the baby up triumphantly, not towards Barry, as expected, but facing forward for the cameras.

'Smile, little one,' she grinned, 'smile.' And she looked mischievous, like a tufted Madonna.

How they cheered and clapped. 'This girl's a natural,' somebody said.

She gave them exactly what they wanted, and of course they loved her for it.

FOUR

Apart from the enquiry team – particularly Heidi, the WPC with special training – the only other visitors to the flat are Annie and Barry's mum, Cath.

Barry and Cheryl are under constant surveillance, probably Annie and Cath are, too. The flat has been searched from top to bottom, sensitively, with the kindly explanation that this is required procedure.

During the long, long days the conversations are sporadic, dealing with the inconsequential. Sometimes they stray into difficult territory . . . The kids come up, but Cheryl's reaction is so hysterical they struggle to avoid the subject.

Barry and his mum read the letters, some from other parents, whose children have gone missing, a few from crackpots who say serve you right, but most are from people who call themselves 'friends'. We feel we know you, they say, after the documentary. 'It's almost like losing kids of our own.' Many say that the Higginses are constantly in their prayers.

Pale, wan and exhausted, Cheryl survives on tablets and tea, her nights are spent fighting dreams so hellish that waking up to the nightmare is almost preferable. Thoughts of the children control her dreams.

How long can this go on?

The general public begin to believe that the poor little kids are probably dead. Some sicko. Hanging's too good.

But DCI Rowe is more hopeful.

Barry's dad, Bill, stays home. Not for him the daily trip to the flat in the Harold Wilson Building to console his desolate son, a depressing experience at the best of times, and he'd only get in the way. This is women's business, and Cath, with compassionate leave from work, always takes round a casserole or a bit of cold ham on the bone. Well, whatever's wrong you've got to eat, you can't let yourself fade away, can you?

He never saw much of the grandchildren anyway. It was six months since they'd last been in touch. The Higginses weren't that sort of family. Living as they did out in Harlow, and him retired with a bad back from ACE Electronics and Cath still at work in the council canteen, their weekdays were taken up and their weekends busy at various Caravan Club conventions . . . A hobby they had pursued for years, since Barry was little.

Their son was a grave disappointment.

He had always been a difficult kid. Truanting, vandalism, that sort of stuff, to the bewilderment of him and Cath in their neat little home with its open-plan garden. Hailing from the bad old East End, haunted by memories of squalor and grime, they had both come to Harlow as kids in the sixties, a new town of cleanliness and opportunity, open spaces, new schools and library books without snot on the pages.

Barry met Cheryl while working part-time in McDonald's up the West End. He was seventeen at the time, and Cheryl a fifteen-year-old who washed up at weekends to make ends meet.

To the horror of Cath and Bill, Barry had truanted on the very day he was due to take CSE woodwork and art. They went up the school to protest, of course, when they learned that that was all he was worthy of, and had been assured that their son was average but seriously hampered by non-attendance.

With no qualifications and an ongoing recession, Barry's future looked worryingly bleak.

Bill can hardly bear to think about this . . . Barry could have made the big time, everyone told them that. He should be in the first division, a top-rate striker by now. Aged twelve, he was offered a trial for Spurs, all Bill and Cath had ever dreamed of. Rain, hail or shine, Bill had encouraged him, standing cheering on the touchlines, scrubbing his boots while Cath washed his kit and sliced oranges. Year in, year out they supported him, raised funds for the team, organized fixtures. And then the magic moment arrived, but it was as if, suddenly, their son had cowered away from the challenge in case he should fail them all, the coach, his parents, his mates and the junior league itself.

He was that stubborn, he never said why. Just clammed up and sulked. Cath and Bill were heartbroken. It was the death of all their hopes. And then he went haywire, turned delinquent. Skived off school. Mucked about.

Sixteen. It was time he found a job.

But 'it's all a con', he used to moan, lolling around in his scruffy room. 'Why should I want a job, nine to five, mortgage, HP? So why shouldn't I travel, see something of the world? You've only got one life.'

'To travel you need money,' they said.

Barry sneered. 'I'll get money.'

'It doesn't grow on trees,' said Cath.

To travel, of course, you need more than money. The spirit of adventure helps, a certain confidence in yourself and a yearning for new experiences. Barry, like his mates, possessed none of these. Their idea of a good time was conning small shopkeepers into selling them booze, sneaking into pubs under age, staggering home shouting obscenities, waking sleeping children and upsetting late-night dog-walkers. Occasionally they would scrape the odd car, remove the hubcaps and chuck them away. Smash garden ornaments or start small fires in hedges.

They went to watch Harlow Town on a Saturday, but rarely ventured farther.

Happily for Barry and his crew, the police were too busy to bother with them.

Their behaviour, for the times, was considered an acceptable nuisance.

Zero tolerance had not been invented.

The trouble with Barry and his mates was that they knew too much. After the recession, a good many of their hard-working, responsible families had found themselves up to their necks in debt and made ill by the terrors of penury, the very penury their parents had come to the new town to escape.

The royals were a laugh a minute.

Teachers were striking.

The Church was for mealy-mouthed losers and paedophiles, and politicians were hogs at the trough with their legs over anything in trousers or skirts. They also knew that the law wouldn't touch them.

And unless you had a brain the size of the millennium dome and the contacts to go with it, you might as well give up.

But Barry's balloon of negative lethargy was burst early one morning, when he heard the cops were after him for causing an affray in a local pub.

So he had been there, OK, and he'd watched some mates get rat-arsed that night. They'd started a fight, nothing unusual, but one of the bar staff was seriously injured – a billiard cue had pierced his lung.

Later that night, the guy died.

Barry was wanted for questioning.

Or that is what he was led to believe.

So when Bill and Cath, dismayed and ashamed by the behaviour of their delinquent son, arrived home on Sunday night from the Caravan Club meet in Skegness, he was gone.

Scarpered.

No note.

Nothing.

And if that misunderstanding had not happened when it did, Barry would still be getting up at midday and hanging around the market square causing trouble. Or inside, like some of his cronies. Jail fodder, no hopers, the dregs.

It was not until two months later, when Barry finally dared ring home, that Bill and Cath were able to tell him that Nathan and Jake Nolan had confessed to manslaughter and were awaiting trial. There were so many witnesses that night that Barry's statement had never been used.

So Barry had legged it to London, got himself a job of sorts and found himself a girlfriend. Of sorts. And all unnecessarily.

It was Cheryl's mother who was the shock. Not Cheryl herself, although she was a little no-hoper, anyone could tell, and so young. Very pretty, though, in a fragile, waif-like way.

After the first baby arrived the council gave the young couple a flat.

The circle had completed itself.

The Higginses were saddened.

He could have made such a name for himself, but their son was back in the rat-run of a life from where they had all started. And because of his back, which had forced Bill to give up work that year and scratch a living from Cath's low wages and his own disability allowance, they were quite unable to help the lad.

The April wedding was a harrowing experience from which they have never completely recovered.

This was the first time they met the Wattses.

And in front of all those cameras.

They knew that the cameras would be there and they were, naturally, nervous. They might well be blazoned all over the telly in front of all their friends and neighbours. Cath borrowed a posh hat from Glo, the supervisor in the council canteen, who had recently worn the fancy confection for her own daughter's wedding that spring.

The hat was a fat little nest, daisies scooped out in a netting of voile and far too stubby to suit tall, thin Cath.

Cheryl was a picture, although wearing white at a register office with a three-week-old baby parked beside the radiator and a crawling toddler was hardly what one would expect. It was good to see Barry out of jeans. He had hired his suit from Moss Bros, same as Bill, and they both looked smart, although suits did tend to make Bill appear even smaller than his five foot five.

They met their own friends and relations outside, hovering on the pavement between two overfull litter bins. It was the usual nervous, superficial chat you expect before a wedding, quietly fiddling with buttonholes, having the last few puffs on a fag, the snapping of the odd powder compact as lips were dabbed and pressed together, looking up the road for the bride and checking watches.

Lorries changed gear at the roundabout beside them.

'I expect it's quite nice inside.'

They thought they had seen it all when Donny arrived dressed for the Arctic in three heavy coats and with brown sandals with the toes cut out. There were no words to describe the colour of those filthy feet, and you wouldn't believe bunions could grow that large.

'She can't be a guest, can she?'

'Surely not.'

They turned away uneasily.

'She is an old friend of the bride,' they were

finally informed, to their horror. 'She's got a problem, OK, but Cheryl likes her. She's known her since she was just a kid.'

Then Big Annie arrived.

Like a slag.

Like a blowzy madam from a whorehouse stinking of Woolworth's fiercest scent, and in an astonishing black leather skirt that hardly covered her arse. The white frilly blouse was totally see-through and revealed a low-slung brassiere overhung by gigantic, wobbling breasts. She strutted towards them on stiletto heels, chuckling through her bright red lips.

The cameras followed her all the way, from the moment the car door opened to reveal a crotch in black nylon, to the sticky, sweaty embrace she gave Cath, dislodging her hat with her own forthright one. A black straw, with violets, like the packaging on a box of Black Magic.

Before Cath could stop him, Bill went inside with a couple of fat-lip lipstick impressions on both his very close-shaven cheeks. Because of his back he escaped the arrival of the rest of the family of the bride.

Dear God, this was a mockery. No doubt the great British public would find this wedding hilarious. Could nobody else see this but Cath? Were they all so keen to perform for the cameras? Or was it that they were so totally tasteless they had no idea how else to behave?

Men with tattoos across their fingers, studs in their ears and noses, heads close-cropped to the point of shaven, shirts without ties, beer bellies, bad teeth.

Peroxide-haired women with bold faces, bulging calves, glittered cheeks and black eyes. Snappy handbags of see-through plastic and sparkling earrings that stretched tortured lobes. Girls and boys in the latest gear, no colour, certainly none in their faces, and trainers or clumpy platform shoes on each huge foot. Spotty. Pale. Ill.

While Cath and Bill might have risen in the world, most of the Higginses had risen even higher . . . A driving instructor graced the family now, Sue's husband, living in Bishop's Stortford; Doug had done well in the navy and was here impressively uniformed; Connie had risen as high as she could in the high-powered world of loose covers and David ran a successful business in do-it-yourself garden sheds. And so it was in front of these people that Cath had to smile and act pleased that her only son, the handsome Barry, for whom they had once had such very high hopes, had brought the Harlow Higginses to this.

This, unlike Barry's previous behaviour, couldn't be blurred in the trivia of occasional telephone calls.

This, unlike messages on cards, couldn't be laughed off behind exclamation marks. *He has gone to London to seek his fortune!!!!*

This could not be diverted: 'Oh, Barry's fine, how's Lindsey?'

This was for real. This was being photographed. This would appear on the telly.

Sebby concentrated on the bride while Leo covered the family and guests.

Cheryl was lovely; she was a natural, and the nasty piece of scum who had conned her at the

72

photo shoot had been a fool to turn her down. But these stupid little wannabes are so desperate for fame and fortune, they'll believe every word they are told so long as the guy has a card with a name like Paramount or Mecca stamped on it. Told they are having a screen test, they give these ponces their bodies for free and then wonder why they've been rejected.

But, Sebby thought to himself as he followed Cheryl along the pavement, giving her a wink for good luck, he and Leo were no better. They were there to report the truth. What truth? Whose truth? The truth the director wanted them to see and, in this case, that meant the bizarre, the eccentric, the pathetic, the humorous, and you could call that life, except that Sebby knew full well how scenes could be manipulated, mannerisms exaggerated and dialogue vetted to suit the occasion.

Cheryl was the victim here. They were filming her at her most vulnerable in order to milk public sympathy. They would build her up for their own purposes in order to cut her down when it suited. Some subjects could deal with this. A few nutters thrived on notoriety, or being seen as number-one buffoon, or portrayed as hard-nosed, or vain. But Cheryl Higgins was different. For one, she was too young, and second, she was too genuine.

Take this wedding, for instance. When the average bash cost twelve grand, when Mrs OK watching at home had spent at least one thousand on a dress, she was bound to be mawkishly fascinated by the antics of these losers. The worst part was the copycat aspect. Why do have-nots insist on mimicking those who have? Why not play by their own rules?

73

Why have a reception at all, with nibbles and sickly-sweet sparkling wine? Why not stick to beer and beefburgers? Why wear a hat if you can only afford a cheap copy from C&A? What the hell was the point of a dress of white nylon when you'd look just great in cotton? And why the Barbara Cartland make-up when you'd normally do it more naturally?

The money being spent on this farce was depressing.

Why, in these kids' circumstances, would you want to get married at all?

None of these people were being themselves, apart from the bag lady. And knowing about the cameras was fatal. They were all performing. Showing off or hiding. Playing into the cameraman's hands with no idea of their true intentions. Trusting in their integrity.

Leo has no reservations, Leo is more of a cynic than Sebby, but Leo is a genius with a unique style and technique, and to work with him is a chance no-one in the profession would miss. His openness and charisma charm his helpless subjects; they instantly warm towards him without his appearing to make any effort. He has an extraordinary knack of making people feel special. People confide in him. People expose themselves. Already Sebby has noticed how Cheryl has fallen under his spell, and unfortunately there is no doubt that Barry has sussed this out, too.

When Sebby learned that Leo had asked specifically to work with him on this project, he had felt flattered and a little surprised. There were more experienced, more talented guys than him working for Griffin just then, and it was only recently that Sebby had started wondering if Leo's motives had been professional, or if he had been chosen for more underhand reasons.

Certainly there were those in the company who would never have agreed to use the porn. And at one time neither would Sebby.

He glances over the top of the camera and sees Leo over the road. Even from here Sebby senses that his colleague is working tongue-in-cheek.

Everyone at Griffin was aware that Alan Beam, the series director, was a cold fish, unscrupulous, and biding his time with the company until he could start on his own. Only a couple of years ago a teenager had topped himself after Alan reneged on a promise and outed him in front of five million people. He'd shown the lad's face on a documentary which featured Clapham Common. Not only had the camera singled him out and turned him into a sex machine, but he was fooled into giving an interview believing his voice would be changed. Then there was that court case when Griffin had to cough up huge damages. And it was rumoured that sometimes money changed hands when Alan needed a particular angle. And it was surprising how many faces Joe Public could wear for the right price.

Jennie St Hill was a new face to Griffin and therefore an unknown quantity. Kate, Sebby's partner, would like her: they were of a similar type, both educated at Wycombe Abbey but five years apart. Aware of his studious, slovenly image – Sebby preferred to buy his clothes from Oxfam, and campaigned energetically to save the earth – he constantly puzzled over his luck at attracting a sophisticated looker like Kate. She was fun. She was sweet. She was kind. Best friend and lover in one. They had been together for five years now, since he left university, so she must see some good in him.

Jennie St Hill had been headhunted from Red Carpet Films, so she had to be good, she must be the best. Why she should pander to Alan's devious schemes was certainly a mystery, but perhaps, in these pressurized times, that kind of subterfuge comes with the territory.

Sebby cringes at his own hypocrisy. But, in his case, his excuses were simpler. The Covent Garden flat had been a huge mistake. Here was Sebby, criticizing this lot for copying their betters but without style, while he and Kate were doing just the same in his third-floor flat in Neal Street.

But Kate had been working then. She had prospects. They felt secure when they signed the lease. *Tone* magazine, topical, tasteful and intelligent, was launched in a welter of media applause, and the high-street sales soon overtook their nearest rival, *Marie Claire*. Until then he and Kate had been stuck out in West Hampstead, and they managed to convince themselves that, for the sake of both their careers, they needed to be more central.

But success, these days, is a transient business, and about the same time that *Tone* sank without trace Sebby started hearing disturbing reports of downsizing at Griffin.

He was hardly in a position to turn down the chance when it came, of making a series that had every chance of securing his immediate future. How could he fall back on his integrity when Kate was finding it almost impossible to find the kind of work she wanted? She was too choosy. She was aiming too high. But how did you tell someone that?

But Cheryl really did look lovely.

The registrar, like a fifties presenter, had bouffant hair and mellowed tones with a *Muffin the Mule* TV accent. The flowers were plastic, the music taped. But the kiss the couple gave each other was real, genuine and full of young love.

'Perhaps it won't last,' said Cath's sister, Betty, rather insensitively, Cath thought. I mean, it was her only son's wedding day. 'After all,' Betty continued, 'they're both too young to know their own minds.'

Outside the reception venue, two dogs humped in the car park and a splatter of caramel-coloured vomit decorated the wall.

Liza Donnolly, as was, sat down on the pavement and waited, muttering, until the door was unlocked.

At this point Cath gave up. Inside the Bunch of Grapes at last, and she laid her bag down on the table with her money and wallet inside it. If they nicked it, they nicked it – she'd had enough.

Bill had given up earlier, but he bore these things better than she did. He might be small but he was hardy, apart from his troublesome back.

This was a serious booze-up. Few of the guests would leave here upright. The Higginses' party pushed four tables together and kept strictly to their end of the room. But little conversation could be had over the roaring disco music and the raucous bellowing of the family of the bride. Their throats grew sore from shouting. Their tables grew sloppy from dancers thudding their glasses and bottles down as near as was convenient, and stubbing out their fags in wet ashtrays in this mainly non-smoking part of the room.

They bopped and hopped like gormless gibbons. And all the while the cameras whirled.

And all the while Cath stayed smiling, with a red-wine stain on her powder-blue suit, aware of how she was looking, concerned that any thoughtless expression might give away her revulsion of the Wattses and everything they stood for.

But in one matter, and one matter alone, the Higginses stood shoulder to shoulder with Big Annie. Both Bill and Cath considered the venture for Griffin TV not only absurd, but dangerous.

'If they're determined to make nerds of themselves, they ought to be doing it for money,' stated Annie.

'But all the money in the world wouldn't compensate them for their loss of privacy.' Cath attempted to persuade Big Annie that money wasn't everything. 'And the subject, poverty, it's so embarrassing. You'd think they'd both be ashamed.'

'There's nothing shameful about being sodding poor.'

'Oh, I know, of course there isn't, but you don't normally advertise the fact.'

'I told them that,' admitted Big Annie, 'but Cheryl's that obstinate. I think she's been over-whelmed by the thought of going on telly. Someone might spot her, that sort of thing.'

'I never knew Cheryl had leanings in that direction.'

'Don't we all?' asked Big Annie, surprised.

'Cheryl used to dream of being an actress, and she's got a lovely singing voice.'

'Perhaps she'll get to sing lullabies,' said Cath hopefully, disturbed by the new and terrible knowledge that the birth itself was to be made public. She did not want to see her daughter-in-law's private parts. How could she look her in the face again, knowing those things about her? A wedding is bad enough, but a birth . . .

Trust Barry to get himself mixed up with this distasteful sort of thing.

After Scarlett was born, a good nine months before the programme's transmission, Cath and Bill visited the Harold Wilson Building bearing gifts of grapes and flowers. Their second grandchild – and a girl. Scarlett, rather overdramatic; Diana might have been nice – in memory. They were troubled by the lack of facilities, the seedy nature of the place, which seemed to have worsened since their last visit, and the statements of violence on the walls outside, dripping in aggressive red paint.

The presence of the camera crew was a strain.

As Cath told Glo, her supervisor, afterwards, 'Cheryl and Barry took no notice, but the visit was ruined for me. I felt that damn zoom lens on my face when I first saw little Scarlett, when I picked her up, when I kissed her. Well, how can you begin to be natural, knowing you are being filmed like that? I'm sure I kept on patting my hair, and I worried that my nose would be shiny, and I've only got one good side and they kept going round to the other. I can't imagine what's going to come out of all this . . . I dread it, Glo, I honestly do.'

'You'll have to go away when they show it,' was Glo's unhelpful comment.

'For twelve weeks? How? You're talking about the whole of the winter, and Bill couldn't sit for long on a plane.'

You would think that the film crew, Sebby and Leo, lived in that flat they were so familiar, helping themselves to chocolates, nibbling the gifts of fruit. Two young men, one smart, one a slob – they stayed there all night sometimes, Barry said, and they had the nerve to call Cath by her first name as if they'd known her all her life.

They all laughed fondly together like a family when Victor attempted to crawl.

'I don't know how you live with the strain,' Cath said to Cheryl. 'Especially with a newborn baby.'

She had seen, but not commented, on the brazen way Cheryl displayed her breast with its enlarged areola, unconcerned about whether the cameras were rolling. Cath wanted to ask if they filmed them on the toilet or in the bath; it was all so horribly intimate that it seemed perfectly possible.

But Cheryl, the show-off, was over the moon. 'Everyone's so nice to us, all the neighbours, they know what's going on and they're worried we might say something nasty about them. It's wicked, it gives you power. Some of them keep calling, they want to be on the box. And Barry at the jobcentre, they've stopped mouthing off at him. The cameras go with him now – they daren't treat him like scum any more.'

'No luck on the work front, then?' Bill asked Barry, hoping the lad would redeem himself before the filming was over. 'You're a father twice over now, you know, son.' And Bill gave the cameras a knowing wink. The one called Leo smiled back at him. Men of the world to men of the world, or lads, in this case.

Little did anyone know that day that Cheryl was already brooding, already dreading the day when Sebby and Leo, her heroes, would pack up their equipment and go.

FIVE

Back then . . .

When the filming began in earnest, Leo and Sebby were with the Higginses almost every hour of the day, and some nights. One or other of the directors called on a regular basis. Alan made Barry nervous in the same way that Jennie affected Cheryl.

Sometimes one of them hung around for a whole morning, and their critical presence affected the kids. Victor in particular would act like a real pain in the arse, and you could be sure Scarlett wouldn't settle. Perhaps this was because they sensed their parents' tension. Having Alan or Jennie just sitting thoughtfully watching or making suggestions turned the whole thing into a kind of ordeal.

'You don't like Alan because he's a poof,' said Cheryl. 'Men who have tendencies of their own in that direction can feel very threatened, and that's why they turn aggressive.'

Barry snorted. 'Dream on. He's too clean to be real. See the way he clears the sofa whenever he wants to sit down. Watch him check the mugs for stains whenever you give him a coffee. He thinks he's superior. I've never seen such shiny hair. He hates it when Victor goes near him.'

'But you're always trying to impress him. Yuk! Using big words, like impeccable. You said impeccable this morning . . .'

'I never.'

'Barry, I heard you. Alan thinks he's better than you because you treat him that way. And when Jennie's here you hardly speak.'

'OK, OK. Now she *does* scare me. So does that mean I secretly lust after really classy birds?'

'You tell me.'

'She doesn't like us.'

'What makes you say that? She couldn't be nicer. She's friendly. She's funny.'

'The trouble with you is you're one of those prats who have no judgement at all when it comes to people. You're born with it or you're not, and I'm sorry, but you don't have it. Just because she kisses you whenever she sees you and pretends to be a fan of *EastEnders*. When Jennie asks you out to lunch with a couple of her fancy friends, or to the ballet, then I might change my mind.'

Sebby and Leo had settled in quickly. They soon became part of the furniture.

It was easy to forget they were there, embarrassingly easy sometimes. From the start of April until July the cameras followed Cheryl and Barry whenever they left the flat. Wherever they went, people stared and small crowds gathered. They came with them round the supermarket, to the children's area of the pub, to Annie's house back on the estate, on their walks through the park. They sat with them on buses as the kids screamed and whined and licked the dirty windows, they joined them in the Safeway canteen when their table was left covered in orange, they accompanied them to social services where they went to try to scrounge a new cooker, to the clinic with the kids, to the doctor with Scarlett's chest, to the fair in the park, and on Victor's birthday, Sebby and Leo helped them wrap his presents.

All from catalogues.

Bringing their debts up to five quid a week.

Nosy parkers would wend their way up to the fifth floor of the building to see what was going on, and sometimes even have the nerve to gawp at them through the small window, barred because of vandals.

'Wanna bun, Trunky?' Cheryl would yell, and they'd fall about laughing.

When the guys weren't filming they sat chatting, smoking, reading the papers, telling jokes. Leo liked to muck about, Sebby was sweet, and so serious, his huge brown eyes always watching behind those solemn lenses. The telly was hardly ever on. They felt like family. Very close. If only she could have brothers like this, instead of those cretins Bobby and Shane . . . But it wasn't all brotherly feelings. Did they fancy her, did they find her attractive?

In childlike awe of both of them, to Cheryl they came from another world. They were exciting, they had presence, they mingled with celebrities sometimes. Leo had been a photographer for the *Mirror*, he had met Madonna and Diana, he had been invited to Scary Spice's wedding. They'd both been to university. Sebby had ridden on the *Rainbow*

84

Warrior. During his short, brilliant career he had visited Antarctica, he had swum with dolphins and ridden on elephants. They named a few documentaries, some of which she had heard of, but which were mostly for BBC2.

She fantasized over what she would do if one of them made a pass at her. Sometimes Leo flirted with her. Stupid, she felt herself heating up. Blushing. Acting daft. But they wouldn't want someone like her . . . thick as a plank, boring, mostly stinking of baby sick or with her arms in greasy washing-up water. Did their pity make them dislike her? They made her feel like rubbish, sometimes, like leavings, like potato peelings. If they did make a pass it would be for a laugh, something to kill time, and anyway, Leo was married and expecting a baby and Sebby had a posh girlfriend.

She needed to know about their women. She stared at the photographs they showed her. So easy, relaxed and beautiful; even with her lack of experience, she could tell the clothes were expensive, and the backgrounds were always beaches or ski runs or small country pubs full of friends.

She stared at the pictures, tantalized, amazed to feel the jealousy there. It grew until she was needled by envy.

She tried to make herself pretty for them. She tried to make herself witty and quick.

She wondered what they told their women, how they described her and Barry.

They probably didn't bother.

But seriously, would Cheryl cheat on Barry if Sebby or Leo wanted her? Look what sort of life they could give her, look at their energy, their

85

talents. She would turn into a different person, with designer haircuts; she'd be able to drive. She would be surrounded by sophisticated people, she would eat out, she would fly. No more dull days, no more debts. And how about making love? They would probably indulge in erotic methods which her and Barry just giggled about. They would probably take her to the sorts of heights she read about in magazines.

She was flummoxed by these feelings, so strong, more like an addiction to something they represented, more like a crack habit than a straightforward crush.

What made her think like this? Certain looks they gave her? Some inflection in their voices? Some tremor communicated from them to her, or was it plain self-deception? A passion for self-destruction, or just the flattery of their attention? Whatever it was, it left Cheryl bewildered. They had no room in their lives for her. They would most likely think that she would be an easy lay. In this strange relationship they were active, she was passive; they made suggestions, she followed their lead. And although Sebby and Leo acted relaxed and friendly, they had a superior air – theirs was the power, the glory. But would she chuck Barry and go with one of these guys if they asked her?

No. These were dream thoughts. Barry was real. Barry was safe and hers, as neither of them would ever be.

When there were small disagreements, Cheryl and Barry were outwitted.

Mainly they rowed about privacy.

If Cheryl and Barry had a slanging match, or if

Cheryl started to cry, exhausted, or if she was up in the night all baggy-eyed and cold and they were still there, pointing the camera, that's when sparks were likely to fly.

'Sod off for God's sake, you perverts,' Barry would shout. 'Leave us alone! Get stuffed.'

Sebby and Leo mostly stayed cool. Their way was to try to reason.

'Look, I know this is difficult, I know it's traumatic to have us here like this, but we have to record the bad times, you know.'

'They're all bad times here, stop messing about. You come here slumming it, so full of shit with your sleeves rolled up, your designer jeans, your cars outside . . . And Christ, you must be laughing.'

'Barry, loosen up. You know it's nothing like that.'

'Oh, yeah? Oh, yeah? So I'm a right dickhead, am I?'

And Cheryl would cringe for Barry, not because he had lost it but because he sounded like such a fool. He made himself look smaller, he couldn't win. This was his world, and he and Cheryl were stuck in it while Sebby and Leo could go down in the lifts and pass through some magic door into another lifestyle, one that Cheryl secretly craved.

Hell. What was the password?

She felt ashamed and embarrassed for Barry because he was the specimen pinned in the dish, and Leo and Sebby were dissecting him.

There was nothing sacred any more.

Not even the bedroom.

'OK kids,' Leo might say, 'let's get some shots of you dossing down.'

And although it was a suggestion, you understood it was really an order. They had the power of Griffin behind them, they had the power of knowledge and skill, and to her surprise and shame, Cheryl discovered that it was a turn-on. She couldn't help it. She liked being submissive – it felt so safe with Leo and Sebby.

The first time this happened: 'You've really got to try to forget that either of us are here.'

'You must be joking,' said Barry, 'telling us to strip off.' And he stood against the bedroom door looking small again, being loud. There was no way he could win.

'If we want this to be real – and we do, and the executives at Griffin do, and our producer does, and even, you know, Alan does – then we can't muck about. We're not going to zero in on boobs and pricks and arses, this film is going to be carefully edited, but it's got to be natural, it's got to be right. Our reputations are on the line. We don't do fiction, OK?'

'Just get them off and get into bed,' said Sebby quietly behind the camera. 'In your own time. I'm ready.'

Cheryl and Barry looked at each other. 'Jesus Christ,' said Barry, hunching, 'is this real?'

'It doesn't matter,' said Cheryl. 'What does it matter, anyway? You and me, we're not going to turn anyone on, let's face it.'

And she made the first move by unzipping her jeans and stepping out of one leg, then another. 'Cheryl, give over . . .'

'Shut up, Barry,' said Leo, 'we're shooting. Just get on with it, please. We're all tired, we all want some sleep.'

Cheryl turned her back to the cameras when she removed her bra, and slipped her nightdress over her head before she took her pants off. She gave Leo a quick, nervous glance and slipped under the covers, pulling them up so only her face could be seen.

'Well at least that's a start of sorts,' said Sebby uncomfortably, and Barry took off his shirt and jeans and kept his underpants on.

'You don't know,' Barry whispered to Cheryl after the lights went out. 'They could be fudge-packers too, for all we know.'

'They're not,' said Cheryl.

He turned his head so it faced hers on the pillow. 'How d'you know that?'

'I just do,' said Cheryl, stopping right there.

After that, of course, it went further. It always did. Everything.

'Make a fuss of her, then,' Leo ordered. 'You're young, you're randy, you're macho. At least roll on top of her, show the viewers you're not just a stiff lying in bed beside her.'

'Sod off,' growled Barry, furious.

'D'you need me to show you?'

'Jesus,' Barry moaned.

'Come on, kid, play the game.'

In the end Barry did. He had no option; they had signed the forms, hadn't they? He rolled on top of her, groaning. 'What a farce,' he muttered under his breath. 'They'll demand that I get a hard-on next.'

But as time went by it was no big deal. There was hardly any modesty left. How could they be so uninhibited? It wouldn't take much to persuade them to roam round the flat half naked if that's what was wanted of them. They had grown so used to the camera's presence. And this, of course, is what Griffin TV had aimed at all along.

It was such intrusive stuff. The Higginses were so eager to please it was getting pathetic. And Cheryl's great need to be liked was sometimes unbearable to watch.

How could the directors consider playing such a cheap, despicable trick?

Maybe the filming would go so well there would be no need for the sick pics. Perhaps Alan might decide to drop the soft porn idea. Cheryl and Barry were so likeable, what was the need for such intervention? And as every day went by and Sebby grew closer to the family, their vulnerability hit him harder and his own sense of power seemed more shameful.

Sebby consoled himself with the thought that the pictures would not change public perceptions. Except for a few Mary Whitehouse loonies.

He watched Leo working with admiration. He watched the way his colleague charmed and wormed his way into the young couple's confidence, so that in the end one word from him and they happily jumped to please. The methods he used on Cheryl were so glaringly obvious. It didn't take a week to win her round, and the danger was, naive as she was, that she would read Leo wrongly. Barry was a different proposition: not overawed by the gift of the gab, or affected by cool good looks, or impressed by Leo's name-dropping tactics, he was beaten in the end by the matey ploy. All lads

together. Changing-room jokes. Men of the ter-
races. Team spirit.

And Leo, who had only ever attended a match to
cover it for the *Mirror*'s back pages, slotted into the
role so neatly you would think he was Tottenham's
number-one fan.

On a half-day's filming they used to finish at the
Painted Lady pub round the corner. Didn't Leo
have any idea of the dangerous consequences of his
flirtatious behaviour? Sebby had to confront him.

'She's a real sweetie,' Leo casually drawled over
his half of lager. 'It's no act on my part, and I don't
see the problem.'

God, he was an insensitive sod. 'She's taking it all
to heart,' said Sebby.

'That's not my fault,' Leo scowled.

'It'll end in tears.'

'She's not that simple-minded.'

'It's not a question of being thick, it's to do with
low self-esteem, insecurity. You're a hero in her
eyes. Yes, it's that simple. She's easily impressed
and you don't have to look far to see why.'

Leo leaned back and smiled. 'She's knowing
enough to have posed for those pictures.'

'Take another look at them, Leo. That's not
knowing. That's a kid being conned. There's nothing remotely erotic about them.'

'So what are you getting at?'

'Ease up, that's all. You've got her where you
want her.'

Leo stared at Sebby, still grinning. 'Do I detect a
concern here that's something more than professional interest?'

What was the point in talking to the man? It

might have been better if Sebby had left it. 'You can turn them on easily enough, it's turning them off that can be a problem.'

'I presume you're speaking from personal experience?'

'It's a well-known human condition, Leo. Cheryl is particularly vulnerable, that's all. And if you can't see that, I can't convince you.'

'You underestimate her,' said Leo drily, getting up to buy another drink. 'You underestimate them both.'

But it wasn't just Cheryl and Barry that caused Sebby such concern, it was the little boy, Victor, and the effect their intimate involvement would have on his life after they left. They were at the Higginses' flat in a professional capacity, but there was no doubt that their presence created a very different atmosphere from the one that Sebby suspected existed in their absence.

Even Leo, a father-to-be, played with the child, who was trusting and friendly and easily pleased. They bought him toys – nothing much, but it was hard to resist the temptation when you saw how little he had. They provided two more sets of arms when the going got tough and the baby played up. They were not averse to heating bottles, to popping out for pizzas, to working out complicated Lego constructions or bringing up the odd burst of wind.

Even outings that might have proved hellish were more light-hearted with the cameras around. In Sebby's eyes, it was depressing how helpful and friendly strangers could be the moment they realized they might be on telly, people who, in other circumstances, would probably shrug and pass by if they saw a mother trying to cope with a pram on a crowded bus. There was no doubt that he and Leo smoothed out some of the choppier waters in the Higginses' bleak puddle of life.

Leo could be hilarious. He made Cheryl laugh till she cried. Barry rose to these occasions, and together they clowned around, mimicking the pompous, outrageously rude, giggling like kids over silly situations. Anyone seeing them together might think they were four friends on an outing.

Except for the accents.

Except for the gear.

Except for the fact that Leo went first and never carried the shopping.

There was the deep kind of talking Cheryl loved, and had never indulged in in her life before.

'But how do we get out of this? We're stuck. Barry gets work and that's it, they stop all our benefits. There's no work round here pays that much.'

'You get some education,' said Sebby, rolling two fags and handing her one.

'Oh, yeah? Barry and I have got nothing. No qualifications at all.'

'That's no fault of yours. But it is your fault if you just accept it.'

'What sort of qualifications?'

'Well . . . whatever you think you'd be good at. What about nursing?'

'Don't you need maths?'

'You could get maths. You could be a nursing auxiliary. You don't need anything for that.'

'I can't even do my nine times table.'

'Neither can I. Don't be so negative, Cher. You'd get through maths if you really wanted to. And what about young Barry here? What about a mechanic? You like cars, don't you?'

Barry's face reddened. 'Your wife, is she a nursing auxiliary?' he asked Leo sarcastically. 'And how about Kate, Sebby, what does she do? And why don't you work in a garage yourself?'

'Ah,' Leo said, laughing, and he had such a sexy laugh, such white teeth, not one out of line. 'So your horizons are unlimited, Barry? Well, where do you want to start, you tell me?' But Barry couldn't tell them anything. He knew nothing about qualifications; going back to school he would call it. A waste of time, a con. But he came out with a big word for him. 'You patronizing bastards.'

'Only trying to help,' said Leo, winking slyly at Cheryl. 'But you can't possibly live here for ever. You can't survive on this pittance. You must have some ambitions. Good God, I'd go mad.'

'But it's difficult with the kids,' started Cheryl, pitying Barry's dilemma.

'That's crap,' Leo snapped. 'There's government help if you look for it. Especially if you're trying to better yourselves, as they like to put it.'

Cheryl would spend hours trying to explain. She loved these discussions, she loved the fact that they were talking about her and concerned about her future. 'It's lack of self-confidence,' she used to stress, over and over again. 'Barry and me, we're not like you. I mean, think about it, here we are taking part in a film about mega-losers. We were chosen, we were actually chosen to represent the poor and oppressed. So it's not that easy to believe you actually have the power to make things happen in your life.'

Once, when Barry was out, Leo said, 'Why him? What the hell made a girl like you shack up with the likes of him?'

Sebby got up and moved away. He fiddled with the lighting in the corner. Cheryl was shocked; she giggled. 'Barry? Why did I marry Barry?' For an awful couple of moments she couldn't think of an answer, and Leo's smile widened, his eyebrows rose and almost met. 'He's funny, he's kind, he's great-looking, he tries his best . . . He could have played for Spurs, you know, he was offered a trial.'

'But he doesn't play for Spurs, does he?' was Leo's quiet answer. 'Let's face it, he does fuck all.'

After clearing his throat, Sebby interrupted. 'Leo. Can you come here a minute, and take a look at this?'

But Cheryl, absorbed, pressed on. 'He's funny and kind and gentle, and he makes me feel good about myself, not small, like you do . . .'

'Hang on, hang on, how do I make you look small?'

Cheryl blushed. 'Just by being here.'

Leo sounded amused. 'Well I certainly don't mean to.'

She controlled her voice; it had started to tremble. The heat that surged through her body was fiery. Could he see it? Was he aware of how he made her feel? She loved this close, suggestive kind of talking, she loved it but it frightened her.

'You make him sound like a friend. Where does love, where does sex come into it?'

95

Cheryl was stumped for an answer. He seemed so condemning, so contemptuous of her. She merely looked up at Leo, confused, and he smiled at her knowingly so that her heart contracted again.

'And now?' he asked her. 'And in the future? Will you always be satisfied by the second-rate?'

'Yes,' she stated simply, in order to take that smile off his face. 'He's not second-rate. He's first. I love him. And he loves me.'

There were none of these awkward complications before the cameras started rolling.

When this was finished, when the work was all over and Leo and Sebby moved on, would they cut the Higginses out of their lives for ever? Was this merely work for them, was their friendship so superficial?

Cheryl could not believe that was true.

If Barry and Cheryl got to be stars, maybe the crew would include them in their circle of equals. Maybe they, too, would have evenings out with Leo, Sebby, Sophie and Kate; maybe they would go skiing in France, have a villa with friends in the summer, and eventually Victor and Scarlett would rub shoulders with their children . . . Go to the same schools, the same parties, the same universities.

Barry would have to change, of course. Barry would have to learn to feel less of a failure, less defensive, less of a joker. But give him fame and fortune, and who knows what might happen to Barry?

Thoughts of the crew's eventual departure began to obsess poor Cheryl. Two more months to go, and then the flat would go quiet again. There would be no-one to talk to, no-one to bring her the odd avocado, to fry up crisp bacon sandwiches, to start the morning with some real life. There would be no point in getting dressed to look pretty or bothering to turn off the telly. There would be no reason to wash her hair or put on mascara.

OK, next January the documentary would be on TV, and that would be just brilliant. That would make people talk – and that might be the making of them. They could be invited to take part on chat shows and attend charity events. They would have to buy the papers the next day to see what the critics said, but never mind the critics, it would be fascinating to see for themselves how they came across on screen.

Cheryl had never seen herself on video before. You couldn't count the post office or C&A, they're mostly fuzzy, and back views anyway. The Higginses had no say in the editing process, and nobody had mentioned that they might get a preview before the finished documentary series was shown. Would the Higginses come across in a sympathetic light, or would they look like a couple of pricks?

Only time would tell.

But she hoped, oh, how she hoped . . . There was nothing wrong in dreaming.

And in his own supercilious way, Alan Beam was reassuring. 'You come over very well,' he said. 'You are both marvellously photogenic.'

'But can I see?'

'Not yet.'

*   *   *

She'd been nagging about a baby again.

'You're joking,' Barry said, over the racket of kids screaming.

'No, I mean it. I can't bear the thought of everything finishing. Barry, I feel frightened. As if life will end when they go.'

'But another kid won't help. Christ, Scarlett's only eight weeks old.'

'It *would* help. Believe me, I know for certain that if I was pregnant there'd be something new going on in my life.'

'You're mad. You can't mean this, Cher.' Barry was almost crying.

'I wouldn't be saying it if I didn't mean it.'

'How would we cope with another kid?'

'Like we cope with two.'

'But we don't cope. We hardly survive.'

'Well then, we'd survive.'

All this was a very different matter when Barry was on the job. He was brain-dead, he was desperate as he bonked maniacally up and down. Then Cheryl had the upper hand. Then Cheryl could demand the earth, and he would swear he would get it for her.

She knew she was being unreasonable, she knew she was putting him under pressure, and she knew that he was afraid she might slip into that old depression again. Have to go back on the pills. Stay in bed most of the day. Cry over nothing, cry over everything, leave him to look after the kids, do the cooking, the washing, the cleaning.

But she was so afraid of oblivion . . .

And what Cheryl did not know was that her silly maternal longings – her quest to create something grand and beautiful, akin to a work of art – would be the massive mistake which would light the touch-paper and turn the popular Higginses into the most reviled couple in the land.

The fool was playing straight into their hands.

SIX

A brilliant sun blazed.

Five floors down, and the trains give their two-note manic shriek as they leave for destinations unknown to the watchers far above them. Sometimes, when there's no wind, you can hear the echo of the station tannoy, voices sounding out of the distance, one immense blended murmur. Comforting at night, when you think you're alone and there's nobody else awake except you.

'Tell us again, Cheryl,' says DCI Rowe, a man of ice who brought a chill like the air round a glacier into the tiny flat, hunched in a chair with a sagging bottom which social services had provided free, 'I know how painful this is, but let's go through it just one more time.'

He is suspicious. He does not believe her. Why?

Where is she going wrong? Her teeth are close to chattering.

Every day the fuzz come round, every day there is this sort of pressure and every day Cheryl fights to recall what she told them last time.

'It was just gone nine . . .'

'How d'you know that?' he asked, with his strange, slightly sour smile.

'Because the news was coming on telly.'

'What channel?'

'BBC1. And we always flick it to ITV when the news comes on. Anyway, I wanted to get there early, so I kept checking the time, like you do . . .'

'And Barry helped you down the stairs?'

'Yes, because the lift wasn't working.'

'And then he left you and came back up here?'

'Yes, he came back to clear up. The breakfast stuff, the beds, the kids' night things. They were all over the floor.' Cheryl sniffs and stares the cop deliberately in the eye.

He stares back until she is forced to capitulate. 'Why did you take all three children? Surely it would have been far easier to take only Cara, as she was the one who had the infection?'

'They like to go to the clinic. There's toys there, boxes of them, and a tractor and trailer that Victor can ride on.' Cheryl adds angrily, 'They don't get out much. They're mostly stuck in here, bored, like us.'

'But surely Scarlett is too young to know?'

'No she's not, she's moving around on her own now. There's more space for her there, and if she goes out it means we can put her down straight after.'

'Put her down for a sleep?'

'Yes, the fresh air makes her tired,' says Cheryl patiently. She has told him all this ten times before, but he insists she might remember something which has eluded her so far.

'And the walk to the clinic from here takes ten minutes?'

'Yes, more or less.'

'But you still can't remember seeing anyone you knew – neighbours, shopkeepers, regular passers-by, other mums with kids . . .'

'You know that I didn't see anyone. I would have said if I'd seen anyone.'

'OK, Cheryl, OK, just try to be patient with us.'

Heidi, the WPC who spends the most time at the flat, offers to make them a cup of tea. This is all so different to how it was when the film crew were here. This is so complicated, so loaded with tension, and Cheryl just wants to sleep, to get her kids back, to tell the truth, to get it over and done with.

She'd never dreamed it would get this bad. She'd never imagined they'd hassle her like this. She'd thought they would be gentle and comforting, not hovering like a pack of wolves to isolate her and tear her to pieces.

Back then . . .

Three-quarters of the way through filming Cheryl had announced she was pregnant in a manner she thought would appeal to the viewers.

The cameras were rolling, and she and Barry were in the kitchen cooking egg on toast. She sidled up to him sweetly and said, 'Barry, Barry listen . . . You know I said I wanted a baby?'

Barry flinched from the spitting fat. He was too focused on the pan to hear her.

So Cheryl looked directly at Leo and smiled at her invisible audience. 'Well, it's worked. I am pregnant.' She said this with a breathless sense of being on the brink of a marvellous discovery.

Barry heard the last remark and straight away

102

turned off the gas. His face was a picture of horrified disbelief. 'You can't be, we only did it once.'

'I went to see the nurse yesterday. She gave me the results this morning . . . I'm nearly eight weeks on.'

Sebby stopped filming. His mouth was tight, his eyes were angry. 'You *are* kidding? Tell me this can't really be happening?'

She ought to have picked up on those first vibes. She ought to have noted this first reaction. When Leo took over, there was scorn in his voice. 'You deliberately went and got pregnant? Living here? In these conditions? In the state you both are in?' He went on filming. His eyes were bright. He closed in on Barry's reactions.

Cheryl, shocked and hurt because he had ruined her special moment, said, 'What the hell has this got to do with you?' But she didn't know what to do. She couldn't take it back now. And she caught a glimpse of herself as the cameras would see her in the mirror over the fireplace – head up in an attitude of defiance and a glare of white in her eyes.

'Oh, Jesus Christ. Must I spell it out?' Leo smacked his forehead. He rolled his eyes, stirring things up. 'This beats everything. You brainless little fool, you're going to be stuck in this hell-hole for ever, two kids already pale and whiny with stress and damp. Is this some masochistic, freakish behaviour you're both locked into?'

'Shut up,' Barry yelled, defending her. 'We can still do something about it, if she's only eight weeks.'

'What the hell d'you mean? This is a baby we're talking about,' Cheryl pleaded with tears in her eyes. 'This is a new life, a miracle.'

'Get real, Cheryl,' said Leo, in a tone he had never used before.

He was goading Barry on. Getting him all agitated. Why didn't he stop and shut up? What had this got to do with Leo? OK, this flat was not ideal, all right, Victor and Scarlett were underweight and cried a lot, and she agreed that she had problems with stress and that Barry was always tired. But one more kid wouldn't make that much difference . . .

Suddenly she wished that she had told Barry the news in private, that she had kept the secret to herself until the filming was over. This was a very domestic scene to be sharing with millions of strangers. Suddenly she felt all alone in the world. Was this some dire premonition?

More likely, it was a belated awareness of the irresponsible cow she would look.

They didn't seem to think she was special. No congratulations were forthcoming. Instead, the camera crew watched her with a mixture of scorn and pity.

'Well, God help you,' said Leo, turning away. 'You are so stupid.'

Sebby stood silently now, and looked sad.

'That's great,' said Cheryl in rising rage. 'That's really great, you bastards. So what if I'm pregnant. There's not much else when you look at it, is there? You've seen how we live, you know what it's like, and now you're thinking that we've got to miss out.'

'My brother's got kids,' said Sebby wearily. 'He waited six years for his. He waited until he got on his feet and could give them the life he wanted for them.'

'Good on him, then,' shouted Cheryl. 'What a sad wanker he sounds like.'

'We all thought things would start going right for you. Once Victor and Scarlett were a bit older, you and Barry could start again. You both seemed so brave and determined.'

Cheryl grew louder and more defensive. 'And why don't you shut your mouth too, Leo? Your wife's expecting.'

'Our first, yes. And we're at least ten years older than you. With money. Dear God, it's a cliché, but you are your own worst enemies, people like you.'

'We don't have to have the kid.'

Everyone turned to stare at Barry, who looked embarrassed, harassed, ashamed.

'Well, it's true,' he went on, gathering courage, 'we don't have to have it. Thousands of women these days have abortions.'

'Thousands might, but I'm not one of them.' How could Barry do this to her? She felt disturbed and humiliated. This was a direct result of Leo's hostile reaction. Barry knew how she felt about abortion unless you'd been raped or your child was deformed. And he knew why she needed this baby. He understood how she dreaded those endless, dead days again.

'Barry's right,' said Sebby quietly.

'You can't bring another kid into this.' Leo's eyes took in the flat and the dingy dreariness of the place. 'Be honest. How can you? You'd have to be mental.'

And that's when she and Barry began the furious argument that was to help top the ratings and divide a nation of couch potatoes.

*　　*　　*

'You can't use those pictures now. You've no need to use them, there's enough drama going on naturally to keep the thing alive.'

Sebby had to get through to them somehow.

Alan and Jennie were watching the rushes. They exclaimed with undisguised glee when the pregnancy announcement was made. 'That's it!' said Jennie. 'That'll do it.'

'So what's the point of using the pictures?'

'Ever heard of the gilt on the gingerbread?'

'But you're conning the public.' Sebby started stuttering, as he usually did when he was stressed out. Kate used to laugh and bring him out of it.

'Where does the conning come into it? Are you saying the kid didn't pose, are you saying she's the innocent victim you and Leo have portrayed her as so far?' Alan's dark eyes narrowed. 'If we left it at that we'd be doing half a job. If the truth is so damned important to you, then why are you against showing it?'

'Because we owe them.'

'We owe them nothing.'

'They're going to be in deep trouble anyway once this pregnancy comes out, once the viewers get wise to that, and the sad fact is they don't even realize. For God's sake, isn't that enough for you?'

Leo, relaxed in his chair with one leg casually crossing the other, pointed out to his troubled friend: 'Public opinion will come down on them, yep, but gradually they'll be forgiven. They're inadequate, people see that, all sorts of losers have kids when they shouldn't. But these pictures won't hurt them. Christ, take a look, she was only fifteen.'

You might have thought Jennie would be more

understanding. Privileged, like Kate, intelligent, as far from the downtrodden Cheryl as another woman could possibly be, you would think she might let the series go without putting more problems Cheryl's way. She swung in her chair, easygoing and confident, a top executive in the making. 'It will be very interesting', she said in her clipped, superior tone, 'to see how the couple react.'

Sebby coloured, his voice rose. 'Christ! They sound like animals to be used for some vile experiment. See how much pain they feel. See how they bleed. This is bloody victimization.'

'Now you are being absurd,' said Jennie. 'When we started this project you knew what we'd planned, and you went along with it.'

'Reluctantly, yes.'

It had not helped Sebby's anxiety over the last couple of months to be faced day by day with the sort of poverty that Kate, in her privileged world, had always dreaded. Because of her irrational fears, he had kept the details of *The Dark End* from her and missed discussing his work with her, something they both used to enjoy. Although she had been shortlisted three times, Kate had still not landed a job. The public crash of *Tone* magazine had tainted her, she said. But she was still aiming too high, a suggestion Sebby didn't dare make. She had borrowed heavily from her parents to help pay for the lease on the Neal Street flat, but now her father was recommending that they attempt to sell it.

'What Daddy's really saying', she told Sebby tearfully, 'is that he's paid out enough. I just can't ask him again. He thinks we should deal with this sensibly, and that hanging on in here is foolish.'

107

Sebby's family couldn't help out. They had just remortgaged their house to convert three downstairs rooms into a self-contained flat for his younger sister.

But what if they couldn't sell the lease?

What if they were evicted?

What if Sebby lost his job? Hundreds did, every week, in this industry.

These fears kept Kate tossing and turning at night. Sebby tried not to burden her; she was frightened enough as it was. She was not used to making do, and pulling in her belt was a concept she had no experience of. He'd get home at night. She'd have been to Marks. There'd be wine on the table. There'd be prawns, or chicken, or strawberries and cream followed by delicious fresh coffee. She'd come home with a plush carrier bag and flourish a brand-new outfit as if she was challenging fate to do its worst, despite her. She had to look good, she told him with freshly highlighted hair, a new jar of Clinique on the dressing table, if she stood any chance at all of getting the job she wanted.

And in the morning he would be faced with the Harold Wilson Building, and the climb up to the fifth floor through the stench of urine and hot concrete.

Kate's greatest fear, for no obvious reason, had always been ending up in a mobile home in some godforsaken caravan park. How could Sebby tell her the unpalatable truth that there were worse fates in store than that, the Harold Wilson Building being one?

God knows what Cheryl's reaction would be when she caught sight of those seedy photos. When she realized that he and Leo had always known of

108

their existence. When she found out that Griffin Productions were intending to include them and that she had been set up. If she guessed that public opinion might well turn against her.

She'd be like a child abused by a friend.

She would be inconsolable.

Broken-hearted.

But nothing he said at that meeting could change the directors' minds.

'When did you have these taken?' Leo dropped the bombshell, having carefully placed the photos on the coffee table along with the crumbs and a half-chewed dummy Sebby zoomed in in close-up.

Totally unprepared for the shock, Cheryl thought Leo was talking about the latest pictures of Scarlett which Cath had shot with her Instamatic. She knew they'd been lying around since her mother-in-law's last visit. Leo must have found them and picked them up. He lifted one eyebrow and smiled faintly, not that lovely smile of his – this had a glint of steel in it. He was holding one picture up to the camera.

'Let's see?'

She knelt on the floor beside the table, Scarlett in her arms. She felt her eyes swell in her head, her cheeks puffed up around them. She looked up at Leo with dread on her face, she bit her lip, she felt cold, she shivered.

Her voice sounded lost. A lost little voice in a cave full of echoes. 'What's this all about? Where did you get them?'

'One of our researchers found them.' His eyes did not convey his contempt, they merely looked excited.

Why, why, why? 'How can they have done? They were never used. The photographer told me they weren't any good.'

'Well, you were conned,' said Leo.

'When did you get them?' was all she could ask. 'And what have you brought them out for now?'

'We've had them from the beginning.'

'Why?' she asked. 'Why would you do this?' She looked at Sebby for confirmation and he looked away, avoiding her eyes. 'Has everyone seen them then? Alan? Jennie?' Cheryl swallowed hard. There was a dry lump stuck in her throat, like shame. 'You're not going to use them? You can't use them . . .'

Barry came in. 'What's this?' He sauntered over to the table. He picked up one of the photographs, the one with her feet on the top of the stool. Balancing for that one had been difficult. Every part of her was on show.

'Hey?' He held it down to her eye level. 'Hey? This is you.'

Cheryl nodded dumbly.

It was Barry's turn to ask questions. Neither Sebby nor Leo volunteered anything. Sebby was behind the camera with Leo holding the mike.

'Did you know about these?' Leo asked Barry, calculating, expectant.

Barry shook his head. Stayed silent. Picked up the others, six in all, and glanced briefly at each one.

'I never told you,' said Cheryl from the floor. 'I made a right mess of it, anyway.'

'Did you get paid?' Barry asked.

'Did I hell.' She was defensive. 'If they'd paid me I'd have done it again.'

110

'When?' Barry cleared his throat and repeated the muffled question.

'Soon after I met you. Soon after I left home. I was washing up in McDonald's. I saw this advert, models wanted. I went to the place after work, some kind of basement. The thing is, I thought he was genuine. He took some normal pictures to start with and then he asked if I was prepared to do swimwear for catalogues.' Cheryl kept her eyes on Barry. His reaction was all-important. At the moment he didn't seem shocked, just puzzled, confused.

'But you must have sussed—'

'I didn't! I didn't.'

'You're not that thick.'

'I must have been, then. I was really desperate for money, Barry.'

'So what happened?'

Sebby carried on filming. How he could focus through the tension in the room was hard to figure. Leo leaned against the wall, watching, listening, coolly detached.

'He didn't have a bikini, did he? So would I strip to my bra and pants.'

'You nerd. You—'

'I know, I know. And then, once I'd got used to that, the next step didn't seem so bad.'

'But . . .' Barry picked up the pictures and squinted at them again. 'These positions! These poses!'

'You weren't there, Barry. You can't understand. This guy, this old bald guy, he kept saying, "That's lovely, that's great, that's exactly what they want to see, you've got it all, baby, you've got a great future in this, turn this way, turn that way, rub your tits,

111

open your legs . . ." ' Cheryl looked away. 'I honestly thought I was going to make it. And then he said he would let me know, and I never heard anything again.'

'You didn't go back, then?'

Cheryl lowered her voice. 'I think I knew by then. It only took a few weeks. And looking back on it all, I began to think it was all so odd.'

'He must have paid you something,' said Leo. Cheryl jumped. For a moment she had forgotten he was there.

'Nothing,' she admitted. She got up and slumped on the sofa, hiding her face in her hands. 'But I never realized he would use them without me knowing. I never imagined that's how they did it.' And then, suddenly, the real shock hit her and she tensed up and shouted at Sebby, 'Stop filming! You can't use this! Don't think you're using this! This isn't fair. There's my mum to think of, and Cath and Bill, and . . .' she looked around desperately, '. . . the kids. They can't grow up knowing that their mother once did this.'

'But you are going to use them, aren't you?' said Barry. 'It doesn't matter what we say. You were always going to use them. Right from the start. Is that why we were picked for the job? Because you had these? You fucking bastards . . .' and he took a step towards the camera, raising his fist as if to smash it.

'Hey. Hang on. You're taking all this too seriously,' Leo tried to laugh. 'Come on, come on, in this enlightened age nobody's going to bother about some mistake Cheryl made years ago. Now, if they were the real hard stuff . . .' He walked over and took them from Barry. 'They're quite tasteful, really. Very nice, anyway. Very nice.'

'You bastards,' roared Barry, fists clenched. He made a move towards Leo. 'If they make no difference, why have you sodding well got them?'

'No, Barry,' Cheryl called out, struggling with the sensation of being stuck in deep, cloying sand. 'Don't, don't. Wait. Please.' How could she believe the worst? If she had a sense of danger it was only for a few seconds, and to go along with Barry just now would be like being swept away by rapids, with all those hopes rushing past on the banks. 'Leave it. I think Leo's right. Nobody cares these days. People know enough about me to realize I've got you now, I've got kids, I'm a different person, I'd never think of doing that now.'

Barry whirled round. 'Jesus, Cheryl. These sodding people. They can do no wrong in your eyes. Don't you realize they've had these pictures from the start? They were always going to use them against us. They've rigged this whole bloody thing.'

'I just think we musn't over-react,' Cheryl said, not knowing what Griffin's intentions were but quite unable to accept that they were anything but benign. The alternatives were too painful. 'The only opinion I care about is yours, Barry. That's the truth. And if you understand how it happened, that's all that matters.'

'You're kidding yourself, Cher,' said Barry. 'I wish I could believe you, but there's no way you mean what you're saying. You care more about what people are going to think, you care more about how much they're going to love you, than you care about anything else.'

'That's not true,' said Cheryl defensively.

113

'Listen, Barry,' said Leo at his smoothest, his most convincing. 'There's only one likely consequence of showing these pictures, and that is public sympathy. They prove just how desperate Cheryl was at the time she had them taken. They show real spirit, true determination . . . This young kid was prepared to do anything she could to survive. Just as you're doing now. They are very human. People will empathize with Cheryl. We kept quiet about them because we suspected your reaction would be hostile, but hang on a minute, think about it. These pictures signify strength, not weakness. There are all sorts of bastards taking advantage of people like you, and the public have to know what it's like. So Cheryl sinned a little. So what? Who hasn't?'

And Leo sounded so damn genuine that even Sebby was impressed. Barry was silenced, taken aback, bewildered by his suspicions. Maybe the guy was telling the truth. But even so . . . It was bloody insensitive. As it happened, Barry wasn't too fazed, but how were they to know he wouldn't have blown his top? Lots of blokes would have. For seconds he was able to see down under the mirror's surface, the dangerous realities, floating, submerged, the threatening menace. And if looks could kill, Sebby and Leo would be on their way over the balcony and down five floors, to end up smashed on the hot tarmac.

Cheryl tried to forget it had happened.

They were using the pictures in a positive way.

They would add more intriguing layers to her character. That's what they said. She had to believe them.

*   *   *

They had a kind of party in July when the last reel had been shot.

The crew did not invite them out, as Cheryl had hoped they might, to the pub they were always talking about, or even the Thai restaurant, where they all seemed to meet and be known.

No, it wasn't remotely like that.

Alan Beam showed his face for ten minutes, then left protesting that he had work to get on with. Jennie St Hill rang Sebby's mobile – she couldn't make it. But two technicians they hardly knew arrived and stayed for an hour.

It was just Cheryl and Barry, Sebby and Leo, and the tension that had existed between them since the flare-up two weeks ago. But even though this had marred a relationship which up until then had been close and intense (Barry had never forgiven them), Cheryl still could not believe these two were going to disappear from their lives. It was the natural bonding that persuaded her otherwise, the lovely intimacy that had linked them, the confidences she had trusted them with and the strong belief that they liked her and therefore would never hurt her.

Sebby presented her with a bouquet, compliments of Griffin TV.

The wine they brought was 'good', they informed her. She wouldn't know. But she downed it desperately while they drank beer with Barry.

Then they started talking about the next job they were on.

Cheryl could hardly stand it, let alone express any interest.

Their joint enthusiasm sliced like a sword. Their new energy lanced her.

She looked and she saw what she would be missing, and her heart plummeted like a shot bird. Leo's shining, collar-length hair was like a curtain drawn back from his face. The way he flicked it. His special wink, hardly noticeable, when she'd done something which had pleased him. The tan of his forearms, the way he caught peanuts and crushed his cans of Coke when he'd finished them.

And Sebby, with the gentle brown eyes and that compelling smile. He could dress as shabbily as he chose, he could underplay his sexuality as much as he liked, he was still a turn-on behind those glasses. His washed-out shirts smelled of hot leather that must come off his old Morgan. She had buried her head in them so many times when things went wrong. The irritating Westminster chimes of his blasted mobile phone, his Greenpeace badge, his expensive cologne. It must be Kate who made him wear that. Would he marry his Kate and live happily ever after?

Cheryl couldn't help it. She was jealous. She hoped not.

'*The Dark End* was a pretty predictable series, but this next one's going to be way out,' Leo went on blithely, quite unaware of the stun effect of his words on Cheryl, who was losing her centre position by the minute. 'There's this guy who owns a private island somewhere off the coast of Eigg, and they reckon he's sired twenty-three kids between eight wives . . . He calls himself king . . . He's declared independence, a right screwball . . .'

But Cheryl had stopped listening. 'You'll be going there then? To this island?'

'We can hardly zoom in on Eigg from here.'

'For how long?'

'It's a four-week stint.'

'When d'you start?'

'We get a couple of weeks' break, then we're off.'

Cheryl felt a cold boulder take up position on top of her heart.

But maybe she should not be so fearful. Maybe she was thinking the worst. They would probably call in the next week or two, and after the job was over they would be in touch again. Nobody could get this close to each other and then sever the bonds so completely.

They were friends.

They were soulmates.

Never had Cheryl enjoyed such company, despite all their ups and downs.

And when the series started in January, a new closeness might form. They would probably watch the programme together, she and Barry, Sebby and Leo, and drink hearty toasts to its success. That would be fun. She looked forward to that.

They went. And she missed them so.

The weeks and the months passed by. Once she rang Griffin TV, asked for Alan Beam, the director of *The Dark End of the Street*. 'Who is it?' asked the receptionist. She gave her name. The girl didn't know it.

'I was the subject of the programme,' Cheryl explained from a phone box inside Paddington station, a perspex affair with no privacy and the man in the next booth playing with his prick. 'Me and my husband and my two kids. They were here

117

for four months . . . I just need to talk to Alan, that's all. Or Jennie, she'll do.'

'Hold on a moment.'

Muzak. Classical. And her money was running out.

'Hello? Mrs Higgins?'

'Yes?' she clutched the receiver expectantly. She had rehearsed her introduction. She was going to ask how the editing was going, and did they have any idea, yet, of the dates the programme would be shown? And if Alan responded positively she was going to ask if she and Barry could come and have a look.

'I'm sorry, Mrs Higgins, but Alan's not available at the moment. Can I give him a message?'

Cheryl banged the phone down and blinked away the tears of frustration, the passionate anger of a child.

You would think she and Barry had never existed. Not a word since Sebby and Leo left, not a note, not a visit, not even a postcard from Eigg.

She felt possessed, like a stalker.

In desperation she redialled, and shoved the last ten pence in the slot. 'Griffin Productions, can I help you?'

She tried to sound super-confident. The kind of person who would ask this question: 'Could you give me the home number of Sebby Coltrain, I need to get hold of Sebby quite urgently . . .'

'I am sorry, it is not company policy to give out personal information.'

Once again, defeated and mortified, Cheryl smashed the receiver down.

'I don't see the point.' Barry, mystified, was

unsympathetic when she got home, full of hopeless misery. 'They are bound to let us know when it's coming on telly. They've got other things to do, Cher, they're busy people, not like us. To them this programme is just another job.'

'Well it means a lot to me.'

'Of course it does. It will do, because you haven't got other stuff going on. And anyway, why do you want to phone Sebby?'

'Because I sodding well want to know why he hasn't been in touch.'

Barry seemed quite bewildered. Stupid and insensitive, he didn't have a clue how she felt. He was so much more self-reliant than Cheryl, and anyway, Barry had a thing about those pictures. Oh, no, he wasn't angry with Cheryl. He understood why she'd had them taken and he seemed to take that in his stride, but he was worried by how Griffin would use them and what effect it would have on his wife. Barry could be stubborn, determined, especially when he was angry. Look how he'd turned his back on his talent, just to get back at his mother. 'Why would Sebby be in touch?'

Didn't he understand? Cheryl staked everything on the belief that a friendship as deep as theirs, and an association as close, reached down to the very roots of self and could not be destroyed. 'Sod you, Barry. Because he got to know us, that's why, because he and Leo were part of this family for four months, and it's pretty shitty that they have just dropped us.'

'Hang on, Cher, hang on. You're right out of line here.'

'I know what you're going to say,' said Cheryl,

standing at the sink, arms akimbo, regarding her husband's scrawny form sprawled across the sofa at two-thirty in the afternoon when outside the sun was shining. For a brief and frightening moment he was the emphasis of her loss. 'For them this is work, they can't get involved, they have to move on. I stupidly thought they were our friends and that's just because I'm a sad old cow. OK, OK?'

'Yep. That's about how it is. And there's nothing you can do to change things. Ringing them up would make it worse, you'd just make a bigger prat of yourself.'

When Cheryl flung back the curtains she almost pulled them down with helpless anger. The flat felt like a sickroom, the germs of stagnation were everywhere.

The kids weren't dressed.

Their nappies needed changing.

The washing was piled up in a corner and someone had to heave it down the steps to go to the bloody launderette again.

She stormed to the telly and turned it over, switching channels till she found a chat show instead of those endless cartoons.

'What you do that for?'

'Because I want to hear people talking.'

'Don't be a jerk.'

Fresh tears formed, she couldn't control them. 'I miss the talking. Don't you understand? I miss those real conversations. Not about the kids, or the TV licence, or the crackheads next door, or who's going to have a bath first. I'm sick of it, Barry, just bloody well sick of it.'

Cheryl was hurt.

Cut to the quick.

She would not accept the fact that she might never hear from them or see them again. It wasn't just the talking she missed but the laughter, the witty backchat that went on between them, the lightened atmosphere in this miserable place, the sense of being important, essential, and the energy having them round seemed to give her, so that sometimes she even began to believe that it would be possible to change her life.

With their help and encouragement, she might have done it.

But after this blatant rejection, her self-esteem was lower than ever.

'It's not over, Cher,' said Barry, trying his hardest to understand. 'Apart from the baby, there's the programme to come. Anyone else would be dead excited by the thought of what it's going to be like. Everyone's going to know us; Griffin are bound to be back in touch. All sorts of things are going to happen, you've got to think about all that.'

Cheryl sighed. She tried. But the pain inside her would not subside.

For a short moment in time she had felt her own radiance coming from deep inside her, like a glow coming through a fog. All gone. It was as bad as being chucked by some guy you were besotted with . . .

It was a craving, an addiction, denied.

An empty future.

A life of no particular interest and no more joy.

SEVEN

Barry listens while his heart sinks lower.

The cops won't leave them alone. They are quiz-zing Cher in the other room again. He puts his ear to the door.

It's not as if Barry hasn't tried to succeed. He has been a fool in the past, he knows that, but his big break came too early. His turning down of the trial for Spurs, the sort of chance some kids would kill for, was the only way he could break free. Twelve years old and a mummy's boy, he raged against the chains that held him, her insistence on his neat haircut, her choosing of his clothes, her criticism of his friends, her smelly medications for every ailment, his long waits with her at the doctor's over a cold, a bruise, a strained shoulder.

From the age of seven he had lived for football. If he couldn't be out with his team he actually felt physically ill, and Cath Higgins used this fierce need and turned it to her own advantage.

He loved football more than his mother and Cath knew that, she played on that, in spite of the fact that it was she and Bill who basked in the afterglow of praise more than their son did. Although Barry enjoyed the applause, the attention and having his picture in the local paper, the games and improving his skills were the lures that proved so addictive. But only if Barry kept his room in the spotless, germfree state she demanded, would he be able to play on Saturday or go to the Tuesday-night practice.

He washed all the surfaces, moved his books, tidied his drawers, re-folded his clothes.

He bowed to the pressure of a regular haircut.

He agreed to wear his anorak to school.

He allowed his mother to iron creases in his jeans.

He never ate chips in public.

He stayed away from the mates she deplored so toe-curlingly loudly. Instead, he went round with the geeks.

The bullies only left him alone because of his sporting success. That was the saving of him.

When the Spurs trial came up, Cath curled over the phone like a mantis, reminding all the marvelling relatives that without the input from her and Bill, such a miracle could never have happened. 'He had our unflagging support,' she said, sounding like a martyr. She had washed his kit, cleaned his boots, raised funds for the club at car-boot sales and jumbles; she had stood on sidelines getting wet and now, she bragged, it was up to him to make the most of this opportunity. And look how hard Barry's father had worked, organizing tournaments at Caravan Club conventions so that, even when on holiday, Barry had the chance to practise.

Their son had talent, they granted him that, but without his parents he would be nothing.

And then he let them down so badly they had never been able to forgive him.

And when Barry startlingly turned his back, not only on the trial for Spurs but on the game of football itself, he had felt such a burst of relief it was like coming up from underwater after holding your breath for too long. Gasping. Fresh, untainted air. But a sadness, too. Like coming back from a near-death experience, seeing the light and pulling away.

Cath didn't speak to him for two whole weeks, and went about with her mouth all puckered as if it was pulled tight by a drawstring.

Dad played hurt. He sulked. That's when he started on about his back. Like he had been physically injured.

Barry was right to do what he did. But he wished he hadn't had to do it.

And now DCI Rowe and Heidi are taking Cheryl through it again.

Have they heard something? Did the shrink they made her see yesterday come up with something peculiar? He doubts that very much. According to Cheryl, she hardly spoke. She resented the fact that it was her, not him, who was hauled up in front of the brain doctor. She detests shrinks, she's phobic about them, after what they did to her mum. But the way they are talking to Cheryl now, it sounds like they think she might be mental.

That small recorder is always on . . . to catch her out, to trip her up, to snare her into some trap.

Cheryl is tired.

She aches for her children.

Barry's sense of protectiveness and strength overlays his immediate panic. He wishes he could help her. Stop her trembling. Stop her ripping at her lip like this.

'So you arrived at the clinic with the children in the pram. Tell us about that, Cheryl. How were you feeling that morning? Positive? Worried? In a hurry? Did you have too much on your mind?'

'No,' Cheryl answers patiently one more time. 'I had cystitis. All I could think about was finding the loo.'

'That was your main concern?'

'Of course it was my main bloody concern. The burning was driving me mad. And I thought that while I was seeing the nurse with Cara, for her chest, I'd tell her about the cystitis and see if she could give me something, save me going down the doctor's and waiting for hours on end.' You can feel the discomfort in the atmosphere. Cheryl is trying too hard.

'I know how much it hurts you to go through that terrible moment . . .'

'Then why put me through it again and again?'

'Just in case', says Heidi sympathetically, but with a studied carelessness, 'there could be something you might remember, some tiny, unimportant detail that hasn't registered with you so far.'

'I've lived through it so many times, all night, all day. All I do is try and forget it in case I can't deal with the shit any more. Don't you think if there had been anything I would have thought of it by now? Don't you think I want my kids back? Don't you think I would give my life just to see them safe and happy and home again?'

125

'Was the clinic door open or closed?'

'I can't remember. I just can't remember.' And Cheryl drops her head in her hands, hoping they will have pity and stop.

'But you saw nobody. The place was empty?'

'Of course it wasn't empty. There were cars in the car park, and I'm sure the waiting room was full, but there was nobody in the toilets, nobody waiting outside the toilets, and if there had been I might not have seen them because of the state I was in.'

'You left the children in the pram in the small entrance area?'

'I parked the pram against the wall.'

'You didn't feel this might be risky?'

Cheryl sits right back in her chair, her head resting on the cushion, eyes closed. 'No. This wasn't a shop. This wasn't the arcade. This wasn't the bus stop. This was the clinic. The only people at the clinic would be other mums with kids. And nurses. If you can't leave them at the clinic, where can you leave them? And anyway, I knew I'd only be gone for a second.'

'Tell us what happened when you came out.'

'I had a paper towel in my hands. I know that because afterwards, you know, after it all happened, I found I was pulling it to pieces.'

'How long did it take you to realize the pram was gone?'

'No time, no time at all, and I ran through to the main waiting area and shouted at the receptionist.'

'Why didn't you check outside the door?'

'I suppose I thought it was more likely that someone might have pushed them inside. It didn't cross my mind, that first second, that someone must

126

have taken them . . .' And here Cheryl pushes her
hands through her hair. They stop at the top, they
pull so hard it hurts, and her sprout in elastic bobs
like a spring.

'So how long, and let's get this right, how long
was it before anyone went outside to see if the
children were there?'

'Only minutes. Two or three minutes. An ambulance had just pulled up. The two paramedics
started searching immediately.'

'But by then there was no sign.'

Cheryl doesn't bother to answer.

Barry, listening, sighs in relief. It sounds as if it's
over with . . . until tomorrow, that is.

Months had gone by since their filming on Eigg. To
get away from the stifling atmosphere of the Harold
Wilson Building, with all the disturbing implications that experience brought with it, had been a
massive relief for Sebby. When his conscience tormented him with thoughts of the Higginses abandoned so abruptly and exploited so crudely, he
forced himself to work harder and concentrate on
the matter in hand.

Leo had no such qualms. 'No, Sebby,' he answered, surprised that Sebby should raise the question. 'No, I don't think we should have kept in
touch. What the hell's the matter with you?'

Sebby stumbled over his answer. He was confused himself. 'I think Cheryl believed we were more
involved than we were.'

'Then she should get a life. We're not to blame if
she's needy. We can't go round counselling everyone we work with.'

'I think we gave her the wrong impression.'

Leo bridled. 'You're blaming me.'

Sebby searched for the right way to say it. 'We grew very close to the family.'

'If we didn't do that we'd get no results. You know that as well as I do. If you want to bring the best out of a dog, you have to gain its confidence, and that's all we did.'

The lease of the Neal Street flat had been for sale for six months. No takers. During that time Sebby and Kate had reviewed all sorts of options. Sebby had been encouraged. They were a long way from down and out; on his wages alone they would have a range of choices. Not so central, not so prestigious – poor Cheryl would sneer with scorn if she knew how anxious they were. Sebby might have been encouraged, but poor old Kate, bored and still jobless, was determined they could do better. She, who had once been so independent, now expected Sebby to be there, to show the punters round, to view endless properties, no matter how unsuitable. He started to turn off his mobile because of her unreasonable demands on his time.

With these sorts of problems at home, it was harder to concentrate on his work at the very time he needed to produce his best results.

Leo had no such handicaps. If both he and Sophie lost their jobs his lifestyle would hardly change. Sophie's trust would see to that. A trust her grandfather left her after his great supermarket successes. A trust which would keep her in clover for life. It wasn't for money that Leo worked, it was for prestige, career advancement and professional excellence. Sometimes, at his most disillusioned,

Sebby compared the opportunities Leo's unborn child would inherit to those denied the Higginses' kids. Depending on the angle Griffin decided to take, *The Dark End of the Street* might have helped to break the vicious circle for that little family. Instead, it would compound it.

Sebby took the videos home when they were finally edited.

'You've had them hanging around for a month. Isn't it time you watched them?'

But he had been reluctant to show this stark picture of poverty, with Kate so agitated and fearful.

But now she insisted, he had no choice. He had not discussed his misgivings with her, and now he would be interested in her reactions. Blissfully unaware of the manipulative nature of the filming, she could watch them impartially. No prude, open-minded and honest, her response would be enlightening. He had put off this moment for too long, but twelve hours of television would take several sessions. He would watch her emotions with interest as her familiarity with the likeable Higgins family would build to a peak, as intended, before turning to stark disillusion.

Barry's guess had been right. They heard nothing from Griffin until mid-December, just one month before the transmission of *The Dark End of the Street*. But then they received a letter inviting them up for a preview.

'I told you they would. Better late than never.'

Cheryl was still smarting from her imagined cruel rejection, but at least Barry had managed to stop her making a fuss and a fool of herself. It was hard to tell which future event kept Cheryl's spirits so high, the birth of their baby or the documentary.

She talked obsessively about them both.

Mad Donny was babysitting. This always required some persuading from Cheryl before Barry gave in. But, as Cheryl said, 'Donny might be dirty, she might be peculiar but she's great with kids.' She'd had them before. They'd been OK.

The preview event was in central London. The day was cold and bright, and so was Cheryl.

But nervous, very nervous.

She had bitten her nails to the quick.

They were early. They sat in the small park in the middle of the square where office workers in scarves and gloves were eating their sandwiches in patches of sun, kids were chasing the pigeons and frost patterns ferned the grass. Nervous but happy again, Cheryl was full of a new desire to laugh and to live.

'Look at me,' she giggled, 'I'm shaking.'

'I'm dreading this,' Barry admitted. 'We're going to come over like real freaks.'

'Cretins. Specially you.'

'It's too late now. And it's all your fault.' Barry's teeth chattered. 'Jesus, I wish we'd never done it.'

'But if they wanted to make a film which showed real poverty, they wouldn't muck about with it, would they? They'd want to get it across. They'd need people like us. So everything's biased, when you think about it.'

'So you reckon they might do us a favour? They might airbrush my acne.'

'No machine could do that.'

They were all there, Cheryl saw with a gasp.

130

All friendly and informal, with grub that was out of this world. And champagne to drink. Strawberries and cream. Smoked salmon, melting pastry tarts, asparagus, avocados – you name it, it was there on long white tables. Barry's last job had been waiting at tables. The company went bust and never paid him. Before that he'd been cleaning cars, then painting yellow lines on the roads, then helping a mate doing window-cleaning, then baggage-loading at Gatwick. The list was so long it was hard to remember all that he'd done since meeting Cher. They took him on as self-employed. That's how they got away with it; that's how they hired and fired at will, and he was always the last man in. They didn't give a toss how hard he worked, how early he arrived to try to impress, how polite and helpful he was or how eager for overtime, evenings, weekends. Not a day went by without Barry studying the evening paper, circling all possibilities, going over to the station to phone. Not a week passed but he visited the jobcentre, and scrutinized any new cards.

'Hi, guys,' said Leo, wandering casually over as if they'd seen each other last night. As if half a year had not gone by. 'How are you doing?' And he threw his arms around Cheryl and gave her a smacking kiss. 'You're looking great, anyway.' He turned to Sebby and said carelessly, 'Don't these kids look great?'

'I really missed you,' Cheryl said quietly, draped in her maternity dress and noticing the lack of comments.

'I'm just that sort of guy,' Leo joked.

'How's Victor?' Sebby asked in his serious way, just as Alan Beam rushed over with a wild-haired man at his shoulder.

'This is Matt, our producer,' he said. 'You remember him, sweeties. He wants to tell you how pleased he is with the way the whole thing's turned out.'

The wild-haired man's handshake hurt, and went on longer than normal. 'You two have turned out to be real stars,' he told them, still gripping. 'Wait till you see what we've got. This is one hell of a good film: sensitive, subtle, intense, and it's got its funny side too.'

'But will we know ourselves?' asked Cheryl, hurt when she saw Matt's eyes wandering. 'Hang on a minute,' he said. 'Got to see Joel. See you later. Enjoy.'

Who were all these people?

'I tried to ring you, Alan,' said Cheryl, sipping her champagne carefully. She didn't want to get pissed, and it didn't take much to floor her. 'It's been five months. Soon after the filming was finished, I tried to ring you.'

'Did you leave a message? I could have got back to you.'

'We don't have a phone.'

Alan slapped his forehead. 'I'm an arsehole, of course you don't have a phone. I hope it wasn't anything important. But this is always happening to me, people always say they can never reach me. Use my mobile number in future.'

'I don't have your mobile number.'

'I'll give it to you later. Now, I don't know about you, but I'm starving, and if you don't get in early these gannets will finish the lot.'

They were all here to watch *The Dark End of the Street*, but you wouldn't have thought so from their conversation. Cheryl kept trying to turn it round, but Sebby and Leo were chattering on about their latest project, company gossip, digital TV and the tight-arsed attitude of the Arts Council.

And how could they join in? In a world they knew nothing about?

Cheryl deflated as the minutes went by, as odd strangers stopped for a word and passed on flippantly; as Sebby and Leo, who at least stayed near them, started talking across them, and Leo made three calls on his mobile.

How many of these special events did these people attend every year?

How many launches, how many parties, how many lunches, how many dinners?

At least Cheryl and Barry did not have to explain who they were. That was a blessing, that was a start. If they had been actors it might have been different, but they were merely the necessary subjects to put across a point of view, to shock and harrow the apathetic, to make a statement, to make some money.

'So what have you two kids been up to all summer?' asked Leo, breathing garlic and champagne.

Cheryl was taken aback. Had Leo forgotten how it was already? Tanned and taller than she remembered, Leo's white collarless shirt and crumpled linen trousers made him look like a star of Kay's catalogue, the outdoor type who would model thick sweaters with designer names across the front. Sebby would be the cross little boy forced into school uniform, scowling.

Well, what had they been up to?

'We went to Italy,' she said, suddenly brightening, turning her back on Barry's frown. 'We went to a hotel for a fortnight, the Italian lakes, you know.'

'That's great,' said Leo thoughtlessly, and Cheryl knew then that she had lost him, that he had never been hers. She would have to go through it all over again, all the hurt and the emptiness, and Barry watched her eyes mist over and felt more useless than ever before.

Barry tried to hold Cheryl's hand as they took their places in the small cinema, but she pushed it away. 'Don't be silly. I'm OK.'

Alan Beam stood on the front of the stage. He looked and sounded like an actor. 'Welcome, everybody. I know how much you have all looked forward to this, and I'm pleased to say it's turned out even better than anyone expected.'

Cheryl fidgeted nervously in her chair. Barry wished he could go home. He would rather not see any of this. He'd had enough already.

'What you will see this afternoon are a number of clips we have joined together to give you all some idea of the finished product. We are expecting the first episode to go on on January the fifteenth. It's got a good slot, a Thursday evening at nine to nine-thirty. Peak time. So as you can see there are high expectations of it.'

Would he mention her and Barry?

'Every one of you worked terribly hard on this project, I know, especially Sebby and Leo, who found the strain quite something. Who can blame them if, at times, they were eager to chuck it all in? So it's thanks to you all for coming together and combining all your special talents. The result goes to prove, as you'll see in a minute, that in the field of documentary, Griffin outclass all competition.'

He left the stage and the curtain went back.

The music faded in.

The aerial cameras focused on the mean streets around Paddington station. The Harold Wilson Building stood out in its ugliness even here, and below it the myriad crazy criss-crossing lines of the trains, the littered sidings, the corrugated shacks, the cinder tracks that led nowhere.

And here was their very balcony, with a row of nappies hanging across it like white flags of surrender.

'We're riding on a strange boat . . .' grew louder.

Barry's eyes closed. This was bad enough. He longed to get up and shout *Stop!* This was their home, their special place, their refuge from the world outside, where privacy ought to be paramount. How could they have done this dangerous thing? How could he have ever agreed with Cheryl?

Her face, in the dark, was no happier than his. She seemed to have stopped breathing. He felt her tense and frightened beside him, but thought it better to leave her alone. She never liked to admit she was frightened.

And then there was Barry, with Victor, sleepy, half on, half off his shoulder as he arrived at the maternity ward last year, with Cheryl waddling along beside him.

There was nothing about the induction. It looked

as if she'd arrived in a rush. This had been a set-up job, but nobody would have guessed.

She looked so young, but then so did he. Her voice was like a stranger's. He had forgotten all the chatting they did when she was lying there and nothing was happening.

'*You OK, Cher?*'

'*I will be when I get rid of this sodding lump.*'

'*Victor's asleep in the nursery.*'

'*There someone with him?*'

'*'Course there is.*'

'*Go and have a fag. Go on, Barry, this could take hours yet.*'

'*No, I'm OK.*'

'*You look lost.*'

At first she looked like a little girl lost – far too young to be dealing with this, too young and too innocent with her little snub nose and her impish chin. As the contractions grew stronger she appeared to grow older, harder, even too knowing, until it seemed oddly natural to dismiss the person and concentrate on the bodily aspects, like she was a corpse, and therefore past feeling.

Barry turned away.

Beside him, Cheryl flinched.

The little theatre was perfectly quiet.

He had never seen her so exposed. The mother of his child was anyone's. Any weirdo who fancied a leery perusal of some woman's most private place, anyone with tea on a tray and a couple of dunked digestives, anyone having a late TV supper, anyone cleaning their shoes, anyone hooking a rug while they watched, anyone sweeping the carpet, opening chocolates, comforting a child, painting by numbers, plucking their eyebrows, cutting their toenails, folding the newspaper, papering the walls . . .

In the darkened theatre, Barry groaned and covered his face with his hands.

EIGHT

'They think I'm mad, don't they?'

'No, Cher, of course they don't think you're mad.'

'Then why did I have to see that shrink? You didn't have to go. Just me.'

High on the fifth floor of the Harold Wilson Building Cheryl stares out of the window for hours, not at the birds with their startled faces that drift on London's feeble breezes, not at the white scribble jet streams that blot their way across the grey skies, but down at the tangle of railway lines, the skeletal bridges, the snailing trains that hiss and spark their two-note shrieks as they disappear to other worlds across the stillness of an eternity.

She wishes she could go with them.

'Come away from the window. There's no point,' Barry says.

'I've had enough, Barry. I don't care what happens, I'm way past that. I just want my kids. I want them back now.'

And the strong, urgent way she clutches at herself is what her arms long to do to the little people she loves most in the world. One tear follows another, like wet baby kisses on her cheeks.

The Harlow Higginses were horrified when they watched the first episode of *The Dark End*.

They were gathered in their neat front room, with two sets of neighbours and colleagues of Cath's, a little concerned maybe, not entirely proud that their son and his wife were the stars of a series which dealt with serious poverty in Britain. The situation was a curious one . . . In one breath you were telling folks that your nearest and dearest were on the telly, but after the oohs and aahs of excitement, you were forced to explain the downside.

'Of course, it's through no fault of their own,' Cath would point out quickly, pursing her lips to go on, 'but Barry could have done so much better.' This gave Cath the chance to prepare the ground for the common, vulgar Wattses, and to let it be known to all and sundry that she found them grossly unacceptable.

She did not want folks thinking that she and Bill approved of the family.

'It happens to so many these days,' Cath would go on, trying to fit it all in and absolve herself of any blame. 'They get in with the wrong crowd at school, miss out on a proper education because of the poor standard of teaching, and before they know what has happened to them they end up below the breadline and wondering where the next meal's coming from.'

Everyone would agree, as they do. Nodding knowingly. Clucking sympathetically. But no-one would hear what they said behind their own front doors.

'I have to hand it to Barry,' Bill would put in supportively, 'the lad has tried everything to get some sort of decent work. But there's no apprentice-ships these days, it's all technical stuff. Yes, I'm afraid that theirs is a generation of kids that's missed out on life's opportunities.'

So there they sat in their front room, with a tea tray prepared for eight in the kitchen which Cath would sort out during the ads, and their friends prepared for the worst and the central heating due off at ten.

They all fell silent as The Waterboys played them in. 'Strange World'.

They moved from the skies above Paddington station to the maternity suite at St Mary's. They moved from Barry's drawn, pale face straight into Cheryl's front bottom.

The silence grew as thick and puffy as the beige velveteen curtains.

In the house where Cheryl grew up, Big Annie had no such qualms, not over poverty or losing face. But when confronted by her daughter's pink parts she yelled at the boys, 'Get upstairs, you two; Go on, get lost!'

My God, this was porn.

And the thought of her enemies on the estate chuckling lewdly into their lagers was more than she could tolerate.

But Annie, a strong and resourceful woman (she was forty, she'd been to hell and back), kept faith and kept watching, and after that initial shock, matters evened out until all she was concerned about was the successful arrival of the child. In her peach dressing gown and matching slippers she gasped with the rest of the nation, she clenched her teeth with them, covered her eyes with them, lit another fag with them, gripped the cushion with them, until finally, to her great relief, a Caesarean was suggested.

She couldn't get over how cute Cheryl looked – the top end of her, that is. Even Barry, that scowling loser, managed to look almost friendly as he comforted his struggling wife. A good-looker – no wonder Cheryl fell for the boy, and wouldn't listen to anyone when they told her she was too young. I mean, she was sixteen when she had Victor. Barry could have been hauled through the courts if Annie had been that sort of mother.

But her bright little Cheryl could have had anyone.

Fair enough, Cheryl had warned her about the birth scenes. Cheryl had been to the preview and told her how explicit it was at the start, how she and Barry had suffered agonies, sitting there with the bigwigs and Cheryl exposed like that.

'But that bit doesn't last long, Mum. It gets better. We look wicked, different. They make us seem quite with-it in a boring kind of way.'

When poor Barry left the hospital with little Victor in his arms, when he returned to that grotty flat, Annie almost wept. OK, her own house was a mess: dirty plates, overflowing ashtrays, curtains with holes in and half off their rails, but at least she could catch sight of some grass if she really wanted to see it; at least she was on the ground; her windows opened, she had carpets, she had a garden of sorts. Her own small, stunted weeping willow.

And then, to cap it all, as she watched, the meter ran out and poor Barry, exhausted after the birth, up half the night, had to traipse back down the steps again and walk half a mile to the all-night garage to pay for a few more units to keep him going till Friday.

With Victor in his arms.

You would think the film crew might have helped. Fancy them standing there watching like that, same as in those wildlife programmes when they allow those poor wildebeest to be ripped to pieces by lions. Who knows? The awful thing is, they might set them up.

Barry's ordeal was a shocking disgrace. No-one should have to go through that, no matter how feckless. Or daft.

It was easy to forget that Cheryl and Barry were Cheryl and Barry. So compelling was the programme that Annie felt she was inside a soap. Unconnected, yet close, very close. She was so totally absorbed by it all that she felt cheated when the credits rolled.

If only they'd been on the phone, Annie would call them up straight away. Congratulate them on a brilliant performance. She needed to get in touch with them anyway. She hadn't seen them since Cara's birth, and that had been, oh, months ago. Time flies.

She shuffled to the door, cursing. Who the hell's that at this time? Kids? Vandals. Trouble, no doubt. 'What d'you want?' she shouted, arranging her rollers.

'Only to talk about the programme, love,' said that cow from across the road. 'Can I come in? Just for a second?'

Well, you wouldn't believe it.

In half an hour the house was full.

It felt like a proper party.

Even the kids were behaving themselves.

Everyone was full of it.

They wanted to know what came next, and was Annie going to be in it, and she said she was and they made her describe what it was like to face the cameras. Did she know she'd be famous, and all that sort of nonsense. She'd never known anything like it before.

'There'll be a lot of talk over this,' someone said.

'It's wicked, it really is, when you think what some of them are earning.'

'How much do we spend on weapons?'

'And then there's the bloody royals.'

'Your Cheryl's such a sweetheart.'

'She's had it hard, poor kid. And three kiddics now, didn't you say?'

Annie basked in it all, relished it, sent Randall out on his motorbike for supplies from the all-night supermarket.

They stayed up till after midnight, some folks who never spoke to each other, some neighbours who'd sworn eternal vengeance. Cheryl and Barry had brought them together in a way Annie never thought possible.

And nobody appeared to remember that Big Annie and her kids were the scourge of the street. That ceased to matter. She would be famous, and that's what counted. She, with her stained dressing

gown and her fag stuck to her lip; with her two
delinquent sons and her sweaty fat threatening
every seam. She could be forgiven at last.

She was the mother of poor Cheryl Higgins.

The morning after, there were two journalists at the
door of Cheryl's flat.

Barry was out, up early for once, to go and buy
some papers to see what the critics said.

'How did you know where we lived?' Griffin had
assured the Higginses that they would not give their
details to the press.

'Get real. Everyone knows that, sweetheart, we
zoomed in on your balcony last night. Us and
several million others. Good thing your frillies
weren't hanging out there, but who gives a toss
about frillies after what you showed us last night?'

'Go away,' said Cheryl, embarrassed. But the
thin man had his foot in the door.

'All we're after is a few words, darling. Then we'll
leave you in peace, won't we, Chris?'

Cheryl picked up Scarlett, who was clinging to
her legs, trying to get out in the passage. She had left
Victor sitting at the table. She was worried he would
climb on top and knock the hot teapot off.

'I can't talk to you now.'

'If we could just have five minutes,' and the men
were inside before she knew it.

Cheryl rushed about, quieting the kids, protect-
ing her modesty, tying the cord round her loose
dressing gown.

The flash of the camera woke Cara up.

'No. Look. You can't take pictures.'

She put her hand to her face.

She thought of Princess Diana, and how she had envied her lifestyle. She remembered she'd said to Barry, 'How could Di have bothered about being surrounded by the paparazzi? I'd swap places any time.' She'd been so puzzled, at her death, to think that she had still been trying to run away. But surely Di's pursuers could not have been as rude or aggressive as this?

'We might be the first but we won't be the last,' the thin one in the leather jacket warned her. 'The thing is, darling, you've got appeal. You've gone down like a sweet dose of salts. You're everyone's sweetheart this morning.'

And he showed her the crumpled front of the *Mirror*.

'Shame,' read the headline across the page. And there, underneath, was a picture of Cheryl coming home from hospital, with a Tesco carrier in one hand and Scarlett in a baby seat in the other. The picture was a still from the film. They had used a photo of foraging rats, blown-up, graphic, nasty, and it looked as though Cheryl was walking through them.

Well, there were rats in the Harold Wilson Building, you could hear them at night, but Cheryl would hardly go casually past them, or see one without screaming.

'We can't talk to you,' she told them again, remembering what had been drummed into them over and over by Griffin, 'it was in our contract.'

'Stuff contracts,' said the one called Chris, still taking photographs, moving around the flat with a cocky air as if he owned it. 'You and Barry could make a bomb.'

'How? Talking to you?'

'Yep. We could come to some arrangement.'

'We'd have to check with Griffin.'

'Listen, darling,' said the thin one, his ratty face turning toothy, 'if you really have signed a silence clause then you're a right bloody mug.'

'We had to.' Cheryl was confused. Griffin had made it clear at the time that the silence clause was part of the deal. No silence clause, no contract.

'Cheryl! *Cheryl!* Look this way, sweetheart. At least you can give us some idea of what you thought of last night's introduction.'

'It was OK,' she said, mainly to get rid of them. 'It was a bit dodgy at first, but after the birth I think it went fine.'

'And how d'you feel about being famous?'

'Huh! We're not famous. Where did you get that mad idea?'

Chris laughed. 'You'll see. Now, can you tell us how you came to take part in the series in the first place?' And he shoved a recorder in her face.

'We answered an ad,' Cheryl said simply, comforting a fractious Cara, patting her back, moving her to the other shoulder.

Cheryl was agitated, felt threatened.

Where was Barry?

What the hell was he doing?

Once she had got this door closed she would make sure she kept it locked. 'Lots of people did. We were chosen. Listen, can you get out of here?'

They had snapped enough pictures to fill an album.

'You want to check up on that contract, darling, find yourself a lawyer, quick.'

'Take this card,' said Chris, thrusting it into her spare hand. 'And if you want to get seriously rich, ring this number.'

'I'm sorry, I'm sorry, I couldn't help it.' Barry, red-faced, flustered, with an armload of newspapers, threw himself down on the sofa. 'Shit. They're all down there, searching for this flat. A couple of them recognized me as I was coming back and I started running . . . It was hell. I didn't have a clue who they were at first, I thought they were muggers.'

He laid the papers out on the floor among the mess of dried rusk and Smarties. He had trouble finding the TV pages, especially in the broadsheets. Come on. Come *on*. Cheryl's voice trembled, 'Get off, let me.' She put the baby down and knelt on the floor next to Barry. She was more efficient at this sort of thing.

Gradually, impossibly, like an origami pattern unfolding, they learned what an impact the programme had made. Not because, as the papers told them, the subject was an original one, nor because it was the most popular theme, and, without a recession, not because it was particularly timely either.

No, it was nothing to do with that.

They called the film effects 'sublime', and the sensitivity 'a lesson to all who would make entertainment out of real people's lives'. Of Cheryl and Barry they said many things, but the comment that made Cheryl most happy was 'they are truly natural and endearing young people, treated abominably by a civilized country and worthy of our highest respect'.

There was not one adverse review.

Everybody loved them.

'They shone with the kind of hope that should make us all ashamed.'

'Brilliant,' said one.

'Television at its best,' said another.

'Well done Griffin.'

And all that sort of thing.

Luckily the doorbell was broken.

But the banging went on endlessly.

The Higginses were suddenly in great demand. If it wasn't for the grey metal security plate that the council had been forced to provide for all the flats in the building, Barry reckoned they'd have bashed it in.

In the end they all went to bed. In the middle of the morning, with the light on. They took the newspapers with them. Cheryl read and reread them. She wasn't hungry. She didn't need food. The energy and adrenalin that surged through her was the same as when she'd tried that charlie Barry brought back when she was low, when she was on her antidepressants.

'But what sort of money were they talking about?'

Cheryl couldn't help him much. She'd told him all she could remember of the reporters who came to the flat. 'They just said it was serious money. And that we'd been mad to sign that clause.'

'It was you who said get on with it. It was you who refused to ask anyone.'

'Barry, listen. If we hadn't signed, we wouldn't have been picked.'

Barry frowned annoyingly. He would not leave

the subject alone. 'I'm not sure I believe that. There's probably ways of getting round it.'

'Ring that number if you like.' She gave him the card the journalist had given her. 'But if you bugger anything up, if you make them withdraw this series . . .'

'Don't be a jerk. They wouldn't do that.'

'They might if it went to law, and that sort of stuff.'

'I just think we should know where we stand.'

It would be ace to have money, too, but for now Cheryl was flying high, above such grubby behaviour. She had all she had ever dreamed of: she had total approval, the love of strangers, the respect of professionals, the envy of thousands, and what was more, it wasn't finished yet.

How she loved them.

There were no words.

Euphoric, she hugged her children, she kissed Barry, she laughed, she sang, she tickled, she played as happiness distended her heart.

'I'm not dreaming, Barry, am I? Tell me I'm not asleep.'

Gone was that awful, aching hunger.

She could think of no other time in her life when she had felt more fulfilled or special.

She knew how dazzling the stars felt, the athletes who broke records, the footballers who scored at World Cups, the astronauts who went to the moon, the poets who found that elusive word.

Every single person, she thought, should experience this one perfect moment, when everything seemed to come together and make one exquisite whole. She could die now and not feel deprived.

She could go blind and not feel the need to see. They loved her.
Everyone loved her.

But pride comes before a fall.

And don't count your chickens before they are hatched.

The videotapes that Sebby took home had been so compelling that Kate had watched six hours on the trot before staggering to bed.

'They're wonderful,' she said blearily.

Sebby watched her reactions closely.

There were tears as well as laughter. She cried when she saw the toys all wrapped and ready for Victor's birthday. The Higginses had overdone it of course, trying to make sure the kid wasn't deprived. She remembered Sebby insisting they buy him a Thomas the Tank Engine set.

'But it's far too old for him,' Kate had said. 'He'll never work the remote control.'

'He'll grow into it.' Sebby wouldn't budge.

'You're fond of that child, aren't you?'

'You would be if you saw him. He's great.'

This was the sort of poverty rarely portrayed in depth. Everyone knew about sink estates from superficial newsflashes, programmes about neighbours from hell and MPs' propaganda visits when the criticism became too dodgy. What hit home most was the wearying minutiae of it all . . . Nowhere to dry wet socks, Camp coffee, vandalized phone boxes, broken furniture. There was nothing lovely to look upon, to taste or to smell.

'We could never end up . . .?' Kate started dispiritedly, terror all over her face.

150

'No. No, we couldn't. No matter what happened.'

But how could Sebby promise her this? It could happen to anyone.

Kate wept when she watched Cheryl up at night in that damp flat, trying to keep her baby warm, holding it tight against her. 'It's wicked,' she whispered, wiping her eyes. 'Where were you when you took this?'

'Wrapped in overcoats.'

'You might have given her one.'

'We did, before we started filming. She took it off.'

'Surely you could have paid for the gas?'

'We can't do that. We can't interfere. Not to that extent.'

'But I bet you did,' said Kate.

'We'd be monsters if we didn't.'

Kate laughed when Barry's pants fell down during a silly dancing session. She held her breath when they hid from the bailiffs, and laughed hysterically when they succeeded. She tutted over their poor diet. She groaned when she saw the mould in the bedrooms. She wasn't too sure about Annie. 'She can't be that bad,' she argued. 'You must have built her up.'

Sebby shook his head. 'She was that bad. Really. Believe me.'

'Leo must have hated it. Being there, dealing with them. He's such a snob.'

'He's good at hiding his feelings,' said Sebby, knowing how appalled Kate would be if she knew about the planted photos. She'd never believe he'd agreed to it. She'd think he was off his chump.

151

'You can tell she likes you,' said Kate. 'It's almost a performance.'

'I know,' said Sebby. 'But you can't really overcome that.'

'Barry's more realistic.'

'He's a good bloke.'

'That comes across.'

Sebby knew the series was good by the way Kate stayed riveted through every sequence. It was he who had to get up and make the coffee, it was he who fetched her nightdress and he who loaded the dishwasher. In the recent worrying months, he couldn't remember her being so diverted by anything, not so intensely and for so long.

It was Kate who suggested they watch the second half the following night. She'd prepared a special TV supper, and Sebby sighed when he saw it . . . Lobster thermidor, fresh pineapple and a couple of bottles of wine. The poorer they grew the more she spent. Still, she didn't mention the sale, and she didn't throw him any more piles of estate agent's blurb.

'I feel I've always known these people,' she said when the second half started. 'It's uncanny, the way you've done that.'

'That's down to Leo.'

'You always put yourself down. I know what Griffin think of you, you're one of the best and you've heard that, too. And don't start denying it. It's true.'

When Cheryl started ranting on about having another baby, Kate showed her annoyance by drumming her nails on the sofa arm. When Barry urged her against the idea, Kate was a hundred per

152

cent behind him. 'They'll never get out at this rate,' she muttered. 'She must see that. She's not stupid.'

Then came the pregnancy announcement.

'I don't believe this,' Kate muttered. 'And after everything she said. All those promises to herself. It doesn't make sense.'

'It happens,' said Sebby mildly.

'I know that, I know, I just thought she was different.'

Kate started twisting and turning. Her crossed leg swung agitatedly up and down.

Almost at the end of the session Sebby was tired, Kate was exhausted. The soft porn pictures had been doctored so the intimate bits were censored. The story was, they'd been lying around and Leo happened to pick them up. Cheryl acted quite brazenly about them, bragging that she'd do it again if there was money in it, and Barry didn't give a damn. And even Cheryl's face seemed different, as if shadowy effects were in use, lighting, angles. It was hard to pinpoint. Now that this pleasing young woman appeared grabbing and bitter, it was hard to take. 'I feel I've been duped,' said Kate. 'She's a good actress, that's for sure. But whatever happens to them now serves them right. They're a hopeless case. No, I just feel sorry for those little kids.'

Sebby took off his glasses. He wiped tired eyes. 'How can you change your opinion like that over two small mistakes?'

'Two small mistakes? You're joking. Griffin have been had. If you believe that couple aren't after all they can get and don't care who gets hurt in the process, then you're more deluded than—'

'She's only got herself pregnant, for God's sake.'

153

'Deliberately. For money.'

'Where's this money going to come from?'

'From the viewers she thinks she's conned. She's taken this serious documentary, which could have done so much good, and used it for her own purposes.'

Sebby sat back. 'Kate. You amaze me.'

'And don't tell me those pictures were taken when she was fifteen. I'll bet you anything that one's on the game and into far worse than you managed to discover.'

'But what if she is? They're desperate.'

'Yes, I see that. And that would be fine, if she hadn't made out all along that she was God's little innocent.'

'Did Cheryl do that?'

'Well, somebody did.'

There was despair in his eyes when he asked, 'So do you think the majority of the viewers will feel the same as you do?'

'I don't know. But they'll be damn fools if they don't.'

At the preview, Sebby had handled the meeting with Cheryl and Barry badly. He should have given them some explanation as to why he had not been in touch for so long. He could have made something up. At least they deserved some effort from him. But, knowing what he knew, he had gone along with Leo, pretending not to see the hurt that showed so clearly in Cheryl's eyes, chatting away about anything but the subject in question. But the way the Higginses were sidestepped, patronized or ignored was too obvious to miss.

How many people here knew about the twisted ending?

Not many, Sebby guessed.

And it certainly hadn't been shown that night.

Certainly, Cheryl and Barry went home under the illusion that their portrayal was fair and positive. Apart from the intrusive beginning, which would leave any woman chewing her fist, these edited sequences showed a young, attractive, cheerful couple coping as best they could. Sad. Funny. Fast-moving. Fascinating in places. And the upbeat way the audience had reacted proved to Sebby beyond any doubt that the documentary would have been a success without any devious doctoring. He could only hope – and he knew this was hopeless – that the Higginses would be strong enough to cope with triumph *and* disaster . . . though how those impostors of Rudyard Kipling could ever be the same was something he'd never understood.

NINE

A plea for the children's safety is broadcast on the eight o'clock and nine o'clock news.

Cheryl and Barry are taken by car to the press room at police headquarters, accompanied by Heidi Trotter and DCI Rowe. They are old hands at this by now, but every time Barry finds it so gruelling he's not sure he can stomach it again.

The room is full, as usual, when they walk in after the police, Cheryl first, Barry trailing nervously behind. He feels lanky and slow. He thinks he looks gormless. This place has an enclosed and echoey feel, the heat is sticky, the lights are bright. There is no hiding from anyone here. And it's not just every expression, but every movement of the body that counts. Even the flutter of an eyelash.

With Heidi's help, they composed a speech last night to suit this new situation. Ten days have now gone by since the children were taken. Their appeal must now be directed at neighbours, relatives, friends, who know of a couple who have, for any reason whatsoever, suddenly acquired three extra children.

Guest houses, hotels, caravan sites and B&Bs must be alerted and asked to keep a close watch on their customers.

A hazy and enlarged photograph of the two older children, taken by Cath's Instamatic last Christmas, will yet again dominate the screen.

Unlike some lesser cases, which have to wait to be picked by *Crimewatch*, because of the exceptional circumstances of this particular case, because the Higginses are as well known to the audience as the newsreaders themselves, this crime is receiving unparalleled publicity – a fact which both irritates and delights DCI Rowe, who has had to do some heavy persuading in his time.

Barry finds it hard to deal with the change of attitude of the national media.

Where once they were so cruelly condemning – drumming up public hatred, hassling him and Cheryl around, criticizing their every move – now they couldn't be more sympathetic. Everything they are writing these days is positive and helpful. Taking Barry back to those first glorious weeks when public opinion was glowing.

He and Cheryl were royalty then.

Every passer-by was a fan.

'Make the most of it,' some presenter warned them, Barry can't remember which one, 'the British public are a fickle lot; this could change overnight.' What Barry does remember is that they smiled at the time, and considered him crazy.

But now it's as if nothing has changed.

And at times, back then, as Cheryl sobbed uncontrollably, he had felt that her pit of need was bottomless. She seemed to be leaving him completely, and going into some blinding desolation where he would never reach her again.

'But not everyone feels this way,' he used to try to remind her. 'Most people don't give a damn . . . Most people are sympathetic.'

'Well it doesn't feel like that,' she said. 'I'd like to meet some of them, if those people are real. They certainly don't live round here.'

But now the faces of their former hunters are full of pity for their prey. There are no coarse shouts, no angry demands or cruel insinuations. Instead, a silent hush falls, there is an expectant stillness as the Higginses sit down at a table which bristles with microphones.

'Good morning, ladies and gentlemen.' DCI Rowe efficiently states the immediate position. He will be the scapegoat this morning; he will have to defend his force for making no positive progress, for still having no definite clues and no persons 'helping the police'.

Cheryl begins her prepared statement.

They both agreed that Cheryl should do it, and the police did advise that the grieving mother generally had more impact than a tight-faced father trying to be brave.

'I know how some of you feel about me,' she starts, 'and I understand why. I'm not here to defend myself, I can't help being who I am, and everyone watching has made mistakes. It's just that mine happened to be made in front of millions of people.'

She pauses. Bites her lip. Runs her hand back over her hair. Barry puts his arm round her. She sniffs and swallows before going on. 'But one thing you know from watching the programme is how much I love my children. My children are my life. We've struggled, Barry and me, we never could give them much, but we gave them all the love we had. It was hard for some of you to understand why I wanted another baby so badly. Today, all I can say to you is that my babies brought me so much happiness that perhaps I selfishly wanted more. It doesn't matter now. What's done is done. I've been punished in the way no criminal should ever be punished. There's no crime bad enough to merit this kind of heartbreak and pain. Every night I scream out to God, if you're there, God, please, please help me.'

And her face crumples before she collapses, exhausted, white and shaking.

Cheryl is bewildered and frightened, and her brain refuses to work any longer.

She sits there staring vacantly at her audience, gazing into seeming emptiness as if she has forgotten why she is here. The pity and indignation of the press beat upon her like thundery rain as DCI Rowe takes the paper from her hand and continues to read in a calm, quiet voice.

'So if anyone has the slightest idea where these children could be, if anyone thinks they know anyone . . . a woman, perhaps, who has lost a child, parents refused adoption, anyone suffering from mental stress which might lead to this kind of behaviour, any ideas, any clues which might help to bring these children back home, please don't hesitate to contact us. Any information we receive will be treated with the strictest confidence.'

'Mrs Higgins? Mrs Higgins?' One keen young reporter tries to ask questions.

'You will all understand, in the circumstances, why we are not encouraging questions at this point in time,' says DCI Rowe sternly.

In the good times . . .

Back then . . .

. . . After that first brush with the press, when they made their first impact on a welcoming world, Barry insisted they see a solicitor, in case there was a way out of the silence clause they had signed with Griffin.

Even the lawyer they went to see embraced them like his own children as he led them into his office and studied that fatal contract.

All he seemed truly interested in was what was coming in the next episode, as if he was expecting some major event in their lives instead of the tedious monotony of court fines they could not pay, giro cheques that failed to arrive, rifling through supermarket skips between the departure of the day staff and the arrival of the night cleaners, waiting for buses in the rain.

The fact that the programme was such a hit was a puzzle that baffled them both.

What was the fascination?

'It's the same as viewing an accident,' was always Big Annie's immediate reply. 'The more gruesome it is the better.'

But sadly, the contract was watertight. Only after the series was finished could the Higginses benefit from the publicity. Only then could they give press interviews for money or get paid for appearing on TV.

'It's a bugger,' the solicitor said, 'but don't worry,

160

it could work out to your advantage. If your popularity keeps growing like it is, there'll be more of a demand when the documentary is over.'

That knowledge made Barry feel brighter. That made it seem like less of a con. Everyone knows what the press pay celebrities, and so he began to plan for a future whose promise he had never imagined, not in his wildest dreams.

The idea that their fame might wane, or even turn notorious, never occurred to either of them.

Well, why would it?

Griffin sent them all the cuttings, all the reviews, all the articles.

Cheryl bought a scrapbook and spent hours sticking them in.

'Lest we forget,' she said.

'As if,' said Barry.

Requests for interviews and public appearances arrived as often as final demands. They started in a small way: on local radio, choosing six records between the chat, a humble version of *Desert Island Discs*.

There was no need to cultivate an image.

Being themselves had brought this acclaim, so they stayed themselves when they went on TV, nervous at first but gathering confidence as the interviewers used tact and kindness to bring out the best in them both. These were popular figures; nobody wanted to be accused of giving the Higginses a hard time, so nobody delved into anything dodgy, none of Barry's murky past was exposed, or Cheryl's mother's notoriety, or the fact that her two young half-brothers were frequently up in juvenile court.

161

Nobody knew about a third child yet. Cheryl wore baggy jumpers. The interviewers stuck to the docusoap, and the shocking facts of such ugly poverty at the start of a new millennium. 'The children' were referred to as a collective, and everyone assumed there were two. The possibility that there was a third just never arose. That fatal fact would not be revealed until episode number eight.

The Higginses' 'bravery' in the face of adversity was one aspect the public admired. They had never considered themselves 'brave', didn't understand it. And Barry's determination to find work people saw as almost heroic, given the overwhelming odds. Here was a couple with unusual appeal: they were attractive, natural, childlike and wonderful with their two little kids, and it played a huge part in their popularity.

Griffin informed them that the generous-hearted viewing public were sending in disturbing amounts of money, in spite of announcements made in the press that such donations should be sent, instead, to the relevant charities.

Barry and Cheryl were naturally cut up – who wouldn't be? The fact that there would be no fee had been impressed on them from the beginning, but surely this was different?

If people were sending money directly, it was unfair that they weren't allowed to have it.

'It was the wider aspects of poverty in this country that we were addressing, not just yours,' said Alan Beam when they rang from the station, trying to hear him above revving trains and screaming children. 'And we haven't the administrative facilities to deal with anything of this magnitude. We are not a financial institution, we just make programmes.'

Barry went hairless. 'But people ought to know that their money isn't reaching us.'

'Don't worry, they do know. We're sending back their cheques with a list of more appropriate recipients. We feel, after long discussions, that letting through gifts of money would be turning you into the kind of freak show we most wanted to avoid.'

'That's such a bloody nerve.'

'Barry,' said Alan sternly, 'believe me, I do understand how you feel, and that this must be difficult for you to accept—'

'We weren't paid for doing the programme, but now the ratings have gone crazy we should get something. Right? You could have paid us wages, you could pay us now if you wanted. And you forced us to sign a contract which stopped us talking to the press.'

'We were very reluctant to become the catalyst which might have interfered with your lives.'

'Oh, yeah? And you know best, do you?' It was the kids Barry felt sick about, the thought that he'd let them down. If he had been sharper, if he'd ignored Cheryl, he might have made their futures secure. Why did he always follow her lead? Why was he so keen to pacify her? The thought of how he had been stitched up kept him awake at night. He had been a right dickhead, he'd been walked all over. He wanted so much to take care of them properly . . . He would die for his kids, and for Cher.

'No, we don't know best, but we are responsible—'

'Sod that.'

'It is precisely because of your feelings that we did not want you to turn into public exhibits.'

Barry banged the phone down in fury. 'It's no bloody use,' he told Cheryl. 'Tight-arsed shirt-lifter.'

A success beyond anyone's dreams.

But the moment he set foot in the door of the Harold Wilson Building, Sebby wished he had listened to Leo. But no, he'd nagged on in his guilt-ridden, self-righteous way. 'They've got no-one to talk to about all this . . .'

'You don't know that. They've both got their families.'

'That's neither here nor there. We know what their families are like. Alan and Jennie don't give a damn. Those two kids have been engulfed by a storm of publicity. How the hell are they coping? Are they getting any advice? What sharks have gone in after them to muscle in on the action? My God, Leo, don't you feel the vaguest niggle of responsibility here?'

Leo was equally sure of his ground. 'So what support are you planning to give, once the shit hits the fan?'

This was a question Sebby had asked himself many times. So far he had reached no conclusion. But face-to-face with Leo's indifference, he answered it there and then. 'I'm going to stick around,' he said. 'I might not be any help, but it's the least I can do.'

'You are far too involved with that family. Your behaviour is unprofessional. They'll cope without you. You can't always be around to pick up the pieces.'

But Sebby had insisted they call – to share in the Higginses' brief celebrity if nothing else.

Cheryl fell at their feet as if they were visiting royalty, and Sebby's heart sank. He wished he hadn't come. He had never seen her looking happier or more sparkly. If only Cheryl would get wise. She was euphoric about the programme's success, wallowing in the press attention, absorbed in the brilliant reviews. Starry-eyed, exuberant and gushing with gratitude, this was the best thing that had happened to her in her whole life. She honestly believed that the airing of the sordid pictures, which she knew was about to happen, would not damage her credibility. The smooth-tongued Leo had made sure of that.

The change in her was remarkable. She looked fitter, younger, full of life and hope. His fears had been unjustified. The Higginses were dealing with their success without any help from him. Far from being the reluctant star, Cheryl was relishing every minute. But Barry seemed concerned, although he said nothing about his misgivings. He wanted least of all to cramp Cheryl's new style.

Leo was the first to admit that they had no idea *The Dark End* would take off the way it had. 'We knew it was good, very good,' he explained, 'but nobody had any idea how big it would get.'

Cheryl listened to everything he said with wide-eyed adoration. 'We've got you to thank,' she said fawningly. 'The way you did it, the bother you went

165

to to get things just right, the stuff you saw as important, and the little details . . . Even the rows make us seem OK.'

The programme was up for an award, Sebby told them. Sir Art believed it stood a good chance.

'Maybe they'll decide to do another series,' said Cheryl, pouring the wine they had brought into a selection of chipped glasses. 'D'you think they will? Is there a chance? We wouldn't mind, would we, Barry? We'd be better at it this time, now we know how it's done.'

Her attitude towards them was too pathetic. If Leo hadn't been sitting beside him on the springless sofa Sebby would have tried, somehow, to prepare her for the worst. But all he could say, in all honesty, was: 'But it's not over yet, far from it.'

'What do you mean? We've seen the preview,' Barry said complacently, 'and that seems OK. We don't turn into werewolves, or anything?'

'We'll have to see,' said Leo, and Sebby thought he might add something else, because he paused and started to frown, but the moment passed and they moved on.

'That was nice,' said Cheryl when they'd gone, 'to see them again like that.'

Barry said nothing. He was happy for her.

It was like she had exorcized some demon.

Their appeal was wide, especially to charities. They opened fêtes and flower shows. They could only go if their fares were paid, and Donny agreed to sit with the kids.

They cut tapes at marathons, they led sponsored

walks, their picture appeared on an ad for the homeless, they used it on the tube.

The kids were too little to go anywhere with them.

At one point, even Cath volunteered to have them. That was a first. They were after the kudos, but getting to Harlow was too expensive, and too much of a hassle. Anyway, the kids hardly knew her.

They were far too busy to go to see Annie.

They spent wonderful hours by their broken gas fire, discussing how it would be when they could finally talk to the papers. They were even approached by a publisher; they were talking about a book. And so charismatic were the young couple that Bob Carnaby, the game-show host, asked if they would appear on his panel when their contract conditions were up.

A house would be their priority, if the money ran to that.

What sort of house was the question. It was hard to believe this part would come true, but that didn't stop them dreaming.

And a car, of course, but what make?

They might even manage a holiday, and Cheryl came home with an armful of brochures. 'We can look,' she told Barry. 'There's no harm in just looking.'

He was more cautious than she was. He said France, she wanted Barbados.

He said an Escort. She said a Jeep.

He said a semi. She said a cottage with a pond in the garden.

Their poverty was a temporary state, and so the

despair that normally dogged them failed to haunt them as it used to.

'Not for much longer,' Cheryl would say as she poured on the saver tomato sauce. 'Heinz . . . nothing but Heinz. And Kellogg's.'

And when they climbed the endless steps under the arch of ugly graffiti, humping the box-pram between them: 'A crazy-paving path, or a gravel one, which would look better at our front door?'

But best of all was the popularity.

Cheryl was in her element, happier than ever before.

Strangers would stop them in the street to ask for their autographs, blank-eyed checkout girls would smile, bus drivers stopped complaining about the ungainly pram and helped them on with it instead, and the passengers didn't give them hard looks when the kids played up.

Even the yobs round the flats gave up yelling after them, and stared with admiration instead.

The only person who did not change was Donny on her seat in the park. She had never heard of the programme; she didn't watch telly and she didn't read papers and she treated them just the same, sharing her chips with Victor, cuddling Scarlett and babysitting when needed. This was oddly reassuring, like a tried and familiar shepherd's pie. Not everything had to be covered in sauce in order to enjoy it again.

And thus a blissful winter went by.

Only two episodes to go, and they could cash in and realize their great expectations.

There was just them and the kids in the flat when

they watched the row about Cheryl being pregnant. She looked fiery, defensive, as she announced her great news. Barry seemed more tired than usual.

'*We can't cope,*' said Barry.

'*We can.*'

'*What are we going to do now?*'

'*We'll get by.*'

'*On what?*'

'*How we always do. We'll survive.*'

'*I thought we wanted more than that?*'

'*This is a baby we're talking about, Barry, how can you be so mean?*'

'*Because we can't look after the ones we've got, Cher. Victor's got a bad ear and the electricity key will run out in a minute . . .*'

'*We'll get more money.*'

'*Huh, that'll help.*'

'*They'll have to pay us more. We need it. We deserve it. Let them pay.*'

'*Who?*'

'*The suckers out there who've got it. They owe us.*'

Then came the abortion suggestion, and Cheryl's outrage at the very idea.

'*It's not my fault,*' she whined. '*How can I help it? If I want a baby I'll bloody well have one. It's the only thing that comes free.*'

But having a baby isn't free, is it?

And they went to bed that night quite contented.

There had been worse moments than that. They had had more violent confrontations; at times she had sworn like a fishwife. Once, Barry smashed down the kettle so it broke, and even she was worried when she got hold of Victor one night and shook him when he refused to stop crying, and the rain was wetting the bedroom wall.

But the public had understood.

They had taken the Higginses to their hearts.

That young couple could do no wrong. They deserved better, and their sad plight was everyone's fault but theirs.

Until episode number eight . . .

TEN

*Magic and witchcraft are the Devil's own work, with
which he not only causes people harm but also, when
God allows it, brings about their destruction.*

Martin Luther

A dawn grey with morning.

Thirteen days since the children left home.

A one-legged pigeon coos on the balcony in
welcome of the day.

Below, in the black shadow cast by the Harold
Wilson Building, the whirring life of the station goes
on under echoing roof structures as soulless as
hangars.

The poor make a straggled army: the dispos-
sessed, the addicts, the underpaid, men and women
in overalls and thin anoraks with blank faces,
hurrying and scuttling for the trains. Not until after
eight o'clock will the station expect the angry middle classes, suits, macs, umbrellas and briefcases,
women with sensible court shoes, young women
with kingfisher blue on their nails, in quiet rebellion
against nature.

Cheryl and Barry leave the flat.

171

No torch.

Hardly breathing.

Something has gone wrong with the plan. The kids were due back yesterday. All day Cheryl and Barry had waited for the wonderful news. Cheryl was so excited Barry had to keep warning her, 'Chill out, they're still watching us. You've only got to keep the act up another couple of hours and then you can let go.'

All the lies. All the deceit. No-one will ever understand.

The minutes dragged on. Sometimes Cheryl sighed. Sometimes she put her hands in her pockets and fiddled with her fingers, or ran her hands over her hair.

What compelled them to do this, what obscure impulse drove Cheryl to this reckless deception, still eludes her. Those last weeks had been unendurable; she'd begun to doubt her own existence. Her face stared anxiously back from the mirror and she scanned it nervously, afraid that there might be no reflection. They had taken away her identity with their cruel smears and their insinuations. She did not know who she really was. In the sunlight her reflection was dull, as if a film of dust was over her skin, and the vacancy of her expression frightened her. She looked haunted. She looked mad.

Their plan had been a simple one. On the twelfth day Donny would get out the box-pram, cover it with a blanket and push it onto the main concourse during the eight o'clock rush hour, and leave it beside the paperbacks inside John Menzies.

If she was accosted during this process, she would say she had found the pram abandoned. And she would not leave her favourite bench until she saw that the children were safely in the hands of the station authorities.

A familiar sight on the station, so long as she pushed them into the store without detection, it wouldn't matter how long she loitered or who she trailed after. She was like the pigeons, like the yellow mechanical sweepers, part of the ambience of the place.

But time went on, and nothing happened.

Yesterday, every communication that came on bleeps through Heidi's walkie-talkie, every knock at the door, every distant siren they heard, might signal the end of this nightmare. From the window they could just see the siding where the buckled coaches were hidden from view, behind a twelve-foot-high wall topped with jagged glass. The broken carriages on one side, the comprehensive school with its tarmacked playground on the other. But the tragedy of the train had taken place six months ago. Six passengers had been killed in the crash, forty-four injured. The experts had finished investigating, so now it was just for the scrap-metal merchants with their giant cutters to clear up the mess.

But these things take time. The legal process is slow, the administration procedures move at a snail's pace, the organization is lackadaisical. For weeks those broken carriages had perched there in that dirty siding until little bundles of greenery had taken hold round the wheels, hungry brambles had begun their climb and pigeons had spattered the once shiny roofs.

Twelve days, they had decided.

On the twelfth day, Cheryl and Barry were rarely free of their friendly WPC Heidi, so it was not until late evening that they were able to console one another, and that was in nervous whispers under the candlewick cover. Something is up. Cheryl is close to collapse. Nothing can stop her from going to find them, and Barry needs no convincing. Either something has happened to Donny, or she has forgotten, or she can't bear to return the children – any number of real catastrophes are flashing through their minds, and, in spite of the danger of discovery, they have to get their children back.

It had all been so ridiculously easy. During Cheryl's dramatic visit to the clinic, Barry had cut a hole in the railway fencing large enough to accommodate Donny and the box-pram with the kids and provisions.

Donny had been impressed by her new and novel refuge. 'I might just stay here, after,' she said when she first saw it. 'It looks as if the pushers and crackheads haven't managed to find it.' This, to Donny, was a priceless advantage after several savage encounters with the razor gangs, psychos and freaks who roamed her regular stamping grounds. Many times since she went on the road she'd been cut, threatened and sexually assaulted.

The very location of the wreck was the reason the searchers had missed it. Pressed between two high walls, it could only be seen from above and, ironically, it had featured quite prominently in the opening aerial shot of the documentary.

When the outrageous idea first struck Cheryl – the idea of an abduction to appeal to public sympathy

174

and end this unendurable ordeal – Donny answered the first obvious question, and the abandoned carriages the second.

She and Barry, still disbelieving but willing to go so far to please her – no further – had left the kids alone in the flat, and avoiding station security and maintenance, had gone on a furtive sortie like crooks in the night.

Barry's previous experiences of petty thieving and vandalism came in useful.

Kids had broken through under the security netting which was all that cordoned off the lines from the bit of scrub grass behind the flats. Cheryl and Barry crawled under, squeezed through the jagged hole avoiding the needles, jam rags, rubbers and dog turds, checking out details in the dark. The lights were bright but sporadic, there were patches of darkness, and they scuttled from patch to patch, across the tracks, behind the shacks, through broken walls, over cinders and sleepers until they reached the vast and foreboding outline of carriages.

They were out of their minds.

This was madness.

This was driven behaviour, but Cheryl stayed in a dreamlike state, thinking that, not so long ago, these actions would have seemed crazy.

This was the final result of months of ugly persecution, probing articles, public outrage and contempt.

Everything had begun to work in reverse of all that initial benevolence.

They were despised, reviled, condemned.

Their fame had been a nine-day wonder, but their infamy promised to last for ever.

If only, if only – how many times had Cheryl wished that – if only she had kept her pregnancy a secret. And the photographs had not worked to her advantage at all, as Leo suggested they might. Quite the reverse. They had slain her.

Her pregnancy, along with that tacky porn, was the straw that broke the back of nationwide understanding.

It had started with one vitriolic attack by Susan Holmes in the *Daily Mail*. The substance of the piece was predictable: here we all were, the compassionate British public, lovers of dogs and down-and-outs, being taken for a ride by a couple of irresponsible cretins who had no intention of pulling out the finger and getting down to a decent day's work. Oh, no, far from it. This sly young pair of scavengers not only milked the system and deprived other more needy recipients of a decent giro, but expected the hard-working taxpayer to subsidize their diabolical stupidity. And another thing: as far as being good parents went, what 'good' parent would stoop so low as to pose for porn, or consider bringing another child into a world of need and deprivation?

They should be forcibly sterilized.

They should be locked up in special institutions and taught the facts of life.

Their children should be removed from their care, to prevent these innocents from being infected by the same depraved dependency culture.

And from that one article the outcry spread, until every newspaper and chat show was demanding their heads.

The people believed that they had been hoodwinked.

176

Conned by Griffin and by the Higginses.

And those who had been most moved by their plight were the ones whose anger spilled over now.

They were shunned, as though they carried some unspeakable plague.

They were spat at in the street.

Their windows were broken.

They had shit pushed through their door.

Rabid media discussions were held as to whether abortion, in some rare cases, should be enforced by law.

The subject was brought up on *Question Time*.

Cheryl discovered a useful talent which she had forgotten she possessed. She willed herself into a kind of trance, which worked to protect her against the ugly people with their faces pressed up against the glass of her life. She had used this talent before in hospital when she was seven years old, and during the year she was fostered. But sometimes reality forced its way through the flimsy barrier, and then she was awed by the horror of it.

The pro-life brigade rose up in its most fanatical, fiendish form. Its devilish shape shadowed Barry, stalked him, maligned him, cornered him, slayed him. How easy it was for that sex-crazed brute to demand abortion, when all he lacked was a free rubber. How little life meant to such foul-minded men. Debauched, the pair of them, him and his promiscuous wife. That moral degenerate should be forced to have the child which should then be offered for adoption.

The Harlow Higginses were shunned at two Caravan Club conventions.

They arrived to discover that their favourite spot had been taken over by some new member.

One morning they awoke to find their awning torn, and it wasn't the wind, it was deliberate.

The phone calls from their more elevated relatives ceased.

Bill's back problem escalated, until he found it a struggle to leave the house, and even Cath's friend and supervisor, Glo, whose hat she had borrowed for Barry's wedding, cold-shouldered her for a while.

'But you weren't honest with me, Cath,' she told her when they had it out in the empty council canteen after lunch. 'You must have known what those two were up to. You must have known all along. All their sort are after is milking the system.'

'But I didn't know, Glo, honest to God. Barry was never like that before he got mixed up with Cheryl. Look at us, Bill and I, we've never had a hand out in our lives.'

Glo was silent, no doubt wondering how much Bill was claiming weekly for his so-called bad back.

Cath picked up on it at once. Ultra-sensitive, these days. So many people had started avoiding them, she just couldn't bear it if Glo did the same. 'Bill has got MS,' she lied, forcing tears into her eyes. 'I never said anything before . . . We're not the sort to go seeking sympathy.'

'Oh, Cath, I'm so sorry,' cried Glo, flinging her arms round her old friend and colleague. 'You should have said something. I had no idea. It's just that, with all this going on in the media, you begin thinking that all sorts of people, even those you know . . .'

They cried together, close friends again, and were still sniffing when they wiped the tables and collected up the cruets.

The news spread round Harlow like wildfire.

When Bill's doctor heard of the new diagnosis, he raised puzzled eyebrows, but of course his lips were sealed.

The response of Big Annie Watts to the turn of the tide was more robust.

Annie was used to being despised and picked on by her neighbours.

The short lull, the unexpected popularity had been more of a rest than a pleasure, a time for the drawing of breath, for rearming for the next fray. Having Marge Smith for a friend had proved somewhat unnerving, being the toast of the estate. The herald of compassionate change through the persona of her daughter had never sat easily on Annie's broad shoulders. Nor did Annie trust any unexpected run of good luck.

And she had warned Cheryl – she can't say she didn't.

She had told Barry that he was a fool.

That programme sounded like bad news.

Stick your head above the parapet of life, and you are bound to be shot down. Listen, it happened to everyone, nobody lasted for long. Even Di, before she died. They didn't have a good word to say about her.

But bad luck had its upside. Bobby and Shane, teenagers now, of whom she was beginning to despair, were chucked out of their gang, were terrorized by former mates and now spent most of their time cowering in their bedrooms, sticking models together with superglue . . .

She tried to offer her support to her demoralized daughter, but Cheryl was so traumatized it was hard to get through to the girl.

Annie would travel to the flat, sometimes punching her way through cheeky groups of reporters, bearing sweets for the kiddies, and all she got was tears and a cup of tea if she was lucky. She never even got to see her new granddaughter. She feared that Cheryl might be blaming the child for her dreadful predicament. After the birth, when Annie called, Barry had the kids out in the pram to give Cher a rest. The next time, when Cher said she'd be in she was out, so Annie missed her. Cher didn't seem to want to talk, so Annie didn't push it. There was something about her daughter which reminded her of her time in hospital, the time she flipped, after Fred. It was Cheryl's constant pacing, her moronic stare, the wringing hands and the shuffling.

'Come on, Cher,' she would say. 'Life goes on. This'll pass. One day you'll probably look back and laugh.'

'Shut up, Mum,' Cheryl said. 'You don't know anything.'

But it was true, they were putting up with a lot. Some of the lies the papers printed made Annie hoot with laughter.

The rat pack came round to her house several times, right jerks they were, they stood out a mile off. If they knocked on her door Annie soon gave them what for, so they went to the neighbours instead.

She watched them.

They were inside Marge Smith's house gossiping for hours, quite a crowd of them once, a curse on the woman, and the next day they came out with such crap Annie thought she could probably sue.

'But it's all true, Ma,' warned Shane. 'Stay out of it.'

And the picture of her they used, bleeding hell. Leggings. Curlers. Bra straps. Fag on, one finger stiff in the air, and her face took up the whole front page, every wart and hair on it. Huge.

The headline said, 'With a mother like this . . .' and left the rest to speculation.

It was a crying shame. These people, honest to God, they were sick, real sick. There were no depths they would not stoop to in order to crucify poor little Cheryl.

But that was the past. That is over and done with. This is the morning of day thirteen.

This is deep night, two hours before dawn.

When finally they reach the third carriage, they hear a child's soft crying. Cheryl stumbles in the darkness; there's something heavy lying on the make-do ramp. 'Donny? Donny?' she calls out through chattering teeth. Already the chill of impending menace has frozen the blood in her veins.

She can't climb over the obstacle, she kicks at it with desperation. Why would Donny leave a sack . . .? 'Shine the torch! Here, Barry, quick, here.' She's got to reach that sobbing child . . . And why is the coach in darkness? They can't have run out of gas. Where's Donny?

Donny's body seems smaller in death. Her eyes stare open, surprised. Shocked? The black length of her is draped the length of the ramp Barry set up to make access for her stumpy legs possible.

'My God!' The screech, like that of a screaming train, is torn from Cheryl's throat. 'My God, we have to get in there!'

Before Barry can move her friend with quivering and clumsy hands, without a second thought Cheryl scrambles over Donny's soft overcoats, balancing on one outflung arm, stepping on the mottled face in order to reach the door. She struggles to wrench it open, pounding against the repulsive resistance. 'I can't . . .' she screams. 'She's in the way. Drag her down, Barry. Victor? Victor? Scarlett?'

The little sobs from inside grow louder.

Cheryl, insensible with terror, bangs on the door with impossible strength. Her own screams tear at her ears. 'Hang on, Victor, we're coming, we're here . . .'

With a slithering motion, with a crackle of plastic, Donny is dragged from the door and onto the grimy cinders beneath like a stinking fish being landed. An iron bar falls out of the bag lady's hand with a clunk, iron on iron. Cheryl snatches the torch from Barry, shines it on the No Smoking sign, wrenches the door and falls inside like a late passenger taking her life in her hands. The door is not fastened. It has been prised open.

Who by, and why?

The circle of light encases Victor, eyes wide open and thumb in mouth, streaks of dirt down his tiny face . . . *My God, how long has he been like this?* Alone. In the dark. Terrified. She flings her arms around him and holds him so close it hurts. The gas lamps have gone out. Scarlett, asleep in the bed in

182

the corner and seemingly unaware of the drama, is woken by Cheryl's wet tears. She's alive. Thank God. Thank God she's alive! She fingers the pudgy baby arms. She strokes the forehead sticky with curls, as if she is touching a small miracle.

Cheryl can't speak. She can hardly breathe. She struggles for breath in hysterical panic and the sound comes out like strangled gasps. The dirty dry rain on the windows mingles with pigeons' droppings, and the table is a mess of half-empty tins and plastic bottles. She fights to stand on rubber legs and forces a smile for Victor's sake but the smile, when it comes, is a sick, rictus grin in a face that has lost all shape and colour. All she can do is sob and hold them, revelling in their smell and their softness and never, never let go her grip.

'She can't have been dead long . . .'

Who? Who is he talking about? Barry is making no sense. How can he talk at a time like this, how can he reason, how can he think through his agony of dismay?

'She's still warm.'

She remembers the body at the bottom of the ramp, heavy and dark and stinking, with a death sheen as white as the moon. Donny's face is swollen, one eye has disappeared between puffs of poisonous yellow and one of her teeth, never her best point, is missing and the next one is loose, half hanging out of her mouth. There is dried blood, like vampire lipstick, stuck in obscene crusts round her lips.

'And the kids . . . Look, they're OK. Look, Scarlett's smiling.'

But Cheryl's voice comes from another place. Her temples beat, her limbs shake and her eyes rest wildly on objects without seeing. Two large bottles of gin, one half gone, one still full, and empty gin bottles lie under the seat like abandoned luggage. 'But how long, Barry? How long? God, God. And to think what might have happened.'

But Barry just shuts his eyes to block the horror out, his brain refusing to work any more.

'Cheryl? And Barry?'

The police are at the door of the twisted train. Their heads appear at floor level. Some are in uniform, those behind, and their buttons gleam in the torchlight. Some are in casual clothes, and DCI Rowe does the talking.

They should have known the police would follow them.

Cheryl's misery is complete. They did what they did to change public attitudes, and now the condemnation will be fiercer than ever. She rails against the perversity of fate.

'Cara's gone! *Cara's not here!*'

And it's true. There are only two children in her arms.

Barry glances her way. Cheryl looks half crazed with grief, the culmination of massive pressures over so many months, and now this appalling result . . . He opens his mouth. He tries to speak, but shock and the weight of his thoughts keep him silent. 'And Donny is dead,' he mutters miserably.

'OK, OK,' says DCI Rowe, whose intuition has not let him down over these last hair-raising twelve days. He'd had them under close surveillance every second since the kids went. From the start there was something wrong about this so-called disappearance, and in his chats with the police psychologist who has met with Cheryl on three occasions there has been a mention of Munchausen's syndrome by proxy. 'Of course I can't be certain, going on three brief sessions,' the psychologist had told him. 'I could be way out. But in some severe cases attention-seeking behaviour can involve sacrifice of the children in order for the sufferer to achieve her aims.'

There was always something odd about this one, but there had been no alternative but to go through the motions just in case. 'One thing at a time,' he says. 'Let's get these people out of here and into the cars immediately. The kids to hospital, get them checked over. Cheryl and Barry, take them in, we'll deal with them later.' And then he makes arrangements for the scene of death to be cordoned off.

But Cheryl is begging, Victor in her arms. 'Let us go with them, please, you've got to let us go with them.'

'Give us the kid now, Cheryl, please, we don't want to cause further upset. I think these little ones have been through enough.'

'Someone must have come in the night, beaten Donny and taken Cara . . .' The stupid oaf, can't he hear, doesn't he understand the enormity or the horror of what might have happened to her baby?

'The door has been forced. What's the matter with you? Why won't you listen? This is outrageous.'

She will shout until he shuts up his bureaucratic mouthings and begins to confront the real issue here.

Donny is dead. The kids are OK. But, dear God, where is Cara?

She might be dead.

Dear God, dear God, they could bury her alive.

They could abuse her . . . Some of these thugs are monsters. You see what these freaks do to animals for a laugh, they are stoned out of their minds half the time . . . Listen to me, you fucker. Listen . . .

But DCI Rowe is like an iron general, his orders are quick, his decisions unquestioned.

Before Cheryl knows what has happened, she is out of the carriage, she has stumbled behind the railway police with their gnome-like lanterns along the curves of uneven sleepers and to the brightly lit rear of the main station, and into a car, handcuffed to a WPC who sits stony-faced beside her.

Barry's gone.

Where?

She never saw where they took him.

At least Victor and Scarlett are together. They are carried across the rails by strangers to an ambulance which is silent but with its blue light flashing chaos, confusion. Cheryl strains to see after them, but it's hopeless, so she buries her head in her hands.

DCI Rowe passes her window and bends to stare at her briefly. In a voice as cold as the metal rails which stretch into the dark black distance, he says softly and menacingly, 'You sick bitch. What have you done? If anything happens to that baby of yours, I hope you suffer for the rest of your life.'

ELEVEN

At the trial of Mary Spencer in 1634 there was such a row that she could not hear the charges that were brought against her.

The English. A Social History 1066–1945

Cheryl feels like a terrified rabbit run to earth in a spinney.

The chill breath of helplessness overwhelms her. If she can only convince these people that Victor and Scarlett will be lost without her.

'It would seem that that thought never crossed your mind thirteen days ago,' says Paula Lake in her hard voice with her ivory keyboard smile. She's CID, frighteningly competent, and seems to be playing a leading role in DCI Rowe's new interviewing technique – he stays silent but watches from the back.

'That was different.' Cheryl, shattered, shaken and tremulous, is only just able to concentrate on these pointless questions.

How many times must she state the obvious? She hates the sound of the policewoman's voice. She tries to shut her ears to it, to listen in another direction, to wish herself standing far off in the distance, somewhere before all this hell started. 'How do I know what happened to Donny? She's dead, that's all, and Cara's gone,' she gasps, hardly believing what she is saying. 'Someone must have attacked her and taken away my baby.'

'But how could you think of leaving your children with such a soak, a down-and-out? It beggars belief, it really does. Who knows what sort of scum she might have attracted. Didn't you stop to consider the dangers involved? Those carriages are wrecks, broken glass, torn metal, broken seats, my God, what sort of damn mother are you, anyway?'

Cheryl shakes her head. Her behaviour is as outlandish to her as it must seem to Paula Lake, this obstinate, disapproving woman. 'But we didn't kill Donny. Oh, God, oh, God. We didn't kill Donny. I swear it.'

'That's for us to find out. We don't know the cause of death yet.'

'Why would we do that? You saw the state my kids were in. Cara's gone. I suppose you're going to start saying we killed her, too?'

'No. But it's not outside the bounds of reason that you've still got her hidden away somewhere, playing to the audience, sympathy-seeking, anything to ensure you're off the hook.'

Cheryl longs to lean forward, grip this woman by her beads and break them. She is lost in a dark and endless night and there is no way out. 'How many times must I tell you this? We went to get the kids back. Why would we treat Cara differently?'

'You tell me, dear,' says Paula Lake, sitting back. And tap, tap, tap goes that cursed pencil.

Cheryl gets up and paces round the interview room, the stone in her heart so heavy she can hardly draw breath round the lump. At least here she's got someone to talk to. What she finds so utterly unbearable is when they take her back to the cell and she's left there for hours on end – for her own protection, they tell her – pale, dulled and defeated, yearning to be with Victor and Scarlett, to fold them into her and comfort them.

Of Cara she dare not think.

In the cells the walls press overpoweringly close, the soundless air threatens terror and madness.

Her throat closes up.

She wants to spew her guts out, she wants to bang her fists on the door like a wild-eyed, witless creature.

What must the kids be feeling now?

Where are they?

And, Jesus Christ, why won't they tell her?

A new thought leaps at her out of the heady confusion.

What if they keep her in here tonight?

What if Victor and Scarlett are kept in hospital? They would be so horribly frightened.

They know that her baby is missing, so why are they so condemning and indifferent to her fears?

Paula Lake's matt, powdered face with the trace of orange lipstick transforms itself into angry creases. 'You abandoned your three tiny kids in two squalid, dangerous carriages with a gin-soaked dosser for company, and now you tell us that you could not have foreseen any tragic consequences? Is that what you're honestly telling us, Cheryl?'

Sitting tipped up in his chair by the door, DCI

Rowe says nothing. Lake is his ventriloquist's doll. He merely concentrates on his hands with that same disgusted look on his face, as if he finds Cheryl too wicked to contemplate.

'I know, I know what it looks like, but we didn't know Donny was a lush.'

'Come on, come on, she was a dipso, she stank of the stuff.'

'And the carriages were only ten minutes away, and we kept watch on them whenever we could. We checked them out first. We made sure they were safe.'

'Whose original idea was this, Cheryl? Yours or Barry's?'

'It was mine. Barry didn't want to know.'

'But you managed to persuade him round?'

'Where is Barry?' Cheryl panics. 'When can I see him?'

DCI Rowe's cold smile is quickly replaced by passive dislike.

Tormented, Cheryl checks the clock. It has been four hours now since they first bundled her in the cells, and dawn has overtaken the night through the thick, opaque glass in the window.

'My mum, Annie, do they know that Mum will look after the children? Has anyone told them?'

'How did you persuade Barry round?' snaps Paula Lake impatiently.

'He thought I was cracking up.' If she answers the questions quickly and sensibly, perhaps they will stop pestering her.

'And why were you so upset?'

'You know that already. Because of the way we were being treated by everyone, even strangers.'

'And that was as a result of the programme *The Dark End of the Street*?'

They think she might have killed Donny. They suspect she is some kind of psycho. Cheryl must be careful to appear as sane as she can, but in these circumstances it's hard. Paula seems devoid of any emotion other than permanent annoyance. Maybe Cheryl can disarm her, appeal to her better nature. She must stop being so defensive. She must try to be calm and sensible.

'When you got pregnant with Cara? That's when you say public opinion turned against you, yes?'

'It was deadly. It was like everyone hated us. Like we'd done some sort of terrible crime instead of just expecting a baby. Everyone thought it was their business. Everyone thought we were dole-scroungers, and when the porn pictures came up they thought I was into that crap, they thought I was scum. If I'd pose for those I'd be on the game, and it all took off from there . . .'

'You couldn't take this unpopularity, could you?'

Cheryl covers her ears. She can hardly bear to remember. 'It went on. It just didn't stop. At first we thought it would stop after a couple of weeks, but they kept printing the articles and they kept snapping pictures of us and we kept appearing in magazines with all kinds of lies.'

Paula Lake is unmoved. 'And how about Barry? How was he affected?'

'The pro-lifers, they hated him, but Barry wasn't the one they blamed. It's always the woman, isn't it, when they want a hate figure it's always the woman.' Perhaps Cheryl can appeal to Paula Lake's sense of fairness. Perhaps she, too, has suffered from sex discrimination, they say it's rampant in the police.

They must be out in force searching for Cara by now. Especially now that it's daylight. 'Look, can't we drop this and talk about Cara? Whoever took her could have dumped her already. I'm out of my mind with it, for God's sake. You would tell me, wouldn't you, if anything had happened?'

The memory of the last moment Cheryl had seen her baby suddenly flashes before her eyes. She'd been dressed in a rosebud babygro with a white cardigan with . . .

And what are they doing to Victor and Scarlett?

Is there anyone with them who loves them?

This gnawing anxiety is driving her mad.

Her only relief is to play with hope.

She must get out of here . . . *she must*.

There are sounds of voices and traffic outside. A new shift must be coming on duty. Maybe Paula Lake will go and someone more sympathetic will take her place.

'On three occasions you and Barry appealed to the public on television. You were so intent on this deception, you lied in front of millions of people in order to succeed with your sick little scheme.' Paula Lake sits back and taps her perfect teeth. 'Did it never occur to either of you that people were upset and alarmed? Not only the general public, but police forces all over the land have been wasting their scarce resources looking for these three children of yours. Thousands of pounds have been spent in order to prop up your fragile ego, and the holiday trade has been inconvenienced by having to check up on their customers. Businesses have

192

conducted extensive searches of land and buildings.' She flings down her pencil in unconcealed anger and raises her voice to a shout. 'And all for the sake of your selfish image.'

'I know that. Of course I know and I'm sorry, I'm so sorry. It was just that at the time I never realized how big it would get.'

'And you've done it again now, haven't you?'

'No,' Cheryl sobbed and rocked in her chair. 'How many times . . .?'

'You and your husband meticulously planned this obscene abduction, which you could have ended at any time, but you chose not to do this, didn't you? You chose to carry on with the scheme in spite of knowing very well the desperate efforts of everyone involved.'

'When can I go home?'

Paula's earrings tinkle musically as she throws back her head like a happy horse. 'Go home? *Go home?* Don't make me laugh.'

Cheryl feels sick, the way she says it. 'What d'you mean?' With her right hand she steadies herself, then rests it on the table.

'You're not going anywhere, Cheryl. Except to court in the morning.'

DCI Rowe looks up suddenly, as if this is what he's been waiting for.

His moment of triumph at last.

Cheryl has to sit down. Her legs won't hold her.

'Cheryl Higgins,' says Paula Lake crisply, 'I am arresting you for wasting police time. You are also being charged with child neglect involving Victor Higgins, aged three, Scarlett Higgins, aged two, and Cara Higgins, aged six months. You do not have to say anything, but anything you do say may be used against you if you fail to—'

'No. No . . .'

But Paula calmly finishes her sentence. 'You might yet be charged with murder. Someone can take your statement later, and we'll talk again tonight when you've had a chance to think,' she says, getting up. Her job is done and she has got more pleasant things to do than sit here listening to some sicko. DCI Rowe slams the door behind him, and only the listening policewoman who has not spoken during the session is left in the room with the prisoner.

When Cheryl begs her for information, the woman refuses to answer.

Back in her cell, she has hours to think.

What will Cath and Bill say when they hear what she has done?

Well.

Let's see.

It was bad enough when the programme went awry, and all that popularity which had seeped and bubbled over the Harlow Higginses suddenly gurgled away down the plughole like a slither of old soap.

Mob hysteria.

For a while, for a couple of months, Cheryl had been accepted as a worthy daughter-in-law. Because of Cheryl, their standing in the eyes of their family had soared.

During their brief appearances on the programme, Cath had come over as she had hoped she would – a decent middle-class woman of principle who was not to blame for her son's decline. And Bill was a staid, dependable person, or was until his back started playing up.

The Harlow Higginses had been invited for Christmas dinner with her upwardly mobile sister and her husband in Bishop's Stortford . . . a first. Of course, they never went because the Caravan Club hold Yuletide meets which they never like to miss.

Cath met Sue for a day's shopping in London, lunch in C&A.

They had Christmas cards, that year, from everyone, even those she had tippexed out. Some names Cath could hardly remember; she had to buy another pack of twenty in order to accommodate them.

Bill had felt so much better, he'd been able to get out in the garden again and plant the baskets with winter pansies.

And they had been most impressed to hear of the kind of money Barry and Cheryl were likely to make after the series was finished. Who knows, some might find its way in their direction. After all, Barry did owe them something, some small gesture, for all the hassle he caused them during those difficult teenage years.

Annie Watts, they were told, typically revelled in the brief popularity.

Pushed herself forward. Minded the kids when Barry and Cheryl went off to some public function. Tried to muscle in on the limelight. Never caught on to the fact that her appalling standards must have somehow influenced Cheryl – her lack of ambition, her ignorant behaviour, her loud mouth – all these must have contributed to Cheryl's low self-esteem, and as for those useless sons of hers . . .

Of course, when the series backfired it all came out, didn't it?

Oh, she and Bill were OK, they couldn't rake up any muck about them. They were decent, they were safe enough, although suddenly the phone calls and the invitations had stopped, and no doubt this Christmas she would not have to buy extra cards.

No. It wasn't the Higginses the press rounded on, it was the Wattses in all their abysmal squalor. They grubbed about until they discovered that that seemingly rough diamond with her messy if homely house in Hackney was in fact a bully and a tart, whose sons were constantly up in court and whose survival on the estate was a matter for council concern.

'*With a mother like this . . .*' was the headline that said it all.

Cath could have told them that – she'd been saying it herself long enough.

And as for the blame which was heaped on Barry by those pro-life campaigners and their like, couldn't they see that the poor, harassed lad was merely trying to be helpful?

Those revolting pictures of Cheryl needed no explanation as far as Cath Higgins was concerned.

Once, during this awkward time, Barry had rung up his parents and asked if they could stay in Harlow for a couple of days, 'just to escape the pressure', he begged. 'It's hell here. We need to get away.'

'Hang on, Barry,' Cath said, while she turned to consult Bill.

'I can't hang on long,' Barry shouted, 'I'm nearly out of cash.'

Bill, as usual, was not helpful, such a slow man to make decisions, so Cath came back to the phone with her mind already made up. 'Maybe just for the day, Barry,' she said. She could hear the blare of trains in the background. 'It's Dad's back, you know, he's up in the night and what with the kids, I just don't think we could cope. But we'd love to see you all for the day.'

'But we need a break, we must get away,' her only son had pleaded.

Cath was forced to harden her heart. 'Well, I'm sorry, Barry, I really am, but we're just not very well placed at the moment.'

They had not heard from him again until those poor little kiddies went missing. And then, of course, everything was so different. It was hard to keep up with it all.

Public emotion changed course like a twister.

So be it.

But the papers were unkind, there's no denying that.

There was no need for such vicious attacks.

Every morning when the debate was at its height, Cath would go round to the newsagent's and buy the tabloids before work to make sure she and Bill didn't feature.

When the press came round they kept their mouths shut. They were always polite, but they distanced themselves. And if that common Annie had done the same, maybe she could have avoided the hounding.

'What will happen to their moneymaking plans,

now they're the scourge of the nation?' Bill asked Cath one evening between *The Holiday Programme* and *EastEnders*.

This had already occurred to Cath, but she'd thought it tasteless to bring it up.

'Maybe they'll be more in demand,' she said, stirring her tea and clinking the teaspoon into the rosebud china saucer. 'Real life confessions are always popular.'

Caged in her cell, Cheryl can hear quick footsteps, voices, shouted orders, the jangling of keys and cell doors banging.

Cheryl and Barry were approached by the media during their long months of persecution, but had turned down every offer for fear of more reprisals. If it was known they were making money, the public would be enraged.

And neither of them could have dealt with that.

She wipes moist hands on her knees. The right one is jumping, it won't stay still. Why doesn't somebody come?

She must keep her mind on something else to overcome this claustrophobia.

So what will Cath and Bill say, once they know the full story?

Cheryl paces her cell. Desperate to stop the hate campaign, in a world that seemed so suddenly unreal she could have been acting in a soap, she had never considered the consequences should their plan fail. It had seemed such a simple, safe thing to do. Like it always happened on telly, no matter what anyone did, things would be OK in the morning.

They have told her to sleep.

How can she sleep?

Donny's dead, maybe murdered. She weeps for Donny, whose death she has caused, probably the best friend she had in the world.

Where will she be tomorrow night?

And where are her children?

TWELVE

There is a detective at the door of Sebby Coltrain's Neal Street flat. Sebby was just about to heat the croissants that Kate has left in the bread bin, and he opens the door with an oven glove, feeling like a fool. The smell of fresh coffee fills the kitchen, and Kate's little touches are everywhere, giving proof of her aimless existence: bunches of wild daffodils, childish paintings in bright reds and greens and a half-knitted shawl in expensive cashmere taken apart many times and wept over.

'No, it's OK, come in, come in,' says Sebby overeagerly. This must be something to do with him, but what crime he might have committed escapes him.

He listens open-mouthed, forgetting the coffee, ignoring the croissants, as the Higginses' tale of woe is laid out before him over the table like a badly stained cloth. He had known about the missing kids, everyone knew about them . . . And after the family themselves, Sebby's misery must have ranked second. He'd been too riddled with guilt to approach them. But the story of Cheryl's appalling deception is too bizarre to believe.

'They knew where the kids were all along?' He repeats the information he is given like a rewound videotape.

'Are you sure? Are you certain?'

It takes some time to convince him that the law isn't playing tricks. But the reasons he is eventually given for Cheryl's outrageous action finally strike some familiar chords.

Contrary to what he told Leo, contrary to the promises Sebby had made to himself, he had not returned to the Higginses' flat during all those months of persecution. He did not provide a shoulder to cry on, or a supportive voice. He had failed them, he had failed himself, and it wasn't hard to understand why. Never in his worst nightmares had he imagined the public response would be so extreme. It was a kind of religious mania, a purge . . . Only Cheryl didn't have a wrinkled face, a furrowed brow, a hairy lip, a squinty eye, a squeaking voice or a scolding tongue. In every paper Sebby picked up he saw Cheryl's face, usually with parts of her body blocked out, and generally under some screaming headline, some new demeanour the press had picked up on, some new focus for hatred, some novel line of attack. *Witch! Witch!* He felt weighed down with inadequacy; surely any efforts of comfort from him in the face of this farce would prove futile. The knowledge of his contribution to this lynch-mob mentality slayed him. If he called on Cheryl and she forgave him, that would be worse than downright contempt. And when the Higgins children went missing, Sebby put pen to paper on at least four occasions, mostly at four o'clock in the morning having woken again in sheets of sweat. But there was nothing he could say, no words that didn't reek of hypocrisy. No sympathy that would acquit him of the terrible guilt he bore.

No-one waited so breathlessly for a positive outcome than Sebby.

He and Leo, Alan and Jennie might as well have snatched the kids themselves for the pain they had brought that couple.

And now it turns out that she did it herself.

The relief he feels soon turns to anguish with the news that the baby, Cara, is missing.

The reasons given by DC Moss for Cheryl's manic behaviour make sense when he has time to digest them. When you bear in mind Cheryl's desperate need to be loved. When you remember how hurt she would get when anyone made a two-finger gesture if she crossed the road without thinking, when a shopkeeper spoke to her sharply, when some passing yob called her names. Sebby and Leo often teased her about this raw sensitivity, sometimes putting it to their own use when they wanted to influence her. God! What cheap power games they had played,

Somehow this young detective has been given the impression that Sebby might know about Cheryl's mental condition. 'You were with that family, you lived with them for four months, and there's so much mess around this case the DCI suggested you might be able to throw some light on it.'

'And you are telling me you really believe Cheryl might have killed Mrs Donnolly?'

'The pathologist's first guess is that a coronary seems to be the cause of death. But whether the woman was attacked or whether she fell won't be known until after the post-mortem, if then. Her face was a mess, but conceivably this could have been the result of a drunken fall, or her efforts to jemmy the carriage door which had certainly been forced. Her body was covered with cuts and bruises, but the old ones suggest that this was partly to do with her rough way of life.'

'There must have been fingerprints?' Shit. This is unreal. Like taking part in *The Bill*.

'Unfortunately the gloves Mrs Donnolly always wore meant that her prints were hard to find, even inside the carriage. We found no others on the iron bar that had small samples of her blood on it, but that means nothing. If there were any assailants they would probably have taken precautions.'

This is unbelievable. Sebby could well be smiling. He hopes not; the last thing he wants to appear is a fool, but, hell, this takes some swallowing. 'Why would Cheryl and Barry want to kill Mrs Donnolly if they were so close to the woman that they trusted her with their kids?' He thinks back for a minute. 'She was a guest at their wedding. When Leo and I were working with the Higginses, they saw a fair deal of Mrs Donnolly. We got to know her. She was like a second mother to Cheryl. She'd known her for years, you know, since her childhood.'

The tall young man in the ultra-white shirt nods towards the percolator. 'Don't let me stop you having your breakfast.'

Sebby jumps out of his self-induced trance. 'Oh, sorry, I should have asked.'

'Black with two sugars, if you're making it.'

He watches silently as Sebby pours, and then, 'That's just it. There are so many anomalies here. I

mean, why would any sane mother risk her kiddies'
safety by abandoning them in a railway carriage
with a no-hope down-and-out?'

'That's different.'

'Oh?'

'Yes.' Sebby sits down, still clutching the teaspoon which he uses to make his points. 'I don't
know why nobody worked it out, but in hindsight it
does make sense.'

'Maybe to you . . .'

'To anyone who knows Cheryl.'

Too eager, the DC burns his lip. Cursing mildly,
he recoils from the rim of the cup. 'You're saying
she's sick?'

'Who told you to come here?'

'Someone from Griffin.' He checks his notes.
'Tarbuck?'

'Oh, Leo? Yes. But he knew her too. He was with
me all through the assignment.'

'He said you were closer to Cheryl than he was.
He said you were the understanding type. Less
superficial. Something like that.'

'Oh, did he?' That is interesting. 'Cheryl . . .'
Sebby pauses, searching for words, 'wanted everyone to love her.'

'Most people do, don't they?'

'For Cheryl, this was not just a whim, it was a
driving factor. We had a talk once. I asked about it.
At first she denied it, got quite defensive, but later
we both agreed it could be something to do with
being ill as a child.'

The DC looks nonplussed. 'What are you saying?'

Sebby considers before going on. Will this make

204

any sense to the detective? Is this worth mentioning? 'When she was a kid, Cheryl spent months in hospital. She was only seven years old. Her arm was virtually torn off, by dogs, did you know?'

Sebby's visitor shakes his head. His coffee has cooled enough. He looks like he's addicted, the way he slurps so eagerly.

'She had six painful operations. Occupational therapy that can't have been pleasant. She tried to explain how it was. If the doctors liked you, they might not hurt you, they might try harder to make things easier. She said that most of the kids sucked up to the doctors . . . smiles, you know, little gifts like favourite teddies, affection, trying to make themselves special. That's how kids think, I suppose. That's how they are with each other . . .'

'And this is the reason, you reckon, why she's got this pathetic need for approval?'

'That could be one reason, yes. This behaviour grew into a habit, and that's why she might risk so much to change public opinion, and why all that aggro the series caused her hurt so much.'

The DC looks unconvinced. 'This is all fairly hazy stuff.'

'You asked me. I'm no shrink.'

'Part of the reason I'm here is to try to work out if the baby's been taken, or if Cheryl and Barry have stashed her away somewhere else. We don't want another fiasco on our hands. We had a psychiatrist check her out when the kids first went missing. DCI Rowe had some misgivings. The shrink suggested she might be affected by . . .' the copper refers to his notes, 'Munchausen's syndrome by proxy. Ever heard of it?'

Sebby nods. 'Attention-seeking.'

'Extreme attention-seeking.'

'The intense need to feel important, willing to do almost anything, even injure your children in the process.' Sebby shakes his muddled head. 'I doubt if she'd ever do that.'

'We haven't got time for deep analysis, that's why I'm here,' says DC Moss. 'For your general impressions. As an outsider, an impartial observer. She's a bloody good liar. She conned a nation.'

'She's a bloody good actress.'

'I know, I watched the series.'

'Where is she now?'

'Down at the station. We can't let her go till we know more about Mrs Donnolly.'

'She's not violent,' Sebby says, with total conviction this time. 'Nor is Barry. Some other bastard must have beaten up old Donny and grabbed the kid . . . But why?'

'That's easy,' says the detective, staring down meaningfully into his empty cup. 'If anyone knew who those kids were and where they were being hidden, a more perfect hostage would be hard to imagine . . . and that's why we're concentrating on that angle. Although it's the worst-case scenario. But with such a lack of forensic evidence, we're stuck to prove what really happened.'

That same afternoon, they unlock Cheryl from her wretched cell with its immovable walls, its crude lavatory and its feeling of claustrophobia, and she follows a humble constable along soulless corridors, ruthlessly clean, through numberless swing doors. The walls to the offices are made of plate glass.

She is the star of the show today; she is the force that draws them, and although these people must have seen it all, the worst – serial killers might have walked this way, and the station is certainly old enough to have played host to some household names – keyboards go quiet, conversations cease and chairs are swung round in her direction.

Everyone thinks that they know her.

They have seen her private parts.

She has disinherited her body.

Waiting in the interview room is Ernie Eales, solicitor, in a dark, snappy suit that shouts a jaunty confidence, seated at the screwed-down table. Cheryl has time to think, with a dull, glum interest, of the hundreds of other souls in torture, like herself, both guilty and innocent, who have sat at this very table and planned their desperate bids for freedom while they waited for the rusty wheels of justice to turn.

A youthful figure, Mr Eales is one of the army of professionals who march through Paddington station each morning, with so much elevating their lofty minds that they take no notice of the irritating crowds of lesser mortals.

They rise above them.

They have their umbrellas to defend them.

There are people in this world with eyes like cows, some like sharks and others with the beaten eyes of old dogs, but this man's eyes, intelligent and knowing, are the eyes of a human being well satisfied with himself.

No doctor looks quite like him, no social worker either, no teacher, and nobody down at the job-centre resembles him even slightly. With sudden surprise Cheryl realizes that she has never actually spoken to anybody remotely like this in her life before.

He is paid to listen to her.

He has to be on her side.

She hopes to God he is good; she has watched enough police dramas to know how much this matters.

He can help her.

'Ah, Cheryl, good to see you. I hope they have been treating you well?'

His voice is plummy. Public-school.

But doesn't he understand, this is no time for chat?

'Is there any news about Cara?'

She knows what his answer will be. His blank eyes tell it all.

'Don't bother to answer. Don't tell me. But do they know who killed Donny yet? Surely they've got some ideas by now?'

'Sadly, I can't enlighten you on that. But I can tell you that they are searching hard, just as they were searching until yesterday for all three of your children.'

The criticism is subtle. But clear enough to stun her.

'Listen, Mr Eales. I know all this is my fault, I know that if I hadn't done what I did Cara would not be missing now. Donny wouldn't be dead. I know what I did was wrong, and I'd give anything not to have done it.' He is as smart and controlled as the knot in his tie. His shirt is so white it looks blue. Who does his washing? Who can iron like that? Maybe he uses a laundry.

'Sit down, Cheryl, won't you?' His is an unhurried, organized pace, unimpassioned, unperturbed. 'I have to explain that tomorrow morning, you and Barry will go in front of the magistrates. Now this may seem cruel in view of your tragic situation, but the law is the law, justice must be seen to be done and I'm sure the bench will go easy with you. They have dropped the charge of child neglect, that would never have stuck. And murder is out of the question, there's not one shred of evidence. But it would be sensible for you to plead guilty to wasting police time. I am representing you both, as long as you are happy with that.'

'What's going to happen?' Her voice is breathless.

'Nobody, least of all me, can be one hundred per cent sure, but if you plead guilty and reassure the court that you are never likely to commit such an irresponsible act again, I would guess you will be given probation. They are not likely to hand out a custodial sentence when all you are facing is a charge of wasting police time. And the consequences of your actions, the extraordinary media attention and the reaction of the general public, can hardly be laid at your door.'

Thank God for that. *Thank God.* 'You're going to see Barry?'

He nods. 'Right after this. Can I give him a message?'

'Can't I see him? Please? Just for a moment?' She needs him so badly beside her. If Leo asked her now, that same question that had stumped her when he asked it one year ago, she would be able to answer without a moment's hesitation. 'I married him because I love him, totally and utterly, because he is funny and gentle and sad, because I know one day he'll make good and because I can't live without him near me.'

'They wouldn't look too kindly on that, I'm afraid.'

She pauses. It's hard to know what to say. 'Will you tell him I love him, and that I am sorry?' She quickly pulls herself together. She can't dwell on that just now. 'And how are Victor and Scarlett? Where are they? Who is looking after them?'

'Victor and Scarlett are in care at the moment, until a court decision is reached.'

What? What did he say? He must have got it wrong. 'What do you mean, in care?' Tears of frustration burn the back of her eyes.

'You must understand that social services have to act in your children's best interests, and it is too soon for them to know if their best interests lie in returning them to you and Barry at the flat.'

Fear shakes her as if she's a skeleton on a hanger. 'You mean, this is something they do automatically if both parents are up in court? So when this is over, they will return them to us?'

'No, I'm afraid I have to be honest with you. I don't mean that. This is more serious than that. You are in danger of losing your children until the authorities feel satisfied that you are a competent and stable mother.'

'What, we might have to fight for our kids?'

'It's looking like that at the moment, yes.'

Her cheeks flare and steam. 'But they've no right to keep them from us. Surely— Can't you get them back?'

Ernie Eales sits back, as calm and collected as ever, as if they are discussing the weather, not this nauseating outrage.

Dear God. *How can they do this?*

How can they even contemplate removing the children from her and Barry?

They are good parents, the documentary proved that. Anyone who knows them can tell the experts that she and Barry worship their kids. To take them away would be scandalous.

Anyway, there's Annie, there's Cath . . . Why should they palm the kids off with strangers?

'That is not in my remit, I'm afraid. My job is to present your case and get you probation tomorrow, and, with that end in sight, we must go through the reasons why you acted so dramatically. We must make sure they understand that you were driven to do this with no evil intentions, that the whole thing got out of hand and that the vitriol of the public finally caused this fateful reaction.'

'But when? How long? For God's sake, why can't I talk to them now? When do I get to see social services?'

'Calm down, Cheryl, calm down. Hysteria isn't going to help you. One step at a time. Let's get you over this obstacle first.'

After Dill was savaged by the dogs, when Mum got ill and Fred left and Cheryl was seven, and discharged from Princess Margaret's with an arm heavily bandaged, she went to live with Mrs Bradbury in a tall, thin Victorian house with two floors. The bedrooms all stank of cat's piss.

There were two others being fostered at Mrs

Bradbury's at the time, Sonia and Barbara, older than her. They went to the comp.

They were friends.

They shared a bedroom.

They were both fourteen.

'But how long am I staying here?' Cheryl asked her social worker, Sue, talking quietly in Mrs Bradbury's fussy front room so as not to appear ungrateful.

'Well, we know that Mummy's not well, don't we? We understand that we can't go home until Mummy is quite better.'

Fear quivered inside her like a tadpole. 'But how long will that take? And does Mummy know where I am?'

Sue raised her eyebrows, and her eyes met Mrs Bradbury's across the dark patterned carpet. How could she come right out and say that Mummy had lost it, Mummy was unhinged, Mummy was the first Mrs Rochester and didn't know her own whereabouts, let alone her daughter's?

'Of course Mummy knows where you are,' said Sue, obviously lying.

'But why can't I go and live with the Donnollys?'

'Because Mrs Donnolly's house is unsuitable.'

Mrs Bradbury's was in Shepherd's Bush, so Cheryl would have to change schools.

She would have to make new friends and find her way round strange buildings. She would have to get used to coming home in the afternoons through somebody else's gate, eat tea at some stranger's table, sleep in sheets which were crisper and colder than the sheets at home, and where the shadows in the bedroom were different.

On her first day at Parkwood Junior, Sonia and Barbara were instructed to take the younger child and make sure she was all right. Cheryl thought this meant leading her in, staying with her, telling the teachers who she was.

But on the pavement outside the iron railings Sonia said, 'You'll be OK, won't you, kid?' There were fags in her satchel. If she hung around here any longer, there would be no time for a puff before the registration bell.

'Yep, I'll be OK.'

'Don't forget to sit on the wall and wait for us at three-thirty. Don't you dare move from there. Just stay on the wall until we come to pick you up. OK?'

'OK.'

She stood on the pavement and watched the children, chewing, mucking about, some with their arms round each other, as they disappeared inside the studded oak door.

Like the giant's castle in *Jack and the Beanstalk*, a favourite story that Mummy would read over and over until Fred came. But there was no beanstalk here that she could hurry towards and grip and climb down, no dumpling mother waiting at home with a wooden spoon in the cooking pot, no cow with a crumpled horn and no garden spiky with sunflowers. There were no magic beans in Cheryl's pocket. Just the coupon for free dinners and twenty pence for crisps.

She had left her own 'shire'.

There were always shires in the stories. Some giants could stride from shire to shire, and Cheryl just hoped against hope that Mummy knew which shire she was in.

But it was right and just that she should be suffering so.

She was guilty, after all; guilty of Dill's savage death, of Mum's illness, of Fred's departure and the cause of her own long ordeal of pain as she underwent hours of surgery in Princess Margaret's, followed by weeks of therapy. God knew what she was, God with his all-seeing eye. Cheryl knew what she was. She would never be forgiven.

She would never forgive herself.

Suddenly, out of the cold, a warm hand pressed hers. The prettiest person she had ever seen. Clean brown hair. She smelled of Christmas soap. She wore a bright red dress and a reassuring smile. 'Cheryl! Hello, sweetheart! What on earth are you doing out here? We've all been expecting you. Come on, come with me, and I'll show you round the school and introduce you to all your new friends.'

Cheryl loitered behind Miss Tandy, open-mouthed as she was bombarded with all the colours and sounds. Crazy pictures littered the walls, and round one door hung string puppets made out of papier mâché. She did not have to find her peg and change her shoes in the cloakroom, which is what she had been dreading.

The classroom was brightly lit. It smelled of modelling clay and varnish. All the tables were in different colours, and Miss Tandy's table was covered with a blue and white spotted cloth, wipeable and plastic, good to feel and run your hands over.

'Now then, everybody,' started Miss Tandy in a high and excited voice. 'We are all very privileged today to welcome Cheryl Watts. Now Cheryl has not been too happy just lately. She has been in hospital for a very long time having operations on her arm. And worse than this, Cheryl has had to leave home and go and live with somebody else because her poor mother is not very well.'

A sigh like a breeze fluttered through the classroom.

'Now, I'd like anyone who thinks they know how Cheryl is feeling just now to put up their hands and tell me.'

'Frightened.'

'Hungry.'

'Pretty.'

'Lonely.'

'Wants to go home.'

'Yes, excellent, very good indeed. I am sure Cheryl is probably feeling all of those things right now. So it's up to us to take care of her and make sure she is happy here. Now, who would like Cheryl to join them at their table?'

Thirty hands immediately shot up.

'Well now, let me see. I think Josie and Matty would be the most appropriate. They are both very grown-up and can be trusted to behave sensitively.'

In the playground, Cheryl was surrounded.

She told her awestruck audience about the dogs and her arm, and about her mother who was in hospital having her leg amputated. She would have to wear a wooden one in future, once they managed to fit her up.

Her days at Parkwood were happy.

She was picked first when teams were chosen, while at her old school she was near to last.

She was a little celebrity.

215

She was pretty and petite, and that always helps.

She was given a leading part in the play. She was the good witch, dressed in white netting with sequins on her skirts. All the parents and teachers applauded her more than anyone else. Cheryl revelled in their praise and in her role of victim. She advertised it and exploited it and she learned a lesson that, bearing the future in mind, it might have been better if she had not.

But all the time, seven-year-old Cheryl knew that she was a fraud.

A sinner. She was fooling them all, but it worked. It made that year bearable.

But she never forgot the heart-squeezing loneliness of living with Mrs Bradbury.

Nobody automatically knew how much she hated the shreds in marmalade, the feel of velvet, bathing in somebody else's bath. Nobody knew she was bored with *Blue Peter*, that Marmite made her sick and that she was terrified of garden gnomes. Nobody told her to clean her teeth for two minutes precisely, or to wipe her bottom from front to back, or where to put her dirty socks. For a week she stuffed them down at the end of her bed with her knickers until Mrs Bradbury found them and told her about the laundry basket.

Although Mrs Bradbury regularly came to kiss her goodnight, she didn't know that Cheryl needed to have her pillow fluffed up and made into a plump little nest.

Only Mum knew those things.

And Mum was fat and demented.

'*Night-night, sleep tight, mind the bugs don't bite.*'

* * *

So now, when faced with the threat, the very idea, of her own children spending a day, let alone a week or a month in care, squeezes Cheryl's mind like a crusher.

It is a nightmare, sitting here in this bright little room with this man with whom she is not making contact. Anything she says, any questions she asks, turn into unintelligible words, puzzling, threatening statements. To Cheryl, the future appears as a menacing, impenetrable wall. And her mind refuses to bite on anything concrete. She clears her throat and wipes her hands. Dazed, she can hardly see Mr Eales. His silhouette has gone fuzzy. He has merged with the window.

She can barely concentrate on the details of her own defence.

Which are simple.

She acted impulsively.

She turns towards the window and looks out into the sunlit street. Somehow all this felt more normal when it was dark. She admits guilt, laying it out like a mantra. This is her fault – all of it. She was the instigator of the whole wretched business; it was she who persuaded the hapless Barry to go along with her fateful plan. She had been driven almost mad by public persecution, and although, of course, she should not have contemplated taking such a dishonest and wicked step, if the magistrates would only forgive her, she would be grateful for their boundless mercy.

She worries that she has made a poor impression on this ambitious young solicitor, and hopes to God that it won't make a difference to his defence of her in the morning.

*   *   *

217

How she survives the night, the longest, darkest night of her life, will always remain a mystery to her.

She is told to sleep.

How can she sleep?

She is encouraged to eat.

Why should she eat?

Ladybird, ladybird, fly away home. Your house is on fire and your children are gone.

In the morning, she washes and tidies herself as well as she possibly can – what she looks like in court is going to matter. She wants to present a calm and positive image to the waiting eyes of the public, the papers and the magistrates. The penitent, the can-do-better of old school reports.

The van with dark windows has cages inside, individual cages. She is a bear in a Victorian zoo, and Barry is probably next to her, although everything is happening too fast for her to try to make contact with him.

Outside the courthouse there is a bang on the side of the van, and what sound like hisses and boos. Cheryl thinks she can just make out crowds pushing against barricades, the idle and the curious, when a spray of hisses against her window makes her flinch away from the sides.

The van comes to a standstill, the driver curses and mutters impatiently, 'What it's like to be famous, eh?' while the vehicle starts to rock . . .

'Barry!' Cheryl whimpers, sick with dread. 'Barry! I'm so frightened, what's happening?'

By now, her whole frame is trembling.

Women's voices shriek over men's, and Cheryl blinks automatically when the dull flash of a hundred cameras rebounds against the darkened glass.

THIRTEEN

This cannot be happening.

Justice stinks.

For God's sake, will they get bail or won't they?

That they should pillory Cheryl when she is on her knees and broken like this is typical of a screwed-up system. OK, they messed up (and the true magnitude of that is only obvious to Barry now). OK, they were caught, and OK, they caused aggro and distress, but that does not alter the fact that Cheryl is having to face this ordeal when she is off her head, wrecked, freaked out with all the shit.

So much for mercy.

This happens. On afternoon TV chat shows you listen to doctors with Jesus voices, lawyers who fall over themselves to aid and succour callers in trouble, and money men who advise coming clean if you fall behind with your payments.

Get real. Real life doesn't work that way. Barry and Cheryl are lucky if they see the same doctor twice, and that's after waiting an hour or more. It's the same with social services – you're in luck if you can find a chair, and the housing benefit nerds are scumbags. If Barry and Cher let on that they couldn't meet the payments, the bailiffs would be in before they could leg it back home.

That's why they put in a meter.

Those radio doctors would make out that Cher should be at home being nursed and counselled. That she should be being loved and consoled, not spat on and yelled at and threatened by sickos.

But because the Higginses are public figures, the law must be seen to be done. Because of their notoriety, there is no fear of a public backlash. They are hardly number one in the people's charts right now.

It would be interesting to see if their treatment would have been different during their time at the top of the ratings.

At least they are together now, sitting on a bench in a plain room with a roof light in the ceiling and lewd graffiti splattered on the walls. Cheryl is doubled up beside him, so all Barry can do to help her is keep his arm round her shaking shoulders.

'It's OK, Cher. It'll all be OK.' And his voice moves across like a hand to pat her.

Both of them know what a prat he sounds, but what else can you say when you're out of ideas, and you don't know what bed you're likely to sleep in tonight? Or where? What can he do? How can he help her?

'Did Eales tell you about the kids?' Her voice comes muffled from an unhappy distance.

'Yeah. But maybe that's just court regulations.'

'It didn't sound that way to me.'

'Maybe he's the kind of guy who always looks on the black side.'

'Could be they have to tell us the worst. Could be that's the way they work.'

'That's right. We'll have to ask the probation officers. We can ask them about the kids, they'll know better than Eales.'

'Oh, why are they taking so long? Why can't we get this over with?'

But Barry is out of answers, and only shakes his head.

Barry grasps one wrist tightly to stop any trembling.

The brightly lit courtroom with the high roof is packed and abuzz with interest. With hair as white as angel snow, a sweet faced, twinkling-eyed woman in a jersey dress with pearls to her waist is enthroned between two middle-aged men, both bald and wearing identical rimless spectacles. The clerk reads the charge against them. To the right, the journalists start to scribble, eager to extend the wood-panelled walls to the outer margins of the land so that everyone can hear.

In an even, measured voice the crown solicitor outlines the facts, which are indisputable. It is only the way he paints the Higginses which makes Barry so mad. Cheryl is misrepresented – sly and wicked, they say. This is done subtly, using chosen adjectives like attention-seeking and self-absorbed, like headline-grabbing and publicity-mad. While Barry comes over as some weak, pussy-whipped creep.

As he outlines the rest of the case against them, the prosecutor's speech is as boringly predictable as the weather forecast. He consults his papers one more time; it looks like he's reached the end. He turns his birdlike nose to the magistrates.

Beside him, Cheryl hangs her head and Barry can feel her trembling.

The court is hot and headachy now, heavy with the breath and smell of crowded human bodies. The magistrates listen with knitted brows as the true cost of the police action is revealed.

As reports of the children's health are read out.

'And at the moment, ma'am, the two older children, Victor and Scarlett, remain in the care of social services. This is until reports can be prepared.'

At this point, Cheryl lifts her face and her eyes are shining with tears.

It is a relief when the prosecutor sits down and Ernie Eales gets up with a flourish.

His is one abject apology on behalf of his misguided clients in the dock.

He points out that, because of the documentary, it is impossible for anyone who watched it to see the Higginses objectively. 'We lived with them for so long,' says Eales, 'we feel we know them intimately, we have seen them at their best and at their worst. We know their little foibles, their frailties, their strengths and their weaknesses. The exposing of those unfortunate pictures, along with the announcement of the third pregnancy, was blown out of all proportion, and was never worthy of the public's vicious change of attitude.'

The fragrant chairman of the magistrates leans forward to interrupt. 'I have to admit, I saw it too, my whole family watched it.' She turns to her right to enquire of her colleague. 'How about you, Mr Dobbs?'

Mr Dobbs nods. 'I did,' he admits, and so does the second man on the bench.

Ernie Eales carries on righteously, rapping long,

pale fingers on the desk. 'It was as if these people had committed murder. It was national hysteria, fuelled by the press. Don't forget, Mrs Higgins was pregnant when the media turned her into an outcast. And when the actual crime was committed, she was still breastfeeding her baby, and even the law recognizes that the actions of a new mother can be affected for twelve months after the birth.

'Put yourself in her place.

'And although Cheryl Higgins' actions cannot possibly be justified, they can be pitied and understood.'

Again, it is Cheryl they are attacking, as if Barry is some jellied sea creature floating around at the whim of the waves.

'This couple have already been punished far more, you might think, than they ever deserved. And we have to ask ourselves honestly now about who is really to blame for the persecution of this little family. Perhaps it is every one of us who followed the fortunes of the Higginses, with no thought of where the consequences might lead. But who caused the sequence of events which led to this wretched catastrophe? And have the media really the right to pluck individuals off the street and use them for their own spurious purposes, however well intentioned they might believe themselves to be?

'This project got well out of hand. Nobody predicted its popularity, and no expert can ever predict the reaction of the public. And whatever happens to them now, whether little Cara returns safely or not, this couple are having to live with the worst imaginable horror that can happen to any parent.'

*   *   *

223

'Damn,' thinks Rupert Shand.

The Griffin representative and legal adviser, who sits jammed between solicitors' clerks, flinches when he hears Ernie Eales's summing-up. This is what they have been dreading – it was bound to come sometime – but this is the first occasion on which the company has been blamed so publicly.

And what is more, before he left for court this morning, the meeting had been interrupted by the handing in of a certain letter.

This, too, had been a predicted outcome, but one which everyone had been hoping would never actually materialize.

They were all there, in the Griffin boardroom: the producer, Matt Broomhead; the programme's two directors, Alan Beam and Jennie St Hill; the camera crew, Sebby Coltrain and Leo Tarbuck; Rupert himself, of course; Jim Falkerson, the finance director and, of course, in the chair was Sir Art Blennerhasset, the suave and experienced head of Griffin. Art read the letter out to the group. His voice remained steady yet grim.

'We have the baby, Cara Higgins. For her safe return, we expect a payment of five hundred thousand pounds.'

It was easy to see how sick Art was with the whole abysmal situation. But against his better judgement he had backed the series, and was not a man to slide out of his own responsibilities.

There was tension in the room, natural under the circumstances, but Rupert detected an extra frisson between directors and crew. In their short, to-the-point discussions Sebby Coltrain sat with his eyes closed as if in complete denial, while Leo

Tarbuck, the flash one, was defensive and even aggressive.

Griffin had been informed by the police that the Higginses were not involved in Mrs Donnolly's death, for which they still awaited the lab reports. And forensic were coming up with disappointing results, the ground around the scene of death being thick with unimpressionable chippings. From the moment the couple left their flat on their so-called rescue mission to the moment they arrived at the train, the Higginses had been under surveillance. They would not have had the time to commit such a crime, although certain questions had to be asked – they were first on the scene, and procedures had to be followed in order not to prejudice any future enquiries.

The use of the media in the search for Cara would necessarily be low-key, bearing in mind the first fiasco and the angry reactions of a cynical public. Although superficial enquiries came back with no firm answers to Cheryl's suspect mental condition, it had been decided at the highest level, on the information they did have, to treat the disappearance of baby Cara as genuine. They could not afford to do otherwise. And now that this letter had been received, it began to look as if they'd been right.

Typically, Griffin had received several such sick demands during the time the three children were missing, most of them illiterate, some obscene, describing in gory detail what would happen should their demands not be met. Letters, phone calls and now e-mails were coming in as well. You can never fully comprehend or accept, Rupert had thought to himself, how many diseased and dysfunctional people there really are out there, ready to suck the last drop of blood from the latest tragedy, the misery of others.

But the letter that came this morning smacked of the genuine article.

It was not done in cut-out newspaper words, not in childish felt pen, but printed neatly in black ink. It was short, to the point, and was slipped through the letter box overnight and picked up with the rest of the mail.

When the three kids first went missing it had been agreed immediately that if a demand should be made, then Griffin must meet it, in the last resort. And now, here in court today, their culpability and their irresponsible programming has been criticized by the Higginses' defence. To this they have no public means of reply. The reputation of the company will be more damaged than it was before.

Damn, thinks Rupert Shand.

This is the worst of scenarios.

'All rise.'

'Have you anything to say, either of you?' the chairman asks the Higginses politely, leaning forward slightly so that her pearls get caught up in her motherly bosom.

Eales has rehearsed them on their response, but only Barry is capable of action. Cheryl stands beside him, white, trembling and ready to weep at the slightest suggestion of kindness.

She wants to be alone, quite alone, away from all these people.

She just wants peace in her life again.

Barry must clench his teeth, tighten his fists and hold himself together for her sake. He has never spoken in public before, and the press will want to record every word. He has learned his speech by heart. 'Cheryl and I are very sorry for the trouble we have caused to everyone,' he says, clearing his throat to make his nervous words sound more convincing. It's all up to him. He must save Cheryl. 'And we would both like you to take into account the circumstances that contributed to the mess we have made of our lives.'

He sends a quick glance towards Ernie Eales, who gives him a small and approving smile.

The blue-eyed lady in the jersey dress leans forward to consult the clerk. He gestures to a straight-backed woman sitting towards the rear of the court. The woman approaches the bench with an expert and professional manner, and a series of hurried whispers follows.

Eventually the chairman raises her snow-capped head. 'My colleagues and I have decided to retire for luncheon, and during that break the probation service has agreed to give us a verbal pre-sentence report. Therefore our final decision will be made when we have had time to digest their advice.'

'It's going to be OK,' says Eales, accompanying them to another bare office. 'They won't remand you in custody. It's looking good to me.'

But Barry, heartsick, is only concerned with the state of Cheryl.

Now she can hardly walk, and has to be given a glass of water and led to a hard plastic chair, where she flops like an old rag doll. She makes a total contrast to smart Olivia Sweet, the very person she was longing to question not one hour ago. Now any fight that was in her seems to have drained away in the ordeal of the court experience.

Barry can't help her.

It is up to him to convince this young woman that bail would pose no problem and that, in the long term, probation would be the ideal solution, that both he and Cheryl would benefit from this opportunity and that a custodial sentence, no matter how short, would be disastrous in the circumstances.

Probation Officer Olivia Sweet opens a file and takes the top off a ballpoint pen. She sits in a neatly pressed blouse under a beige linen jacket behind another authoritative desk. She gives Cheryl a concerned stare.

Barry needs to make excuses for his wife's total collapse. 'It's Cara,' he explains, 'Cher can't get her mind round anything else except what's happening to her, and Victor and Scarlett.'

'I am sure you are right,' says Miss Sweet. 'And that is quite understandable. But right now we have to concentrate on the magistrates' orders, and they have given me the task of assessing the likely benefits of probation orders in both your cases. If they adjourn this case for further reports, which is likely, I will be seeing a lot more of you.'

Better Barry should shut up and say nothing in case he puts his foot in it. If Cher was more together she could handle this better than him – she has always been the one to deal with sticky set-ups like this.

'Are you quite well?' Miss Sweet asks Cher. 'Are you fit to continue?'

'Oh, yes, oh, yes,' says Cheryl, but bleakly.

'Just take your time,' says Miss Sweet. 'Now, Cheryl, I would like to ask you if you know what a probation order means?'

'No, not really.' She shrugs, disinterested.

'How about you, Barry? Have you ever been on probation before?'

Barry cannot lie. No, he has not been on probation. And no, by a whisker he has steered clear of the courts. He has been lucky. Most of his mates have not.

'And Cheryl?' asks Miss Sweet, busy writing, 'I believe your two brothers are no strangers to the law?'

How unlike anyone else this woman seems. Dressed as she is with meticulous neatness, she strikes Barry as a birdlike creature with the quick turns of her small head and the way she suddenly pounces on points, like a heron spearing a fish. 'They are her half-brothers,' Barry answers. 'She doesn't have much to do with them.'

'Oh, really? I thought you and your mother were close.' And she darts Cheryl a look from clear, light-lashed eyes that gleam so intelligently, matching that delicately finished nose.

So she knows about Annie, too, thinks Barry, heaving a sigh. The image of Annie put up by a press who used her, like Griffin, as the odious mother of a family from hell, morally bankrupt, the scourge of society.

Some of the pictures they printed of Annie during the worst of those times had made her look like a rutting pig.

'Let me make this absolutely clear,' continues

Miss Sweet with her manicured nails and her care-fully plucked beige eyebrows. 'We are a service that works for the courts. A probation order is not an easy option. A probation order means that you meet your probation officer on a regular basis, and that any neglect of this results in an immediate return to court. It means that you follow the advice of your appointed officer at all times, and that you understand that we make detailed reports of your progress and continually assess your position.'

Barry nods obediently.

Cheryl might well not be listening, fazed by too many words. After this long tirade she can bear it no longer. Her head is aching with the strain of trying to concentrate on what's happening. Poor Donny, poor Donny. She begins to sob uncontrollably, maddened by guilt and impotence. 'But when can we get our kids back? Why have they been put into care? What do we have to do to convince anyone to let them come home right away? We've never hurt them. We love them. We couldn't know what would happen to Donny. We couldn't know they'd be left alone. We were happy, a happy family until this all began. You people, you think you know everything. You don't, you don't. You mess up people's lives, you tear families apart, you don't give a shit about people like us . . .'

She is doing herself no service. Her freedom depends on this interview, and on the decisions of this one woman whose eyes are direct and un-sympathetic, whose scarf is held by a Wedgwood clip and who is obviously aiming straight for the top of her specialized tree.

FOURTEEN

Freedom. Thank God, thank God for that. When you think what might have happened.

But for sanity's sake, Cheryl should not be watching the television news. What is she trying to do to herself? Why can't she leave it alone? Why must she hug the knife that stabs her?

Barry told her to skip it, but after the kindness of the magistrates and their sympathetic decision, after she had collapsed in a passion of anguished tears, hope crept back to her eyes and a glimmer of courage took root in her heart.

There is some good in the world.

Nevertheless, alas, here they are, back in the flat without their children.

'The last thing we intend to do is compound your unhappiness at this terrible time,' the gentle chairwoman told them. 'And all of us would like to extend our sympathies to you both.' She paused here to give Cheryl a sad kind of smile. 'We can only hope against hope that Cara is returned to you safely, and that one day you can put all this behind you and get on with your young lives in peace.'

Her words glowed with sincerity.

Her overwhelming desire was to comfort.

But Cheryl was so drained and drawn, so thread-bare was her nervous control, that her arms were trembling from her narrow shoulders and her fingers fiddled together on the railing of the dock as if she was a prisoner waiting for the judge's black cap.

'We have considered the probation officer's opinion after her initial meeting with you,' the magistrate went on in a more businesslike voice, 'and we feel that, over time, you might find that their help will be useful to you both. For a final decision we need medical reports, and reports from the social services department. Therefore this court will adjourn until a later date. The plea for bail is granted.'

There was an indecent stampede from the press benches, but Barry and Cheryl hardly noticed. It wasn't until, with Eales beside them, they reached the entrance hall of the court that the cameras started to flash and microphones were shoved in their faces, and a hundred voices were demanding answers to a hundred muddled questions.

'No comment,' Eales shouted, 'no comment.'

Someone cried out, 'Witch! witch! What have you done with your baby?'

Cheryl heard it and shuddered, just as persecuted women must have done five centuries ago when 'All wickedness was but little to the wickedness of a woman'.

Eales pushed his way through like a small bull-dozer, with his confident suit and his Hollywood jaw. The taxi driver waiting at the kerb was there at his request. He helped them in. Eales stayed behind.

'To give them a statement,' he hurriedly explained, 'anything to shut the buggers up.'

'But I haven't got enough money,' Barry was forced to stutter as the taxi sped away from the crowds.

'That's OK mate, it's all paid for.'

They should have learned their lesson by now.

News of their arrest had been broadcast on every bulletin on every channel, radio and TV, since early that morning when the facts leaked out. Two of the Higgins children were found, but the baby was still missing. Incredibly, unbelievably, they had hidden the children themselves.

The public asked themselves, what now?

What new malice has that woman done?

In their furious minds they crossed themselves against the evil eye.

She did it. She must have. Who else?

People were talking about it on buses and trains, in supermarkets, pubs and on street corners.

Before Cheryl and Barry reached home to face yet another barrage of cameras, the shocking details, both real and false, were spilling into the public arena and being kicked around by pundits who knew how to dribble and weave and titillate the game.

'No,' Cheryl wanted to howl out loud when the taxi halted outside the Harold Wilson Building and they were surrounded.

'*No!*'

They sidled through the congestion, only to be pursued ruthlessly as they rushed up the five flights of concrete steps towards their flat, their sanctuary.

And then the truth of this new reality hit home

233

hard. If they were out of favour before, what new wrath would visit them now?

Witch! Witch!

Unclean spirit.

Sick with dread as this awful new fear possessed her, Cheryl thought about what Barry had said. Perhaps this defensive reaction of theirs was making matters worse . . . Maybe they should co-operate with the press, stop running, stop hiding. There must be a way of turning this venomous tide into something resembling sanity.

Maybe Barry was right. This might be the time to try it. But each time Cheryl stopped, he pushed her on; if she turned round, he dragged her behind him protectively, believing she had run out of steam or stumbled in the path of their enemies.

'*Wait, Barry, wait . . .*'

But in the chaos he could not hear her.

'Hang on!' Barry's idea was that if, by some miracle, they could get one reporter on their side, if they gave their exclusive story to someone, it might help in the search for Cara. They had their investigative journalists, they had connections, they had money for bribes. If the tabloid readers could be persuaded to swallow their anger just temporarily, surely the hunt would be more successful – helped by millions of eyes, hundreds and thousands of families in every corner of the land.

But who, in this fiendish furore, could be trusted?

At last, they slammed the door behind them and thanked God it was vandal-proof.

Barry makes her a cup of tea, and they sit holding hands to watch the news.

234

The report itself is balanced and fair. It is only the headlines that grab and chill.

'Bail granted for mother who plans her own children's disappearance. Police on a wild goose chase.'

And if these are the banal TV headlines, what the hell will the press do tomorrow?

They ignore every knock on the door.

If they'd had a phone it would be off the hook.

Barry seems to have changed his mind, overwhelmed by the hazards which he spells out, as if she's stupid. 'But every move we make from now on they'll call sly and manipulative. That's what happened last time, and I don't see what will have changed.'

'Victor and Scarlett are safe,' says Cheryl, sitting with her elbows on her knees, head down like The Thinker. 'Although they're not here, they are safe. So the only person who counts now is Cara, and I don't care what they call us after, I need to find out if someone will help us.'

A speck of comfort for her to cling to.

But Barry wrestles with a gnawing anxiety. How much further can he follow her? He watches her face anxiously. The last time he followed her lead, look what happened. She suffered more than he did. Women crave approval more than men. He remembers her hunted eyes, so he says, 'They'll accuse us of going to the press for the money.'

'How can they say that? There won't be any payment. Look, I only want someone to help us.'

'Since when has the truth mattered to that lot? Don't say you've forgotten already. And it's you they're after this time . . . didn't you hear them?'

235

'What's new? I know that. That's why it's me who has to do it. Unlike you, I've got nothing to lose.'

No experience on earth could ever be worse than this one. Her spirit moves in an infinite waste. Oh, my God. There must be some order somewhere behind the riot of this kind of wilderness.

Her memory tortures her with stories of children gone missing, countless words of intolerable pain which she had read and passed over, looking for the TV pages or her stars. Oh, yes, she had paused, and like everyone else she had felt that small stab of agony inside and counted herself lucky, and imagined that she would never have to endure such torment. She had wondered how any mother could experience such desolation without going insane, and her white unhappy fingers trail over her own face now, as if to feel that she is real and not stuck in some intolerable dream.

The following morning, and now it seems certain that Barry and Cheryl are in the fiendish business of kidnapping. Demanding money for the daughter they have hidden away God knows where. A note has been received by Griffin; someone has leaked the precious information the police were so keen to keep confidential.

They are now accused by all and sundry of causing the death of a simple old woman by putting her at serious risk in such an ungodly locality. Grainy pictures of the sidings, with the carriages sagging on their broken lines, underline this point of view. There were six fatalities on that very train. Now, with the ribbons of death shimmering round Donny's last stand, it looks like a scene out of hell.

These accusations leave Barry and Cheryl speechless. But they should have known . . . they should have learned . . .

DCI Jonathan Rowe, a previously reasonable man, nevertheless finds it hard to conceal his anger when faced with such pathological liars. Particularly when such a puny sentence has already been suggested. Probation, my arse. A crime committed for the dubious sake of seeking public sympathy, Christ! Mrs Buckle, JP, dogooder, champion of the underdog, falls for it every time. And her two bald-headed lackeys are no better.

And it does not improve DCI Rowe's temper to know that his specially trained policewoman, Heidi Trotter, still leans towards forgiveness and pities Cheryl, particularly for what she calls this 'hideous trip'.

In the car on the way to the flats this morning, he had stressed the wretched reality of the situation. 'They brought this on their own heads.'

'Oh yeah?' said Trotter. 'They have made their beds and they must lie in them, is that it? As my granny used to say.'

'You are letting your heart rule your head.'

'Good,' said Trotter. 'My head never did much for me.'

And DCI Rowe was reluctant to pursue that line of questioning, because Trotter is not the most alluring of women, chubby and freckled and with three or four eye-catching little stout hairs like tent pegs bristling out of her neck.

Why doesn't anyone tell her about them?

Instead, he persisted sourly, 'I was right the last

237

time, and I still feel there is a very real chance that the Higginses know where Cara is now.'

'Balls,' said Trotter dismissively.

'I presume you have been influenced by Cheryl's apparent distress.'

'Well, that does have some bearing on my opinion, yes.'

'Don't forget she was equally distressed when she knew very well where her blasted kids were.'

'It's the shock element, sir,' said Trotter. 'Being a man, you might not recognize it.'

'If this shock element was missing before, how come you never recognized that? And maybe mentioned it at the time?'

'Because, sir, you would have dismissed it as women's intuition.'

The ransom demand sent to Griffin is being taken seriously by the top brass, so much so that a special crime squad has been called in to deal with the technicalities of that particular angle.

DCI Rowe is not sorry.

He does not feel that his patch has been invaded. Far from it.

He was troubled enough; he had been traumatized enough by the burden of the original search for those three kiddies, and by the dread of the possibility that the kidnap might have been genuine.

So his anger is quite understandable. Those endless nights without sleep, known about only by his wife; his lack of appetite; the black thoughts of what might have happened to those three innocents; all these nightmares he cannot forget. And he is determined not to allow thoughts of Cara to affect him in the same debilitating way. Especially if these miserable lowlifes are up to the same little scam again.

Now Barry paces the flat, frantic with fury. 'We were under surveillance, how could we have sneaked out, snatched Cara and taken her somewhere else?'

'Who's to say she was ever with the others in the carriages?'

'For Christ's sake.'

But one baby's belongings are much like another's. The feeding bottles the team had recovered could have been Cara's, could have been Scarlett's. As the teats were swimming in disinfectant, nothing useful had come from those. The disposable nappies shoved in black bags had been examined by forensics, but as there were no comparisons to make, all that proved was that the food that was eaten was mostly milk preparation and cereal. The babygros they removed could be stretched to fit from six months to eighteen. Cara and Scarlett could both have used them, ditto the shawls and the items of bedding. Skin and hair samples taken from these matched Scarlett's, but some had been washed in a soapy bowl, even scrubbed with an old nail brush – part of Mrs Donnolly's curious attempts at hygiene – so these tests, too, proved inconclusive.

DCI Rowe continues calmly, but there's menace in his tone. 'Nobody is even suggesting that you two did this yourselves. You could have got any local scum to go in there, smash the door down, give the old woman a going-over and stash the kid away. But the going-over went too far . . .'

'No, please stop. Don't say these things,' pleads Cheryl, covering her ears in useless protection.

'Look, for God's sake, listen. We'd never risk Cara anywhere near that kind of psycho. And we'd never let Donny be hurt . . .'

'It seems to me', says Rowe, 'that the first time you gave your kids away you never gave much thought to their bloody safety.'

Where does any chain of circumstances begin? Did this all start with *The Dark End*? Was it that that led them step by step towards this awful moment? Or did the causes go back much further? But Cheryl needs to concentrate on the well-being of her children, not on what might have been, not on the wild accusations of the police. 'This letter, this demand. You think it might be genuine?'

'We can't be certain, of course,' says Trotter, 'but it's got all the hallmarks.'

Cheryl's next question is full of hope. 'So does this mean that Cara is more likely to be safe?'

Trotter runs her hands through her mess of springy red hair. 'Don't be too optimistic about that,' she starts, and then, in the face of Cheryl's distress, 'but if whoever has Cara thinks she is valuable to them, then yes, it does mean that they are more likely to be careful.'

Trotter is talking out of the back of her head, but if that calms Cheryl down so that she is better able to deal with his questions, then Rowe is happy enough with that.

It is imperative that he find out if the Higginses are telling the truth.

They assure him that the crazed Mrs Donnolly was never in on the plot. So of course she had no idea that the Higginses had alerted the law to their kids' disappearance.

And no, while the children were with her, she had no newspapers or other forms of reading matter. They had found none in the carriage.

She never read newspapers anyway. 'Load of crap.'

She hadn't a clue that the Higgins kiddies were the hottest property in the land.

And no, the bag lady did not think it odd to be asked to move into some sordid railway siding and single-handedly take care of three infants who were not her own. She had liked and trusted Cheryl. In the drug-crazed, cardboard-boxed underworld she inhabited, nothing seemed that outlandish. She was grateful for a warm, safe haven. She jumped at the chance. She felt privileged to look after the kids. 'Bless their little hearts.' She had missed having bairns about since her own were taken. Since Winston left her and her world caved in.

'Come on, Cheryl, why don't you admit it? But you're not after sympathy this time, are you? No, this time you're more hard-headed, this time you're after the money, aren't you?'

'But why would we have gone through all that, just to do it again?' asks Barry, still pacing, more frantic to convince them than ever. But he is weakening. Slow and tired, he had one hell of a bad night. 'Why wouldn't we hide Cara in the first place? And demand the cash then?'

'Maybe an additional, more devious deception,' says Rowe, unfazed by their protestations. 'You admit you knew you were under surveillance. You deliberately lead us to the children, feed us all that crap about Cheryl cracking under the strain, and then you hit us with this second disaster and expect us to be taken in yet again.'

'But why would we do this?' asks Cheryl. 'Why would we go through all this hassle for the sake of a few thousand quid?'

'Because you are sick,' says Rowe, looking at them with sardonic pity. 'And grabbing like the rest of the scum round here. Because you need constant attention like most people need air. And because you believe that the rest of us are as gullible as Trotter, that we are as thick as two planks.'

Cheryl's body shudders.

She looks a little mad.

But she lifts her small shoulders and says nothing more.

At the brightly lit end of the street, this is a time for good cheer.

Bring on the Brut.

Let the fanfares roll at their loudest, because this is a glittering occasion.

Now their worst fears have been quelled. Kate, who speaks fluent German and French, has landed herself a job as an interpreter at a City bank. Not the kind of work she had hoped for, and Sebby was surprised when she took it. But it brings in good money and that's what they needed. She sets off every morning at nine, and returns around four-thirty.

On the strength of this, she was able to visit Harvey Nichols and purchase the slim silver creation in which she looks so dazzling tonight. And now she and Sebby sit round a circular table with colleagues from Griffin and their wives in their best, confident of winning their specialized category at this awards ceremony – as long as the judges have not turned squeamish and been influenced by the recent criticism of the genre, and their series in particular, bearing in mind the unfortunate repercussions. Expectant fingers tap liquor glasses, which flash with vivid Caribbean colour.

And Sebby's career looks safer than ever when the suave presenter, Charles Lamb, in his best bib and tucker, slits open the envelope and announces the name of the winner.

Yes, *yes!* Can you believe it? *The Dark End of the Street* has won this most prestigious award. Sir Art Blennerhasset's face briefly disappears behind a hearty puff of cigar smoke. Kate leans forward and plants an excited kiss on Sebby's flushed face. He takes her hand and squeezes it.

Alan Beam and Jennie St Hill, his hair as shiny and rippling as hers, are commended for their excellent direction, and Sebby and Leo for their inspired camera work. This can do nothing but good for their high-flying ambitions. All are represented here. News, current affairs, drama, wildlife, documentary. It is interesting for the humble viewer to know what makes these geniuses tick. They can speculate on what sort of childhoods, education, relationships and other of life's influences have brought these artists together to create something quite so special and unique. While they, the viewers, with their little wasted lives, can wonder what the menu was and contemplate in their long leisure hours the reasons why they themselves have achieved so pitifully little.

But Sebby's low forehead, under his untidy mess of hair, crinkles into a deep frown. He drops Kate's hand from his almost as soon as he's taken it. He twists on his chair with unease. This cannot be right. Although, in theory, they did nothing illegal – the porno pictures were genuine, Cheryl's pregnancy was her own fault – the way they handled the whole affair was manipulative and nasty.

Everything around him looks and tastes stale. He can no longer live with all this, without confiding in Kate.

Lovable, beautiful Kate: the last of the world's big spenders she might be, but at heart she's a kind and generous woman who will share and understand his concerns. And maybe exonerate him of the burden of guilt he drags like a sack of cement over his shoulder.

FIFTEEN

Griffin have been contacted for a second time by Cara's kidnappers. The contact was made by telephone, in a helium, Pinky and Perky voice.

And although the special force suspect that the instructions included could well be the first of a series of tests, nonetheless they will act upon them. They must convince the abductors that Griffin are being amenable to any reasonable suggestion. And who knows   this could be it.

Sir Art Blennerhasset himself, Griffin chairman and man of influence, who still blames himself for this whole ghastly mess, has agreed to make the drop. He is to take the five hundred thousand pounds and leave it in an Adidas sports bag beside the Peter Pan statue in Kensington Gardens, at three-thirty this afternoon.

The area will be buzzing with tourists, the kids are on holiday from school and the coach parties are out in full force with their camcorders, rugs and thermos flasks. This, however, makes it simpler for the undercover surveillance team to mingle with the crowds undetected. The bag will be watched at all times by at least four pairs of trained eyes. Sewn

245

inside the bag will be a low-frequency transmitter. Every road will be covered, every footpath guarded, and the statue itself will house a minute hidden camera.

The Higginses need not know the details of the drop; merely that contact has been made and that some action will be taken this afternoon.

In real fear of physical violence, now the feeding frenzy is at its height, they leave at dawn and hide in a café until late morning, when they take a bus to the case conference which will decide the immediate future of Victor and Scarlett, their two children whose whereabouts are known.

But not to their parents.

Of Cara there will be no news until this afternoon.

Cheryl is beside herself. She wishes she had never been told.

Hopefully, nobody connected with social services will have leaked news of this meeting to the press. But everyone else is turning traitor, so why should these bureaucrats prove the exception? There might well be an angry posse waiting outside the social services offices.

The importance of today's decision looms large enough in Cheryl's mind to lessen the fear of discovery, so now and then Barry reminds her, 'Your scarf has slipped. Come on Cher, hang on in there.' And obediently she adjusts her disguise.

Incredibly, every day since their return to the flat Cheryl had been reading about her past. It was like looking at faded old photographs, people she could hardly remember talking about her so fluently, and with such vivid memories of those times, she could only marvel.

Fred, of all people.

Mum's old boyfriend.

The same Fred whose dogs attacked Dill, who was imprisoned for manslaughter, whose departure sent Annie bonkers. No-one had heard of him for well over ten years. Well, somehow the press had discovered his whereabouts, and Fred recounted in incredible detail his life on the Hackney estate when Cheryl was six and seven. What a strange child she had been: violent, unpredictable, with uncontrollable moods and tempers, the despair of her sick mother, the thorn in the side of a beautiful relationship which might have lasted if it hadn't been for her. And her manipulative ways. And her lies. And her constant craving for attention.

'Anyone who knew me then knows that this is just not true,' Cheryl cried when she read it, a pack of lies from start to finish. 'How could they have believed Fred, he's been inside more than he's been out, he drove Mum mental in the end, he broke her heart.'

And there was a photograph of Fred with his big red face and his ham fists and a fag on his lip, and a small one of her in a group of schoolchildren with a circle round her head.

Not a halo.

More like a satanic stamp.

A class photograph. Oh, God. One of the children she had been to school with must have sold it to the paper.

Barry, helpless in the face of such scurrilous

reporting, could only shake his head and fear that they had not hit rock bottom yet.

And here was Mrs Bradbury, and her fellow foster children, Sonia and Barbara. Some bright spark had managed to root them out of obscurity. 'I've had some children in my time,' Mrs Bradbury told the reporter darkly, 'but never so strange as Cheryl Watts. That one I never forgot.'

But Mrs Bradbury had always been kind to her.

OK, she had been unhappy in her house in Shepherd's Bush, but that was not Mrs Bradbury's fault. It was just that Cheryl had been homesick. So why was Mrs Bradbury saying these unkind things now?

Was it true?

Had she been strange and difficult?

Had she stolen money from Mrs Bradbury's purse?

Had she wet the bed?

Maybe she had.

She couldn't remember.

And if they had managed to find Mrs Bradbury, why hadn't they gone to Parkwood School and interviewed Miss Tandy, the teacher who had been so understanding?

Or Josie and Matty, her special friends?

Or Sue, her social worker?

Sonia and Barbara both looked like tarts, bony and shifty with bad complexions which showed up even in black and white.

Cheryl was stunned to think that either of them could comment at all. She had had so little to do with them. They had been so absorbed with their own lives, and they were such close friends, there'd been no way in.

'She was a nasty piece of work,' said Sonia ominously. 'She was more like a kid who had been in a children's home all her life, disturbed, you know, untrustworthy, into porn and perverted stuff . . .'

What? *What?* She had been only seven years old. Where could she have found porn? She hadn't known what perversions were.

'. . . Nicking stuff from shops, like those brothers of hers, but 'cos she looked so sweet, as if butter wouldn't melt in her mouth, she used to get away with it, like.' And then, in answer to a question: 'Oh, yeah, everything that Cheryl did she did for attention.'

Barbara's comments were worse. 'She'd do anything, go with men, not the whole thing, nah, she was too fly for that, just letting them feel her up round the back of the community centre. Me and Sonia used to worry about her – we told Mrs Bradbury once, but she said what could she do? Her social worker didn't give a toss, so why should she?'

'We tried to act like older sisters,' Sonia went on with the kind of imagination Cheryl had never credited her with. 'We looked out for her, me and Babs, but all we got was foul words and our clothes ripped up and pushed down the bog.'

Of course, Annie's enemies on the Hackney estate, especially her long-term sparring partner, Marge Smith, went straight for the throat.

From the start of this whole affair Annie's warring neighbours had found themselves on quicksand. During the periods of the Higginses' popularity they had wangled their way in; they had quickly formed new battle lines when the third-baby syndrome had clouded the previously bright horizon; they had returned in full force with sweet tea and sympathy when the three kiddies went missing; but now they stood shoulder to shoulder and would retreat no more.

Every weapon was sharp and lethal.

There was money to be had.

The competition was as compelling and addictive as scratch cards, but with more of a chance of winning.

'I well remember the time . . .' was the prologue to stories which beggared belief.

And 'I'm not surprised', was the general summing-up of this latest, heinous behaviour of the hapless Cheryl Ann Watts.

'But I'm just an ordinary person,' Cheryl wept, torn open by so many ugly smears. 'Not good, not bad, just normal. Aren't I?'

'Well, you know you are,' said Barry reassuringly. 'We both know you are, Cher.'

Barry fared slightly better because of the company his family liked to keep. Not the sort of people who would go gossiping to the press. And most of the relatives of the Harlow Higginses, having risen in the world, did not want to be associated with Barry, the family black sheep. Better to do a fisherman Peter and say they never knew him, once, twice or even thrice. Better to deny who they were. Better to leave the answerphone on and check the peephole in the door before answering the bell.

Anyway, they weren't that desperate for the money.

'A tearaway' was the worst they came up with, and in a laddish, *Sun* kind of way, this was not too condemning a verdict.

And although an avid public wrung anxious hands over the fate of baby Cara, the blame was laid at her parents' door, and not one jot of sympathy was extended to them in those desperate hours.

Well, how could anyone sympathize? That poor old woman battered to death, those kiddies abandoned to their fates; and now the baby gone.

'She'll have that kiddy of hers hidden away somewhere, or I'll eat my hat. Devious bitch.'

'And even if she hasn't, let her suffer for a change, like those babies of hers, poor little souls.'

'Shouldn't let her have them back, she's not fit. She's evil.'

'What sort of mother must that slag be?'

When they knew what sort of mother she was.

They had watched her for months on the television, they had seen how she adored her children, they had seen how she tried to keep them nice, fed them the best she could afford, played with them, spoiled them if she was given the chance, gave up her nights for them, wept for them, laughed with them.

Her public had loved her then.

They had admired her guts.

So how could they be so fickle that they could believe all these malevolent lies?

How the people love a sinner, especially if she is a woman.

Witch! Witch!

The deepest tragedy of witchcraft lies in the fact that their own relations desert women denounced as witches, for witchery teaches that they must, through their sorceries, bring distress on their own families.
        Philippe Schmidt, *Superstition and Magic*

But the real question is, what will the experts believe?

Will they, too, have read these vicious articles and interpreted them as fact? Or will they take more notice of the shrink's hastily compiled report, based on yesterday's interview and three previous meetings?

Cheryl and Barry will find out in a minute.

Along with the supervisors and department heads, there are two faces at the table that the Higginses recognize. The hard-faced Paula Lake, who had interviewed them at the police station, is here to represent the police . . . not a good omen. The beige probation officer, Olivia Sweet, in her linens, with whom Cheryl had not managed to develop any rapport, has an open file set before her and a pen between her manicured fingers.

At the head of the table sits a blowzy woman with a button missing off her white blouse, through which a pink piece of petticoat peeps. She introduces herself as Mrs Binnie, the director of social services.

'Do come and sit down, Mr and Mrs Higgins.'

There are only two empty chairs among the six already occupied, and as they take their places a secretary, here to take notes, rises and pours them coffee.

'Now then,' starts Mrs Binnie, 'we try not to

252

make these meetings too formal, but there are set rules which we have to follow, for your sakes. You need to know everybody's feelings. It is only fair that you should understand where our decisions come from and how they are formed.' But the open-handed director is careful not to mention that the psychiatrist's report will remain confidential. There are some things that are best kept in professional hands. For example: the doctor's opinion that there are definite signs of the condition of Munchausen's syndrome by proxy (of course, he cannot be certain at this early stage, but the possibility must be considered). And if this should be the case, it would be a very dangerous move to return the children to their mother. If this diagnosis is confirmed, it is likely that Cheryl Higgins would go to almost any lengths to make herself the centre of attention.

Mrs Binnie goes on. 'If, at any time, you do not understand, please feel free to interrupt. Of course, you will be given a chance to put your point of view when the time comes.' The smile she gives is benevolent, forced and professional.

Paula Lake kicks off the proceedings.

'In the opinion of the police involved, it would be extremely unwise for Victor or Scarlett Higgins to return to their parents' home at this time,' is how Paula Lake begins, not afraid to pull her punches. 'We have come to this conclusion for the following reasons . . .'

But Cheryl, deep in shock, cannot bring herself to listen.

How much influence will this damning report have on the others?

Doesn't everyone realize that the police would

naturally see things this way? How could the police be impartial? They have an axe to grind, and particularly this brittle woman who never took to Cheryl, who condemned her from the start without even trying to understand the pressures which drove her.

'Dangerously irresponsible,' is one phrase being oft repeated in this long and hostile report.

'Mentally unstable,' is another.

'Devious and manipulative.' Well, OK, fair enough. Who has not been devious or manipulative at some time in their lives? And Paula Lake should know.

At last, the first attack comes to a halt.

Only to make way for the second.

Cheryl grips her hands together underneath the table. The nails cut into soft flesh.

Please, please God. She must not lose control.

She must not appear hysterical. At least the psychiatrist's report ought to be neutral. She had hardly opened her mouth in her interviews with Mr Tonge. She was wary. She was cautious. He had listened and nodded and smiled and taken notes.

What notes?

She must maintain a quiet dignity and an understanding of why these so-called experts are so reluctant to trust her.

They have her children's best interests at heart.

If she was on this panel, having heard all the evidence, she would probably reach the same damning conclusions. Cheryl is guilty and everyone knows it.

Olivia Sweet speaks without notes, just the occasional reference to the opened file before her. Her words are convincing, her manner thoughtful and although she admits, as did Paula Lake, that there has been little time to compile any thorough investigations into the Higgins family, it would be extremely unwise to return the children at this moment in time.

'There are so many unanswered questions in this sad case,' she goes on in her persuasive way, 'and finding the answers will take time and patience. At this early stage the probation service would prefer to err on the side of caution. The risks involved are too hazardous to take. We have not yet had time to explore the in-depth situation.'

The most unfair reason of all is given at the end. 'The effect on these very young children of the constant hassling of the media would not, we think, be without damage. And we do know that Cheryl Higgins is not totally averse to this, and could revert at any time to her attention-seeking ways.'

This is too much for Cheryl – just too much. 'No! No! It's not like that . . .'

Shocked faces turn towards her.

'Please sit down, Mrs Higgins . . .'

'But what she said, that cow, it's not true!'

'Mrs Higgins, really, please,' and the director of social services raises a hand with a torn tissue in it. 'You really must allow us to be the judge of that. As I said earlier, you and your husband will have your chance to speak.'

'So I'm supposed to sit here and let these people spout their lies like everyone else is doing, without any way to defend myself, nobody to stop it? I'm supposed to bloody well sit here, while you calmly discuss taking our children away from us?'

'Mr Higgins, please try and control your wife, for everyone's sake . . .'

'Cher! Cher!' And Barry awkwardly hangs onto one arm and tries to drag her down on her seat. 'Please don't.'

'You don't know me!' Cheryl continues to shout, tearing her arm away from his grasp. 'None of you here. You don't know me at all. You only think you do because of the programme and what you've been reading, and the lies they're all telling.'

'Would you like to take your wife out for a little while?' one of the shocked faces suggests. 'Maybe that would calm her down?'

'Well, we certainly cannot proceed with Mrs Higgins in this state,' says the blowzy woman in the Chair, taking another, fresher tissue from the Kleenex box on the table.

And Paula Lake and Olivia Sweet are whispering together conspiratorially.

'You're playing right into their bloody hands,' moans Barry into the chaos, but he can't get through to her.

'Put yourselves in my place,' yells Cheryl. 'I love my kids. I want them home. Don't you think I've been punished enough?'

'Mrs Higgins, this is not a question of punishment.'

'I know, I know, this is to do with my kids' best interests, but I am their mother, I know what their best interests are. They need to come straight home to me and Barry.' And she beats the table with her fists, her eyes wide, dry and fixed.

'Come on, Cher, let's get out of here. Let's have a fag and come back when you're feeling better.'

Gradually he coaxes her away from the table, and it's like he has to unlock her arms and shoulders before she can move. She's like stone. Like a statue to outraged protest.

She throws a last curse over her shoulder. 'Who d'you all think you are anyway, for God's sake, you sodding know-all wankers!'

A chastened Cheryl, ashamed and afraid of the damage she has probably done, is led back into the meeting by Barry ten minutes later, ten minutes which were spent listening to his angry rantings and smoking for all her life was worth.

What have they been saying about her behind her back?

Has she reinforced their resolve? Of course she has, no question. But maybe they had made their decision before they even met her. Maybe her maddened outburst has had no repercussions at all.

'I'm very sorry,' she says, following Barry's strict instructions. 'I should not have acted like that. I don't normally, I promise. It's just that I miss my kids.'

A dig in the ribs prevents her from getting het up for a second time.

Now it's up to Barry, once again, to put a positive case for having his children home. It is best she keeps her mouth shut from now on. She can only make matters worse. And anyway, Barry is doing an excellent job without any help from her. He suddenly sounds grown-up, even forceful, a word Cheryl would never have associated with her twenty-year-old husband before.

Anxiously Cheryl casts her eyes round the listening faces.

Mostly blank, concentrating, giving nothing away.

Barry is afraid of the effect a strange environment will have on the kids. He and Cheryl have been very close to them, closer than most parents, he suggests, because of the very cramped conditions and lack of opportunity for outings that the experts might consider unsatisfactory. But the bond these restrictions have created is what Barry fears they might lose during separation, to their future detriment.

As far as the press are concerned, Barry and Cheryl have, from experience, learned to live with that. He is lying, but Cheryl urges him on. He convinces his audience that the fifth-floor flat, far from being a vulnerable spot, is in fact a perfect location. Unapproachable from two sides, with the lift shaft against the third, the front is the only accessible place, and both the windows and the door are protected by vandal-proof steel.

'Once we get past, once we're safely indoors, we don't hear them,' says Barry, sounding ultra-sensible, 'and they soon go away because the landing is not a good place to stand for hours at a time.'

'But what happens when you go out?' asks Olivia Sweet with her characteristic directness.

'They don't seem to pick up on me, it's really Cheryl they recognize, and if she's wearing a scarf we can mostly get away with it. We know what to look for now. We're experienced. We're streetwise.'

At this Mrs Binnie smiles. After thanking Barry for his help, she sums up the panel's thoughts.

They must have decided while we were out, thinks Cheryl hopelessly, trying to concentrate.

Nothing Barry has said can have made any difference.

He was wasting his time.

They were laughing at him.

But no, it would appear that they have taken Barry's words into account. The last part of the summing-up goes something like this . . . she can't remember exactly . . . only the last few words stick in her heart like a jagged knife that won't pull out, never, ever . . .

'We are satisfied that Victor and Scarlett should be returned into the care of their father, as long as their mother, Cheryl, does not continue to share the family home.'

SIXTEEN

There is a fifteen-minute break in proceedings. They will have to go back in a minute and give the panel their reactions.

'But where will I go?'

This is pathetic.

To have to submit passively, silently, while such monstrous decisions are made.

With his arm tight around her, Barry says bravely, 'You don't have to go anywhere. Don't be silly.'

'But if I stay at the flat the kids can't come home.'

'Well, they'll have to stay away a while longer. You're not moving out, Cher. Those evil crones in there are mad, they've lost it, they can't do this. They can't chuck you out of your home.'

'I'd go to Mum's,' says Cheryl abjectly, 'but I'd be murdered if they saw me there. Mum's in a right mess anyway. If I went there it would make things worse.'

'What about my mum? She'd have you in Harlow.' Barry, at a loss, is grasping at straws.

Cheryl's smile is a weak one. 'Don't give me that. Don't let's kid ourselves. She'd rather have Myra

Hindley than me. At least she's not related. And I can't even use the railway carriages now they've blocked them all off.'

'Who else do we know who could help?'

You have to be honest. You have to face it. 'Nobody.'

'We could make out you'd gone,' urges Barry, looking round, 'and you could sneak back in later.'

'We daren't do that. We can't. They'd only take the kids again and not let them back at all next time. Have them adopted or something.'

This has all turned out so unfairly. Of course Cheryl is relieved that Barry is seen as the sane one, the trustworthy one of the pair, not tainted by the same kind of wrath. And she has to admit that it is all her fault. It was her idea to take part in the programme; it was her idea to hide the children; it was she who couldn't take the flak. Easygoing Barry just went along with it all, and that is why she is the witch, while he, much milder, is just her familiar.

Poor Barry is in one hell of a state. 'I'll just go back and tell them we accept their terms, shall I? I'll go back in and we will decide what we're going to do later. There must be something. We can't let them win. How can they bloody well justify splitting couples up like this, without even offering to provide any help? It's crazy. It's sick.'

'Maybe they could suggest somewhere?' It is just the thought of packing a bag and setting out into the night, leaving Barry in the double bed with Victor and Scarlett cuddled beside him.

'No,' says Barry. 'Those bitches in there might change their minds if they thought we couldn't find anywhere, if we couldn't even make our own plans. Better to lie. I'll tell them you're going to Annie's. They don't know you can't go there. They don't know how bad it is.'

'OK. You go in. I'll wait here.'

So for goodness' sake, how long do they expect Cheryl to make herself homeless?

She supposes she could live out for a week. It is summer time, the nights are warm, but what about after that? Is she allowed to visit the kids? Is she allowed to claim income support?

And do they really believe she might harm her children? Torture them with cigarettes, batter them, tie them down on their beds, put them in boiling-hot baths? And if they do believe that Cheryl is capable of this, it reinforces those newspaper headlines, it adds credence to the chat shows, it supports the disgust of the public, it compounds this hellish new image of a brutal woman who would resort to anything in order to get her own way.

This is so wrong.

Poor Cheryl. The victim. Is there nobody she can turn to for help? There's the Press Complaints Commission, Barry found out about that, but Cheryl is sure they would take no notice of someone as infamous as her. And now all they would have to do would be to contact the local authorities to be told that, yes, in their expert opinion, Cheryl Higgins is not a fit mother.

And how about Barry's idea – should she pick out a national newspaper and plead with the editor for just a few moments of his precious time to put her side of the story? There are risks involved in that, of course, Barry pointed that out, but these are risks she might have to take, given her hopeless situation.

After an anxious ten minutes' wait Barry comes out, pale, from the meeting. 'They think you are going to Annie's. They seem quite happy with that. And Victor and Scarlett will be brought home some time this evening.'

'Maybe Cara, too?'

Barry nods and swallows hard. 'Maybe.'

'But how will you manage with all three?'

'I'll manage,' says Barry, being manly. 'As long as I have to, I'll manage.'

Griffin are expecting their call at four o'clock precisely. By then they might have Cara.

But nobody has invited the Higginses to wait at the company offices, or to be at the incident room at police headquarters to await the news, good or bad. Nobody deems it necessary to provide any special support for this young couple in their hour of awful distress. The Higginses' own preposterous behaviour has forfeited any rights they might have, and caused them to be officially excluded from the heart of the action.

Partly to divert their minds from the see-saw of terrible hope and the dread of this afternoon's drama in Kensington Gardens, and partly through necessity of finding a roof for Cheryl, they spend the next couple of hours searching the papers for live-in jobs.

Staff wanted. Training given. A short walk. A card in a window, a brass sign on the door, Gilwern

Rest Home for the Elderly. A building that looks like a disused hospital with bars on every window.

It is the first local, hopeful opportunity they have seen. Barry and Cheryl stare at each other. She shrugs and turns towards the door – might as well – and the sound of the bell echoes through an empty hall within.

But the door is opened by a cheery young girl in a smart, clean uniform.

'I saw your advert in the window,' says Cheryl.

'Matron is out just now,' says the nurse, 'but if you would like to leave me your name and address I will get her to contact you.'

Cheryl turns to face Barry again. In all the shock and horror of the morning, with the ongoing trauma of this afternoon's swap, this obvious thought had not struck home.

How could they leave Cheryl's name with anyone? It must rank among the most notorious ten in the country today . . . It would leap off any piece of paper, it would strike dread into the heart of any employer, and the fact that she'd had the cheek to apply for any job involving vulnerable people would find its way onto the front pages by morning.

And to lie would be next to useless. Nobody would give her a live-in job without a reference or the right papers.

No sanctuary. Not here.

'Never mind,' says Cheryl, backing away, but too late, slowly watching the recognition dawn in the young girl's eyes.

Her hand flies to her lips. 'Oh, God. You're not . . . ?'

'No, I'm not anyone,' says Cheryl.

Places like McDonald's, where Cheryl and Barry originally met, would recognize her in an instant, and even if the staff didn't know her, ten minutes in there with a tray in her hand and a customer certainly would.

Same with shop work.

Same with a cleaning agency, an all-night garage or a bar.

Everyone has a reputation to keep up.

Everyone likes to maintain some standards.

In the end, out of answers, they sit miserably in a bus stop on a busy road, Cheryl resigned to her fate . . . a night spent roving the streets until dawn, in and out of the station, just hoping she stays safe, and Barry determined to try to force open one of the doors to an empty flat in the Harold Wilson Building.

She scrapes a pattern in dog-ends with her foot. 'It's no good. You'd never get in, you know that. All those doors are specially designed to keep people out. It's not on, Barry.'

He sinks into a weary silence as he watches her mess of litter art, then, out of the blue, in a sudden burst of angry new energy, 'This isn't our bloody fault. If we hadn't appeared on that programme, none of this would have happened. We have to appeal to Griffin. There's no other way. They have to listen to us. They know what has happened. We've lost a baby, nearly a family, Donny is dead and now we're sodding well being split up.'

'They wouldn't speak to us even if we tried. Remember? I did that before.'

'Not the bastards at the top. The crew. The guys who knew us. What about Sebby, or Leo?'

'Why them? They don't care. They wouldn't give

me their private numbers. I tried that too, back
then. It's no good, Barry. And even if I did have
their numbers, why would either of them listen?
They got what they wanted, didn't they? They came
round when things were going right, and they've
stopped away ever since.'

'But I got Sebby's number.'

'What?'

'I got it,' Barry nods. Keeps nodding. Looks
ridiculous.

'How?' He can't have. What is he thinking of,
pratting about when everything is so black, getting
blacker?

'I asked him for it.'

Why is he lying to her like this? What the hell is
the point? 'When?'

'When the filming first started. When it was all
going OK. He said he could get me a ticket to an
Arsenal game. He said to ring me at home, but I
never bothered, I never had the money for the
phone call, let alone a ticket.'

'You never told me that when I was trying to get
hold of him.'

'I didn't tell you because I thought you would
make a right jerk of yourself.'

Cheryl, deep in thought, works it out aloud.
'Even if Sebby doesn't want to help, he might know
the name of some journalist who would see us, and
maybe listen.'

'Could be.'

'Where's the number?'

'Come on, let's go back to the flat, get your
things, have a drink and I'll find it.'

'Can we ring up yet?' She daren't look at her own

266

watch. She hasn't dared glance at it for the last two hours.

'It's not half past three yet.'

And Cheryl can hardly breathe.

It is as the experts had feared. At the appointed hour, Sir Art Blennerhasset parked his BMW and strolled past the lake and the palace (where once he had been an occasional visitor), through to the Peter Pan statue. Concerned about leaving such a huge sum of money in a public place, yet he did as he was bid, safe in the knowledge that at no time would it be out of sight of the police.

He and his co-directors, so aware of the fate of the Higginses and their part in it, have set in place a vetting procedure, overseen by a psychologist, so that for future documentaries, any participants will be subjected to a series of tests.

At one meeting, Art pushed for compensation to be paid to the Higginses in the form of a trust, but that idea was soon scotched, with all its implications as to culpability and the legal aspects of that.

After all, as Jennie St Hill, newly promoted, pointed out, whatever the outcome of the documentary – and the public outrage had shocked everyone – Cheryl Higgins had acted in an utterly disgraceful manner. She must have been unbalanced to start with.

And much to Art's discomfort, this is the angle the Griffin public relations people rely on when they are accused of gross manipulation.

'The woman is daft. We can't help that. We can't take that into account each time we make a new programme.'

Or, 'Everything that has happened to the Higginses they have brought on themselves.'

Even, and this came from Alan Beam, newly appointed member to the board: 'We did a public service by exposing a woman who is too fundamentally flawed to care for her own children safely.'

Since news of the ransom demand was leaked, the authorities have been careful to keep any further developments close to their chests. Although it might well be assumed that the baby has been kidnapped, no confirmation of that has officially been given. But if this grim business has a positive outcome, Griffin the benefactor is poised to make the most of its generous contribution.

Job done, and Art Blennerhasset, sweating profusely, walks smartly away from the Adidas bag. He half hopes this dramatic performance will have to be repeated. He is on an adrenalin high. A decent man, and honest, who nevertheless thrives on power and display, the feeling of walking through the park with half a million pounds in his hand and the eyes of a hundred policemen on him, is very satisfying.

Art is under pressure from his society wife, Sarah, who has even suggested they contact the Higginses in a private capacity and offer them succour and support. A champion of the underdog, a supporter and fund-raiser for many grateful charities, Sarah is a fighter for rights both human and animal. Art agrees in principle; they do owe the Higginses something for their pains, but in his position of chairman of Griffin he has to act with caution. Surely Sarah must recognize this.

'I just can't stand it, Art,' she told him last night as she climbed into her Regency bed in her flowing silk pyjamas. 'The thought of that poor, much maligned couple, and all because you capitulated when faced by a group of arty posers.'

'You blame me, don't you?' asked Art unnecessarily.

'Yes, I do. You should have stuck to your principles. You knew this programme was far too invasive, and yet you let them grind you down.' She applied her night cream with angry movements. 'And it's not like you to be weak, Art, not like you at all.'

Sarah was right. She mostly is. Art dwells on this conversation during the long afternoon's wait.

But when, by four-thirty, the bag is still in its original position, the team retrieve it surreptitiously and give up.

Better luck next time.

The phone call, and its hopeless outcome, has taken its toll on Cheryl and Barry. And it didn't help to be told that the negative result had been predicted, or to be assured that further contact would almost certainly be made. 'This is often a long, slow process.'

Cheryl collapsed on the station concourse. Barry almost carried her to the flats and up to the fifth floor. Poor old Barry. Oh, dear! He felt so powerless, and so useless. Surely there was some medication they ought to be giving Cheryl to help her cope with all this? Maybe he should contact the doctor. But would his reaction be as heartless as everyone else's . . . on her own head be it?

Barry badly needs help. But how the hell is he going to get it?

269

It might help Cheryl if she's given something positive to focus on. He rummages round for Sebby's number – he knows he has it somewhere. Even a visit to Sebby might help.

Cheryl glances at the card. 'It's got his address on it as well.'

'Why not go and see him tonight?'

'Surprise him?' She's not going to risk phoning first, and be given some embarrassed excuse. Frantic over her baby's safety, she has nothing to do this evening, she has nowhere to go. All she can do is stroll pointlessly round trying to keep warm, alienated from her husband, her kids and humanity in general.

'He might be away, filming,' she says, struggling to keep thoughts of Cara at bay. *Oh, dear God, let them not hurt my baby*. She has never been closer to breaking down.

But before she leaves the flat, Cheryl makes it tidy, changes the sheets on her children's beds, puts out their favourite toys and leaves a kiss on their small pillows.

This thing is hurting so hard.

Soon Barry will get to hold them, to make them chuckle and feed them chocolate buttons. Soon he will undress them and bath them, blobbing froth on their noses, holding their little bodies to his, feeling their fidgeting warmth through the towels, drying between their tiny toes. And finally he will tuck them in and listen to their fluttery breathing, watch the dream bubbles form on their lips and push their legs back under the covers where they have flopped out.

It's like there's a glass partition between them.

Dammit. And it's not fair. It is just not fair.

'It's not too late,' says Barry, sharing Cheryl's bleak despair. 'We could still phone social services and get them to keep the kids, just for a while, just until we find you somewhere.'

'They need to be here more than I do.' And Cheryl, the good mother, looks quickly away, for fear he will see her brimming eyes and do something foolish.

She hasn't got much with her.

She is wearing enough to keep her warm until the morning comes. In the string bag she carries a blanket, just in case it gets colder than she expects, and an old *TV Trivia* magazine. In her pocket is their last fifty pence; it will buy her a cup of tea in a stained saucer with two cubes of sugar, and a seat in an all-night café for as long as she can make it last, along with the dossers, the junkies and the piss-heads.

But first she has got some serious walking to do.

This gives her a purpose.

Covent Garden. Where Sebby shares a flat with his girlfriend – or he could be married by now, it's so long since she has seen him. She takes her time, like she did as a child, making a mint Aero last longer by breaking off one small piece at a time. She pauses in Trafalgar Square to watch the jostling people, the theatre crowds and the buskers. So different from the drab streets nearer home. Why were she and Barry never here? How had their lives got so serious so soon? Only a short evening walk, and they could have been part of this no-reason celebration: little groups, families, students, tour-

271

ists, gangs of big kids defacing the lions and late school parties waiting for coaches . . . Chips, burgers, pizzas, baked spuds and a guy still flogging pigeon food.

These faceless crowds are her judge and jury.

They have driven her out of her home.

They have conspired to take her children away.

They are the blessed and she is the damned, and this is the method they use to test for witchcraft – sticking pins into her flesh. *But if she is guilty, they shouldn't hurt.*

And although the evening is mild, a nursery moon on a Wedgwood sky, Cheryl pulls her anorak more firmly round her and makes sure the black hood obscures her face.

SEVENTEEN

For over an hour Kate sat listening to Sebby's confessions, his tone dull, his manner listless, watching him trying to relieve his conscience by passing over some of the weight.

The room is large, with deep-set windows looking out over the street. Faded wooden floors are strewn with rugs. Sebby and Kate sit in two overstuffed chairs covered with fabric in rust, white and slate blue. The coffee table, reading lamps and magazines stacked beside it suggest a place of rest and repose. They are safe here now. The threat of poverty has passed. Safe and sound.

Kate does not take pity on him as he'd hoped. 'Why the hell didn't you tell me before?'

'Because we were in such a bloody mess, because I was worried about your reactions. I had to go along with it, Kate, I had to keep my job, whatever.'

Kate takes a mighty slurp of her wine, as if she tastes it for a living. 'I would have told you not to touch it. It stinks, Sebby, it's sick. And when you think what's happened since.'

'I know,' he says, all hang-dog. 'I know.'

'It was my fault too, though, wasn't it? If I hadn't

carried on spending as if there was no tomorrow . . .'

Sebby shrugs non-committally. 'I was scared of what might happen to us. And if you'd seen the state of that flat.'

'I did see it. I watched it, remember? And I was the first to turn on the Higginses for being so stupidly reckless – another kid, posing for porn – when the whole country was batting for them. It just seemed so . . . ungrateful, you know?'

'It was meant to.'

'Well I know that now. And I wish I didn't.'

'We could have portrayed that quite differently. They could have come out of it almost unscathed if we had handled it sensitively, like we did in the first seven episodes. But no, they were picked because they were vulnerable. They were chosen so those sad little pictures could be used against them and the whole sentiment turned on its head.'

Kate laces her fingers together, making a steeple of the middle two and resting them against her lips. 'You couldn't have known that Cheryl getting pregnant, combined with a few raunchy pictures, could have escalated into this mass hysteria. So in that way, it really isn't your fault.'

'Well, whose fault is it, for God's sake?'

'It's the masses and their love of a victim. It's women turning on women, grabbing the chance to release their bitterness. Lots of those viewers must have envied Cheryl when she was a TV star through no real merits of her own. Why should she have the luck and not them? Everyone secretly likes to see the mighty fallen. Cheryl was getting too big for her boots.' Kate tosses back her long golden hair. 'And the fool plays right into their hands by dreaming up the abduction. They've got something real to hate her for now. The slavering masses were led on by people who should have known better. There was money to be made out of her downfall; that's why the witch-hunters lasted so long. They were in it for profit, it's that simple.'

'And Leo doesn't give a toss. He has always been able to rationalize what he does, if it's in the name of art.'

'Well he certainly doesn't need the money.' She asks him: 'So is it right that they don't know for certain if Cara has actually been kidnapped? That's why they came to see you?'

Sebby nods. 'They did it once. They could do it again. But I just don't believe . . .'

It is hot. The sun blazes in through the windows. Kate fingers her damp forehead and nods while she is deep in thought. Suddenly she interrupts. 'Who says there is a baby at all?'

'*What?*' Sebby stares at her in utter surprise. He can't have heard her properly.

'Well,' Kate goes on, working it out, speaking slowly. 'Think about it again. Try and see it dispassionately. You've told me so much about Cheryl, how she daydreams, how she needs to be loved, but I never saw a picture of Cara on any of those television appeals. And Annie told you she'd never seen her. Her own grandchild? That's extraordinary. Cara is supposed to be five months old. Yes, Cheryl was pregnant, everyone knows that – she announced it in front of ten million people. But who's to say she didn't decide to have an abortion after all? Who could blame her, in those circumstances? Or who's to say the baby lived?'

'But why . . . ?' Sebby stutters. What on earth put this idea into Kate's head?

'Why didn't she tell anyone? Is that what you were going to ask? Well, let's see. At the time she got pregnant, Cheryl had no idea how it was going to go. She didn't have a clue that the public would turn against her, but she did know how you felt, and how Leo felt, her heroes, and although she appeared defensive in the face of your disapproval, she might easily have been influenced by you and gone and had an abortion. It's what Barry wanted.'

'But she was dead against abortion.'

'She was also dead against ruining her image. And I can see why, with the series coming up, if she'd had an abortion she'd not want to broadcast the fact.'

'But that's absurd. She would have told her family, her mother.'

Kate seems not to be listening. She babbles on urgently. 'Not necessarily. Not if she was really afraid her actions might ruin her public credibility.'

'But Kate, she loved being pregnant. That was half her trouble. When she was pregnant she felt important.'

'Not half as important as she was going to be on TV.'

Sebby removes his glasses and wipes them, as if that action might help his understanding. 'You are actually suggesting that she lied to everyone and pretended she'd had a baby? Named her? Made out she'd gone missing along with the others? Come on, get real. She's really not that twisted.'

'No, she's not twisted at all.' Kate gives Sebby a hard look. 'She's just a very needy person who has been horribly manipulated.'

'And Barry? You think Barry would go along with such a fantastic con?'

'I don't see why not. From what you've told me, Barry would do anything that would make Cheryl happy. She's had some bad times in her life, she's not the most stable of people. Barry's obviously been through a lot, and he loves her,' Kate goes on, excited, her words coming faster and faster. 'Listen. Barry agreed to pretend his kids had been snatched in order to change public opinion, so in my book that means Barry would do virtually anything for Cheryl.'

'Right. So what happens when Mrs Donnolly drops the kids at the station without Cara? How were they going to deal with the fact that Cara was still missing?'

'They're dealing with it now, aren't they? They're making out she's been kidnapped. Sending notes. Still playing for sympathy. Only this time, the ending will not be so happy. This time the baby won't come back.'

Sebby says contemptuously, 'And Mrs Donnolly? I suppose they bumped her off in the process? I'm afraid that really doesn't square up. That doesn't fit the picture at all.'

'No, I give you that. That was never part of the plan. She was attacked by persons unknown, some gang of thugs that make it their business to go round picking on dossers and pissheads. They do exist you know, and in that part of London. The walls are scarred with their names – racists, arseholes from the National Front.'

'So how come the police aren't working on this angle?'

'Because they are not centring on Cheryl. The sort of person she is, the kind of experiences she's been through. And the lengths she is likely to go to to get herself forgiven.'

'Forgiven for what?'

'For being human.'

'And that's your theory?' He stares morosely at Kate, and she stares back.

'There are other possibilities, of course. Cheryl might have miscarried and not wanted to face the pain of that. Kept it from both families.'

'Surely there would be counselling to deal with that sort of extreme behaviour?'

'But you said yourself that Cheryl was almost phobic about any aspect of psychiatric treatment after what happened to her mum. When she was interviewed by the police shrink, she wasn't exactly forthcoming. She hardly spoke, is what you told me. Anyway, the NHS don't go round offering counselling for mere miscarriages. They give them a form saying the baby's dead, and tell them to take it back to their doctor.' Now Kate seems almost frightened by her own wild thoughts. She swallows twice before going on. 'Maybe I'm wrong. I have to be wrong. What I'm saying is too upsetting.'

They are silent for some moments until Sebby edges round the idea with reluctance in his tone. 'If your mad suspicions have any substance at all, they could be verified by the hospital.'

'An abortion might be more difficult to trace.'

'Not in Cheryl's case. She would never have the funds to go private.'

'That's true, yes. But she could well have used some other name.'

Kate's look is bleak. 'There is a far worse scenario,' she says hastily. 'But I don't expect it's occurred to you.'

'You're going to tell me, whether I like it or not.' Sebby ruffles his head of disreputable hair. 'Is this some kind of punishment, using these appalling situations to make me feel even worse than I do?'

Kate ignores him and carries on slowly, thoughtfully. 'If there really is a Cara, she would have been born around Christmas, just before the series was due to be shown on TV. Before she got to be three months old, the public lashings would have begun. What effect would this have on Cheryl's relationship with her small baby, the cause of all her miseries? The mind boggles . . .'

'Oh, Kate, for God's sake.' Sebby blanches. 'If there had been a death in that flat everyone would know.'

Kate shrugs. 'I suppose so. Or maybe this kidnapping palaver was a way of getting out of it. The body will be never be found. The blame will be put on persons unknown.'

The gate which protects the Neal Street flats could easily have been utilized in a high-risk offenders' institution. And no wonder: it is under siege. The crowds are packed so tightly inside the piazza it is easy to get swept along, like Christmas time in Oxford Street.

Cheryl envies those protected few who sit at the colourful tables, eating alfresco and watching the mayhem through their bulbous wineglasses. If only

279

she had the money . . . On balconies above sit the elevated young professionals, Thatcher's yuppies, still clinging on to their wrought-iron chairs at their wrought-iron tables in their Calvin Klein and Gucci T-shirts while giant, petrol-smoky bubbles drift past them, blown by a man from Hamleys dressed as a joker with bells on his toes.

Like mega-cool couch potatoes.

The gate is between the entry to a club from which music pulsates – round the door, bouncers like wrestlers in leather body-check the punters as they stream in – and a small card shop featuring London views.

Beyond the gate is an intimate courtyard.

Cheryl breathes deeply before pressing the bell which must be Sebby's – S. A. Coltrain. His surname is on the card. It used to be familiar to her from watching the credits roll upon TV. Sebastian Coltrain . . . Leo Tarbuck.

A pause, and then a voice from the box on the wall. 'Yep, who is it?'

'It's Cheryl. Higgins.' Even now she keeps her voice down, lest somebody in the crowd behind her should hear and arrange a lynch mob.

'Cheryl?' Another pause. Then, surprised, 'Come up.'

At least he remembers. But then he would. There is a reminder of her on every newspaper stand.

She pushes the gate. It swings open like magic and automatically locks behind her. Number twelve. In italics. She goes through the small courtyard – a few listless pots – and starts to climb the stairs.

No graffiti here.

No needles.

No hookers or pushers lurking in the dark corners.

The flat is surprisingly small. Minimally furnished, beautiful, pastel-painted with distressed effects and Persian rugs and weird pencil drawings in neat wooden frames on the walls. It all reminds her of a TV advert of a room overlooking the water in Venice. It must have been for Tampax, because the model was wearing white jeans.

And this girl, looking curiously at her with a bottle of wine drooping in her hand, must be Kate.

Kate, with her posh jobs.

Kate who goes skiing every winter

Kate – whose photographs she once saw, always surrounded by beautiful people – wears skimpy shorts and a see-through shirt and goes around barefoot.

What a grotty impression Cheryl must be making in her cheap jeans and her anorak and her dilapidated, second-hand trainers. No wonder they look embarrassed to see her, as if they've been discussing her.

Kate's smile is brilliantly pretty. 'Sit where you like. I'll get you a glass. Ice?'

'Oh, no thanks, I'm fine.'

'I know what's been happening,' says Sebby, leaning forward on his chair to demonstrate interest and concern. 'And what can I say? I'm so sorry.'

'I thought you might be away,' says Cheryl, her heart pounding in spite of herself for the times they had together, for the fun and the excitement. 'I thought you might be working.'

'No, we're in between jobs at the moment.'

Don't let him start talking about them, please don't let them get sidetracked by that. OK, he is obsessed with his work, but he must know that her baby is missing. This is not the time to bring up Eigg and its king . . .

'I've had to move out of the flat,' says Cheryl, watching for his reaction.

'Why?'

'They reckon I'm a danger to my kids.'

'Who reckons?'

'Social services. The experts. All those strangers who don't know me.'

'This is intolerable,' says Sebby, holding out one hand aimlessly towards her as if, by moving, he is offering help. 'Where the hell will you go?'

'I've nowhere to go,' Cheryl says flatly.

'So that's why you've come to me? You want to stay here?'

'No, that's not why I've come.' And she thinks she sees a flicker of relief cross his boyish, pleasant face, and the meaningful way his eyes meet Kate's as she comes back into the room with a glass.

'Well, you could stay here,' Kate says pleasantly, now she is pretty sure that Cheryl will refuse.

'No, there's no need,' says Cheryl. 'I'll be OK.' But she hurries from the pain of his rejection like a small kid running away from a bully. He could, after all, have insisted she stay. He knows she has nowhere to go, and although she came here tonight with other ideas in mind, she secretly hoped he might volunteer, or at least show more pleasure to see her.

During one brief period of Sebby's life, Cheryl had been all-important.

Now she is nothing.

Nothing but trouble.

Cheryl spends the next half-hour sipping cold Chardonnay and bringing Sebby up to date. He knows about the kidnap, of course, and the demands made on Griffin. The tall windows are wide open, and from the turbulent street life down below comes the rhythm of the buskers' steel band with *Mardi Gras*, which mingles with the drums from the nightclub.

'Gosh, I bet you wish you'd never heard of Griffin TV,' says Kate, 'when you think what's happened to you since.' But the coolness of her reactions, her concern for courtesies and the shortness of her attention span – she keeps getting up to refill the glasses or to bring some more of those nibbles – only show how little she cares about Cheryl's numbing state of affairs.

Anyway, why should she care?

Kate is not involved.

And determined never to be so.

'I'm so sorry for all this, Cheryl,' says Kate. 'It's just too ghastly, isn't it, Sebby?'

Cheryl has not come here tonight for this sort of pretty pity.

She knows they are both uncomfortable, waiting to hear the reason for her visit, but she is wary of raising the subject in case Sebby can't help her, and at the moment, this thought is the only one keeping her going.

Eventually, as the pauses grow longer and there's no more wine in the bottle and she senses Kate's stingy reluctance to open another, she gingerly raises the subject. 'If only there was someone who would listen to me. It only takes one and the rest follow on, I know that now. It's happened so often.'

They still don't know what she's asking for.

'I know what I did was terrible. I even know why they hate me. So I'm not wanting to paint myself as some angel that I'm not.'

Kate's neat eyebrows are arched, waiting for the crunch, while Sebby studies a crease in his jeans which seems to merit his attention.

'You must know all sorts of people who work in the media. You go to parties. You mix with the professionals. You rub shoulders with them at work, don't you?' She hopes to God they do. 'I only need one reporter who's not part of this mass hysteria to take me seriously for just one hour, and give me the chance to give my reasons.'

At last Sebby raises his eyes from his task to meet hers. So that's why she is here.

Phew, he must be gasping under his breath.

She's not after money or accommodation, references or a job, she's not after revenge – yes, that thought must have struck him, thinks Cheryl. And it is quite true. Everyone agrees she is unbalanced, and who knows what she might be capable of? They have all been warned at work to steer well clear of the Higginses, to say nothing if they are approached, to inform the company of what's going on so that their legal people can deal with it. If Cheryl had phoned before her visit, Sebby would have had to say he was out.

To appeal to the press is a great idea. If they find the right person, this could work. The best thing they can do is ask Leo – give him a chance to atone.

He's the one in the know. In spite of what Cheryl seems to think, Kate and Sebby don't circulate much. Now that they know their home is safe, they prefer to stay in it. But Leo is certain to have some hack friends who might rise to this tricky occasion.

'Ring him up now, Sebby.'

'What? Right away?'

'Of course. Do it now,' urges Kate.

Contrary to expectations, Leo is in. He answers the phone. He understands immediately. He wants ten minutes to test the waters, and then he'll get back to them. But don't worry, he will think of someone. Not all journalists are bastards.

Eventually, after an embarrassing wait while Kate struggles with casual conversation, Leo comes back with a name and a number. Nobody on the broadsheets will do – their reporting is already reasonable. It is not they who are inflaming the mob; they don't have such a pull on the masses.

No, Zak Quinn is the obvious one, a feature writer for the *Mirror*. Leo has given him a quick buzz, and the guy says he might be interested as long as it's exclusive. He wants to meet Cheryl later tonight.

'F for Failure. Jesus, what a mess we made of that,' says Kate, closing the door after Cheryl, slumping against it. 'You'd never guess we wanted to help.'

'You were trying too hard. It was awful. After all we'd been saying about her, it felt like being caught red-handed. And everything I said sounded so bloody pompous. Maybe we should have insisted she stayed.'

'She wanted to. I knew that, poor thing. But I

thought it was against the rules. I would have pressed it,' says Kate, 'but I didn't think you'd want me to.'

So. It was as easy as that.

And as hard.

Cheryl leaves the flat armed with a piece of paper with the name of a pub on one side, and *Zak Quinn, ten-thirty*, on the other.

Has Leo warned Zak that Cheryl is unhinged?

To tread carefully?

To check out every word she says?

Or did Leo remember that she had once been normal, nothing like that?

The Seven Stars is not far away. She keeps Kate's directions in her head and wonders why the reporter had not been invited to use the flat.

As they were friends.

And all free tonight.

And even with all this heartache, Cheryl still has time to consider why this thought hurts her so. Why, even now, she is not invited to join their circle, to sit round a crowded pub table laughing with their sophisticated friends. Of course she knows the answer to that. Nobody wants to be seen with the outcast, the vile, the untouchable.

Her unpopularity might well be catching.

She might as well go straight there as hang around in this crowded place. She hasn't got money for a drink – only a tea, much later, to break the long hours of the night. She passes the beggars and considers that choice. But she doesn't have a pitiful dog. And she would look odd, begging with her head hidden and her hood right up. But anyone lucky enough to recognize her and catch her with a camera would make their fortune by morning.

This is not a tourist pub.

There are no beckoning chairs or tables under Guinness umbrellas outside here.

Set in a backstreet, its dingy image has probably not changed since Victorian times. Cheryl has an hour to wait, and while she loiters, she is propositioned by a number of swaying men. She smiles wryly to herself: if they knew who she was they wouldn't want to touch her, they would think her diseased, contagious. Or maybe, ironically, her price would go up.

Summer darkness is falling now, and with the dark comes the menace as the alleys and doorways move into shadow. This alien atmosphere is her world now. She, like her lowly companions, will learn to use the shadows, will pick the most draught-free doorways, will finger the stacks of cardboard boxes piled up outside electricity showrooms and rifle the overflowing bins left by the steaming restaurant grills.

Is that somebody following her? She turns round quickly. Nothing.

A street-cleaning lorry comes by, sweeps her up in its lights and ignores her. Just another piece of life's flotsam washed up on the capital's pavements. Her legs are soaked by the water jets, and her trainers paddle in man-made puddles. A dog with flapping black and white ears comes by and lifts its leg on an old-fashioned lamp-post. She calls to it, needing its warmth and brief companionship. Is it a homeless stray, searching for that life-giving bone, or is it hurrying about some bad business before returning to its place by the fire? It lifts its lip and growls at her, so Cheryl keeps her distance.

'Cheryl?'

Oh, my God.

She jumps, unprepared.

Catches her breath and turns, ready for the expected attack.

The man has come up right behind her.

'Cheryl? I'm Zak. You should have gone in. You could have put your drinks on my slate.'

How could she, when she didn't know?

Everyone knows him in this grim place. He even seems to own his own table. This must be the only London pub which isn't crowded out tonight, and Cheryl can just about make out why. It is dark behind dusty drawn curtains of Christmas red. The atmosphere is stale and smoky, with a background smell which wafts up from the urinals, and the only women in here are old whores with short skirts and stilettos. There are yellowed hunting prints on the walls, a collection of stout iron keys deck the ceiling, and there's no blackboard with today's specials on it.

Only crisps and peanuts served here.

At Zak's table the old beer rings shine wetly.

'What'll you have?'

Cheryl is no big drinker, and the wine at Sebby's was more than enough. She'd better not mix it. She needs her wits. 'White wine?'

'Dry?'

'No, sweet.'

'If they've got it.'

He comes back with a dripping beer mug for himself and her wine in a lipstick-smudged glass.

Can she trust him?

How can she tell?

Will he listen to her, or just use her? This is the first time Cheryl has spoken more than two words to the press.

'You're in a mess,' is how he starts, with foam across his top lip, straddling the stool beside her as if he is mounting an American saddle. Cheryl is on the velveteen seat with a fag-burn pattern of black and yellow. His gaudy shirt looks Hawaiian, and his blue jeans have been cut off at the knee.

'It's my own fault,' says Cheryl at once, determined to prove before they start that she knows where she stands.

'But you couldn't have known that getting pregnant or the existence of a few photographs would change your name to Myra Hindley.'

'No.' The wine is foul. So bitter, she winces. 'No, not that. What I did with the kids. What's happening with Cara now. I couldn't deal with the backlash. It was frightening. Wherever we went they were there, people slagging us off, or staring, letters, threats . . .'

'But now it's much worse?'

'Yes. Now it's unbearable.'

'Now they've got real cause to hate you.'

'I know that. But what you lot are printing encourages them. They'd be violent, I know, if they thought they could get away with it. And the articles in women's magazines, the experts they put on the telly calling my behaviour some sort of sick syndrome. Everyone's got an opinion about me, but nobody understands what that time was really like, after the documentary finished and we were sentenced to hell.'

'And you want to tell me about it? Is that right?'

His dark, intelligent eyes stare directly at her. His tight black curls reach his vivid collar – those jungle scenes of startling colours suit his swarthy complexion and his legs, splayed either side of her, are the hairiest she has ever seen. Monkey-like, Cheryl supposes. Quick, restless and impatient. He could pick you up and run with you . . .

'You want me to vindicate you of your crime?'

Cheryl smiles for the first time today. 'Oh, no.'

'You want me to grant you some respite?'

Cheryl's sigh is impatient. 'I want you to print the truth, as you see it. That's all. That's what I'm asking. And if you don't want to do that, then we are both wasting our time.'

'I thought you had nowhere to go?'

'I don't. But that's not your business.'

'Ah, that's where you're wrong,' says Zak, still mocking. 'If you want the truth to be told then it certainly *is* my business. I need to know more about you, and Barry, and what's been going on. And if you've got nowhere to go tonight, you might as well come home with me and we can make a start. As you so rightly say, let's not waste time.'

Is this the right man for the job?

And, after all he has done, can Leo be trusted?

EIGHTEEN

*Every venereal act outside wedlock is a mortal sin,
and is only committed by those who are not in a state
of grace*

The Malleus Maleficarum

Anything. She is just so grateful to Zak, like you are
to a doctor who saves your child, or to a vet who
cures your pet. Cheryl is prepared to do murder if it
will help to find Cara and remove this notoriety
from all their shoulders.

Anyway, Zak is a serious and genuine person.
Just half an hour at the pub told her that, from the
compassionate, intelligent questions he asked. He is
concentrating on her, and listening. It is such a relief
not to be on her guard. In no way does his manner
imply that her awful fate is justified, and it seems so
long since she was facing anyone who showed a
liking for her that Cheryl is filled with fresh hope.

If anyone can help her now, Zak can.

Her suspicions of his eccentricity are confirmed
by the brilliant red Harley-Davidson on which he
speeds her home, across bridges, through under-
passes, down nerve-rackingly narrow short cuts.

She lets her head fall back and all the lights of London merge into one blindingly brilliant streamer. She hangs on for dear life, with her arms circling his waist tightly. His body is muscled – no spare flab, he must keep himself fit, she thinks. He probably visits one of those gyms where all the top people go.

The reckless speed, the super-confidence of the rider, which once might have brought on a panic attack, now fits with her mood.

What does it matter?

What does she care?

Faster, faster.

She could scream into the warm wind, she could lean out dangerously on the bends as if she was crewing a racing yacht, and nothing could hurt her any more.

Cheryl is too wounded. She thinks nothing more can touch her.

And she has drunk far too much this evening. This new and intense sense of mad release is what she has been struggling to control for so long. Amazed to discover that she is crying, she licks the hot tears that chase down her cheeks, salting her mouth, blowing behind her with the exhaust fumes of the powerful bike.

His flat overlooks the Thames.

Cheryl is unprepared for the bizarre effects within. You would think it was a tenement slum that had been hit during World War Two, and the only way in is up the fire escape, a dizzying climb to the top floor when you are already unsteady from too much booze.

Zak Quinn lives in one room, one room the size of a factory floor. No attempt has been made to paper the walls or to soften the atmosphere. Brick. Metal. Pipes. At the far end is an immense fireplace full of roughly sawn logs. Kerosene lamps dangle from varying heights. And to open the window, he pushes a button and half the wall goes up and under like a vast garage door, with a drop that leads nowhere and no protective railings between you and the deep black Thames below. He touches a fifties Wurlitzer as he passes, and the tinny music absorbs the space, causing an instant intimacy of the kind you might achieve in a small front room.

'Like it?'

Yeah, Elvis. 'One Night With You', if you're into that sort of thing.

'Have you eaten?'

Cheryl shakes her head. But she doesn't want to put this special man to any trouble.

'Are you vegetarian?'

'No.'

'Have a drink.' And he deftly opens a bottle of red wine, not like her or Barry, who have to search the drawers for an opener and make a real corky mess.

His fridge must be American. It's as gaudy as the jukebox. And his cooker is something Swedish, long and multi-doored, with many hotplates under silver domes. With the kind of wilful abandon that she's only ever seen on TV, Zak chops, seasons, squeezes, throws and tastes, and the aroma that fills the cavernous space is like the music – all-engulfing.

The table is like a giant packing case. The chairs are the real thing. But it's the setting that is so awesome, the wide-open windows looking out on barges and pleasure boats spangled with light, and the scents of the muddy Thames waters drifting in and mingling with all the rest. Cheryl could never cook a meal like this. Throw the ingredients together, so confident of success. And nothing she or Barry cooks gives off the smell of anything but fat, or burned crumbs, frozen fish or cabbage.

She has to sip the wine for something to do. And it's nice. They would probably call it fruity.

She wants to be nice. She wants to please him. If he likes her, he won't hurt her, will he?

And it's not just the trouble Zak is taking, the thought of a bed for tonight makes her weak at the knees with relief. Her feet hurt from all the walking. Her shoulders ache from all the worrying. Her lips are sore from all the picking, and to sit at this table and stare out at the night is all Cheryl feels she is capable of.

But this red wine is something else.

Never has alcohol affected Cheryl before, in this out-of-body sort of way. This freedom is a fearful, floating sensation; she has been unpegged from the ground.

She is not too sure of the final result, which he brings to the table with fanfare and flourish.

Arranged in a vast wooden bowl, or gourd as he calls it, Zak slops it out into smaller gourds, and they tackle it with spoons. It is so loaded with chilli, you can't make out what is in it.

'Fish stew. Squid,' he says, when she spits a piece out, unable to go on chewing after the first five minutes.

The 'interview', she supposes, takes place over the

packing-case table where a small tape recorder is set among Zak's strange centrepiece of debris and blanched dead branches.

The unearthly sound of foghorns from the bend of the river in the distance, and flashes of music from pleasure boats passing, perforate the intensity. He is so easy to talk to. He doesn't interrupt, apart from some encouragement, and murmurs of sympathy and disbelief.

Cheryl holds nothing back.

She could go on talking like this all night, and even the numbing horror of Cara's disappearance, which she carries with her at all times, everywhere she goes, like an abcessed tooth, has miraculously subsided into a dull and painful ache.

She never imagined she would be able to discuss such personal stuff with a stranger. Not after Leo, who she thought was an expert. But it all tumbles out as if she has been waiting for this one moment in time to empty her head, like spring-cleaning a cupboard . . . From her sex life with Barry to the loss of her virginity when she was thirteen years old, from her one snort of charlie with Barry to the time she was touched up on the tube, under her knickers.

And Zak's serious eyes never leave her.

He doesn't keep jumping up.

His answerphone rings a couple of times; callers leave short messages, but she is so focused that she hardly hears it, and Zak completely ignores it.

And all the time Cheryl's confidence grows, in Zak, in herself, in the way she looks and sounds, and in the importance of what she is saying. She is no longer a whey-faced beggar girl in shabby jeans and trainers, but a fascinating, black-eyed woman with a streaming waterfall of hair that shimmers like in an advert.

'I will need to talk to Barry too. I'm sure he's got a contribution to make.'

Barry? *Barry?*

'Tomorrow. I'm meeting him and the kids in the park tomorrow. You can come.'

It is after two o'clock in the morning when he finally stops the tape recorder and suggests that Cheryl has a shower.

And then bed.

They both need their sleep.

She is shocked by this awakening. She has never felt less tired. In fact, she feels as if she could party all night. She wants to move her body to music and float on this new level of ecstasy so it lasts and lasts and lasts . . .

But he leads her to a cordoned-off corner. Behind shoulder-high, silver-painted corrugated iron is a state-of-the-art shower and whirlpool bath. 'Put this on when you're ready.' He drapes a Japanese kimono over the peculiar walls. 'I'll stick your clothes in the machine, they'll be clean and dry by morning. OK?'

She is either bewitched or insane, stripping off in some stranger's flat with just a thin layer of metal between them. It feels like being in a film. And the flat makes an excellent set. This whole crazy thing could well be a dream. As the water gushes over her and she wipes it from her eyes, she realizes that there is no detail of Zak's looks, his tone, his every word and his gestures, or any of the emotions which he has made her feel, that is not vividly present, here, with her and her nakedness.

And she wants, so desperately, to please him.

She rests her forehead on the partition to feel its coolness, its common sense, then presses her cheek and finally her lips against it. Not long ago she had been haunted by all the terrible happenings of the last twenty-four hours, comfortless, pitiful and desolate, but now . . . how great the difference is. She flings her arms above her head and lets the water have her, palms open and fingers curled like a child's, eyes closed.

'You're lovely,' he tells her as she walks out, still steamy-damp, with the silk kimono wrapped loosely round her.

She gives a delighted little laugh. Feeling daft. 'I'm not. Not really.'

He bends and kisses her softly. She closes her eyes again as she feels his warm breath on her lips and inhales his fragrance, which mingles with hers. She is growing irresistibly drowsy. 'I'm just afraid,' she whispers, only half aware of what she is saying, like someone slipping under anaesthetic.

Zak laughs softly, and the laugh sounds reassuring, so she follows him to what must be his bed, a plinth of bricks covered with a mattress.

What the hell is she doing?

What is she thinking of?

There is only a deep and humble gratitude that this man, undressing beside her, with his broad brown chest that slopes abruptly to his flat belly and hard, tapering legs, that this man is giving her such shelter and succour. Spreading through her body is a warm and wonderful sensation of ease and fulfilment. Perhaps everything's going to be OK. Deeply and slowly and luxuriously, she sighs. A compliant and voluptuous languor about her makes her feel special and alluring.

'For me. Will you?'

Jesus. Oh, God. She has never done this sort of thing before.

But she must not upset him. He is here to help her. There is only a brief reluctance. 'Don't make me.'

'Don't be afraid.'

His very tone seems to stroke her arms, her breasts and between her legs, tenderly and voluptuously, making her grow warm and feel luxurious. Gently but firmly Zak positions her in various erotic poses. Her initial awkward and horrified shame turns into a welter of vivid sensation. She has become his prisoner, and must remain so until he chooses to free her. She must do his bidding. She lies, her legs outspread; she sits on the edge of the plinth, holding herself apart; she rubs her nipples and he seizes her wrist in a light, strong grip, jerks her arms above her head and holds her there in a pose. This is carnality so intense that her body seems to swell and glow, eager to experience whatever might happen.

What the hell is going on here? Is she all body? No mind of her own?

She is his helpless, passive victim. She wants to show herself to him. She wants to be his – if she belongs to him he might like her. No position is too revealing. He is unrestrained, fierce and masterful. Like someone in a book. Unreal.

Then he moves on her slowly, almost thoughtfully. Their breathing comes and goes simultaneously. The senses of time and motion disappear until there is only a welter of sensation.

Zak fucks her ruthlessly, driving her onwards as she thrashes and moans, pleads and begs, to unendurable excitement. Flesh of my flesh. The walls between them have been destroyed; she loses all sense of herself and fears her own extinction, and she catches a brief glimpse of his face, dark and shining, wearing a strange, triumphant smile.

Cheryl wakes up cold and frightened, with a desolate sense of being abandoned in an alien place. She looks down at her naked body. Oh, God, no! What has she done? What happened?

She rolls herself into a ball, hugging herself to get warm. Her previous despondent melancholy has returned, stronger this morning than ever.

Where is Zak?

The warehouse room seems larger in daylight and even more extraordinary. Despite the room's tremendous size, last night Zak created the impression of being larger than his surroundings, of extending the bounds of his personality until the room contained him, and nothing else.

She hears him coming across the room from between a screened-off area completely surrounded by black curtains, the sort of curtains photographers have, or that were used for the blackouts during the war. The sound of his footsteps on the bare floorboards seems to echo thunderously in the vast, silent room. She opens her eyes and looks at him. Fully dressed, he carries two cups of coffee. He stops at the bed and stares at her. 'OK?'

As some memory returns, her face flames. Stunned and almost too embarrassed to speak, she turns away, nursing a headache which nearly closes her eyes with its force. What sort of drink did he give her last night? Surely this can't be the wine?

Zak smiles and shrugs his shoulders indifferently.

'We had a good time. What's wrong with that?'

'Because I'm married,' Cheryl says quietly, forlorn and perplexed, 'and I don't normally do those things.'

There is nothing between them any longer.

All those frenzied emotions of last night have gone.

'I said I wanted to get to know you.'

'And you did.'

'It was nice. Don't be sorry.'

Gradually, every one of last night's humiliations return with startling clarity, with agonizing vividness. She wants to recoil from her own self as if she has just discovered that she is disgusting and ugly. And what must he think of her now? Unnatural? Dissolute? And her baby kidnapped by God knows who, and doing what to that tiny body? All he is showing is mild surprise that she should be so concerned. She feels a quick spasm of fear when he hands her her clean clothes, tumble-dried.

She draws a deep breath and stops.

Had Zak arranged things this way?

Had he always intended to take her to bed?

Was that why he offered her bed and board?

Had he drugged her?

She had not merely broken her marriage vows, she had forgotten them.

She had never thought herself capable of such wilful treachery. Or such unrestrained sexual abandon.

Best get down to business. 'You said you wanted some pictures. I agreed for you to take some pictures.'

'Don't worry about that now,' Zak says, 'there'll be time for that later.'

'When will the article go in the paper?'

'Sometime this week. I can't tell you the day.'

'I'm sorry about what happened last night.' Does he think she's a nymphomaniac? 'I've never behaved that way before.'

'That's a shame, then,' Zak says in a reasonable tone, his footsteps echoing on the wooden floor as he takes the cups to the kitchen area. 'You should do it more often. It's fun.'

After a nervous breakfast of grapefruit juice and some kind of sour muesli which Zak mixes up in a blender, it's back on his red Harley again, and a more cautious ride through the London traffic.

Cheryl can't wait to see her two children. The no-contact order she feared so much was never put in place. As long as she has vacated the flat, she can see them whenever she wishes as long as Barry is always present. This means that Barry's interview with Zak will have to be indoors, because out in the park with the kids tearing round, there is no way he could concentrate.

Cheryl plans to wait in the park until his business with Zak is finished.

Zak won't mention last night, will he?

He won't let it slip?

So agitated is Cheryl now, that her excitement to see her children is spoiled.

If Barry even suspected she had been to bed with

somebody else, his world would collapse around him.

These fears are overwhelmed by a sudden burst of love, as Victor and Scarlett trail up the path towards her, Victor so sturdy and sure of himself with his Teletubby boots and a broken stick, and Scarlett tottering along, one hand on the battered old push-chair.

She grabs them, talking soft baby talk, and can't stop pressing her face in their hair, eyes brimming with tears.

'Oh, oh. Are they OK?'

Barry hugs them all, in a bundle. 'They're doing great.'

'Do they miss me?'

'Of course they miss you. So do I.'

'Any news of Cara?'

Barry shakes his head.

Then Cheryl remembers Zak, still on the seat where she left him, waiting for an introduction.

Wouldn't this make a good picture?

A little family, almost united?

Why has there been no mention of a photographer? Or will Zak use his own camera later?

But Barry is asking, all concern, 'How was last night? I never slept. I couldn't stop thinking about you.'

'Last night was fine. I went home with Zak. He's going to do an article on us. It worked, Barry! It will be OK. I found Sebby, and Leo called Zak. He's a mate of his, a colleague, we can trust him.'

Unexpectedly Cheryl shudders, a sharp, spasmodic movement that begins at her shoulders and travels right down her body. And she watches, disconcerted, as Zak grasps Barry's hand. 'Hi, Barry, good to meet you.' The edges of his straight white teeth show as the *Mirror* reporter grins at her husband.

NINETEEN

'Of course, Cheryl could be deceiving herself. Total denial. If she lost that baby, with all the stress she's been under she might honestly have convinced herself that the child's still alive.' Sebby muses, still disbelieving, after spending the afternoon delving through last summer's births at St Catherine's House. But he is stumped for an answer. No record of Cara Higgins exists to show she has ever been born. 'Or it wouldn't be too surprising if the shock of finding Mrs Donnolly dead triggered some post-traumatic stress.'

'But what about Barry? Why would he . . . ?'

'He follows her lead,' Sebby says bleakly. 'He always has, and he's doing it again. Probably terrified of the results if he confronts her with the truth. Things got out of hand, and he couldn't deal with the repercussions. Didn't know where to go for help.'

'So what the hell do we do now?'

'We have to tell the law,' says Sebby. 'For everyone's sake, including Cheryl's. But I hate what we're doing, I hate it, we're making out she's insane.'

'Tomorrow,' says Kate. 'We'll wait and tell them tomorrow. Cheryl's ill, Seb, she needs proper help. It's just too awful.'

'OK, tomorrow,' Sebby agrees. But hell, he is meant to be on Cheryl's side. And now it looks as if he is the straw which will break the camel's back – Sebby knows only too well that the inflamed public will not tolerate any more of Cheryl Higgins's crazy schemings.

This time, the special force is more hopeful.

The message is delivered in the same way as before, by public telephone, in a distorted voice. Only the venue is different.

Speaker's Corner in Hyde Park, on Sunday morning at ten.

The question, 'Is the child OK?' is ignored by the caller, who's in a hurry.

The police are still questioning local people. They are carrying out door-to-door searches. The public have been asked to look out for a mum with a six-month-old baby who didn't have one before. That person may appear nervous, the child might cry more than normal. There is probably at least one woman involved.

Doctors and hospitals should stay alert. When the baby was snatched, she was ill with a slight chest infection. The mother did have a clinic appointment. The fact that she never turned up is now beside the point.

Well-known local gangs have been pulled in and questioned. They have a double crime on their hands, a murder and a kidnap, two of the worst in the book.

Every police snout has been sniffing around.

Once more, Sir Art Blennerhasset, man of connections and conscience, sets out, Adidas bag in hand.

Once more he puts it down in the place specified by the kidnapper. Once more he notes the size of the crowd – so many weirdos frequent these places, it would be hard to pick the odd man out. If they only knew what was in that bag: a quick grab, a dart, a few twists and rugby dives . . . no. It would not be possible. Not with so many plain-clothes cops about. So surely these curious rehearsals cannot mirror the real event.

This is beginning to feel like some lingering, gruesome game.

There have been changes on the Griffin board since the success of *The Dark End*. Art is not a happy man. Like all who are balanced at the top of the ladder, he has to keep checking the rungs below. Alan Beam, director and *The Dark End*'s creator, is lording it in his new position. At confidential and important meetings, like the one with the police this morning, his pomposity bores everyone stiff. That he regularly fends off headhunters is rumoured throughout the company, rumours which Art suspects are spread by nobody but himself.

And the programme's co-director, Jennie St Hill, a thrusting woman who sincerely believes that her cracked ideas are paving the way for new 'break-throughs in the industry', is now on a salary approaching his own.

So it's good to get out of the office sometimes, it's good to have time to think.

He stops to pick up the Sunday papers on his way home. They have *The Times* and *Observer* delivered, but it's always useful to read some tabloids, and he considers the sport coverage better, and Sarah likes to read her stars.

Jesus Christ.

What now?

Splashed across the front of the *Mirror* is a picture of Cheryl Higgins in a most unfortunate pose, her lower reaches covered only by a black exclamation mark. This will start Sarah off again with her accusations of insensitivity and caving in to young upstarts against his better judgement. He wishes Sarah would stop ranting on, nothing she says can make Art feel worse. But it's hard to know what sort of help he could give the Higginses now without appearing manipulative, and, worse, a patronizing bastard.

All he can realistically do is come here with a bag full of money, while half the Met are on double time doing their bloody damnedest to get that poor little kid back.

What the hell is going on now?

He sits wearily in his BMW and rereads the headline, 'Mum Poses for Porn Pics in Vanished Baby Scandal.'

Exclusive. And the byline of some salacious rat calling himself Zak Quinn.

Well, Art will wait till he gets home to read the rest of that.

Things can't get worse for the Harlow Higginses.

You think, you hope you have reached rock bottom, and then you sit down with the Sunday papers, rib of beef in the oven on a hundred and fifty, and all hell is let loose.

How could Cheryl do this to them?

And in the circumstances, too.

You would think she would have been satisfied with all that exposure she got during the documentary. Open-legged in the delivery suite, displaying herself to all. Lewd snapshots. And now this.

And since Cath Higgins lied to her friend, Glo, about Bill having MS, that rumour has spread like wildfire and now Bill has to pretend he is feeling worse than he is, hobbling around on a crutch, if you please, with neighbours bringing him videos and rock cakes. Sometimes it looks as if the man is actually enjoying himself.

Maybe it's time they paid Barry a visit.

He's going to need a shoulder to cry on at a terrible time like this, what with little Cara still missing and his wife's brazen disloyalty.

Cara must be dead by now. Poor child.

They are always found dead in the end, and what happens to the beasts that range the streets on the lookout for their tiny victims? A couple of years inside and then out, cocky as ever. Chop it off, is what Cath thinks. Balls and all. No, poor mite, it would have been better if Cara had never been born, as so many people made clear at the time of her unfortunate conception.

Well, if the newspapers need another opinion they've only got to ring Cath. The more blackly Cheryl is painted the whiter Barry appears to be. He's only a man, after all, hypnotized by the slut, besotted with her and her sexual wiles. Cath should have known all along it boiled down to sex. It's so often at the bottom of things, the start of that slippery slope.

*　　*　　*

308

'I need you, Mum.'

'You bloody fool. You've gone and done it now.'

Annie hugs her daughter to her, checks both ways before closing the door, touches the lucky horseshoe with her forefinger and draws her flimsy curtains.

'I spent Saturday night in the park, hoping that Barry would come out and talk to me.'

Cheryl looks as if she has been run over by a bus. Her clothes, though clean, are dishevelled. She hasn't touched her hair. 'He didn't. After he'd been interviewed by that reporter, Zak Quinn, I waited and waited, but he didn't come down. Zak must have told him. I never knew about the pictures, I never guessed he was doing that . . .'

Annie's large arms remain crossed. 'But you were undressed and posing in that man's flat?'

'I was drunk. I was high. He must have put something in the wine . . .'

'You don't look drugged,' says Annie, bringing the paper out from under one of the tatty sofa cushions and eyeing it with disgust. 'I hid it in case the boys found it. You look to be enjoying yourself.'

'I went up to the flat lunchtime yesterday. Barry told me he would come down when he'd finished with Zak. I banged on the door. I yelled. I shouted. I had to see Barry. He's got my kids. But he didn't come out, and in the end one of the neighbours must have complained, 'cos the cops came and took me away and said I was in breach of my probation order.' Cheryl pauses. She covers her face with her hands. 'Of course then I didn't know what Zak had told him. Then I had no idea he must have developed those pictures behind the curtains while I was still asleep, and actually shown them to Barry.'

'You slept with the jerk, then?' demands Annie, her big face speculative.

'Mum, I can't explain it.'

'I'm not surprised.'

Cheryl smiles timidly. 'It wasn't at all like that.'

'That's what they all say.'

'I know. I *know*.'

'And all the while the camera was rolling? God, Cher, you must have had some bloody idea! You're not blind. You're not deaf.'

Cheryl shakes a head made of lead. 'But I didn't.'

'Well, more fool you.'

'He was being so kind.'

'I bet he was.'

'He was going to help us,' Cheryl says dismally.

'Help himself, you mean.' Big Annie rolls her eyes to the ceiling. 'Men. That Marge Smith will have herself a ball.'

'And all the others?'

Annie checks the curtains. 'Yeah, I suppose. The bastards.'

Cheryl jerks her head up. 'Don't worry, Mum, I'm not planning to stay.'

'You can if you like, Cher, you know that.'

Cheryl's eyes are big and staring like someone still in shock. 'I have to get back. I have to stay near in case I see Barry. He's got to come out of there in the end. He must feel so hurt and angry. I know, I'd be the same.'

'Too bloody right.' Annie cocks her head to one side, listening. Listening for spies outside the window? 'You broke?'

'Yep, I hitched.'

'That's dodgy.'

'I kept my hood up.' Her laugh is dry. 'I reckon the driver thought I had a disfigurement.'

Annie lifts the china dog basket off the pine-clad mantelpiece. Cheryl remembers how, when she was little, she used to play with the Scottie, both fascinated and appalled by the toe-clippings her mother insisted on keeping inside – another insurance against bad luck. She broke his leg once, and mended it with superglue without Mum knowing. Has Annie ever found out? No, she would have said.

'Here's a fiver.'

'Cheers, Mum.'

'You can stay if you like.'

'I know. I know.'

Two hours later and back at the flats . . .

'Barry! I know you can hear me. You've got to let me in. Please, please. Let me explain how it happened.'

Those nosy neighbours are gathering again.

Hands on hips.

Arms folded.

The attacking position of angry women clustering like sharp mussels on a rock. Some of these ought to be in the army – one look at their faces would slay an enemy, never mind germs or gas.

'Right little whore you are.'

'Dunno how you've got the face . . .'

'What you done with that kiddy of yours?'

'You shouldn't be here, you know that.'

She lets out a scream. *'BARRY!'*

'Fuck off and leave those kiddies alone.'

'Don't you think you've done enough?'

'I'm calling the pigs.'

Cheryl doesn't run down the steps any longer. Let them take her picture if they want to.

Let the reporters follow her.

Without Barry's support, she is despairing. She has nothing more to lose.

She shuffles towards the park still carrying her string bag with the blanket inside in case it gets cold. She goes to their special seat, so Barry knows where to find her if he should change his mind. She will sleep here tonight, tomorrow night and every other night until she is given a chance to explain.

But what will she tell him?

She wasn't forced to go to bed with Zak Quinn.

She had wanted to. She had found him attractive – no, not just attractive, *irresistible*. And how is she going to make anyone believe there were drugs in that red wine?

Maybe there weren't.

Maybe it is true what they're saying; maybe she is a lustful nympho with no more morals than a farmyard animal. After all, Sonia and Babs told the papers she went with men for money, and that was when she was seven. She wonders how much money Quinn made. Five thousand? Ten? He didn't waste much time. Did Leo make a mistake, or was he in it too?

And Kate and Sebby?

For the laugh?

Or for a cut?

She holds out her aching arms. *Oh, Cara, Cara, where are you?*

* * *

She has to ring Sebby. She has to know if this is some conspiracy.

'Sebby, this is Cheryl.'

She expects him to replace the receiver, but he doesn't. He pretends to be as aghast as she is.

'I've spoken to Leo, and he didn't have a clue this would happen,' says Sebby at his most sincere. 'Please believe me, Cheryl, we would never have dropped you in it like this. I've been trying to catch Zak all morning but he's not at home. I just don't know what I can do. I feel so bloody responsible.'

What's the point of going on with this? The damage has been done.

'You told me I could trust that man.'

'And I believed that. Honestly. Kate did, too. We really believed Zak was the best person to take up your cause. As Leo says, he is an excellent journalist.'

'You can say that again.'

'Is there anything we can do, Cheryl? Anything at all?'

'No, Sebby, it's too late for that.'

'Where are you spending the night?'

'Why? Have you got any mates who might take me in?'

And the pips tell her the money's run out.

Darkness begins to fall.

Cheryl sits in silence, waiting, all hope gone.

Couples come and lie down on the grass. They wouldn't lie there if they knew what was on it. It's difficult enough to keep the kids out of the sea of turds.

The odd drunk comes weaving by.

She becomes aware of slow footsteps shuffling towards her. When the seat gives slightly, Cheryl takes no notice. It isn't Barry. She knows his walk. Whoever it is is large and heavy . . . probably some bag-snatcher after Cheryl's spare blanket. Well, she doesn't possess anything else apart from the clothes she is wearing, and no-one would give tuppence for them.

But that smell seems familiar . . .

Just another dosser, like Donny.

If only Donny was here now.

Cheryl's sad eyes stare into the distance as she picks out a chip and blows on it. Her thoughts take her round and round and back in that old vicious circle. Unless somebody stumbled on those railway carriages by accident, which is very unlikely given their unique position, somebody knew the kids were there.

How?

Some dubious friend of Donny's? Had her tongue run away with her? Had she left the kids and come out onto the streets, driven by a need for booze which neither Cheryl nor Barry dreamed she still had?

Other than that possibility, only the residents of the flats knew those carriages were there. And the railway workers, of course. Only the people above the fifth floor, and there's only two floors above that, and only the ones overlooking the station . . . so that narrows it down.

Only a desperate need would have driven Donny to leave the kids. Only booze would have loosened her tongue; Donny normally played her cards very close to her chest.

Is that a shadow behind those bushes? Cheryl tenses and stares.

Who else could have known? Cheryl's brain burns with the pressure. Who? *Who?* As the awful thought strikes her, as she tries to dismiss it from her head, Cheryl walks over to the railings. She screws up the empty chip bag. Throws it down. No. *Not Barry*.

Oh, no, not Barry.

But Barry could never have done this alone. Somebody must have helped him.

For what?

For the money?

Or was he intent on driving her mad?

She must have lost her mind completely to be even considering such paranoid notions. And then she remembers the company he used to keep before they met. Scum, Cath calls them. Lowlife. The pits. And they've moved from being teenage tearaways to serious crime – some are in prison.

Funny how Barry comes out of this as white as snow, while she is left to carry the can. And he didn't fight very hard to stop her being made homeless, did he? Surely he could have done more to help her – unless?

She leans heavily against the railings and grabs the spikes that run along the top. Nobody knew the children were there, no-one but her and Barry. Barry had Sebby's card. Spurs is Barry's team, always has been. She never knew he was interested in Arsenal. *He never mentioned that before*.

Could Barry, with Leo's help, have actually planned this farce with Zak Quinn?

But why, why, *why*?

When a woman thinks alone, she thinks evil. The Malleus Maleficarum.

She dismisses these terrible thoughts from her mind. That way lies madness.

She grips the spikes with all her strength, pulling on them for all she is worth as if she is in great pain, giving birth.

TWENTY

'Come on home, son, I'll have your old room made up for you. You can't stay there cooped up day and night with that madwoman raving outside. You need a rest after all you've been through. Come on home to your mum and dad.'

'I dunno how you'll stand the kids.'

'Don't worry about the kids, son. We'll manage, we always have. Don't forget, I'm a mother myself.' And Cath Higgins gives a satisfied laugh.

Barry had left the flat deliberately early this morning, to avoid bumping into the press and Cheryl, who he suspected was lurking outside in the park. He had run out of supplies, he was making his way to the newsagent/grocer's just five minutes down the road. The freedom he should be feeling, once he rounded the corner, should be something like growing wings and taking off, swooping and gliding with the thermals, friendly faces everywhere, not one aggressor in sight.

For he is the wounded party now.

But he feels like he's been nailed to a cross. How could she? How could she do that to him? And to

317

have it splashed all over the papers . . . He never would have hurt Cher this way. He was shocked enough, he was hurt, to be honest, when those photos of Cher naked came out in public, but he managed to act grown-up. This is different. Between them they don't have much, but without faithfulness they have nothing. If it wasn't for Cher and her insane ideas, Cara wouldn't be missing now. They would never have gone on that damn programme. She would never have got mixed up with Quinn.

She is the impulsive one. Cher is the one with the energy, the one with all the ideas. But why does he always follow her lead? Why does he always give in, against his better judgement? Could it be he's afraid of women after his mother's domination, which he put up with meekly for years until he rebelled in that damaging way? In Barry's limited experience, women are the leaders – in all the game shows they make the decisions. He must have been certifiable when he agreed to hide the kids, and yes, he supposes, at that time they were both close to breakdown. But that's no excuse for such lunatic behaviour. Sod her, sod her, sod her. Is it because he's inherently weak? Maybe he would be stronger if he worked, if, as his father puts it, he brought home the bacon. It's amazing how many nursery songs talk about Daddy coming home . . . Pockets full of plums, diamond rings or even bloody fishes . . . shit.

He has already had offers. Two journalists arrived at the flat to ask him for his story: The Man Who Lived with a Witch.

So far he has refused. He wouldn't sink that low.

But now he needs to use the phone. He will go mad if he sticks around here any longer.

That is why he had pulled the box-pram alongside the station telephones and called up his mum – to test the waters.

No wonder Cath is so eager to have him. Her telephone has not stopped ringing since Sunday morning when the *Mirror* came out.

Interviews, radio, TV, tabloids – Barry is now in constant demand since Cheryl has been 'outed'. They want him to tell them in black and white that she always had led him a dance, that he wasn't surprised to see those lewd pictures, or to hear of her attempted blackmail of the freelance reporter in exchange for sex.

She had flirted outrageously with the Griffin crew during their months of filming.

The camera crew had all they could deal with trying to fend her off.

He had never wanted to start a family, it was she who had insisted, although she was under age, wasn't it?

She was far from virginal when he met her, wasn't she?

She knew all the tricks in the book, didn't she?

And wasn't it true that he would never have married Cheryl if she hadn't threatened suicide, if she hadn't screamed that she and Victor would jump out of the window if he refused? Her mother, Annie, had bullied him into it. Paid for the whole affair, didn't she? Had told him in no uncertain terms what would happen to him if he let Cheryl down.

Most of their ideas were rubbish. He wondered where the hell they got them from. When Cheryl declared in front of the cameras that she was pregnant for the third time, did Barry suspect the child was not his?

That she had been out on the tiles again.

Picking up men?

Casual sex. But because he was a decent man, he probably felt he had to support her, especially when the public turned nasty and he saw what extreme effects that had.

Poor man. He must have acted out of concern for the safety of his children. He can't be blamed for anything. Her moods were so unpredictable in spite of the tranks she took. Her depressions were awesome, weren't they? Her tantrums terrible to behold?

What strength it must have taken to stand by Cheryl through the so-called abduction.

What loyalty he must have felt, to aid and abet her wicked schemes.

Only the thought that the children were safe – safer with Donny, perhaps, than their mother, so manic was Cheryl at that time – made his actions bearable. And the knowledge that at any time he could have gone and checked them out. He realizes now what a fool he was, doesn't he? He was half demented himself. Not driven by public disgrace, but by the antics of his wife.

All he wants now is his baby back and a little understanding.

He never wants to see Cheryl again.

Tell us, Barry, tell us. Open up your heart.

So when does he plan to divorce his wife and go for custody?

Choosing his moment, that same afternoon he leaves the Harold Wilson Building with the minimum of belongings. Most of the furniture is not theirs, and neither is it worth taking.

Cath roots through Cheryl's bits and pieces with many a cross sniff and cluck, and stuffs them in two black dustbin bags which the slut can collect if she feels like it.

What Cheryl does and what she does not do is no longer of the slightest importance.

Having packed two suitcases, mostly with kiddies' clothes and toys, the Higginses are struggling down the steps, are almost at the bottom, when, God help us, that woman turns up like the bad penny. The nerve!

Cath had hoped they might avoid this. And is that a camera? Do these fiends never rest?

But Barry stands his ground. He hands Cheryl the keys to the flat. 'You might as well take them.'

She has the face to stutter, 'But, what's going on? Where are you taking them?'

'Never you mind,' snaps Cath, pushing herself between them, lips pursed. She can deal with this little madam. 'Get out of our way. This is nothing to do with you any more.'

Cheryl pushes rudely past her, confronts Barry so he can't move without knocking the strumpet over.

Her eyes flash and her voice rises. 'I said, *where are you going?*'

'I don't want to hear your excuses, Cher. It's too

soon. Please leave me alone. I've got to work this out myself.'

She starts sobbing, of course. Oh, yes, she's the actress right enough. 'I know how hurt you must be, I do understand, and that's why I've been waiting out here. We must talk, Barry, you can't do this . . . *I can't bear it* . . . Don't be like this, please, please . . .'

'You heard what he said.' Even Bill is getting hot under the collar. 'Now please get out of our way. All you are going to do is upset the children.'

'Huh! Since when has that one cared about doing that?' snaps Cath, trying to get by the cameras.

Cheryl splutters, threatening hysteria, working her face into ugly shapes. 'But I can't just let you take them and go.' And her mad eyes dart this way and that.

'Cheryl, you have no option,' says Bill with an angry flush, and for the first time in years Cath feels proud of him.

'Barry doesn't want you,' says Cath with a glorious, airy confidence. 'When will you get that simple fact into your stupid head? Little whore.'

'Barry,' Cheryl pleads, 'please tell them to go. This is between you and me.'

The cameras close in, but nobody seems to notice.

'I can't handle this, Cher. Right now I just can't take any more.'

Cheryl collapses against the pram, and while Barry tries to manoeuvre it past her she clings desperately to Scarlett's hand, upsetting the child, as she no doubt intends. She sobs as if her heart is breaking. 'Please don't do this, Barry, please, I love you, I love you, *I love you.*'

322

What an amateurish, transparent display. And, of course, the crowds start gathering, but this time Cheryl has underestimated their distaste. To a man they take Barry's side.

'Poor bastard. Living with that.'

'The woman's sick.'

'Mother from hell.'

You see these sorts of people on *Crimewatch*.

Well, Cheryl has asked for this all along. She can't expect any sympathy now.

By now, of course, the kiddies are screaming. All Cheryl's doing, the selfish slut. Goodness knows what effect this attention-seeking display will have on them later. And who will have to cope with the fallout? Barry, of course, and Cath and Bill, while they're living in their house.

At last, defeated, with the odds against her too great, Cheryl lets go of the child and slumps against the wall. No more fight in her. At last. Thank goodness for that. Cath steps carefully over her, making sure that the case on wheels gives her daughter-in-law's legs a wide berth as it squeaks behind her towards the taxi.

They are only just indoors after a hideous train journey, with the children playing up all the way and people staring and rustling their papers; they are only just beginning their first cup of tea when the telephone rings.

It is for Barry.

'I told you,' whispers Cath, pleased, handing it over. 'I told you it would be like this.'

With Barry's attention given over completely to the reporter on the end of the line, Cath swoops

about her tidy living room removing glass ornaments, pictures, books and letters, anything below
three feet, within Victor and Scarlett's grabbing
reach.

'No, Victor,' she says strictly. 'We mustn't touch
Granny's precious things. No, Scarlett, *give that to
me*. Don't let them play with the TV buttons, Bill,
they'll upset the controls.'

But Bill just sits in his chair and regards their
antics with horror. Have they never been taught
to behave? Have they never heard the word no?
And now Scarlett has banged her knee, and you'd
think she'd been operated on without anaesthetic
the way she raises the roof with her screams.
Piercing, nerve-shattering screams that put his
teeth on edge.

But Barry is still stuck, helpless, on the phone.

How did he cope with this on his own?

Cath attempts to lift the child up but Scarlett
grabs her glasses and pulls them from her nose,
hurling them to the floor and kicking her little legs
so hard they are going to bruise Cath's kidneys.

'Stop it, Scarlett, *that's enough*. Daddy's on the
telephone. Shush, he can't hear what he's saying.'

'That child needs a good smack,' says Bill.

Right. So Cath gives her one, just a tap on the legs,
just like she used to smack Barry, but the results are
not the same. While Barry would creep behind the
sofa and cower, Scarlett just yells louder.

'Takes after her mother,' says Cath, rescuing a
lead-crystal eagle from the coffee table beside the
sofa.

And there is no peace that evening, either.

Eight o'clock, and still the adults have not had

their tea. Cath couldn't concentrate on *This is Your Life*. Up and down, up and down like a yo-yo goes Barry to comfort that spoiled pair.

'Leave them,' says Cath. 'We always did. Leave them. They'll stop in the end.'

'They've been through shit,' moans Barry, exhausted. 'They've had a bad day.'

They're not the only ones, thinks Cath, stomach rumbling. Was this such a good idea after all? What will happen when visitors come? A sturdy playpen might be the answer.

'This is that woman's influence,' says Bill.

But 'that woman' could now be the vehicle through which all comforts flow, if Barry would only handle this properly and agree with what the reporters are saying.

When finally they have some peace, after they've eaten and washed up, when Cath has replaced the fish knives and forks carefully back in their case, they discuss the three generous offers Barry has received this evening.

'You should think hard about this, son,' says Bill, propped on cushions to rest his back. 'They'll only give you so much time and they'll be off after some other bugger. Take the money while it's going. I would.'

But Bill knows nothing about making money and keeping it. Look at him lying there, such a timid man with his greying hair and his dull, tired eyes, everyone at his beck and call, no job, disability allowance, useless round the house and no companionship, either. Cath doesn't know what she would do if it wasn't for the Caravan Club.

'Yes, take the money. You shouldn't need to think twice about it, Barry,' says Cath.

'I know what I'm doing, Mum,' says Barry.

'How? How do you know? You're as out of your depth as we are.'

But at this Barry goes silent, just like he used to as a child when he'd done something naughty – spilled a drink, broken a cup – and was obviously lying about it. And later, in adolescence, when he was out of control, that's when he would go surly, that same look of defiance on his face when he sneaked out to meet his cronies, came home late, drunk, stinking of glue, and Cath would find stains on his underpants.

Even thinking about that time makes Cath go cold all over.

He had spoiled it all.

He had ruined everything.

It was like losing a loved one.

One minute he was pliant and obedient, with the whole world at his footballing feet, the next he had spots and was into open rebellion, and there was nothing they could do. He laughed at her puny punishments, he was too big to hit, too strong for Bill. He scoffed at their threats to withhold his pocket money – somehow he'd always raised enough to go and do whatever he wanted, wherever he wanted.

But he was out of work.

He was too young for the dole.

He never stole money from her – she checked. She always kept a tally of what she had in her purse. She could only assume his mates helped him out. Huh, mates! That's what he used to call them, when in reality they were using him, teaching him bad ways, leading him into temptation and turning him against his parents.

No wonder he failed at school.

No wonder he ended up with Cheryl.

Now, maybe, he can make good at last.

Come to his senses. Talk to the press. Tell them what they want to hear. This is no time for high principles, especially when you can't afford them.

Perhaps this is a defence mechanism he was forced to cultivate for 'that woman'. And who can blame him, when you think what the poor boy has had to endure?

They had expected this.

Gone ten, and the phone goes.

You can tell by Barry's face that it's Cheryl.

Dill gets up to wash the teacups, but Cath stays in the room making out she is tidying the cushions, picking the papers up, turning off the lamps.

'Put the phone down on her,' she hisses in the direction of the hall.

But Barry turns his back on her and hunches over the receiver, so Cath has to wander closer to hear.

'I'm not ready to talk yet, Cher. Give me more time. It's a shock. It's like having your face smashed in. I don't want to talk yet. Please.'

So she is still ranting and pleading. She won't give up, that one, she will hang onto him for dear life. Where else is she going to find a decent, caring man who she can manipulate to her own ends? Courage to the sticking post! Barry has got to be strong and hold out. It was too good of him to give her the flat keys. Cath wouldn't have, if it had been left to her. Let the hussy sleep out on the streets, best place for her.

'No, Cheryl, no, I don't want to meet.'

And Cath wouldn't put it past that one to be after him for the money he'll make, once he comes to his senses and speaks out in his own defence. Cheryl's not daft. She'll have worked out how things stand. She will know the reporters are after him now, to come clean and betray her. The meek will inherit the earth – how true. The worm will turn, she must realize that. Barry will no longer be trodden on by Cheryl or anyone else.

Cath breathes a sigh of relief when the phone finally goes down.

'Horlicks or hot chocolate?'

Barry shakes his head and Cath sees that he is pale, trembling. 'Neither, Mum, thanks.'

'What did she want?'

Barry shrugs. 'To talk. To explain.'

'She's got a bloody nerve . . .'

'I know.'

'At least have a plain digestive. Don't go to bed on an empty tummy.'

But that same old reticence is there, it's in his eyes, that woodenness of expression she had learned to fear not so very long ago.

TWENTY-ONE

*What else is woman but a foe to friendship, an
unescapable punishment, a necessary evil, a natural
temptation, a desirable calamity, a domestic danger,
a delectable detriment, an evil of nature painted with
fair colours?*

St John Chrysostom on St Matthew XIX

Confusion, darkness and pain.

Knotted ropes of horror, and worse.

Cheryl has lost everything. Baby, children, home,
husband and any self-respect she might once have
had. And she's done it to herself. She can't blame
Barry for his reactions to her now. If he had been
caught fooling around with some other woman,
Cheryl would probably kill him, let alone deny
him the time of day.

But is she being manipulated by some unseen, evil
hand? Could her downfall, so swift and violent,
have been planned for some macabre reason?

Cheryl is not alone in her suffering.

Bitterness swept over Sebby Coltrain almost like
physical nausea. 'If anyone ought to be paid off by

Griffin, it ought to be that family,' he said, flushing darkly, fists resting on the desk in DCI Rowe's office. 'Jesus Christ, when you think what has happened. And all that crap they talked about choosing a positive archetype! Balls. They soon put paid to that, if the Higginses ever complied with it, which is doubtful to put it mildly. It started off as an upbeat programme, and descended into in-depth squalor.'

'That might well be, but it's beside the point, I'm afraid,' said DCI Rowe doggedly, staring back at the crumpled man and the suave but angry woman beside him. He was as bad as the rest. Working with those arty-farts who cared only for their work, part of the vulgar scramble where people pushed and exploited and traded on others' trust or love to make big money and hit the headlines. 'What is important now is that the search for that non-existent child is called off immediately before there're too many red faces.' Since Sebby's arrival at the station that morning with his extraordinary information, Rowe had doubled-checked St Catherine's House for records of Cara's birth and, to his fury, had found none. Barry, at his mother's house, was being questioned at that moment, but Cheryl Higgins could not be found. Wretched woman. If only he had paid more attention to those psychiatrist's reports. If only he had given more credence to the views of the Griffin board . . . That Cheryl Higgins was unhinged. That they could not be blamed for her unreasonable reactions. There was no way of knowing, when she was chosen, that she was a mental case, a sex fiend, a compulsive liar and a sufferer from Munchausen's.

He stared at Kate, Sebby's partner, impressed by her cool demeanour. Her anger remained well concealed. 'What gave you the idea that there was no Cara?' Rowe was impelled to ask. Damn, damn, damn. He should have suspected something like this, but he was fixed on the more likely idea that the Higginses had Cara hidden away and the ransom demands were from them. If DCI Rowe was not careful, if he failed to get it right this time, he would have no credibility left.

Kate tried to explain, but with every word she said she sounded as if she was betraying the woman whom her husband and his colleagues had set up so cruelly. 'I just listened to what Sebby told me, and formed a picture of Cheryl in my mind. I asked myself what I might do if I was in her position. And I have to admit, I might have behaved in a very similar way.'

'Oh, no,' said Rowe, 'I don't believe that for one moment.'

'No. But then you're a man, and men don't have the same imagination,' said Kate. 'But where Cara is concerned, I feel that Cheryl is not trying to con you. I'm afraid she might be terribly ill – as I would be, given her situation.'

Mrs Donnolly's body had been released for burial. It was to be a pauper's funeral. At last the forensic people had come up with some positive conclusions. Mrs Donnolly was not attacked. A large woman, she had fallen heavily in her efforts to jemmy the carriage door. She had fallen and crawled some distance, causing the injuries and the heart attack. Strangely, there were no signs of long-term alcohol abuse, which corresponded to Cheryl's

331

belief that the bag lady was not a drunk. But she was rat-arsed when she died, and had polished off two bottles of gin in her last wobbly twenty-four hours.

'The fact that the grandparents never got to see the baby seems to make what you're saying almost a foregone conclusion,' said Rowe, frowning, his jaw thrust forward. He wished he'd never heard the name Higgins. Before any of this began, Rowe would have sworn he could not be duped, not after his years of experience. He knew a lie when he heard it. It was he who had suspected the Higginses the first time round. He'd been right. But no-one had ever questioned the fact that there might be only two kids, not three. To be honest, that idea had never crossed his mind. But dealing with a sicko like Cheryl meant taking nothing at face value, and, dammit, he should have known that.

He heaved a sigh. 'And if that prat of a husband goes on supporting Cheryl's lies,' said DCI Rowe turning to Sebby, 'I'll have him in here so fast, I'll grill him so hard, he won't know his arse from his elbow.'

'I just hope we haven't made things worse,' said Kate worriedly, and DCI Rowe thought how entirely different this couple were, she so neatly dressed, perfectly featured and together, Sebby slumped angrily in his chair, looking as if he'd slept in his clothes. 'Cheryl needs help now, not hounding. If Cara is nothing but make-believe, you can bet there's a reason, caused by the strain she's been under.'

He wasn't prepared to argue with that. But Rowe had no time for these kinds of excuses. These days everyone was at it. Nothing was ever anyone's fault.

'She will get all the help she needs,' he said, sounding ominous, 'I can promise you that. The moment we find her.'

That last horrendous meeting with Barry, outside the Harold Wilson Building with Bill and Cath muscling in, had given Cheryl no chance to talk. Her knees had been trembling so much she could hardly take another step. She'd had no opportunity to see Barry alone. Victor and Scarlett were there in the box-pram, crying for their mother. Cath was triumphant in her self-righteous coup – she had her son back at last, undamaged if she could keep him away from further contamination.

Even Bill mounted a weedy attack on his wicked and wanton daughter-in-law.

In no mood to listen to her garbled explanations, Barry was unreachable, locked up inside, his castle wall too high to breach. She had hurt him too deeply. But she went on and on, humiliating herself, begging, clinging . . . *Don't do this, please, please don't go.* The pain of his rejection and lack of pity was expected, but intolerable. Barry, who had been so gentle and kind, who had loved her, the father of her children. They had been through so much together. If only he'd give her a chance to explain. Instead, he told her to move out of his way, with his eyes flinty-hard and his voice cold with dislike.

In the end she had let go of Scarlett's small hand, helpless with sorrow, knowing she had lost them all.

Oh, God help me, help me and show me what to do.

Had the whole world gone mad? Or was it Barry who was losing it?

'But you can't call off the hunt for Cara! What are you saying? Christ, I can't understand. Cara was born at home. At the flat. She came very quickly. There was no time . . . And anyway, that's what we wanted.'

A brief flash of that long, hot night flickered through his mind. From the start, the pregnancy was different. Having confirmed the fact by herself in front of the TV cameras, it was as though Cher had achieved all the attention she needed, but not the sort she'd anticipated. Barry's abortion idea had upset her terribly. Leo and Sebby had not been impressed. They had not disguised their disdain. Cath was disgusted by the news, and even Annie quibbled, 'You fool, you silly fool. On your own head be it.'

She made two clinic appointments and failed to attend. Throughout those months, she was so unhappy about being abandoned by her two yuppie heroes, the pregnancy took second place. And then there was the build-up of excitement before the series was transmitted – the preview, the start of all that publicity. The baby started coming early when Cher was in the bath. Two hours and it was all over. Barry cut the cord with his Swiss Army knife soaked in Dettol. He felt he was an expert. He'd watched it done twice before. And after the birth both Cara and Cher seemed to thrive without any medical interference, no long waits at the clinic with whingeing kids, stupid instructions about diets and exercise and getting the right kind of rest. The series began soon after, and the Higginses' lives were turned upside down.

'We didn't want a big fuss made, not after the last

time. St Mary's might have told the press if they recognized me and Cher. She knew that the public birth had upset me, and so we agreed to keep this one quiet.' Barry looked round at the faces turned on him, all featuring disbelief. 'So what the hell's wrong with that?'

'You never registered the birth. That's against the law. You're a father already. You must have known that.'

Barry shrugged. This was madness. 'Me and Cher, we don't really care that much about forms and registers.'

'I think you are lying, Barry,' said DC Scott aggressively, 'just as you've lied so many times. It was you who sent those notes to Griffin, it was you who . . .'

Cath poked her head round the door. 'Coffee, anyone? Tea? A biscuit?'

'Even your mother admits she never set eyes on this mystery child.'

'But we rang her after Cara was born. Tell them, Mum. I rang from the station. I told you she'd been born at home, and you said she was lucky to be alive.'

Scott ignored Cath's nodding head.

'Did she die, Barry? Is that the truth? Was the baby born dead? Did you panic and try to keep it quiet? Is that why your mum never saw her?'

'Barry would not lie about a serious matter like that,' said Cath, her face all prim and tight.

Scott laughed at her expression. 'He's done it before, love. Don't give me that.'

Suddenly Barry turned to DC Scott and exclaimed, 'She was pregnant at the preview. She went

335

in a maternity dress. You've only got to ask the people who were there. For God's sake, somebody must have noticed.'

DC Scott seemed unimpressed. 'You were telling me why your mother never saw her grandchild.'

'From the moment *The Dark End* came on telly we never had a moment. You can't imagine how it was. And time went so quickly. We kept meaning to invite Mum and Dad over, but they weren't keen on visiting the flat. We were never that sort of close family.'

'What do you mean by that?' Cath's voice was icy. 'Of course we were close. You'll make people think—'

Barry shouted an interruption. 'I'm sick of caring about what people sodding think, don't you understand that?' He gestured around him futilely. 'None of this shit would be happening now if we'd ignored people's nosy opinions.'

'How about your family doctor?' asked DC Scott severely. 'Cara must have been checked over, vaccinated and so on. She must be on the surgery records . . . Your wife even made out she was at the clinic with Cara on the day the kids were supposed to be missing.'

'We never took Cara to the doctor,' said Barry resentfully, using up the last of his self-control. 'We never had any reason. It's not like your first, when you're always worried.'

DC Scott laid his hands flat on Cath's well-polished table. 'Well you tell me, Barry. I'll leave it to you. Tell me who I can go to who can vouch for the fact that this child exists.'

Oh, dear. Poor Barry felt helpless. He had no

336

answer. Most of the neighbours were a transient lot. Directly next door lived a bony old man who they could hear coughing at night. He rarely left his flat. He wouldn't have noticed Cara. On the other side, it was hard to tell who the tenant was and who were his visitors . . . Sometimes there were three guys, sometimes a hard-faced woman came round, there were knocks on that door all through the night. Everyone knew the guys were pushers. With amazement Barry realized that Donny was the only person who could have reliably confirmed Cara's existence.

'Tell him, Barry,' urged Cath eventually, ignoring the bawling kids in the kitchen. Let Bill sort them out for once in his life. 'Go on, son, tell him.'

DC Scott's round face turned triumphant. 'You can't, Barry, can you? Why don't you admit it? That child is either dead and buried or she was never born alive. You made her up, you sent your sick notes to Griffin. How did you plan on doing the swap without a baby to barter with? Come on now, Barry, this has gone far enough. Was Cheryl too sick to know what you were up to? Did you use her too?'

'It was her,' screamed Cath Higgins, breaking down horribly and sending a chill of shock all the way down the policeman's back. Her fishy pale blue eyes started strangely from her head. 'If what you are saying is true it was her . . . that bitch. It was Cheryl. She needs locking up, she needs brain surgery, she needs sterilizing . . .'

Five minutes later Barry Higgins, incoherent, was in a police car heading for the station.

* * *

That night, Cheryl walked. Just walked. *Dead man walking*, is what they say when they lead a man to the electric chair. Well, she felt like that. She walked mindlessly through the railway arches and between the viaducts that converged towards the river, where the only sounds were her own feet and the deep sigh of tugs on the distant black water. The arches, as low and long as corridors and hung with black lichen, were a fitting gateway to the paved alleys of low, flat-fronted houses with broken windows and tottering chimneys and roofs of broken, fluted tiles.

There was a scuffling in the dark. She had a strong, heart-stopping feeling that she was being followed.

There was a yard behind barbed wire, the meeting place of one of London's most notorious razor gangs and a no-go area for the police, and here was a wall daubed with the names of some of London's most wanted thugs.

She kept whipping round to check the shadows, and the more she did that the more nervous she felt.

If she was being followed, who could it be? Some skulking flasher looking for his main chance? Some pisshead, shambling his own way home? An overenthusiastic photographer hoping she'd do something sly, worth snapping? Or someone obsessed by her public image, some violent deviant seeking the sort of painful revenge the letters had so often threatened?

There were people out there like that, Cheryl knew from experience. Cranks who ring up with false information, or confess to crimes they never committed. Nutters who send cards to the soaps, mourn the deaths of folks they don't know and cry at the weddings of strangers. Sad bastards who get off on vicious videos, who love nothing more than a victim, like prisoners who beat up paedophiles, glad there's someone alive worse than themselves.

Cheryl walked more quickly. Or could it be one of the gang who've got Cara? Someone trying to communicate. She slowed down. She waited. But the footsteps stopped when she stopped. The shadow slipped and then disappeared.

An ambulance siren blasted past and the silent fabric of night shivered. As she shuffled on through the streets, Cheryl's plight was brought home to her with a force that threatened to drain all her energy and leave her slumped against a wall, like so many losers she passed on the way.

Cheryl Higgins was a waste product.

What was the point of going on without Barry at her side? And now even her own mum thought she was a whore.

The public perception of Cheryl Higgins was that she was a wanton woman of untold evil.

Thou shalt not suffer a witch to live. That's what the Bible says.

A group of young blacks, five or six, loomed out of the distance and walked towards her purposefully. Did they know who she was? Were these kids out to get her, the woman everyone loved to hate? 'Cross the street,' Cheryl told herself. 'Don't even look in their direction.'

These lads were no more than sixteen years old, but they were big and angry. Two of the group peeled off and deliberately blocked her path. Cheryl just stood with her head down, awaiting her fate like a victim. The one in the baseball cap pushed her and Cheryl tottered and almost fell, but she righted herself and said nothing and they moved on.

Pity, perhaps?

She was not even worthy of their serious attention. But what might have happened to Cheryl if those kids had recognized her?

Because of her inner corruption, maybe this was what Cheryl had always deserved. A kind of leaden resignation began to dull the pain. Maybe her goals had been set too high. Perhaps the kids were better off without her. Perhaps Barry was relieved to have a reason to desert her. He must have wanted, so desperately, to escape from his situation.

Cheryl was nothing now.

She had no further to fall.

She thought she heard footsteps again. Turned. Stared. Stopped breathing. If only this night would pass, with its great sweep of darkness. The line between nightmare and reality was blurred. Cheryl glanced miserably from side to side. She had no idea of her whereabouts. She ought to be heading for home.

And then she remembered Donny, who had no home. Donny who died because of her. She had passed a funeral earlier today, in an untidy churchyard. The birds had been singing in the limes, fluttering the leaves as they hopped from branch to branch, and the voices of children came up from the market and a flawless summer sky arched over the open grave. There was only the vicar and two men in suits, their hats in their hands . . . a lonely send-off. For whom? In the silence Cheryl noticed many things: the strong scent of roses from a nearby grave, the overpowering smell of pine. She waited and watched. The mound of turned earth gave out a mouldy scent of its own.

She wept for Donny, as she'd done so many times.

If it wasn't for her and her stupid idea, her friend would be alive today.

Cara would be at home, safe.

Her children would be with her.

Was it booze that caused Donny's man to walk out on her? Did booze make her kids reject her? Did it make her turn her back on the world and inhabit this lonely subway of life, a loneliness intense and complete, avoiding civilization as a wild animal cringes from a light in the forest? Was she trying to deprive the world of its ability to hurt her, by pretending to be dead already? Donny must have been forty. Same as Mum. And yet she had looked thirty years older. People must have looked at her and said, 'Poor old cow.' Would they say the same about Cheryl one day?

The footsteps were getting closer . . .

And then, almost miraculously, she was back on her own territory again. Thank God there were no press around. She felt in her pocket for the flat key. How lonely and cold it would be inside, but she needed sleep, she felt exhausted. She crawled up the five flights of stairs and let herself in to her empty home. She gathered together the few belongings Barry had left behind, the children's small bits and pieces. She took them to bed and curled up round them, like she used to cuddle her Uncle Bulgaria when she was a child. So loved and handled, it had smelled of Persil, but tonight her

341

children's rejects smelled of loss and longing, baby powder and puke – such an evocative combination.

Thirty minutes gone.

First thing in the morning, Cheryl was going to find Barry.

She must make him listen, he had to give her a chance to explain. Zak Quinn meant nothing. She fought with the blanket. She kicked. She sweated, unable to rid herself of that palpitating fear. She sobbed pitifully in the darkness.

Why, why, why?

Two and a half hours gone, and still no sleep.

Someone banged hard on the door, but Cheryl ignored it.

What if Barry divorced her?

Won custody of the children?

Perhaps he would refuse ever to see her again.

This thought slayed her.

Four o'clock in the morning, no birds, but bumps and burps in the corridor outside mingled with the increasing traffic, the dawn chorus of the city. Doors banged. A woman shouted. Cheryl sat bolt upright in the darkness, and brought the *Mirror* article as close as she could to her eyes.

Six-thirty, and Cheryl gets up with the same permanent ache in her head. She can indulge it in only one way – by going to Harlow and begging forgiveness. But wait! My God, she nearly forgot – her first probation visit. If she misses that, they'll arrest her. She has to see the probation officer, but after that she'll go and find Barry.

This one sustaining thought gives her hope and stops despair from gathering round her.

TWENTY-TWO

There is no doubt about it now. Cheryl is being followed.

Someone was loitering outside the flat when she left it this morning. She managed to catch a glimpse of him as he scurried down the steps in front of her, but when she arrived at the ground floor he must have gone behind one of the pillars. Was it the press? But why would they hide? A garrulous lot, they would rather step out in front and block her path completely, yelling questions as they flashed their cameras. No, this was a more secretive business. This was obsessive behaviour. This was the man who'd pursued her last night during that desolate walk to nowhere. This man's presence was no sudden impulse, no spur-of-the-moment attack. Pale now, and sweating with fear in spite of the fact that it was broad daylight, the hairs on the back of her neck stood on end, and again she felt that chill breath of terror.

If he wanted to hurt her, why was he waiting? Why not get it over with?

He'd be a hero in the eyes of the public. Probably get off with a warning.

She tried to throw him off by backtracking, taking her life in her hands and crossing busy roads suddenly, disappearing into shops, stopping at the café where she sometimes used to sit with Donny and share a cup of tea and a bun. She chose a table with a view of the window. In order to lessen some of the fear, she needed to see him, she needed to know he was not just a shadow or an illusion created by her distress.

She managed to glance sideways without raising her head. A man she had seen strolling past the window wandered by a second time. She half expected him to come in. She sat pretending to read the article she carried with her everywhere, Zak Quinn's titillating version of that humiliating night. She didn't need to read it. She knew every word off by heart, every crude description of her naked body, all the come-ons she was meant to have made, every groan, all the sex talk. Her fascination with it was awful. Out of the corner of her eye, Cheryl saw the guy in the denim shirt cross in front of the café window again.

This time he paused and looked in before moving on.

She was fiddling with a sugar cube. If only Donny was here. How she missed her. Donny used to empty the bowl, stuff her pockets with cubes and then make a start on the neighbouring tables . . .

Then the man crossed the street and pretended to be waiting at the bus stop. He was still there after the bus came and went.

Cheryl was torn. Should she get up and run, and grab him and quickly tell him she didn't care, he could do what he liked, she probably deserved it?

But before she could think it out he was gone, and five minutes later she had to leave to keep her appointment with Miss Sweet.

She twisted her way between cars and buses, she changed direction, she dodged into side streets until she thought she had lost him. At the entrance to the probation office she stood in the foyer, hid to one side of the door and looked back outside, against the sunshine.

She staunched a stab of terrible fear. She was friendless. She was vulnerable.

He knew where she lived. Of course he did. So did fifteen million others. If only she had money she could get away, take a train, lose herself, pay for protection, but all she could realistically do in her desperate situation was persuade the authorities that her fears were not attention-seeking behaviour or an attempt to stir up more publicity.

She saw him.

Across the street from the probation office.

Half inside a greengrocer's shop, pretending to test the grapes.

He was about five foot ten inches tall, about twenty-five years of age. He had reddish hair and a young, open face and was dressed all in denim, even his boots and a small rucksack that hung off one shoulder. It was bunched, oddly, under his arm, as if there was something important in there which needed extra care. Cheryl took in every detail, in case she needed to describe him to the police.

In her fright she nearly called the receptionist over to get a look at the guy herself, to ask her to call the cops, to lock the door, *to protect her*.

But no, no, she mustn't do that. That would only

confirm her instability and love of drama they'd made so much of. She must wait until she was in Miss Sweet's office, and then she must tell it calmly and sensibly: no panic, no hysteria, just a careful summing-up of the facts until Miss Sweet, surely an intelligent woman, was convinced of the danger.

Many phantastical apparitions occur to persons suffering from a melancholy disease, especially to women, as is shown by their dreams and visions. And the reason for this, as physicians know, is that women's souls are by nature far more easily and lightly impressionable than men's souls.

                                        The Malleus Maleficarum

Miss Sweet has only just put the phone down when Cheryl knocks at her office door. She has received her instructions. She knows she must handle this carefully.

Cheryl is mad. There is no baby. There's even a chance that the Higginses might be quizzed over a suspicious death. The authorities are concerned that the public hounding of this woman could well result in physical violence. A custodial sentence is not an option, but it is imperative that Cheryl be detained, for convenience's sake, until she can be dealt with properly.

Cheryl's words come out in a rush, so eager is she to persuade Miss Sweet that there is a man outside who has been stalking her for at least two days.

She listens intently for several minutes, and then Olivia Sweet leans back in her probation-officer chair of hard canvas and regards her new client across the table. Cheryl is certainly very distressed.

346

This is Cheryl's first appointment, and Olivia is quite surprised that she has turned up at all, after all the scandalous stuff she's been reading. She might as well go along with the girl – play for time as she was advised. 'Now why would anyone want to follow you?'

Puffed up with anxiety, Cheryl gasps, 'I dunno. I just don't know. But somebody's been following me, and it's either a psycho who's after my blood, or something to do with Cara's disappearance. Whoever it is I'm scared, I really believe they might kill me.'

Olivia's voice softens slightly. She regards the girl with startled interest. 'I know you're under terrible pressure at the moment, Cheryl, and I do understand how hard it is for you—'

'No, no, you're not listening. *Please . . .*'

'Cheryl,' continues Miss Sweet carefully, looking uncomfortable in the heat, although the window is open and she is wearing a cool, sleeveless blouse, prettily embroidered, blue on white. 'Why would anyone want to do that?'

Cheryl is suddenly aware of the delicate way Miss Sweet is handling this interview. 'There are lots of reasons,' she says quite simply.

'Really?' Miss Sweet pauses, consulting Cheryl's file and clearing her throat, but not before Cheryl notices several newspaper articles that are clipped underneath the weight of white sheets. So she's read them. Miss Sweet goes on quickly, 'Cheryl, now listen to me carefully. Has anyone suggested you see a doctor?'

Cheryl reddens. 'You mean a shrink? You think I'm barking?' She has messed this up completely, getting upset when she meant to stay cool.

'No,' Miss Sweet says slowly and meaningfully, leaning across the table and stretching out a bangled arm. 'No, I am suggesting no such thing. But you have been through such a stressful time, faced so many troubles, that I do believe you might need to talk to somebody . . .'

'A shrink. Like I said.' Cheryl pales. 'I've seen one already.' How she hates them. How she mistrusts them. And thoughts of childhood visits to Annie, who was sectioned in that grim, closed ward, come back uninvited. Those few visits she made to St Hugh's with her social worker, Sue, will never leave the locked cupboard of her memory, and she has never found the key to rid herself of them.

That shiver of fearful anticipation as they waited.

The presentiment of coming pain.

The slack-jawed faces of the utterly solitary, the Mogadon shuffles, the empty eyes. Each time they visited, Mum was fatter as the doctors gradually changed her with drugs, formed her like a plasticine person into the woman she was to become.

Miss Sweet detects alarm from Cheryl's lost expression. 'And not just because I think you are using these peculiar ideas as a defence mechanism. Unable to deal with the loss of Cara, it is quite understandable that you have gone into some sort of denial.' Her glib tone lowers into one of trustworthy confidentiality, as if she is swapping some red-hot gossip. 'Naturally it is easier to fantasize . . .'

Cheryl listens to this open-mouthed. She stands up abruptly and goes back to the opened window. The woman has got to believe her.

It is imperative.

This is too real.

She leans out of the window as far as she can. 'He's still there,' she urges Miss Sweet. 'The guy who followed me here. He's still there. If you come and stand where I am, you can see his shadow under that tree.'

Miss Sweet sighs heavily. And stays put. This is beginning to look more worrying than she was led to believe. Mental health is not her forte, but it doesn't take a Master's in psychology to recognize insanity when it's staring you in the face.

Cheryl returns to the table. Her heart is beating fast, but she manages to speak as calmly as if she is discussing something impersonal. 'You're saying I'm imagining this. You're saying I need help, aren't you?'

'But why would anyone be following you? And why would they want to hurt you?'

Dear God, isn't it obvious? Cheryl fights down her desperate fury, feeling her new-found strength ebb away. 'What planet are you living on? You've read the articles, you've seen the pictures. There are people out there who feel it's their duty to punish women like me. And now Barry's gone it's much easier for these cranks to act out their sickness. If you'd read some of the letters we got, if you'd heard some of the stuff they shout, if you'd seen their faces . . .'

Miss Sweet's face settles itself into one long, worried frown. Cheryl needs help. Specialist help. And quickly.

There is a peculiar edge to her voice. 'Why don't you calm down, Cheryl? Relax. We can deal with your stalker later. And I do believe you. Really.

349

And I intend to do something about it. But in the meantime, why don't we talk, let me see, I know. You could tell me more about Cara.'

'About Cara?'

'Yes. I want to know more about your baby. I think it might help.'

This case is high priority because of its risk of negative publicity.

The dilemma Olivia is faced with this morning is very, very serious.

All along the experts have suggested that Cheryl might be suffering from Munchausen's. So far, nobody has had a chance to investigate this matter further. But now Cheryl is demonstrating such disturbing symptoms she could well be a danger to herself or others. Particularly if she finds out that the search for Cara has been called off.

And the authorities need to know very quickly if Cheryl's baby ever existed. For that she has to be detained. But the proper channels are the best way to go in this very public arena.

Miss Sweet twists her made-up face into an expression of kindness. 'Tell me what Cara looks like, Cheryl.'

Baffled, in spite of her resolution to stay calm and collected, Cheryl's voice rises, cold with anger. 'You haven't been listening to a word . . .'

'You are wrong. I have listened.' Are the girl's pupils distended, or is that just fear on her face? 'But you are here now, and you are safe. Nobody is going to hurt you. No doubt the police will give you protection after hearing the accusations you are making. But for now, why don't we just sit quietly and talk about your children?'

Cheryl looks blankly back at Miss Sweet. 'It's not me who needs help, it's you,' she says rudely. 'If you think I'm going to sit here chatting with all this chaos going on . . .'

'Why are you so frightened to talk about Cara?'

'Frightened? What the hell d'you mean?'

Olivia Sweet carries on gently. 'Some people, Cheryl, when they've been very hurt—'

'I don't get any of this. What's going on?' Cheryl breaks off, frowning. 'Why are you talking in that strange way, as if I'm a dopehead? I've never touched drugs.'

Cheryl is highly charged. Frightened. Angry and bewildered. What if she went and did something silly, and the press discovered that Olivia Sweet had seen her client this very morning?

And taken no action?

Of such stuff are nightmares made.

Thank God she had been warned, and her responsibility officially removed.

'All right, all right Cheryl. What you have been saying to me is very serious indeed. And as I said at the start, I think I must take it further.' Miss Sweet clasps her hands in her lap in an effort to stay calm and give nothing away. 'But that involves several telephone calls. Would you mind waiting in the next room until I can get this sorted out? I will bring you a cup of tea. Cigarettes? Ah, yes, I think Mandy smokes, the copy-typist in reception. I will be as quick as I can. Be patient. And hopefully before very long we can get this sad business sorted out.'

Thank God, thinks poor deluded Cheryl, *thank God for that*.

*   *   *

Wondering what is holding things up, waiting for the law to arrive, hoping the nutter is still outside so she can lead them to him directly, Cheryl waits for over an hour in the small room next to Miss Sweet's office. Miss Sweet brings her a coffee as promised, and Mandy the copy-typist is generous with her cigarettes. At least now she feels safe. At last something is going to be done. Miss Sweet, although unconvinced, is worried enough to take action.

She has no ashtray. She uses the flowerpot.

The coffee is bitter, not like Nescafé.

The double-glazed window is locked; she tries it. She wants to check if the man is still there, and get some fresh air into the stuffy room.

The footsteps are swift and determined. When the door flies open, Cheryl leaps up and a man clad in white comes to stand beside her. A male nurse from the hospital, although she doesn't know that yet. The other two men are both in suits, and follow Olivia Sweet inside. She closes the door behind them.

'So this is Cheryl,' says one of the men in a voice you would use to a backward child.

'Cheryl,' says Miss Sweet soothingly, justifying her actions, 'we don't want you to be alarmed, we don't want any trouble, we're all here to help you, remember that. This is Dr Franklin and this is Dr Hart, and they are both doctors who would like a few words.'

In her first flush of terror Cheryl backs against the window.

'Now, why don't you just come and sit down? Nobody's going to hurt you, I promise.'

Shrugging helplessly, Cheryl obeys, and one of

352

the doctors takes the opposite chair. She wants to break into furious tears, but knows that will not help her. She must try to stay calm and unruffled, but how, how? She's a beast in a trap. She gazes at the sunlight streaming through the window, hoping that might dilute the terror she knows must show in her eyes.

With a studied carelessness, watching her narrowly, Dr Hart asks her to repeat the fears she confided to Miss Sweet.

She feels the rush of blood to her face. She has to gulp twice before she can speak. Is this what she fears it might be? Are these people really here to diagnose her as insane, so that they can forcibly take her against her will and imprison her in some hospital ward?

'Sod off,' says Cheryl. 'I'm not saying anything.'

Miss Sweet's tone is falsely cheerful and ingratiating. 'Now Cheryl, please don't take this attitude. I've explained to the doctors how frightened you are and that you feel someone's going to hurt you. They know all about that. So it's up to you to help them decide what best treatment they can offer you.'

Cheryl stares but refuses to answer. Her brain is revving like a hot engine in an effort to find the right response. She tries to speak, but her voice won't come. She clears her throat and it is anger which finally blows out the words she needs. 'Fuck off. Leave me alone. I'm not going anywhere. I'm staying here.'

Miss Sweet gives Dr Hart a knowing and meaningful look.

The room seems full of watching eyes.

With her heart no more than a sickly blob, Cheryl

353

is very aware of the man in white standing directly behind her.

Dr Hart leans forward gently. 'You see, Cheryl, we are all afraid you might do something you might regret.'

'Like what?' Cheryl demands.

Dr Hart shrugs. 'If we knew that, we would be in a far happier position. But the fact is, we do not know, and I doubt very much if you know either. But we are all very aware how much strain you have been under lately.' He speaks in low and reverent tones, feeling it incumbent upon himself to gather the solemnity of the room between his folded hands and express it in voice, movement and word.

Cheryl's eyes turn to Miss Sweet's, which are all solicitude and sympathy. How could the woman have betrayed her like this? How could she have persuaded two doctors that she is so deranged she needs to be restrained? How is that possible? There are lunatics wandering the streets, the prisons are full of dangerous psychos, there are schizophrenics clamouring for treatment in hospitals all over the land, and yet these experts have decided that Cheryl Higgins is more in need of their care and attention than any of those.

This is madness. But not hers.

And suddenly she sees that whatever she does, whatever she says, will be useless. Their decision has already been made. If she fights them off she will lose control, and another nightmare will be made real.

So Cheryl keeps her manner subdued when the nurse asks for her arm and dabs it with cotton wool before inserting the syringe.

'Good girl, good girl.' Like she is a dog.

Stunned and stilled, she follows the group of three to the waiting car. Miss Sweet peels away in the reception area.

And is it only Cheryl who notices the red-haired young man with the rucksack standing on the pavement, watching their departure?

Little is said on the short journey which was quick, quiet and businesslike, but she feels the eyes of the doctors on her all the time. Dr Hart and the nurse sit in the back, either side of her, like jailors. Dr Franklin sits in the front with the driver. There is no way she can get out.

But it is when she arrives at St Hugh's, so massive and merciless, that the real hell begins.

TWENTY-THREE

We know from experience that the daughters of
witches are always suspected of similar practices,
as imitators of their mothers' crimes; and that indeed
the whole of a witch's progeny is infected.

The Malleus Maleficarum

Perhaps insanity runs in the family.

It looks pretty much like it, because here is Annie
Watts at her worst, approaching the Higginses'
house in Harlow, determined to have things out
with Barry once and for all.

And what is more, *where is her daughter*?

She went to the Harold Wilson Building yesterday and spent some time hammering and banging,
but either Cheryl wasn't opening the door (which
was doubtful, to her own mother), or she'd gone.
Done a runner. There was no point asking the
neighbours, the old man and the druggies.

Now Annie is after some answers.

She has read some pretty grim things in the
papers – the source could only be Barry.

This particular area of Harlow is inhabited
mostly by older people with standards, net curtains

and no children. The houses are all of a pattern. They stand in pairs, hiding their secrets, presenting a pretty face to the world. The gardens are carefully tended: here is a wishing well with a gnome eternally fishing; here is a miniature picket fence painted in brilliant white; there is a picturesque rockery with wheelbarrows full of busy Lizzies trailing in rainbow colours between the miniature pansies and petunias. And the cars parked outside, though not new, are shampooed every Sunday and maintained in pristine condition, as are the lawns, as green as groves in the very best public parks.

No broken toys in the gardens here; no chained-up dogs; no boarded-up windows. No burned-out cars or black skid marks mar the smooth, unpotholed tarmac.

At the gate outside number forty-one Annie pauses. Loud screams and raised voices come straight from the door which bears the house name, *Ambiance*, on a piece of polished wood, surrounded by a circle of glossily painted holly.

'But I'm just not having this, Barry,' storms the tight voice of Catherine Higgins.

'Calm down, Mum, *calm down*, if you shout at them they get worse.' And that's Barry, Annie knows his voice.

'But what am I expected to do? And now the police coming round with their accusations, parking the car outside my house, hauling you down there for questioning.'

'You're not expected to do anything. For God's sake, I said I'd cope and I will.'

'Oh, yes? And what if they lock you up next time? What if they fit you up for murder?'

'For Christ's sake, Mum, shut up.'

Annie bangs at the door, ignoring the knocker and using the flats of both her large hands.

'Now what?' comes a quieter voice from inside. And a curtain is shifted, eyes peer out and come face-to-face with Big Annie.

'*Where is my sodding daughter?*' she yells, and two more curtains in the close are twitched. 'And how dare you spread those ugly lies, suggesting she's a dirty cow, sex mad, a pain in the bum, a head case. Oh, yeah, oh, yeah, I've read every bloody word you've been saying, Barry bleeding Higgins.'

'But I never—'

'Get rid of her,' mutters Cath inside, falling back limply onto her floral sofa. She can just about cope with the daughter. The mother is another kettle of fish. 'I don't care how you do it, but get rid of that woman, Barry, *now.*'

For one blissful moment the children fall silent, shocked by the ferocity of the pounding and the ribald voice from outside.

Since the moment they arrived at her door, Cath has regretted her offer. My goodness. It is so true what she and her neighbours are always saying, and those acquaintances the Higginses meet up with while shopping on a Saturday down at the Harvey Centre: kids these days are out of control, and it is the fault of the parents.

They are no longer taught respect, they have no idea how to behave. If you smack them you are accused of child abuse, if you raise your voice you are traumatizing them for the rest of their lives. And it's so typical, Barry forever telling them, 'Cher

358

doesn't do it that way. Cher likes to turn it into a game.' And, 'Mum, it's easier and quicker if we tidy up when they've gone to bed. Victor's only three, he can't be expected to put each toy away after he's finished with it.'

'You did,' Cath kept protesting. 'You always put things away. You were made to,' while treading over bits of Lego, plastic cars, pull-along dogs, and all strewn around so anyone could break their necks, no respect for their possessions, thrown around the room at whim, it is quite outrageous.

And as for bedtimes, they don't exist.

'Children need a routine. They like to know where they stand. And that is why discipline is so important,' Cath goes on. And on.

Well, she has to try.

For the children's sake.

What sort of adults will they be? They haven't yet been taught about the Queen. And she doubts if they know what a church is, let alone God.

Bill, of course, has gone into himself. Hides behind the paper. Turns up the sport. His back is so bad, or so he makes out, he can't do anything positive to help.

Barry is constantly plagued by the press. He is rarely quoted correctly. They turn his words round and write what they like, whatever he says. And that, according to Cath, is just as well, because he still won't say a word against that Cheryl. The fool. It gets worse and worse. Now, astonishingly, they are making out that he has been sending ransom notes, that he is involved in some scurrilous business over a baby who never existed. As if. All Cheryl's doing . . .

Barry, incredulous, still in shock, roars back at these accusations like a wounded lion, but he is helpless in the face of the expert opinions being bandied about, and the fact that there is no record of Cara's birth. The abandonment of the search for the child has affected her son's senses. Sometimes Cath hears him up in the night, pacing, down in the kitchen. The walls of *Ambiance* are thin, so she knows that his outward calm belies his inner turmoil. But as Cath told him last night, 'You cried wolf once too often. And this is what happens. You can't really blame them for taking this line.'

He shouted at her. Said things. It was awful. Really awful.

Even she and Bill have been interviewed by the local telly. Every day they tune in hoping to see themselves – nothing yet. All the camera seemed to be interested in was their reaction to the kidnap, to Cath's great disappointment. She could have contributed some colourful opinions of her notorious daughter-in-law. Perhaps the film is being stored for some more appropriate time – like when or if little Cara is finally returned to the bosom of her loving family.

But therein lies the rub.

She and Bill were quite happy to welcome Barry back into their home. I mean, the circumstances were such that he needed a secure base, someone to help mind the kids, a permanent contact number from which to keep track of police progress and a more pleasant backdrop for the cameras than that dreadful Harold Wilson Building.

But neither Cath nor Bill had imagined that

Victor and Scarlett would have such a disastrous effect on their lives.

It is virtually impossible to have people round.

Her last coffee morning had proved a disaster: conversation interrupted, coffees balanced on nervous knees as the kids shrieked and banged round the floor using the occasional tables for boats. When she suggested Barry put them to bed for an hour or two, 'a little rest, that's what you used to have, gave me a break in the day', he told her that would mess up the night. They wouldn't be tired. They wouldn't sleep.

They had the neighbours round for drinks so they could watch the England match together. You could tell what Rowena and Nigel were thinking. They missed every goal that was scored. They even missed the penalty. The kids were up and down like yo-yos, spoiled with cups of tea and biscuits. 'You are encouraging them,' she told Barry. 'Of course they're going to get up when they know you're going to let them do whatever they like. And pamper them.'

'What they need is a good smack,' was all Bill was capable of saying before turning the sound up once again so no-one could hear anything at all because of the distortion.

Some interviews Barry gives pay money, but where is it going, Cath would like to know? She knows he has opened a bank account, and she had rummaged through the things in his bedroom to see how much was accumulating there. She found nothing. He must carry the statements on him. And when she came out and asked him outright, he looked sheepish and muttered secretively, 'I'm putting it by for a rainy day.'

A rainy day?

And here they all are, surviving on social security, child benefit, Bill's disability allowance and Cath's meagre earnings from the council canteen.

Perhaps Barry ought to be approaching Harlow Council for a house for himself and the children. Yes, there is a waiting list, but surely in Barry's case the authorities could make an exception. Maybe hold back some teenage mother, a couple of queers, a family from hell, maybe get their priorities right for once in their lives.

Cath had mentioned this to Barry, but he had been evasive. Put that look on his face again, that rebellious look that locked her out when all she was doing, when all she had ever done, was look out for his welfare. But surely Barry isn't planning to stay with her and Bill for much longer? He is a single parent now, and as such has rights. Soon, when the present crisis has died down, surely he will apply for a divorce and Cheryl will be out of his life for ever.

The washing machine churns endlessly.

The Hoover is at full stretch.

The kitchen floor needs resealing.

And the sofa covers must go for a clean.

And now, to cap it all, that vulgar woman is at the door. Ranting and raving in her loud, crude way so all the world can hear her.

And where did that camera come from?

How did the press know Annie was coming? The awareness that this is being filmed will only egg the harridan on, like mother like daughter, anything to get on the telly.

Barry nervously opens the door.

'You bastard,' screeches Big Annie.

'Annie, calm down . . .'

'Don't you tell me to sodding calm down, you lump of shit, you scrotum.' She pushes her large face towards his so that they are virtually nose to nose. 'Come on, come on, you piece of piss, come on out here and tell everyone just what you think you're up to.'

Barry holds up his hands like buffers. Annie smacks them down with her huge ham fists. 'Listen to me, please, this isn't the way,' Barry begins . . . but it's hopeless.

She gathers him up by his T-shirt, hauls him along the path, kicks open the gate and throws him into the road. As Barry rights himself, the man with the camera zooms in.

'That's right, that's it,' shouts Big Annie, apoplectic and purple in the face. 'Here he is, the wanker, get a good look at him. Not quite so cocky now, are you, matey? You little toe-rag. You scum.'

Barry just stands there, limp, like prey, like a stunned impala waiting for the predator to spring.

While Cath, still indoors, nose pressed against the window, turns to regard Bill with contempt. 'Well, you're his father, are you just going to sit there? Aren't you going to help him? That woman could kill him, you know.'

'I didn't want to leave you with the kids,' is Bill's feeble answer.

'Get out there,' says Cath, 'or believe me, I will.' But Cath has no intention of putting herself in such danger. Annie would eat her for breakfast, and besides, there's neighbours watching.

'Tell him,' Annie nudges Barry, and almost

knocks him for six. 'Go on, go on, tell the man what you've done with my daughter.' And she turns her son-in-law round so he faces the camera again.

'I don't know what you mean.'

'Don't give me that,' warns Annie.

'Annie,' Barry splutters, 'honest to God, I don't know anything about Cheryl.'

'But you know enough to slag her off at every God-given opportunity. You turd. You tosser.'

'I haven't.'

By now the neighbours have trickled out into their tidy gardens. They hover beside their water-falls, they study the creeper in their crazy paving. However, their doors remain open and their postures suggest they are poised for flight should flight become necessary.

'As far as I know, she's in the flat.'

'She didn't answer the door to me.'

Some of the neighbours titter, but quietly. Who, in their right minds, would open their door to Big Annie?

'Annie, Annie,' pleads Barry, cringing, 'you've got it all wrong, and the kids are in there hearing all this.'

'Good. I'm glad,' roars Annie. 'They need to know. They're not too young to understand what their tossing father has done, how he has savaged their mother . . . And as far as you and that tight-arsed cow of a mother of yours go, the fact that the kids are in your care is a right laugh, a right bloody rip off.'

Inside *Ambiance*, Bill bravely dials nine-nine-nine.

Annie, beside herself now, looks around her and

364

rips a standard rose out of its little patch of earth. Frail and whippy, it can only recently have been planted. Along with its supportive bamboo cane it makes a handy weapon, and she raises it high in her great arms and brings it down with all her strength again and again on Barry's head and neck, until he is beaten to the floor. 'Take that and that and that, you bugger!' The neighbours are finally forced into the road in their bedroom slippers to try to restrain this devilish woman from committing murder in the close. From tainting its reputation further.

But the man with the camera does not intervene. He merely steps back and films on, saying nothing.

Back at the station, Annie rails on. 'You bleeding lot, you're as bleeding bad,' she screams as her handbag is emptied onto the desk.

The duty sergeant sniffs. A worn pair of tights. An open lipstick, shredded with bits of tobacco and old face powder. A pot of rouge gone to jelly. An assortment of tissues and old receipts. A plastic purse with the zip gone containing two pounds twenty. A box of Lil-lets, a rain hood ... And so the motley collection goes on.

'You can't charge me,' yells Annie.

'We can and we will,' says the sergeant. 'Assault, for a start.'

'Sod you,' roars Annie, making a break for it. 'What about my grandchild? What are you sodding doing about her?'

'And resisting arrest,' says the sergeant calmly, while the two constables grip her arms more firmly.

*   *   *

Inside *Ambiance*, Cath is in tears. 'We can't have this,' she sobs, 'we just can't have it.'

Barry, white-faced and still shocked, admits, 'I should have known she'd come. It's funny Cheryl hasn't been round by now.'

'You should have gone and been checked out at the hospital, Barry,' Cath cries abjectly into her handkerchief. 'You should have done what they advised. Who knows what internal damage she's done.'

'I'm OK,' he tells her, seeing to the whimpering kids. 'Just shocked and a few cuts and bruises.'

'They should lock her up, people like her, and throw away the key,' says Bill from the kitchen, filling the kettle.

'And you, you weren't any help,' Cath accuses her husband. 'You just sat there and watched it all happen.' She dabs angrily at her eyes.

'I called the police,' says Bill defensively. 'I couldn't have done anything to help out there with my back. What could I do? I'm disabled. I'm a cripple.'

'And loving every minute of it,' cries Cath before she can help herself.

But Scarlett's screams bring an instant halt to a conversation which could have proved damaging. Instantly Barry is at the child's side, picking her up, rocking her as if she is the only one affected by this afternoon's dreadful debacle. Cath's nerves are close to snapping, but nobody thinks about her, oh, no, she is supposed to be able to cope. The children are quite obviously the only ones who matter.

'She was frightened,' says Barry, observing his

366

mother's impatient face folding in. 'That was her granny out there. She's fond of Annie, they both are.'

'Don't be so silly, Barry,' snaps Cath. 'Stop fussing. Fuss, fuss, fuss. They were in here all the time with me, they saw nothing. And they're far too young to understand what goes on between adults.'

'Well,' says Bill, sensing the tension and coming through with a tray. 'More grist to the mill, I suppose. Best to look at it that way, I say. The newspapers will be interested to hear of this latest little escapade.' He puts the tray down and rubs his hands. 'It all adds up, doesn't it, son?'

'Don't put it there, you fool,' snaps Cath. 'Move that tray or they'll have it over.'

So when the phone rings with a shriek, it merely adds to the chaos.

Bill can't get up. He reckons he's fixed. Lifting the heavy tray has worsened his back. Cath is in no state to talk to anyone. Barry is forced to abandon Scarlett, but the child follows him through to the hall, clinging pathetically to his jeans.

Cath speedily thrusts a piece of white chocolate (the only chocolate she will allow in the house) straight into Victor's mouth, lest the child set up a racket and thus prevent her from hearing what might be going on. He does this so often, she suspects that his behaviour is possibly deliberate. A learned response to the telephone. A cunning bid for instant attention.

But Barry is disappointing. Apart from saying who he is, his only response is yes, I see. Cath senses this could be important – his voice is low, his back is to the door, the old familiar ploys he used when he was a boy and out of control.

When the phone goes down there is a pause before he returns to the room.

'Well?' asks Cath. 'What was that all about?'

He seems to consider before he answers. 'That was Olivia Sweet. It's Cheryl,' he starts, with a shutdown expression.

'What has that woman done now?'

'They've taken her into hospital.'

'What's she done? Broken her leg trying to pose? Arranging herself into one of those pornographic positions?'

'Not that sort of hospital,' says Barry quietly, rescuing his cup and putting it on the mantelpiece, right out of the children's reach. 'She's been committed. They rushed her in. Two doctors. They think she could be a danger to herself or to others.'

'Well, that sums it up in a nutshell,' Cath snorts. 'Best place for her. And Barry, here's a tissue. Please wipe the arm of the sofa, Victor has sicked up the chocolate and it looks like his orange juice, too.'

TWENTY-FOUR

If Sebby had realized that his and Kate's discoveries at St Cathcrine's House would have led to this further attack on the Higginses, he would have kept his mouth shut. If he had hoped that their findings would lead to the hapless Cheryl receiving the help she needed, he was badly mistaken. So much for good intentions. Instead of that, the plot has thickened, with police and press immediately assuming that this couple's evil knows no bounds, that this was their plan all along . . . Five hundred thousand pounds in exchange for a child who never existed.

'It's true what they say,' he said to Kate, so distressed over his part in this trauma that he could hardly discuss it rationally – his spectacles were all steamed up, 'once you've been branded by the tabloids your number's up, there's no mercy.'

Kate insisted they try to help Cheryl, but what the hell could they do?

Today Sebby and Leo, flies on the wall once again, are filming a series on children's homes, but Sebby senses a lack of commitment to this project on Leo's part . . . Odd for Leo, who's normally so single-minded. It's probably because it's run-of-the-mill stuff with not much room for manipulation.

'You can't blame yourselves, either of you,' says Leo matter-of-factly, seated at the refectory table in the home's expansive, comfortable kitchen while Sebby stirs the coffee in two large homely mugs. Everything in here is designed to compensate for the lack of the real thing.

'Dammit, Leo, you know Barry and Cheryl. You know they are incapable of carrying out this kind of charade – ransom notes, a safe place for Cara, holding out against intensive interrogation . . . and that's without persuading a group of thugs to snatch the baby. OK, they hid the kids for two weeks, but that was stupid, desperate behaviour and it went disastrously wrong. If Donny had lived, their plan would have worked – Scarlett and Victor would have come home unharmed, and public opinion would have softened towards them. But this . . .'

Leo rolls a cigarette and licks the paper slowly before he gives his considered answer. 'So why did they mislead everyone by saying three kids were missing, not two? Why would they include Cara, unless they meant to extend the deception?'

'Because everyone assumed that they had three kids, and they didn't want to get into the business of explaining away an abortion, or worse, a death which they hadn't reported.'

'OK. OK. But that would have come out in the end, when Donny brought the children back and left them at Paddington station as planned. Everyone would have wanted to know where Cara was.'

'That's precisely what makes Kate and I think

that Cara probably died after birth, and they were too scared to report it because of the publicity. That's the awful tragedy. And Kate believes they were going to keep up the lie about the lost baby as a way of getting out of a hole.'

Leo reaches across the table into the ample biscuit tin and picks out a chocolate digestive. Sebby has time to wonder what sort of father he is. It doesn't seem to interfere with his work pattern. He still works the long hours he used to in spite of the fact that he has a new son. They probably have an au pair or a nanny – Sophie can well afford it. 'So where's that baby's body?' demands Leo. 'Oh, come on, Sebby, this is so far-fetched,' he says contemptuously. 'Two children safely returned by person or persons unknown, but the baby disappears for ever? Pretty convenient, isn't it?'

Sebby will not be budged. If only he knew the whole truth. So far, he and Kate have been floundering around in conjecture, yet still believing firmly in the innocence of the Higginses. 'Why not? It's a fairly simple device when you think about it. Nobody could ever prove otherwise, unless the baby's body was found. Either that, or Cheryl was driven out of her mind by the constant harassment and actually convinced herself of Cara's existence.'

'Oh? And Barry went along with that? Knowing that, at the end of the day, the truth was bound to come out? Come off it, Seb. Get real. Those two knew exactly what they were doing. They're in this up to their necks and they've been caught red-handed, all thanks to Kate and her female intuition.'

'And now they've put her away.'

'For her own good,' says Leo. 'If your theory is right, she's in the right place. She's a head case. Maybe they'll sort her out.'

'Do you never worry that we caused all this?'

'Do I hell,' says Leo. 'Cheryl was always the perfect victim. She did it to herself.'

The hospital is Victorian, the next on the Government's list for demolition with no replacement: the land it stands on will be used for housing and the medical, geriatric and surgical patients will be transferred. Those in the psychiatric unit will either be sent elsewhere or scattered like ashes within the community in bedsits, hostels or B&Bs.

Although poor Cheryl is confused because of the drugs they've rammed into her, her brain is still conscious enough never to forget her shattering nerviness, or the bed of fresh linen waiting for her, one in a line of ten, in a room with cream-coloured walls and a fish tank in the far corner.

They order her to undress.

They never bother about a screen.

They never mention what they are doing.

They bundle her over, naked, and push a needle that feels like a skewer into the muscle at the top of her thigh.

She squirms and yells with the pain.

They hold her down. They spread her legs to do the internal.

The male nurse with the rough hands says he is checking to see if she's brought something danger-ous with her, razor blades, drugs, scissors, what-ever. He checks her mouth and her hair, in the same way they used to grade slaves for their value. He

372

takes samples on a spatula. Testing for drugs, he informs her.

She can't move.

She feels so small.

Fear grips her heart like a fist, but Cheryl refuses to break down and reward them with the gift of her utter helplessness. She disinherits her body.

The world as she knows it is falling away from her. The high windows are barred. The doors are locked. But Cheryl knows nothing of this as she slips into grey unconsciousness and sleeps for over twelve hours. When she wakes up, her clothes and her handbag are gone and inside her locker is an old lady's nylon nightdress and a pink dressing gown.

With the same sick terror in her heart, she dresses and makes her way to the day room. She approaches a nurse. There has been a mistake. With a casual lift of the eyebrows the nurse consigns her to her fate. 'It's nothing to do with me,' she says. 'You'll have to wait till you see the doctor.'

Don't panic. Mustn't panic. 'But when will I see the doctor?'

'How do I know?' the nurse tells her coldly, but she takes a quick, sharp interest in her. Even in here she is notorious. 'They'll let you know when they're ready.'

As she passes the window on the way to the day room she sees the man who had been following her sitting on a seat in the hospital grounds. There is no mistaking him, his red hair, his denim, his bag. She shivers but says nothing.

She goes to sit in a plastic chair, one of the many in the brightly lit room arranged to face a television set. The television is set high in the wall with what looks like a child-safe fireguard around it. Cheryl knows this place well. She has been here before. This is where they kept Annie.

The food would arrive already cut up. She would have to eat it with a spoon.

She knows when she is beaten.

Cheryl's eyes dart this way and that but, anxious to give no trouble, determined to show no emotion at all, her agonized cry of 'set me free' stays un-uttered.

Will she be kept in here for ever? Will she ever again feel a soft sofa or a cushioned chair? The windows are so tightly closed she is cut off from the sounds of life – birdsong, the wind in the trees, the laughter and movement of normal people. She obediently accepts her cocktail of drugs while her eyes stare into her own private thoughts. If she does not accept her medication meekly, she knows well the kind of violence that will follow. She saw it many times in the days when she visited Mum, how patients would be manhandled down to the ward, outnumbered and defeated.

She takes little notice of those around her, avoiding them with frightened eyes because she knows them of old. They people her dreams, and have done since childhood. They have no expectation of life and no thoughts of death. They are lucky. They are zombies.

Done with the brotherhood of man.

But then . . .

It must be him. She can't mistake Leo. *And he is coming towards her*.

Oh, no, let him not see her here, not like this, not

Leo, and anyway, how did he know? It must have been Barry, who else but him? Cheryl's heart sinks even further.

But despite herself, her eyes brighten. Out of the guys in the two-man crew, Leo was the comic, the sexy one, the flirt. And during those exciting times, when she was at her most impressionable, it was Leo who attracted her; it was Sophie, his wife, whom she sometimes envied. But these were fantasies, like you'd worship Oasis. And now here he is, as large as life, and even more lush than she remembered.

He looks so normal in here, his overlong fringe split down the middle, that same stylish swagger, that sexy grin on his face. She sees the nurses glance at him with undisguised admiration. She sees his eyes roam over her clothes, her drawn white face and her unwashed hair. 'Hey kid, what the hell's going on?' And he dumps a *Viz* magazine on the table and hugs her tightly just like he used to. 'It's good to see you, really good.'

At one time she might have misunderstood. In fact, naive as she was, she did, many times over. What a fool she was. What a prat.

Why does he bother to ask? He can see very well what is going on.

What must she look like?

She used to try so hard . . . for Leo.

And anyway, where is Sebby?

They have taken her clothes. The pink hospital dressing gown – blue for boys and pink for girls – buttons up shapelessly to the neck, no ties for these At Risk patients. Her slippers are merely rubber flip-flops that hang off the ends of her heels and

375

make her shuffle like she's drugged to the eyeballs. Underneath this drab dressing gown, her nightdress is exactly the same as the ones the old ladies wear, nylon for a quick wash and change, bobbly from overuse, hot in this overheated ward so she thinks she smells of BO from the mix of medication and sticky humidity. And she has already been informed that only two baths and hair-washes are allowed each week. With supervision, of course.

Cleanliness seems not to matter in this ward, with its sparsity of visitors.

'Cheryl,' says Leo, so out of place in this so-called sanctuary for the insane. A prison more like, a medieval jail. 'What the hell are they doing to you?'

'Is there any news about Cara?'

Leo is careful, like everyone else. Round here it's weird; when Cara is mentioned they close up their faces and change the subject. 'How would I know? Surely they'd tell you? You and Barry would be the first to know, surely?'

'I just don't know any more. If they think I'm so mentally deranged they might think I couldn't handle it.' She tries to compose her face into a picture of perfect sanity, whatever that might be. She only ends with one eye doing a Pink Panther Dreyfus twitch and a jaw that feels like it's sagging as badly as if she's the victim of a stroke. She decides to carry on anyway, and repeats what she has been telling the nurses over and over again. 'I don't know why I am in here. I'm not mad. I don't need treatment. What I told them was all true, I was being followed, and what's more, I've seen the same man out of the window walking round the grounds.

Barry wants me out of his life, and I don't know when I'll see my children again.'

It is easy to forget how close Sebby and Leo once were to her family. She had gone to Sebby for help, and been sold down the line. What does Leo know about that?

Leo knows Zak Quinn.

Is he a trustworthy friend of his?

Does he come to supper with him and Sophie?

'So what's it like in here?' says Leo looking round, dumping his duffel bag on the table between them. 'Tell me what drugs they have put you on. How are you coping? Who is your doctor?'

In the past, in the good old days, there was much comfort in talking to Leo. Perhaps it might work here. She can open her heart to him and he will understand. 'It's hell. I'm on a cocktail of God knows what. I'm not coping at all, and I haven't seen any doctor yet.'

'That's bad.'

Under Leo's warm sympathy, Cheryl is fast filling with tears. 'I've not been in here twenty-four hours.'

'Even so, you should have seen someone. Bloody NHS.'

'They gave me an injection. It hurt like hell. They held me down and stripped me. They gave me an internal for some sick reason, probably to humiliate me and make me feel worse. Then they put me out for the count. I only came round two hours ago. God knows what's going to happen, or when they're going to let me go.' Cheryl stares at her visitor, her heart thudding with despair. 'You've read the stuff Barry's been saying. He's never out of the news with new scandals about his wife from hell. You know they're lies. He's taken the kids and he's gone to his mother.'

'You can't believe what you read in the papers – you, if anyone, ought to know that. Anyway, I've got my own theory.'

'Oh? Aren't you going to tell me?'

Leo is as kind, companionable and well-meaning as ever. 'You thought you couldn't handle the flack. Well, I think you dealt with it better than Barry did – you always were the strongest in that relationship. And I think he just couldn't take any more. The blacker he paints you, the more the public are going to forgive him. And that's what he is after – forgiveness. And to be loved.'

'And money. Don't forget money. They're clamouring to hear from him now. All the dirt he can dig.' She might be safer changing the subject. That one is more than she can handle. 'How did you know I was here?'

'Sebby told me. I couldn't believe it.'

Cheryl stares at her fingernails, trying to make her next question casual. 'How did Sebby know?'

'I didn't ask. Should I have done?' Leo shrugs, gazing thoughtfully at her. 'About Zak Quinn. You must blame me for that, and I want to explain. As far as I knew, Zak was a decent guy. Straight. Honest. An investigative reporter, ideal for what you wanted. He's unearthed some important stuff in the past. How was I to know that the jerk had sold his soul? But it happens.'

'Not in my world it doesn't.' But isn't Barry doing the same?

Now Leo sits quietly, observing Cheryl's distress.

378

There doesn't seem to be anything more to say, and she has been talking for over an hour.

He picks up his bag and makes to leave.

'Please get me out of here.'

'I'll do what I can, I promise you that, but I'm not sure who's going to listen,' he tells her, falsely bright.

'I'll say anything – do anything . . .' and she drops her eyes to the newly mopped floor. How she hates to beg like this, of anyone. But she knows that his hopeful attitude springs only from the desire to comfort, and not from any real belief.

Why did he come? He hadn't come near her during those months of terrible publicity. He hadn't offered any support – he was probably overwhelmed by the public response to the porn pics, which both he and Sebby had assured her would do her no damage at all. No one from Griffin had been near her. She can never quite forgive him for that, but nevertheless, she is touched and surprised that he has come to visit her here.

What does he want?

Does he feel he is to blame for her situation?

'By the way,' he says casually as he gets up to go. 'They have called off the search for Cara. They think you have been lying. They are saying she never existed. That she was never even born.'

'*Sorry?*' She can't be hearing this. Cheryl looks up at him, white and shaken, while a roaring sound starts in her ears.

'It was something Sebby discovered, apparently. Went to dig around in St Catherine's House. Doing his Good Samaritan bit, with the lovely Kate.'

'Sebby?'

'None other.'

They've called off the search? She doesn't believe it. How can they think of doing such a thing? Surely Barry wouldn't let that happen? Cheryl is frantic to get out of this menacing place and into the sunlight, where there was once a radiance. But she cannot move. Her feet are clamped to the floor, there is only darkness and faces around her.

Her misery is complete.

TWENTY-FIVE

Cheryl's blood-curdling screams of despair echo along the corridor long moments after she's left it, dragged, buckled, half on her knees, arms forced behind her back, by nurses who responded to the urgent pressing of the emergency button in the hospital's only locked ward.

Leo follows with an air of concern, unnoticed in the breathless drama of tugging, shouting and pushing. Patients turn as the party goes by, they continue to pace, blink or chew with busy, toothless gums. He watches as she is roughly manhandled into one of the segregation cells. The walls and the door itself are padded with a thick flock mattress material. The floor is totally bare. They bend down over her and buckle her into a canvas corset, so she takes up the pose of a graveyard angel, arms crossed, head held high, but dead-eyed and as pale as marble.

Her reaction to his confidences was more violent than he had anticipated. At first he thought she was going to pass out, the way her eyes rolled in her head. Unseeing. Glassy. She was like a woman possessed, chattering like a maddened monkey through jabbering jaws. But then she started to scream, and it was the scream of a woman gone mad. Hundreds of sounds and words were mixed up, so that only occasionally could anyone catch what she said . . . Cara . . . my baby . . . who is doing this to me . . . let me go . . . Barry . . . let me out . . . dead . . . dead . . .

Three nurses rushed to her side. She was banging her head against the wall. She was strong; she fended them off. Her eyes were glazed over, not seeing or understanding.

'There. Give her a chance to cool off,' says a nurse, puffing heavily after the door clangs closed, rubbing her hands as if to rid them of something that might be infectious.

Sir Art Blennerhasset cracks his knuckles angrily at the briefing in his offices this morning.

Dammit. Dammit. You would think he was the tea boy.

Here they all are, the police top brass, the token psychologist, members of the crack force brought in to handle this latest crisis, and across the conference table, that jumped-up woman Jennie St Hill is filing her goddamn fingernails. While beside him, all got up in a silky jacket and toting that vulgar briefcase, which has to take pride of place on the table – must have cost an arm and a leg – Alan Beam has the nerve to adopt the role of spokesperson for Griffin.

Art is not having this.

Rumours are abroad that this supercilious pair are subversively plotting with various financiers about forming a company of their own. Even the name has reached Art's office, via his underground network. Marigold. I ask you. At every opportunity these two power-mad activists rubbish Art's management style, which they reckon is prehistoric. It all gets back to him on the grapevine. They regard Art himself as a fossil, and the programmes produced by Griffin Productions well past their sell-by date. But if this is the case, why the hell don't they stop and ask themselves why Griffin is one of the most successful production companies in London?

That Beam and St Hill are two highly talented members of the Griffin set-up is not open to question. Neither is the fact that Art would be sorry to lose them. Much of the credit afforded to Griffin would go out of the window with them. But they are too egotistical. Both original thinkers, they lack team spirit, and their motivation is too often directed at self-promotion rather than joint success. Always on about breaking barriers, like some hotheads from NASA.

Every day since the first contact was made with the so-called child abductors, certain board members have met with the police to be updated on the latest situation. Tellingly, Beam and St Hill have never missed one of these meetings, so keen are they to push themselves forward into every aspect of company life. You would think they were running the show by their arrogant attitudes. These meetings are prolonged by their repeated questions: half the time, embarrassingly, they seem to be criticizing police protocol, police motivation or police expertise, as sharp as Paxman on *Newsnight* interviewing some newly corrupt superintendent.

Art is surprised the coppers put up with it. He wouldn't, that's for sure.

Art leans forward and attempts to take charge. 'So now we are certain this is a take-on? Now we know there is no Cara?'

'Yep, everyone agrees that's the situation. The panic is over. The case is now officially closed, leaving us to find out what did happen to the child.'

'Or whether she was born at all.' This needless interruption comes from Jennie St Hill, who is swinging casually round in her chair, inspecting her nails as if she owns the damn place.

The short, dark fellow, Hyde, who was in charge of the exercise, and is probably well used to the idiosyncrasies of pompous people, goes on calmly, 'The ransom notes were obviously sent by the Higginses themselves. Presumably they had some plan for collecting the money without handing over the child. God knows what it was. We've had Barry Higgins in, we've put all the pressure we can on him but the man won't crack. He still insists the kidnap is real, and turns very aggressive when we accuse him of making up the baby's existence. Cheryl's a clever young woman, she must have rehearsed him expertly. And the power she still has over him is really something to see.'

'From what you read in the papers,' says Alan Beam with that supercilious look on his face, 'it sounds more like he's turning on her.'

'That's all pretty predictable stuff. The press know they can say what they like – that poor harassed sod isn't going to sue anyone, is he?'

'Have they got any sense out of Cheryl yet?'

These days Alan Beam seems to have all the answers. 'Leo's going to visit today. I think they're letting her settle in before they start the heavy stuff.

But the internal examination they gave her proved nothing, apparently. Scarlett is only one and a half. If Cheryl'd had a baby since then it wouldn't be detectable because of the closeness of the two births.'

'The parents could have done the child in themselves,' Jennie puts in needlessly. Everyone knows that. That's in the back of everyone's mind. That's what makes it so horrible. No wonder poor little Cheryl Higgins has finally flipped her lid and ended up in some loony bin. All Art's fault, according to Sarah, his wife. 'They say she has brought this on herself,' Art tries to convince her, even against his own convictions. But Sarah will not have that. 'Rubbish. And even if she had brought this on herself, nobody would wish her this. No wonder the poor young father has cracked and is letting himself be used by the press.'

'What is Cheryl's reaction to the fact that the search for Cara is over?' asks Rupert Shand, the company solicitor.

'The father has been informed, as you know,' says Hyde. 'But it was considered that Mrs Higgins would be too distressed to be told. They're not altogether sure if she still genuinely believes her baby is alive.'

'So if this was all one big con, it's the husband who's milking the situation. Is he capable of that? Sending the notes? Conning the public? From what everyone is saying round here, it's Cheryl who's the boss.'

'In normal circumstances she would be,' says the psychologist, whose fees, according to Art, are quite extortionate. 'But if she's in denial it is possible that the subordinate partner would take over and, of necessity, take the lead.'

'What I would like to know', says Art, suffering from intense irritation, 'is why Leo Tarbuck should visit Cheryl in the first place. When you bear in mind that it was us who started this whole ghastly chain of events. Wouldn't Griffin be better keeping a low profile?'

Jennie St Hill disagrees. Cold fish. Insensitive cow.

'Leo knows Cheryl very well, and she trusts him. It might be a good idea to have someone there from Griffin to keep a handle on all this. For the company's sake. After all, we're still involved. There could still be proceedings against us.'

What a weird suggestion. Since when does that woman give a damn about Cheryl Higgins's welfare?

'Cheryl's rather isolated at the moment. Annie Watts is being held on remand to appear in court in the morning – assault, I believe . . .'

How the hell does Beam know that?

'. . . And naturally the marriage is rocky, after what's happened. Barry's not likely to go near her just now.'

'How about siblings, then?' asks Art in a cold, hard voice, annoyed that the meeting has once again been hijacked by these two pushy posers. 'Surely the woman's got someone?'

'Two half-brothers – trash, no good, time-wasters.'

Art's exasperation level must be affecting his blood pressure now.

Oh, God. Beam is such an objectionable queen.

Once he's got his teeth into something he will not let go, just like Sarah. 'I just think, company welfare or not, that it's not in our jurisdiction to be interfering with – *spying* on – the personal affairs of this couple.'

'Afraid of being held culpable, Art?'

'That damn programme was your baby, not mine,' Art reminds him curtly. As if the bounder needs reminding. He and his ambitious colleague are still riding on the back of it.

What is happening to Cheryl's baby?

Is Cara alive or dead, or somewhere in between, in some dark coffin underground with the air about to give out unless the kidnappers have their way? Terrified? Cold and wet? With nobody bothering to search for her? Dear God, dear God. Cheryl's baby. *Her own sweet child.*

And here is Cheryl, powerless, drugged to the eyeballs among the mad, whatever she says discounted as the ravings of a lunatic, and no way to prove to anyone that her youngest daughter ever existed. That seems extraordinary, but it's true. They know nobody round the tower blocks. At the market it's always too busy to talk, and at Tesco's everyone's faceless.

If she screams out her agony she is sedated. If she shouts her denials she is restrained. If she tries to claw her way out of here, they drag her back to her padded cell. Her flesh, her very bones seem to have melted away, and yet another part of her holds her in such iron control she can only just move her clenched hands together. This total wiping-out of herself gives her the feeling of being banished from all society for ever. She sees the office of Dr Hart as the fixed landscape of a dream, and her own voice as hardly more than a breeze tickling the farthest treetops. Her eyes wander uselessly over the psychiatrist's desk, neatly tidy with a blotter, two snapshots, a collection of pens in a leather holder and an opened file in front of him. She nerves herself to look into his eyes and sees puzzled, energetic interest. So she must be in the chair. He has to be looking at someone, and there's nobody else in the room.

'We didn't think you were ready to know about the police's latest findings,' says Dr Hart in his deep, pleasant, resonant voice, his head held slightly back as if to view her more easily, a wedge of shadow under his jaw and pale lashes drooped over his eyes. 'And I'm sorry you had to hear it in the way you did.'

'Leo told me,' she manages to say.

'I know. And I wish he hadn't.'

'Is it true?'

'I'm afraid it is. The search for Cara has been called off.' Dr Hart stares in silence, waiting for an outburst from his patient.

When there is no response at all, when all she does is clutch at her fingers and separate them individually, he tries to press her further. 'Cheryl, do you know why the police are taking this line?'

She humbly repeats what she has been told. 'They don't think there is such a person.'

'And could they be right?' His voice is gentle.

What can she say? If she insists, as she ought to, she won't be believed, as they have refused to believe everything she's been saying. Her talking has only conspired against her to land her where she is. The most she can hope for now is that they think her well enough to stop administering these debilitating drugs, and let her return to the ward again. Cheryl is determined to say and do nothing that might make her imprisonment worse.

'What happened, Cheryl?' Dr Hart's voice is so kind, designed to trap the unwary into all kinds of insane confessions which can only lead back to that hellish padded confinement.

'I don't know what happened,' she says, fighting her way through the daze in her head.

'Was it Barry who made you pretend that Cara was still alive?' And his warm smile invites her confidences. 'Or was it easier for you to make believe rather than face the pain of her death?'

What would the shrink rather hear? What would make her sound more sane? 'It was Barry,' she stutters forlornly.

'I see.' Dr Hart scribbles a note and looks up quickly to assume continuity. If his patient is ready to open up, he must not let this vital moment pass.

'And would you like to tell me what did happen to baby Cara?'

Again Cheryl has to work this one out. She has no intention of remaining in here while her child is out there in such terrible danger. The only chance of escape she has is if she is back on the ward. Although she has no plans as yet, she is willing to go to any lengths – assault a nurse, overdose, prise the bars of the windows if need be.

'I had an abortion when I was three months pregnant,' says Cheryl, closing her eyes as if pained.

'Go on,' says the psychiatrist, his puffy white hands in an attitude of prayer.

Cheryl forces sincerity into her lowered eyes. 'It was my idea to hide the children, that time when everyone hated us,' she murmurs truthfully. 'And then Barry thought, why not take it further? We'd kept meaning to tell my mum and Barry's mum and dad about the abortion. But it's not the kind of thing you like to say on the phone, and so much was happening, we didn't see them that often . . .'

The doctor interrupts. 'Tell me, Cheryl. How did Barry mean to take it further?'

'He said we should pretend there were three children, not two. And then when Cara didn't come back, we could get some money out of Griffin. He knew they'd have to pay up. He knew they'd be held responsible.'

'And you were perfectly happy to go along with this?'

'Barry said if I didn't he would refuse to support my idea. He wouldn't let me hide them in the carriages with Donny. It wasn't so bad for Barry, you see, it was me the tabloids hated, so it was me who wanted to do something to stop it.'

'I see. I see.' Dr Hart leans back and stares at the wall over his patient's head. His initial opinion is that there is nothing mentally wrong with this young woman. He has read the previous reports, the suggestion of Munchausen's syndrome by proxy, and the effects her chequered childhood might have had on this troubled girl. But the reports also stated clearly that Cheryl had clammed up on his colleague, leaving him little to go on other than past experience. The police psychiatrist's diagnosis had been based on very little real evidence. Nevertheless, after one consultation, he cannot afford to make quick judgements. She came here only yesterday convinced there was a conspiracy against her and that she was being followed. This patient could be, like so many, devious and manipulative. It is necessary that she be confined on the locked ward for some time, where she can be watched and evaluated, at least until he can be more certain. And although Dr Hart cannot breach his code of confidentiality, he can usefully inform the police that their decision to call off the search is the correct one, in his expert opinion.

There is no Cara.

There never was.

Meanwhile, in the permanent chaos which is now number forty-one, Barry cannot abandon his much maligned wife any longer.

Leo was on the phone earlier, begging Barry to visit her. 'I know she betrayed you, and she did it in public. I know what you must be feeling,' he said. 'But Christ Jesus, Barry, she is suffering enough. She's in hell.'

Thoughts of what she must be going through, locked up in the ward, chilled him. What was Cheryl feeling now, knowing that the search had been called off, being accused, like he had been, of inventing Cara for her own wicked purposes? Even having to face the suggestion that she was so mentally ill she refused to come to terms with her own baby's death?

What crap. What absolute crap. At least they hadn't accused him of that.

They must assume that men don't feel the death of a child so strongly.

'If Cara has a hope in hell,' Leo told him over the phone, 'you and Cheryl must stand together. And she needs you. She misses you. Hell, you can't switch love off like a tap, no matter what the poor kid has done.'

All afternoon Barry has mulled over Leo's words. Stoked them up, damped them down, poured more petrol onto the flames until he can't hold back any longer. The words burst out of him like a sneeze he's held in too long. 'I've got to get to Cheryl – right now.'

'But you can't, Barry, you *can't*,' says Cath. 'The woman's a danger to herself and to others. What are you thinking of, after what she's done to you? Calm down, calm down. And what on earth's brought about this sudden change of heart?'

'Get out of my way, Mum, I must ring Leo. I told him I'd get in touch if I changed my mind, so he could be there at the hospital when I arrived.'

During that brief telephone call, Cath carries on on a brusque, barking note: 'I hope you're not expecting me and Bill to babysit yet again, while you go off on some madcap jaunt to see a woman who's out of her mind? And that's the most positive thing I can say about that filthy little trollop . . .'

'Shut up, Mum.'

Cath can no longer swallow her wrath. 'Don't you tell me to shut up! I'll have you know your poor father and I have put ourselves out for you, and little thanks we have been given.'

But it's no good.

Barry has gone.

Slamming the door behind him.

Typical.

Leaving the kids to be given their tea, the washing on the line and the toys all over the messy floor . . .

TWENTY-SIX

'Barry's here? I don't believe you.'

Poor Cheryl is not used to good news. There must be some catch. Some trick of the light, some stranger who might look like him. Or he's come to discuss the divorce, or to hobnob with her doctors and suggest all kinds of new neuroses from which he suspects she is suffering. After the nasty things she has been reading, all attributed to her husband, no wonder Cheryl is mixed up, puzzled as to his motives. And all because she screwed up so badly over that meaningless night with Quinn.

To see Barry now will be tantamount to removing the bandages and sticking another knife in herself.

Leo has been a pillar of strength since he arrived two hours ago. They let him in, but only after a staff nurse warned him that his visit yesterday had disturbed what could be a volatile patient.

Two visits in two days, when nobody else has bothered to come near her. Leo's unexpected support is astonishing, particularly after nearly a year when she never saw hide nor hair of him. He has taken the trouble to make enquiries about Mum,

Victor and Scarlett. Annie was ordered to keep the peace; apparently Barry was not in court. An unfortunate phone call to Harlow only resulted in Cath Higgins telling Leo stiffly that the children were fine, no thanks to their mother. 'So we have to assume all is well,' said Leo.

'Nothing changes,' said Cheryl.

'Don't sit there keeping it all inside you,' said Leo with some of his old understanding, seeing her clenched fists, her teeth gripping her lips. And she couldn't prevent them: the tears just poured down her cheeks. 'That's why I'm here, you can talk to me. You must have such muddled emotions after all this time, trust me, use me . . .'

He held her hand. He stroked her arm.

This was so like the old Leo, when they were filming *The Dark End*. So understanding, so uncritical, you felt you could tell him anything and he would be on your side. Even Barry, normally so reticent, had opened up to Leo. That's what made the series so good. It was so totally *Honest*.

In her distress, Cheryl caught his duffel bag and knocked it off the table. Unprepared for his reaction, she jumped with surprise when he shouted, 'Don't touch it. *Leave that alone!*' And carefully repositioned it, like he was obsessive about it.

She broke down then, and confided in him all her hopes and her worst fears. Just like during the months of filming, she didn't care what she looked like or what words she used. It was a torturous business, trying to communicate through the drugs without her shadowy thoughts turning fluid. Bobbing bits and pieces of hope were carried backward and forward like water in a dark, flooded cave, with

395

tides sweeping in and out. Her hopes – these poor drowned things – were all of finding Cara, freedom from this asylum, reclaiming her children and making a normal, happy home away from the public gaze.

It was all so confusing. As if her life was one troubled sleep, sluggish mostly, but feverish at times with periods of nightmare. Her horror was the loss of Cara, further confinement, more hostility, separations from her family and even real insanity. She knew how easy it must be, a prisoner surrounded by madness, to be infected by it, doused with it and even, finally, beguiled by it and welcoming it.

The quiet, white eye of the storm.

Leo listened and encouraged her outbursts with nods and shakes of the head. Without this support from him, Cheryl doubted she would survive. To the authorities, Cheryl was now just a name on the doctors' files. Disembodied, a damaged brain in need of treatment. The dark inhabitant of some medical astral sphere.

Now he tells her that Barry is coming, 'and the hospital have assured me that if the press get wind of his arrival, their spokesman will deal with them outside on the steps'.

Dear God. *Oh, no*. Cheryl hasn't anticipated this. 'Will they never leave us alone?' she asks Leo in despair. 'Will this hounding go on for ever?'

Leo shrugs nonchalantly. 'Until something better comes up. This is the silly season.'

'Until somebody else falls from grace and gets caught in their self-righteous trap.'

'No matter what you might think about them,' Leo tries to explain, 'the great British public are going to go hairless over Cara's return. There'll probably be bunting out in the streets.'

At least Leo seems to believe that there *is* a baby and that she *will* come home. 'No baby has ever had such attention. Even before she was born Cara was gossiped about as if she belonged to the world. And now they deny her existence.'

'It's because, these days, people are cut off from their neighbours,' Leo explains to her gently. 'They need to get involved in something, little dramas they lack in their own lives. That's why the soaps are so popular. You daren't gossip over your garden fence any more, you're more likely to get a string of abuse or a spade brought down on your head. So you turn on the telly and get angry with that.'

'So me and Barry did them a favour. Griffin were providing a public service when they did *The Dark End*.'

Does Leo ever feel guilty, she wonders?

Does he ever blame himself for the fact that Cheryl is here today, sitting in this miserable place, talking to him across a round table, round for safety's sake? Looking back from this grim place, it is hard to make sense of the line of events that has led to this final nightmare. Her memory is more like a paintbrush than a clear, clean photograph. Life had been difficult before *The Dark End*: they had been poor and struggling, but Cheryl is under the vague impression that she and Barry had been young and happy and in love, and this illusion had lasted until that programme began and something had got hold of them both, used them and

397

destroyed them. Had turned them into the comic and monstrous offspring of the media ratings.

So does Leo blame himself? Maybe he, like everyone else, really believes she is mad and deserves all she gets. With Leo, it is hard to tell.

Barry stops dead when he turns the corner and spies the crowd from the end of the street. There must be fifty people or more clustered round the hospital entrance, and it doesn't take a great brain to figure out that it's him they are waiting to see.

But how did they know he was coming?

What more could they be wanting to ask him?

After the way he has been misquoted in the last couple of days, he thought he had made it perfectly clear that he had nothing further to say.

There must be another way in round the side. But as Barry hesitates, one of the group looks up and spots him, shouts and starts to run . . . The trickle turns into a buzzing swarm as, within seconds, he is surrounded by microphones and cameras and eager lookers-on.

'Barry, are the latest allegations true that you killed your baby daughter?'

'Is that why they've called the search for Cara off?'

'When do you expect you and your wife to be charged with manslaughter?'

'Have you seen a solicitor yet?'

'What is the reason for your visit to the hospital?'

How can one man alone be expected to face all this confusion? These stunted, twisted, brutalized people, a collection of starved appetites and low, brute cunning. Something very old and evil is obliterating reality, and these forces are too much for him. The whole of civilization is shaking. Panting, with sweat starting on his forehead, Barry closes his eyes and barges through the human mass, feeling that he is up to his knees in the squelch, as if he is struggling through a bog. He has to make the hospital entrance. He has to get to Cheryl. She has to be protected from this. What if this crowd follows him in and pushes its way inside?

And who has been feeding these vultures these vicious, outrageous rumours?

So much for police discretion.

He pictures Cheryl's skinny shoulders shaking, like they do when she is in pain, her head bent in her hands when she hears the things they are saying. What motives lie behind these leaks, which can only be designed to cause more torture and to stoke more public outrage? Or is it nothing so grotesque, merely poor organization, lack of foresight? Whatever, Barry is helpless against it, his thoughts flying in all directions in a futile effort to make sense of his life. He has no private life any longer: he can move neither hand nor foot without creating a crowd at his door.

It is true that the police have their suspicions, and Barry has done all he can to reassure them. In his last interview with DCI Rowe, he'd been told they were making enquiries. *But what sort of enquiries?* Searching the Harold Wilson Building for the body of a newly born child? Questioning the neighbours? Pouring the direst rumours into eagerly listening ears? And all the while, his baby daughter is out there, maybe alone in the cold.

Jesus Christ, he can't bear it.

Thank God, thank God for that. A friendly face at last. Leo is standing in the doorway, casual and relaxed with his hands in his pockets, and now a dozen security men appear to be dealing with the mob. Before Barry knows it the crowds are behind him, and he's following Leo through long, pale corridors on his way to visit his wife.

At the first sight of Cheryl, Barry thinks of a fawn, a wild, shy, frightened creature hiding from the world and tired nearly to death from the hunt.

There are no more thoughts of betrayal, none of the nervous panic of meeting as he takes her in his arms and holds her, and sees the loneliness leave her eyes.

'Cara?' she says at once.

'I know.'

'They're still not looking?'

'No. No, they're not.'

She doesn't seem frightened any more, just broken, helpless and grateful to have him near her, holding her tight. 'Barry, what are we going to do?'

Barry shakes his head numbly.

'I had to lie,' she confesses, tears suddenly streaming down her face. 'I had to tell them we'd had an abortion. I had to go along with it all so they would let me out of here. But it didn't work. They won't let me go. So it must be my fault they've given up on Cara.'

'It's not your fault. And I understand.' Barry looks round at Leo, because this is a very private moment between two people.

'Carry on. Don't worry, I'm not listening,' says

400

Leo, hoisting his duffel bag onto his shoulder as if he is preparing to leave. But he doesn't.

'And the papers, Cher, those things they said . . .'

'I know that, Barry. You don't have to explain. If anyone understands the press more than me, I want to meet them.'

And it's true. Despite Cath's nagging, Barry has steadfastly refused to say anything that might harm his wife. He reaches into his back pocket and brings out a paper which he unfolds. Cheryl stands back and squints down at it.

'This is the balance as it stood this morning. This is the money we can use if all else fails. We can use it to find Cara. There are people, there are agencies . . .'

'How much?' asks Leo, moving over.

'Twenty five thousand pounds.'

'How did you raise that money, Barry?'

'I talked to the press. I thought it might help. I tried to tell the true story.' Barry shrugs after the pause. 'That was before I realized that whatever I said would be misquoted. That was before I understood that they only wrote what they wanted.'

Cheryl's laughter is as brittle as strands of toffee, not a laugh at all, more a scream. 'And now they think that we made her up. That's rich. That's really rich.'

'And they're not just saying that either,' says Leo, sitting back in his chair. 'The crowd outside are convinced you are about to be charged over the death of Cara.'

'What?' Cheryl pales, her eyes enormous with apprehension. She gives a single shuddering sob.

Barry's unease spreads over his face. He throws

Leo a look of wild appeal. 'I wasn't going to tell her that, not this soon, not here.'

'Barry,' says Leo, firmly indifferent. 'At this stage there is no point in hiding the truth from Cheryl. She'll find out soon enough, and it's better that this comes from you than from some stiff nurse with the evening paper.'

Maybe he's right. Maybe Cheryl should know the worst. So Barry explains the ugly truth as gently as he can, while Leo listens without interruption and Cheryl questions every sentence as if such an enormous lie has to be told ten times before it can be swallowed.

'But it's just not true – so they can't prove it,' Cheryl cries desperately, gripping the Formica table for balance and disturbing Leo's bag. He rights it. 'They'll have to realize the truth in the end, then they'll have to continue the search . . .'

'All they will do, in those circumstances, is follow the abortion line,' says Leo, grim and cynical. 'Didn't they ask you where you'd had it done, so they could confirm it?'

'They asked. I refused to tell them. I couldn't have told them, could I?'

Leo shakes his head while Cheryl groans and sinks to her chair, as if the last of her spirit has been brutally broken.

Is Leo, sitting there between them, aware of the consequences of his honesty tactics? He had always been hard, Barry remembers, and remorseless when it came to the truth, critical of their performances and determined to get things absolutely right. But this isn't one of his films. Barry and Cheryl are sitting here dealing with what could be their child's life – or death.

'What do they want from us?' Cheryl murmurs to nobody in particular in a blurred, childish voice. 'Do they really believe we are after the money?'

'The money or the sympathy. But now they've made sure you won't get either. They simply do not believe you. You cried wolf once, and that's what did it. That was the worst move you made in your lives.'

Barry wants to take Cheryl back in his arms and hold her, but feels he can't because her pain is too much: it has turned her into a battered shell, which might break if handled too roughly.

'There must be something . . .' he turns to Leo with defiant eyes. Let Leo, so smugly satisfied, undo some of the harm he's just done. Let Leo make some positive move. Barry has never trusted the man, never really liked him. It was Cheryl who seemed to need him around.

'You've got to get her out of here,' is Leo's only response. 'She's getting no treatment, she's drugged to the eyeballs, she feels powerless and out of control just when she needs to be strong for Cara. If Cheryl stays here another week, I think she'll go right round the bend. Well look at her, just look at her.'

Instead Barry looks at Leo, astonished. Cheryl's fragile state of mind has not been helped by his attitude. But even so, Barry is worried. To see her in here is not pleasant. 'Do you know someone who could pull that off? What, doctors? Someone with influence?'

Leo shakes his head. 'It's up to you, I'm afraid. It's up to you to work something out.'

Does Leo mean what he seems to be meaning?

'I'd never get away with it.' Barry's eyes scan the ward furtively, noting the bars on the windows with their shatter-proof glass, the doors with their locks and electronic alarms, the nurses in their central office and the patients with their demented eyes. His heart sinks. 'There's no way I could do it.'

'You could with my help,' says Leo.

'Leo rang up earlier,' Kate tells Sebby when he gets home, when he's stripped and on his way to the shower. 'He wants to talk to you about Cheryl.'

He is hot and sticky after a day in town with a party of kids who needed some watching. This children's home project is falling onto his shoulders. It was only first thing this morning that Leo put in an appearance, and then he seemed distracted. He shot off at eleven, not saying where he was going. Not like him. 'What about her?'

'He's spent the afternoon in the hospital talking to Cheryl. He's worried that Barry might do something silly.' Kate follows him through to the bathroom with a cool Coke, tinkling with ice, in her hands.

Sebby snorts as he sheds his sweaty pants. 'Leo? Worried? Oh, yeah? Pull the other one.' He holds his breath at the shock of the cold water and gradually relaxes into it. Kate sits on the loo, on the other side of the shell-patterned curtain. 'Well, what did he say?' Sebby frowns. And why hadn't Leo phoned Sebby's mobile if he wanted to talk to him?

'It's all so ludicrous. That fool Barry is planning to spring Cheryl out of there. Leo agrees that the hideous place is driving Cheryl mad, that she's not getting the treatment she needs. But if Barry does play the knight in shining armour, they'll end up in a horrendous mess.'

'Too bloody right. So?'

'Leo wanted you to know, that's all. Wondered if you had any positive ideas to calm Barry down, maybe knew of some technicality which could be used to help them, or somebody with the right influence who might be able to hurry the process?'

Sebby shakes his head, puzzled. Why would he know something like that? 'Barry wouldn't listen to me, not now he knows it was us who discovered the truth about Cara. As far as he is concerned, Cheryl wouldn't be in there if it wasn't for us and our interference.'

The water cascades through his hair, cooling, refreshing. Strange, Leo never mentioned he was visiting Cheryl, and he knows how concerned Sebby is. 'He should talk to the authorities.'

'What, inform on Cheryl and Barry again? Is that really what you'd do, Sebby?'

'What else, for God's sake?' Sebby, annoyed now, chases the soap. 'You must see how absurd the idea is. Think of the catastrophic results if they got caught. Think of the headlines. Barry could end up inside. Surely you don't seriously believe we should let them go ahead with this lunacy? We've done enough damage already.'

There's a pause from the other side of the curtain, and the sound of ice swirling in a glass. 'You blame me for the fact that she's in there,' says Kate, raising her voice above the water.

This is no good. Sebby cannot relax with this curious conversation going on.

Kate goes on, sounding determined. 'And I blame myself, too. This time we ought to mind our own business. What right have we got to betray them? Barry spoke to Leo in confidence. Leo's seen Cheryl. He's spent hours with her. He knows what it's like in that wretched place. Maybe he thinks Barry could actually get away with it.'

Sebby steps out of the shower with the towel draped over his head. The last thing he needs is an argument with Kate. It's too hot and he's tired. 'Why is Leo suddenly so interested in the fate of Cheryl Higgins, and why tell me about this new development?'

'Because he thinks you care. And he hoped you might have some ideas.'

'I haven't. And even if I had, what does he expect me to do?'

'You'd better talk to him yourself,' says Kate. 'All I know is that he's got Cheryl's best interests at heart.'

There is such irony in this. Since when has Leo given a damn? 'He's won you over, at any rate.' Sebby makes for the kitchen and the ice compartment in the fridge, leaving damp footprints across the floor. 'I'll talk to him if that's what you want, but the only reasonable thing to do is go to the authorities.'

'For Cheryl's sake, I suppose,' says Kate with a cynical smile.

Maybe Cheryl is insane, as they say. She feels insane. She feels demented.

She wants to get out of here, she does. But it could all end up as a fatal disaster, a more dangerous mistake than hiding the children, if anything should go wrong. And if Barry manages to pull it off, will the stalker still be waiting?

If only there was somebody out there she could talk to. Months ago she'd have asked Sebby – he would have given them sensible advice, but my God, not now . . . The very thought that Sebby and Kate caused the search to be abandoned by questioning her own sanity and denying her baby's existence, causes her head to rage with hatred.

No wonder he hadn't come anywhere near her.

But if Leo is in favour . . . ?

Maybe she does need treatment.

There is too much going on in her head, pounding there, heavy metal through the walls.

TWENTY-SEVEN

No more ransom notes. No more phone calls to Griffin. Which rather confirms the suspicions of police and public that now the Higginses' bluff has been called, they have accepted the inevitable and thrown in the towel.

Not that Cheryl has any choice, incarcerated as she is in a high-security psychiatric ward.

Talk of some new secret project is doing the rounds of Griffin Productions, and it has once again been suggested that Alan Beam and Jennie St Hill are thinking of taking it elsewhere. The majority of Art's fellow board members have been seduced by the aura of the pair in a profession in which glamour and success is rated higher than God. Any criticism Art might make is liable to get back to them. He doesn't know who he can trust any more. Since their appointments to the board, appointments which Art felt instinctively were wrong, the old trust and camaraderie have been replaced by nasty cliques and unhealthy competition.

Jilly, Art's sexy PA, with whom he has been conducting a clandestine and satisfactory affair for ten years (it is more of a marriage now, with calm common sense on both sides), edges into his office this morning in a manner far removed from her normal bustling, businesslike rush.

On Art's instructions, for weeks now Jilly has been attempting to infiltrate the tortuous minefield, the sandy foundations of the company rumblings. A competent and bright woman, popular with all, she has been able to separate the wheat from the chaff, gossip from fact, friend from foe, loyal from disloyal.

She lowers her deep-throated, sexy voice. She is thirty-five, and more beautiful now than when he had first known her; a voluptuous woman with an hourglass figure and hair like a Timotei ad, held up in a knot on the top of her head. 'There's something you should see.'

Cloak-and-dagger.

She sounds like a member of the French resistance movement.

This is her best bedroom voice.

'Oh?' Art peers over his gold-framed bifocals.

'Here, in this building.'

And whatever wickedness it is to which Jilly is referring, the fact that it is taking place in the precincts of the Griffin headquarters seems like the most scurrilous part of her undercover revelations.

She sits down in her swivel chair as if she's about to take a letter, or decide on a menu, or take Art through the schedule of another busy day. Art is not a man who prefers to dictate by Dictaphone and conduct his affairs through a system of buttons. A witty and gregarious man – hence his friendship with so many top personalities – he is always happier face-to-face, even in bed, and especially where Jilly is concerned.

'You were right,' says Jilly, 'there is a project, but I don't know any more than that. Jennie and Alan are playing this one close to their chests, and although a few folks are well aware that something's going on, nobody seems to know what.'

Art is disappointed in her. 'So we're no further forward.'

'I know. I know. But I have managed to find out where they're working. They have converted the old paint room into a studio, equipped it with all the necessary cutting and editing and wiring and lighting – mostly out of their own pockets is what I'm hearing – and they come in early mornings to work on it, or stay late in the evenings.'

Art muses out loud, 'Why all this undercover stuff? What the hell could they be doing which would stop them coming to me?'

'Something you might turn down flat?'

'Well, obviously. But hell, they don't know what I might disapprove of. Not till they come out with it.'

'They think you are an establishment flunkey. They might not be working with Griffin in mind. That's what you heard, and that's the gossip. But it must be something big, or else why would they bother to go to these ludicrous lengths?'

Nobody had ever accused Art of being an establishment flunkey until he married his present wife, the daughter of a landowning, right-wing Tory MP. This had, undoubtedly, opened the doors to country piles, but it had never affected his integrity. Until then, he was considered risqué, a thorn in the establishment's side with a vital role to play in the sixties revolution, a keen supporter of satire and the exposing of humbug.

Art says wearily, 'I don't honestly think I want to know much more.'

'But you can't take that attitude.'

'I know that. If only those two would give me some credence. If only they didn't sincerely believe they were God's gift to the media world.' As he contemplates this, his weary eyes meet Jilly's and hold them. 'It's my job to find out what's going on whether I want to or not, but I'm beginning to think these jerks are right – I am too old.'

Jilly snorts in astonishment. 'I've never seen you like this before.'

'I've never had to do this before. I've never been sidetracked like this before, or been considered a censorious fogey. Jesus Christ, I've fought against censorship all my life.'

'They reckon there're others involved.'

'Oh? Who? Go on. Tell me the worst.'

Jilly directs a look of sympathy from under her dark gold lashes at her despairing boss. 'And it is the worst, if it's true. Leo Tarbuck is the only name that was mentioned to me, but there could well be others. I'm sorry, Art. But that's what I've heard.'

This is a hard one to digest. A deepening frown is the only clue Art gives to his great disappointment. Leo, so bright and talented, trained from college by Art himself. He has seen him rise from focus-puller and clapper-loader to researcher and camera operator, virtually left to direct some of the best documentaries Griffin has ever produced, including, of course, *The Dark End*. And likeable. And loyal. Yes, foolish as he is, Art had believed him to be totally loyal.

'It's true what my old granny used to say, a couple of bad apples and they infect the rest.'

'It's no good retreating into a cosy second childhood,' says Jilly smartly, sensing Art's distress. 'The question is, what are you intending to do? And when?'

He could see them, Art supposes.

He could order Alan and Jennie into his office right now, and accuse them of dishonourable practices, or whatever label their offensive activities might best suggest.

He could accompany them to the old paint room in an authoritarian manner, force them to run the tape, confiscate it (legally it must belong to Griffin), argue its merits or decry their efforts, depending on what he saw.

But this has never been Art's style. He is not a dictator. Freedom of expression is essential for the furtherance of the artistic spirit, and he is reluctant to clamp down on any of his employees who, in their work, are expressing their very souls.

And, to be honest, these high principles of his are not the only reason for his reticence to play the high-handed director.

The thought of that disloyal pair ranting on about freedom of expression, accusing Art of having a blinkered perception, influenced by a society wife and the opinions of his 'high-born' friends is enough to make Art recoil from any such confrontation.

He has heard it all before.

He would rather play this one more delicately.

He would rather pussyfoot round it than confront this attack head-on.

If the film is good, he will confiscate it. If it is crap – if, as he suspects, it is so outrageous as to be unsaleable – he can happily let it go and his protagonists with it.

With a heavy sigh Art removes the master keys from the safe. 'I'll stay late tonight and take a look. Phone my wife, sweetheart . . .'

'I'll stay with you.'

'And I still don't really know if there's any sense in what I've been saying,' says Sebby, looking rougher than ever, with one string of curls down over his eyes and his spectacles stuck together with tape.

If he thought he was miserable at ten this morning, threatened with the loss of an excellent team, worried by rumours of illicit goings-on somewhere in the basement of his own damn building, by lunchtime Art is seriously depressed.

Over lunch, Sebby Coltrain airs concerns that defy belief. Art's scrambled egg and smoked salmon remains a yellow mess on his plate, only toyed with, fork prints around the edges.

But if what this scruffy young man is suggesting can possibly be true, at least Art has the wherewithal to put a stop to such scandalously unprofessional conduct, now he knows where the film is being edited.

Is it remotely possible that Jennie, Alan, Leo Tarbuck and who knows how many others could be taking such appalling advantage of somebody else's misfortune, as to be following them round and filming every single miserable moment with cameras and microphones at the ready? Christ. To cash in in the name of entertainment on such traumatic events as kidnapping and mental illness; to be so damn insensitive as to use the young Higgins family as if they are cartoon cut-outs, is descending into a stinking abyss, a gross violation of morality, let alone of every broadcasting standard.

Art's face turns a darker purple.

The revelation that *The Dark End*'s directors scurrilously used obscene material in order to sensationalize the series at its conception now seems almost mundane. This behaviour can be expected from those independent producers whose pay cheques arrive when their programmes are just commissioned, and when changing practices and casuals in the industry mean less factual facilities, but in Griffin's case – a successful company – these arguments cannot be applied.

No wonder Beam and St Hill had not come to Art with their latest project.

No wonder they were keeping it strictly under their hats.

And the young man who sits miserably before him playing with his asparagus, trailing it through melted butter and back, this young man is genuinely concerned that not only are these renegades recording the ghastly mishaps of the Higginses, but in some instances are actually engineering them.

'I've not slept a wink all night, not since I began to work it all out.'

Art can only shake his head and sink more morosely into his chair.

'It was Leo's sudden interest that made no sense to me,' he explains. 'For months we had talked about Cheryl's misfortunes, and Leo showed absolutely no interest, certainly felt no remorse over the way the programme was handled.' His own guilt is clearly consuming him. 'That series was fixed,' he meets Art's eyes. His are red-rimmed behind his glasses. You can tell he's had no sleep. 'Leo's the expert. You taught him well. There was no way that family were going to come out of that series smelling of anything sweeter than shit.'

Deep within his chest cavity Art feels the hot signs of heartburn and swallows. 'But all that intense public interest, and the anger. There was no way that could have been deliberately triggered.'

Sebby shakes his head. 'That didn't reach boiling point until Cheryl and Barry's ridiculous trickery was discovered. Then, of course, there was Zak Quinn, a friend of Leo's. Leo must have thought his ship had come in when I stupidly rang him to ask for advice. But I did, and look what happened. If there was an edge there, between us we pushed the Higginses over it.'

'And since that time, you believe the Higginses' lives have been secretly recorded?' It all makes perfect sense now. That designer briefcase on the table at every Griffin meeting. At the time, Art put it down to Alan's enormous vanity. But it could so easily have housed a concealed camera. All that questioning of the police – some of the questions were so damn obvious they could only have been used for public consumption. The team knew all the official moves that were being made during the search for Cara . . . the drop points for the ransom money, the letters themselves, and they could easily have recorded the telephone calls. And then the focus would switch to shots of the grieving parents.

It had to happen one day.

Brilliant television, even Art has to admit.

A film it would be hard for any commissioning editor to ignore, especially when you bear in mind the infamy of the Higginses.

'And now you're worried that Cheryl and Barry are walking into a malicious trap?'

'That's the only reason I can think of as to why Leo is doing nothing to stop Barry's stupidity. He wants this to happen. He wants the disasters to carry on as long as he can make them. Imagine the frenzy if Cheryl escaped. They think she's mad, and dangerous . . . But this couldn't be further from the truth.'

'She did invent the existence of her child,' Art reminds him. 'Either that, or she was deeply unbalanced.'

'If that discovery had not been made, on Kate's intuition, and if I didn't know that as a fact, I would put it down to more manoeuvring.'

'To what purpose?'

'To bring in the grisly hospital scenes. What else? That's real drama, especially as they took her to St Hugh's. Shades of the dark old asylums.'

'But if that was the case, it would mean Cara was still missing. It would mean she really had been kidnapped, and is probably in serious danger.' No, no, he can't believe that. Nobody would take that risk with the life of a child, just to make great television. 'Dammit, that would mean the Higginses were telling the truth.'

'I know. Jesus, I know. And that's why I had to come to you.'

'But why did Leo let you know about Cheryl's proposed escape? If he was encouraging this catastrophe-in-the-making, wouldn't he want it kept quiet? Especially from you. He knows your views.'

'He wanted to protect his back. He must have guessed I thought his interest was peculiar, out of character to say the least. Perhaps he was worried that I might work it out. When I rang him back he sounded despairing, caring, afraid to interfere in their lives yet again.' Sebby manages a short, sick smile. 'He sounded pretty convincing. He even convinced Kate. And I know he was fairly certain I wouldn't go to the authorities. He knows how guilty I already feel. He was exploiting that.'

Even if they order coffee, Art is not sure he can drink it.

'Good evening, Mason,' says Art casually to the security man on the door. 'Yes, there's some work I have to catch up on.'

And if Mason gives the party of three an odd look, they ignore him.

'This way.' Jilly leads them on, heels tapping, Sebby in the middle and Art bringing up the rear.

This ridiculous subterfuge, no matter how necessary, makes Art feel diminished. Amost fifty, and what is he doing? He is a schoolboy again, at Winchester, afraid of being caught red-handed. But Jilly's eyes are full of excitement – to her, this is an exciting wheeze, meriting nothing more than detention or a warning letter sent home to the parents.

Does she feel this way about their involvement? Art asks himself as he follows his employees down the corridor, through the swing doors, feeling more foolish every minute. Unmarried, a career woman and happy to be so, Jilly risks so little, while Art is gambling the love of his life with this relationship, his prestige, his position, his reputation.

Why does he do it?

Why does anyone do it?

Five turns later, and they arrive at the door of the old paint room, no longer necessary since carpentry, props and costume had been moved to the second floor.

'This is it,' says Jilly triumphantly.

Art stoops to inspect the lock.

'There's no light on inside,' says Jilly, and Art breathes a sigh of relief. To meet his antagonists face-to-face would have meant an unpleasant confrontation, and that would have been the height of embarrassment. He still finds it hard to believe that any serious documentary-maker would lower themselves to these depths.

But there's only one way to prove it.

He opens the door and switches on the light.

The other two trail in after him.

People have certainly been in here lately. Old paint tins are stacked neatly along one wall, and the floor has been freshly mopped over but over there, under the shelf, are some give-away clippings of celluloid. There are three swivel chairs in front of a bench, an empty waste-paper basket, and that looks like new wiring.

But other than that, the stark room is empty.

The project is finished.

The birds have flown.

TWENTY-EIGHT

It has never yet been known that an innocent person has been punished for suspicion of witchcraft, and there is no doubt that God will never permit such a thing to happen.

The Malleus Maleficarum

Nine-nine-nine.

At 10.36 p.m. precisely.

The voice is a woman's, cultured and assertive, not one you'd want to argue with. Janet Foster . . . hospital manager. Just five seconds later, the St Hugh's priority alarm blasts out at the station, and three fire-appliance engines are already revving smoothly.

Back at St Hugh's, on the secure ward, bedlam is breaking out as twitchy patients react to the ear-splitting sounds emitting from the red box over the door, and puffs of grey smoke start spiralling out from one of the segregation rooms. The automatic sprinkler system sprays down like a garden hose on dead roses. It disturbs the confused patients further, while the old and the vulnerable are prised from their beds and hurriedly pressed into wheelchairs.

The set procedure must be followed. There is no room here for personal initiative. No call for heroics. The staff turn into automata as they have been taught, coughing on the acrid smoke while securing the medicines, checking patient lists and moving everyone as calmly as they can to queue in front of the door, which is then automatically opened to allow for extra help to arrive.

In case of fire, do not use the lifts.

With stinging, running eyes the patients, senile, bewildered, in a mixture of nightwear and elderly clothing, are herded past the tempting opening by stern-faced nurses too focused to notice, or to question, the presence of the man in overalls working on the buttons. When the first posse of firemen arrive, they only add to the mayhem as they charge through the milling throng in their heavy boots and startling helmets, going against the flow of fear.

Since Barry's arrival half an hour since, he has suffered from the kind of fear-cum-adrenalin syndrome most common in troops embarking on a battle. The raging, spittle-strewn words of his mother as he departed this morning, leaving her with his children, still echoed in his ears. In spite of Leo's calm reassurances, he expected to be confronted and challenged at every single turn, from convincing the staff to let him in a whole hour before visiting time, to sneaking along the well-lit passage that led to the segregation rooms. *Don't turn round. Act casual.* Most of the doors were closed, as expected, but two of the six were open, and it was with shaking hands that he lit the three firelighters Leo had provided. The sweat stood out on his brow as he slit small holes with his Swiss

Army knife and pushed the burning white wedges hard into the thick flock walls.

What the hell was he doing?

This was arson. This was serious, although Leo had reassured him that the material was fireproof and all it would do when ignited was send out billows of smoke.

There would be no loss of life.

'Well, if you're sure.'

'I'm sure,' he said.

In the exposed and unlockable toilets, five minutes before the alarms were set off, Cheryl flung off her hospital garb and pulled on the cheap new jeans and T-shirt Barry had smuggled in, along with a bundle of old magazines. She was stiff with terror, the slightest move – just to grip the zip in her slippery fingers – seemed to take an eternity. She'd never be ready, she'd be seen, she'd be caught . . . She must wait till she heard the alarm before she crossed the ward, but when she did, her head felt huge, her limbs turned wooden and the manic shriek of the fire bells only echoed her own hysteria.

All this fear she felt inside her. When had it begun to claim her? It was an ugly alien that had moved into her little by little, slowly making room for itself, nudging and edging with its feet and shoulders, pushing out all other feelings until it had the space it needed. At any moment, of course, the thing might grow obstreperous, fling out its arms and spread its feet like a jack-in-the-box on a spring and destroy her entire being. If only she could confront it – defeat it.

She found Barry. She went limp against his

thudding heart. Without his help, she could not have walked.

What would they do without Leo? Gratitude is an inadequate word. That he should risk so much for them . . . He must have always cared, but been unable to show it. Just as he had assured them, Leo is waiting in the service lift directly to the left of the door, looking odd in his ill-fitting overalls with an open tool bag on the floor. When the lift door closes, the claustrophobic, boxed-in sensation is the safest Cheryl has felt in months. Nobody can see her. Nobody can reach her. If only they could remain in this mode, moving up and down aimlessly, up and down for ever.

Nobody speaks.

They watch the red light illuminate the floor numbers . . . four . . . three . . . two. Their faces are immobile as the lift descends gently to the basement floor.

They know what they have to do, and luckily the instructions are simple. They must stick close to Leo, they must follow him. Anything more demanding would be too confusing for Cheryl.

Since nine o'clock, Sebby and Art have been sitting in Art's silver BMW directly outside the hospital, expecting to be moved on any moment by a conscientious traffic warden. Shortly before any sign of fire, a small crowd had started gathering around the hospital entrance. Not press; these people appeared to be the sort of random mixture you might find in a TV audience. But these types are prolific in the daytime, with nothing more pressing on their minds: mothers with pushchairs, groups of layabouts, middle-aged women with shopping bags, a few hospital visitors delayed by some infectious anticipation, but easily identified by bunches of flowers and drawn, anxious expressions. But all of them were waiting for something. You could tell by the looks on their faces.

Sebby got out on Art's instructions and went to make enquiries.

'Dunno,' said the nearest woman, vacantly. She had hennaed hair and big earrings. 'That's what we're all wanting to know. Somebody said there was something happening, so me and Jean stopped to see.'

Everyone seemed convinced that something was in the wind, but nobody knew quite what. Some vague rumour had spread around, causing the first little group to assemble, and after that, spotting a crowd, others had been attracted to it for fear of missing out.

'But this is the hospital where they've got Cheryl Higgins,' Sebby heard somebody say darkly.

'That witch.' There was an accompanying sniff.

Sebby reported back to Art. This morning, both men were hoping that their worst fears were going to be proved wrong. Both were curiously embarrassed by their unofficial surveillance, which smacked of underhand practices and the accusation of spying on colleagues, so neither had uttered a word to anyone about their secretive intentions. Art's good wife, Sarah, would never forgive him if she heard that he had allowed a project like Leo's to take place inside his own company, right under his nose, and Sebby knew that Kate's response would be one of wilting disdain.

423

She trusted Leo. She admired him.

And she believed that Cheryl was mad.

Art felt, understandably, that instead of sitting out here like a spy in a schoolboy comic, he should have grasped the nettle and confronted Jennie, Alan and Leo. But, he convinced himself, there simply had not been the time between the discovery of the empty paint room last night, and the dreadful suspicion that something utterly disastrous might well take place some time today, some unscrupulous treachery engineered by professional people in his employ.

Naturally, between them they had discussed the easier option of warning the hospital management and the police, but to do that would have meant remaining in ignorance and maybe adding to the Higginses' exploitation by allowing this malicious business to continue longer.

Add to that the fact that the very last thing they wanted to do was alarm the authorities and bring more strife to the Higginses, should they be mistaken.

Speed is of the essence. If their suspicions are confirmed, then an immediate stop must be put to these grotesque proceedings.

The first sign that something is imminent comes from within the hospital: a high-pitched screech meets the approaching sirens somewhere in the warm air between.

'Hello,' says Art, turning down the radio. 'This should put the cat among the pigeons. Nobody in their right mind is going to pull some stunt in the middle of this.'

'You don't think this could be part of the stunt?'

'Not in a million years. No-one would go to these extremes.' And as if to confirm his words, five more fire engines siren to a halt, blue lights flashing. By now the gawping crowd has doubled, hoping to see leaping flames and patients being lowered from windows. No such luck. So far, not even a puff of smoke has reached the front of the building. 'No matter how deranged they are, they're not going to endanger lives.'

When Sebby stays silent, staring at the action, Art comes back quickly with, 'Well, are they? For God's sake, we might be dealing with hot-headed fools, but they're not in the league of driven fanatics.'

'Do you want to stay?' Sebby asks.

'Only for another five minutes. In view of this new development, I think we are wasting our time.'

And it's not until the sirens cease their caterwauling wails of alarm; it's not until an eerie silence descends upon the chaos, broken only by the sound of rushing water, the shouts of firemen, the murmuring crowd, that one strident voice pierces the excited morning.

'That's her! That's them, look, coming out of that door . . .'

'It's that Higgins woman. I said she was in there . . .'

'Hey! What's she up to?'

'She's flitting – that's bleeding what.'

The first remarks become even louder and more and more outrageous, until some of the crowd become uneasy and stand back in twos and threes as if in revulsion against persecution at such close quarters. Only for one fleeting moment do Art and Sebby get a quick picture of Cheryl and Barry on the steps – Cheryl, head down, Barry pulling her by the hand – before they descend as if handed down into the milling throng of watchers.

It is a breathless blur, and Leo has disappeared.
Where is he?

Chest heaving, shaking, frightened, never for one moment had Cheryl imagined that one small fire, which is probably out by now, would cause this amount of panic; this army of firefighters, this column of engines, this frenzied activity and this huge fascination.

Did Leo know this would happen?

She moans and covers her face with her hands. And how, in all this sickening confusion, had anyone spotted her and Barry, just two people out of the mass of patients and staff? They should have slipped through unnoticed, shouldn't they? It is as if these people have all been waiting for the star to arrive, and the fire itself is merely a sideshow to entertain an eager public.

The only individual face she manages to pick out of the scrum is the pale, slim, unshaven profile of the man she most fears. There he is, the stalker in denim, with a camera on his shoulder, two back in the trickle that starts to follow their stumbling retreat. The trickle soon turns into a flow of gesturing, shouting people, eager to get a sight of this most notorious of women, and it seems this river cannot be dammed by the few uniformed coppers who try.

'Thou shall not suffer a witch to live.'

There are so many women among them, voices noisy and profane, shouting threats. They jostle her, they give her a hard shove, but she feels nothing.

Growing hot across her face and throat, she breathes in quick, shallow gasps. She feels ugly and she feels a need to be uglier still, to look ugly enough to horrify and frighten them all.

Now Cheryl is running for her life, the pounding of her own feet are hammering out a beat in her head. Her T-shirt is wet and sticks to her back. Her own gasps of breath increase her fear. The stitch in her side hurts as if there's a dagger in her, but she knows she must run for ever if needs be – if she falls the crowd will have her. She knows that they are fleeing from something unbelievably horrible and strange. How could this have gone so wrong, when everything seemed to be succeeding? But Leo's plan had not included a get-out clause in case of failure. She won't let go of Barry's hand: even at the end she will cling to him for dear life. If she's going to die, she wants to be holding him. That hand is her only comfort.

As the pavements whizzing underneath dizzy her, as the lamp-posts and litter bins flash past her eyes, she can only think of that film she saw, the one that made her cry, when John Merrick, the elephant man, was hunted to the ground by a crowd as menacing as this one. In the end he'd been cornered, and all he could do was crouch down like a foetus.

This is the kind of chase she remembers from school playgrounds. She'd been scared then, too, really scared; she had sometimes wet her pants and had to go round in them damp all day. But this isn't a game, this is real. Her heart is pounding in terror. This is unfamiliar territory. Barry is as confused as she is: reeling and dodging, he hasn't a clue where he's going. They could end up against a brick wall, just like in the film. Perhaps, maybe, if she could think of the right thing to say, she could turn and face the crowd, the kind of thing that Jesus did, put up a hand and call a halt.

In the name of God!

Why did these people seem to hate her more than anyone else in the world?

She hasn't hurt them, or their families. She hasn't killed anyone. She hasn't stolen their money. What is this stealthy, steady force which seems intent on tracking her down, overtaking her, destroying her?

They daren't stop in shops to ask for help.

They daren't beg groups of strangers.

Oh, God – somebody – help us.

But as usual, when people call out in pain, the heavens stay silent.

And even if they did find a phone box, pushed inside and closed the door, they have no phone card, no money, and by the time they dialled the police the crowd would be upon them. No: all they can do is run and keep running until their legs, pumping up and down, are as regular and automatic as pistons. Their ears roar with the noise, deafening, hideous, stupefying, the noise of their own panic. They dare not even risk a quick glance over their shoulders. They know their pursuers, shrill, wild and savage, are still behind them, by the curses and threats, the ugly sounds and cries they can hear on the surface of their minds. It feels as though they are being hounded by all the people in the world and will never get free again. The crowd is a remorseless weight which leans on them slowly, steadily, mercilessly, and will soon crush them to pulp. But it's not Barry they're after – no, it has never been him – it is her, Cheryl, the fallen woman, the witch who must be punished.

But how?

What are they planning to do?

Search for her third nipple? Stick pins in her? Duck her? Burn her? Hang her? If she ever looks in the mirror again, perhaps Cheryl will find herself grotesquely altered, hag-like, humpbacked and shrivelled.

Barry is about to circle the front of the silver car which pulls over directly in front of them – just one more obstacle – until he recognizes the passenger who steps out quickly and holds open the door.

'Get in!' shouts Sebby. 'Now!'

'*You!*' Cheryl hisses in a frenzy of rage and hatred, so furiously angry she seems suddenly to have lost all her fear, but Sebby seizes her wrist in one hand and drags her towards the back door of the car. She regains her footing and staggers, and his voice turns sharp and stern. 'Get in, Cheryl!'

'This is a trick . . . a trap . . .'

But all Barry's weight pushes her from behind, and she's in the car with him on top of her, feeling as if her bones are about to break, the door closed and the engine roaring before the front runners can catch her.

Pandemonium breaks out.

Panting, chests heaving and as yet unable to speak coherently, Cheryl and Barry lie back against the luxurious white leather upholstery. The cool, fresh air inside is a balm after all that hostile heat. Neither of their unlikely rescuers seem concerned about anything more than getting them out of the area and speeding them somewhere safe.

It's good that they don't say anything. She wouldn't understand if they did.

Wherever Cheryl looks things are blurred; she might be underwater, so wavy are the outlines of people and streets and rooftops. She wears a fixed monkey grin of terror. Her ears ring steadily, cutting off outside noises, and after three convulsive gulps she bursts into a fit of coughing, spluttering and gasping as if her throat has been seared by acid, weeping and shuddering.

She leans against Barry and closes her eyes, but he is doubled over, breathing hard, his skin wet and shining.

TWENTY-NINE

The worm is slowly turning.

It really doesn't matter now how many fiends are after them; it doesn't matter if the police, the press, the public are all intent on tracking them down, because even if they did trace the Higginses to this fine country house in Surrey, they would never sneak their way in through the systems designed by security experts to keep marauders at bay. Five years ago this superior system was installed at the insistence of the insurance company responsible for the antiques and pictures inherited by Sarah, from her long line of aristocratic ancestors.

Another factor that reinforces their safety is the up-to-date legal position, knowledge of which came equally expensively by way of Sir Art Blennerhassset's London solicitors. The Higginses have not been charged, so far, with any criminal offence, although the accusation of arson, with pictures, has already been splashed across the tabloids. Manslaughter charges won't stick. Under the Mental Health Act, the order for Cheryl's section was only in force for three days – and those three days are up. She cannot be held against her will without a court application made by a panel of doctors and, due to the sensational nature of this case, when push comes to shove, there are few shrinks willing to put their reputations on the line.

If the police wish to question the couple, they are perfectly free to do so, but they must understand that the Higginses are now represented by the best defence briefs in the land, who will only agree to their being interviewed at the country home of Sir Art and Lady Blennerhasset, bearing in mind the dangerous consequences of moving them elsewhere while public opinion is so volatile.

Quite apart from all this, the Higginses are taking out an injunction on the good advice of their new top lawyers, to prevent any more unjustified rubbishing. All this is costing an arm and a leg, but the cat is out of the bag now, and Lady Sarah firmly believes that this is the least the Blennerhassets can do to compensate for the misery that has been inflicted upon this innocent family under the very nose of her husband.

Cath Higgins was torn when the car pulled up outside her formerly neat and tidy Harlow home. She wanted these children removed, of that there was no doubt in her mind: they had brought her precariously close to breakdown, but at the same time she felt unkindly sidelined by the attitude of her son.

'But where are you taking them? Don't I have a right to know? Why aren't they dealing with Cheryl? Are you telling me she's somewhere out there, free as a bird, and that these kiddies are going to be returned to that witch with no thought for their welfare?'

And, 'What am I supposed to say when the papers come hounding me and Bill – offering us money, money we could well do with, to tell them where you're hiding out?'

At least, during those last harrowing days, she and Bill had enjoyed being at the core of things, offering their views to all who would listen, posing primly for photographs, the mother and father of a young man who had been cruelly deceived and ill-used by a fallen woman gone mad. Now poor Cath was in danger of being thrust right out of the limelight, with no thought and no gratitude for the ordeal she and Bill had endured.

And what part had Barry played in the notorious escape of his lunatic wife? This was worrying. From what the papers were suggesting, he had caused that fire himself. Surely not? Surely Cheryl hadn't bewitched him again with her cunning and her devilish guile? Cath had warned him not to go near her . . . she knew a visit to that place would be the downfall of him. What was that man Leo doing, leading him on with such bad advice?

All she got from Barry was, 'They're coming with me. I am their father, they need to be in a safe, peaceful place away from all this attention.'

And all the while that snooty chauffeur stood by, granite-faced, and said nothing.

What was Cath going to tell people now when they asked her for the latest news? And by the looks of things – chauffeur, sumptuous car, Barry's new clothes, even Barry's attitude was curiously more confident – Barry and Cheryl seemed to have found themselves some influential backing. This Cath ought to know about. She could certainly do with some generous help to put her own house in order. A new carpet, new loose covers wouldn't come amiss. Or was she only there to help out in the bad times, to be discarded like an old rag when things turned more interesting? Huh. *Typical*.

Catherine Higgins sniffed.

After such a hopeful start, Barry had turned out to be a grave disappointment.

'I want you to tell me everything, Cher,' said Big Annie Watts from the sagging sofa of her shambolic home, the telephone resting on her stomach, her wayward sons God knows where, but at last her daughter was somewhere safe on the other end of a telephone line. 'I've been out of my wits with worry . . .'

'Mum, you wouldn't believe this house.' Cheryl sounded like somebody else, far from the poor broken thing to whom Annie had last spoken. There was such animation in her voice. 'You wouldn't believe our bedroom, and the kids have got a nursery. If only Cara was safe, if poor Donny wasn't dead, I could honestly say we could be happy, but the police still won't change their minds, and Art thinks that's because they are scared to be taken for fools again. Even Sebby believes us now, but it seems there's nothing anyone can do. At best, there's enquiries going on unofficially, but that's only because of the Blennerhassets' influence. I can't tell you, Mum, they've been so wonderful to us, like real friends, and we've met people, friends of theirs, who hated what was happening to us and we never knew . . . All through that time we really believed everyone was against us. They weren't.

434

And there's people still on our side even now. But the police just refuse to admit officially that Cara is still missing.'

Cheryl sounded so together, as if this discovery of sympathetic souls had helped her turn some important corner. 'I'm sure they'll find her, Cher,' said Annie. 'Nobody could hurt such a little baby.'

Even as she spoke, Annie knew she was talking rubbish. There's hundreds of people out there who would hurt a little baby and not turn a hair. Annie puffed hard on a cigarette and tried to change the subject.

'But when can I see you all, lovey?'

Once again Cheryl gave a positive answer, so unlike her of late. 'They think it's better if we just stay put and don't see anyone the press or the telly are likely to be watching. Even this phone line has been put in specially so there's no way of tracking us down. That's why you can't phone us back.'

'But I feel so helpless, my love.'

'We're all feeling helpless. Especially now we know that all through this nightmare they've been filming us – people we trusted, like Leo.'

'I never liked him.'

'And the two directors of *The Dark End*. Right from the time they heard that Cara had been kidnapped, they've followed us around with cameras and we've all been giving interviews to the project without knowing it. You. Cath and Bill. Me. Barry. We're all there on tape. I never realized there was a camera and microphone hidden in Leo's bag. He got all the morbid stuff he wanted. And it can't have taken him long to persuade his mate Zak Quinn to add some more excitement to the show . . .

probably with the help of the date-rape drug, Sebby says.'

'That snake in the grass . . .'

'No, Mum, he's not. He did believe Cara was dead, he did think I needed professional help. So did Kate. They really thought they were helping me, but ever since then he's been so kind, and done so much for us, it's unbelievable.'

'I'd never trust the bugger again. Or her.'

'Well, even she doesn't know where we are.' Cheryl paused for a moment, considering. 'Sebby seems very protective of her. It's funny, he says the fewer people who know the better, but it seems strange not to tell the person you live with. I couldn't keep that sort of secret from Barry. But maybe he thinks she will worry if she finds that he is so involved . . . His job, that kind of thing.'

'Well, he'll find it nigh on impossible to work with that bleeding crew again.'

'There's no fear of that. And Art didn't get the chance to sack them – that really pissed him off. They got what they wanted from Griffin; they ignored their employment contracts; they formed their own company months ago, and now they are all working together, with Leo. And Art reckons he can't touch them because we signed an open-ended agreement so that if Griffin wanted to do a follow-up series, we would go along with it.'

'But you didn't bleeding know they were doing it!'

'I know. Apparently that's covered. There's a clause, but it's rarely used . . .'

'It's bloody wicked.'

'That's just how it is.'

'So you're telling me these arseholes are free to sell this piece of shit and get it shown on TV?'

'That's why they did it. They knew Art wouldn't have it. They knew they would have to go it alone, but they reckoned it would be worth it. They put their careers on the line, so they must have been pretty sure. They even had cameras at the places where Art went with the ransom money. They knew all the details. They were at all the Griffin meetings. The police videos show it all. A red-headed man all in denim stood there like a tourist in the crowds taking pictures, while Art put the bag in position. He was following me, Mum. For days. I knew I was being followed in the end, and it was driving me mad.'

Annie gasped. Her chins wobbled angrily. 'The nerve of the bastards. Surely they can get them for *something*!'

'No. What they did was legal. And we just went along with it all, like puppets. Doing what Leo told us, starting the fire in the hospital, following him out like a couple of nerds, and all the while there were people in the crowd who were put there to start the shouting.'

'Can't you sue? If they show this bloody programme? There must be something you can do?'

'We've been into all that. The lawyers are still looking. But they would argue that it was all done in the public interest.'

Annie huffed. If she could get her hands on these wankers! 'Public interest, my arse.'

'It's when you start glamorizing people that things like this can happen,' said Cheryl, 'that's what Sebby says. It's when you start thinking they're better than you, and that's my fault, I've always done it. And I wanted them all to like me.' She stopped. Annie heard her daughter's voice break for the first time during the conversation. 'I was so pathetic. I can't believe I allowed myself and the kids to be used . . . and Barry. I was the perfect victim. They saw me coming a mile away. Never again. My God, I've learned my lesson. I'm going to need you now, Mum. I'm angry, really angry. And I hate them so much for what they did.'

'Good,' said Annie, 'I'm glad to hear it.'

At last she was in a position to make something happen.

Doreen Chandler and her daughter, Trudy, browse through the underwear rails at the Lakeside Marks & Spencer.

'But I need something to hold me in.'

'No you don't, Mum. You're not that bad.'

'Just to stop the bulge.' She pats it.

'I can't see any bulge.'

'That's because I'm dragging it in.'

'Do all your bra straps go grey?' asks Trudy, picking up a bargain pack and putting it down again, having noticed the navy and lime-green knickers. 'Even cotton ones?'

'Don't put them in the hot wash. That's what does it.'

Trudy shakes her head. 'God, some people are so thick. Look, someone's just gone and left that baby . . .'

Doreen looks round, and there, between the petticoats and the bodies, looking round brightly with a dummy in her mouth, sits a dark-haired baby in an otherwise empty trolley.

'The mother must be round here somewhere.'

'I know, but wouldn't you think, after all the dreadful things that have happened, that she'd have more nous than that?'

Doreen and Trudy, afraid to appear interfering, continue to finger the tempting silky wares before them. 'When would you wear a full petticoat?'

'Dunno.'

'I've never really known what bra size I am.'

'You should go and get measured,' says her mother vaguely.

'What?'

'You should go and get yourself properly measured.'

'No way. Not on your life.'

'She's still there – that baby.' And Doreen peers over the top of the elasticated all-in-ones. Slowly she edges towards the trolley, looking this way and that as she goes, afraid to be seen as a child abductor, the kind of sad woman who snatches babies. If Trudy hadn't been with her, she doubts if she would have done anything. 'She's very good,' she says, and then, to the baby, in a higher voice, 'You're very good, aren't you?'

The baby gurgles and fixes on her.

'Trudy, come here a minute.'

'What's up?'

'I think we ought to tell someone. She could have been abandoned for all we know. There must be a supervisor around somewhere. Where's that woman in red we saw trying to push account cards?'

'I dunno,' says Trudy nervously, looking round,

still loath to interfere. 'The mother'll probably be back in a minute.'

'And I'm going to give her a piece of my mind,' says Doreen firmly.

They wait another five minutes, circling the trolley, looking anxious.

'I don't care,' says Doreen finally. 'This baby's been on her own long enough.' Her voice moves up five notches. 'Haven't you, darling? You've been on your own long enough. Where's your mummy gone, eh?' As if the child could answer.

A supervisor is alerted, and the child is removed to the offices, where a great fuss is made of her and an announcement put over the store's tannoy system.

No response.

Still none.

And so it comes to pass that half an hour after Cara is spotted, the local police are called in.

Later that day, in the garden, Cara is in the family pram, a huge Silver Cross with multi-springing, Scarlett toddles around with the Blennerhassets' badly behaved pack of retrievers barking and screaming, and Victor is fishing the stream with an 'Art special' butterfly net. Barry draws Cheryl against him and, passing his hand over her head, he murmurs the most romantic words she has ever heard him utter: 'And I wanted to fight the world for your sake. It didn't work. Forgive me.'

He must have rehearsed that, she thinks, when she turns and holds him as tight as she can.

But forgive him for what?

He did the best he could.

She was the one who fucked up, not him.

At last they have a future, and one with more hope in it than ever seemed possible. With the help of so many new friends, most of them influential people, colleagues of Art and Sarah, Barry has been offered a job at a garden centre in Tring, just ten minutes from the house on which they intend to put in an offer, using Barry's ill-gotten twenty-five thousand as a deposit.

A new life.

A new start.

Everyone is of the opinion that Cara was returned because the search had been called off. Just one more perversity of fate.

'So if you had believed us, she'd still be missing now?'

'That's what they think,' Sebby said earlier, when they were all gathered round in Art's historic hall in hysterically happy anticipation of Cara's return. 'The people who had her realized they were onto a loser. Their demands would be ignored. The police were blaming you. They didn't have much alternative other than to give her up.'

'But they're still looking, they're still trying to find them?'

'Of course they are,' Art reassured her. 'And they're not likely to give up, not on such a hideous crime.' He smiled wryly. 'And especially after they made such a gaffe. There will be an investigation. They'll have to prove themselves now.'

When, at last, the car arrived bearing the missing baby, after Cara was put in her arms, Cheryl looked round expecting to have to share her joy, but she and Barry were quite alone for this most private moment. The welcoming party had melted away, leaving just the three of them to enjoy this special time.

No cameras.

No interviews.

No hidden lenses behind the panelling.

'She's perfect,' said Cheryl, through so many tears the child seemed to be sparkling with rainbows. 'They haven't hurt her, whoever they were. Thank God, thank God she's been well looked after.'

Now the only cloud on their brand-new horizon was the threat of a sensationalized, invasive and highly personal story of two people's descent into hell.

Well, they could live with that if they had to.

They were no longer the fools they were.

Far from it.

THIRTY

'More than five thousand Britons died because of the biblical edict, "Thou shalt not suffer a witch to live". And when persecution died away, around about 1750, some two hundred thousand supposed witches were tortured, burned or hanged in Western Europe.'

So begins the controversial documentary much heralded by the press.

It carries on in with all its dire warnings. 'These witch-hunts were little more than mass mania, initiated by the Church and kept going by the vested interests of professional witch-hunters. Confessions were extracted by means of thumbscrews, the rack and red-hot irons, and had little value as evidence.'

Seated in the drawing room of the Blennerhassets' luxurious home, the small audience is tense with anticipation. The narration sounds like Alan's voice – smooth, slightly effeminate – but it's hard to be sure. 'Despite dark stories of sorcery in high places, witchcraft, at least in England, was almost invariably the crime of the very poor.' This is a most extraordinary angle, when you bear in mind the culpability of its executors, but it's not unexpected, given the promotional publicity. 'By 1640, a supposed witch could be brought to trial by an anonymous, unsupported accusation, and it was extremely difficult for the accused to prove her innocence. Evidence for the defence was twisted and corrupted to suit the prosecution. The sentence was almost invariably death.'

The pictures portray a blasted heath, dank with a yellowy, poisonous atmosphere, one Shakespearean witch in all her shabby haggishness landing gracefully on a broomstick. Dramatic pictures. Suggestions of evil. Clever computer graphics. Even in the tense atmosphere of the room, Sir Art can recognize this.

It is four months since Cara was returned (no-one has yet been accused of the crime), and six weeks since the Higginses moved out from his protection. Almost immediately, news of the newly formed company, Marigold Films, had started to reach him in dribs and drabs. Great interest had been expressed throughout the tightly knit media world. No doubt the major backing for the enterprise had been provided by Leo Tarbuck's wife, Sophie, heiress to a supermarket fortune, but the company's credibility lay in the talent of its two young directors.

It was not in the interests of Griffin Productions to broadcast the facts of the split, and nobody else had inside knowledge. But it wasn't long before intriguing rumours spread about Marigold Films' latest project, which was hawked around London's commissioning editors for only two days before it was snatched for an unknown sum. And in spite of Art's most diligent efforts – he used all the connections he had – the lid was banged down so tightly on the secret even he could cast no light upon it.

That was until three weeks ago, when the first bits of blurb were released.

That was until the date for transmission was given to the media, and the critics began to applaud the film as 'wholly original'; 'a tale of darkest foreboding'; and 'a most fascinating insight into the shady underworld of docusoaps.'

'Not to be missed on any account.'

Art and Sarah were worried about the effect the film would have on the Higginses, who appeared to be settling incredibly well into their new life in Tring. They had the house they had always wanted. They were running a small car. Barry was working. But the fear everyone felt was that, given the slightest prompting, the feeding frenzy would start again. That the programme would fan the flames of that fanatical victimization which seemed to be dying a natural death since Cara was found, and the Higginses went to ground.

But the couple themselves, so much more secure, seemed strangely unconcerned. Cheryl in particular seemed to have found some new strength from somewhere. She was very close to her mother just now. They both insisted that, in retrospect, it had been their behaviour that allowed the victimization to happen. If, from the start, they had responded differently, the trap could not have been set. It was their need, their lack of self-worth, that made the possibility of manipulation so easy, and that, they were certain, could never happen again. But even so, Art and Sarah were concerned, and had invited

445

the family to watch the programme with them. Sebby insisted on being there too.

The title, *Witch, Witch*, puzzled them all. During the worst of the persecution, those words had often been thrown at Cheryl, as if there was some subconscious belief still lingering in the hearts and minds of even the most vacant members of the population. It was too incredible to believe that the Marigold team would embroider the myth that witches were alive and well; that Cheryl had indeed made a pact with Satan, could maim or kill her enemies, could ride to the sabbath on a broomstick or fornicate with the Devil. So what was their angle going to be, and how could they retain their integrity if their exploitation of the Higginses was revealed for what it was?

There is total silence in the Blennerhasset drawing room. The programme is also being watched intently by the Higginses' legal team, who will take it apart in their efforts to find some loophole they can use to their benefit. But the Marigold team must know this . . .

'For centuries, the Church and the State have persecuted vulnerable women, those who did not conform in their day, those who could not defend themselves. But today it's no longer Church or State who select their luckless victims. The Church has lost its power. The State has been dishonoured. The media have taken over their role smoothly and effectively, and can decide among its own who to raise and who to fell. Anything will do: sexual preferences, body and boob size, overspending, working, not working, ugly, single, mother or not. And this takeover, as much to placate the discontented masses as it ever was, can be shown in graphic detail tonight as we watch the way one woman in Britain, at the start of this brand-new millennium, was used and abused, tried and convicted, run to ground and finally burned at a virtual stake.'

There is no noise in the drawing room. Just a collective holding of breath.

'And our reporters managed to follow the truly harrowing experiences of nineteen-year-old Cheryl Higgins, from the time her baby daughter was kidnapped until the time she was run to earth . . .'

And now the film begins in earnest.

There is a preliminary run-through, using short scenes from *The Dark End*, as if anyone needed reminding, before the new material begins, at the darkest point of all, when Cheryl and Barry, silhouettes in a half-dark morning, were picked up at Paddington station, Cara missing, Donny dead.

'My God, I don't *believe* it, they were watching you both way back then,' Art splutters, dumbfounded. The sequence progresses with painful pictures of the Higginses' descent into the mire, with a commentary to match the tale of absolute woe. They are shown as they leave the court, as they leave the social services enquiry when Cheryl is ordered out of her flat. The cameras follow as they traipse round the streets, feebly searching for live-in work, zoom lenses working overtime, capturing their despair, even the movements of their lips.

'I didn't have a clue . . .' Cheryl gasps, too stunned to register the depths of this scandalous invasion.

And it seems that no attack by the public has

447

escaped the camera's eye. From every malicious catcall to the crowd scenes outside the court; from groups of people turning their backs to the angry attack at the Harold Wilson Building, when Barry moves out and leaves her.

Over the most sensational scenes, some of the daily headlines of the time are read. The results of several polls are announced, which the tabloids had conducted among their readers, deliberate policies to incite and grip any fading attention.

No, I do not think Cheryl Higgins should be allowed to keep her children. Eighty-nine per cent in favour.

Yes, I do think Barry ought to divorce her after her indecent display, her disloyalty. Seventy-six per cent agreed.

Lady Sarah shakes her head, stunned. 'So they are saying that *they* are the crusaders; that *they* did all this to prove a point, to rectify a wrong . . . ?'

'That's exactly what it looks like,' says Art, crossing the room in exasperation, noisily pouring a brandy. 'These sods are going to emerge as heroes.'

'So are Cheryl and Barry,' says his wife. 'That's one blessing, at any rate.'

'The legal team are going to come back and tell me there's only one villain here, and that's Griffin Productions,' mutters Art, morosely.

Sebby's silence goes unnoticed in this shocked atmosphere of disbelief, and nobody mentions that it's odd Kate is still not with him, but all the while the film is running, he is focused on a more sinister place.

For him, the real trouble started around the time the Higginses found refuge and began the slow process of recovery; around the time he should have, like them, been able to start experiencing some degree of relief. But Kate refused to understand his reticence to share his knowledge of the fugitives' whereabouts.

'But it's me . . . look, it's Kate, I live with you, remember? You can trust me, I am your lover, your friend . . .'

'I know that, I *know*, and it's not that I don't trust you, it's because the fewer people who know where they are the less likely they are to be disturbed.'

She came straight back at him. 'So are you suggesting I might blab?'

'Of course not, why would you? But this is such sensitive stuff, there's so much money at stake, so many people involved.'

'Like Leo?'

'Kate, I know you don't want to believe that . . .'

'He wanted us in with him, you know,' she told him casually.

Nothing surprised Sebby any more. 'You never said so. Nor did he.'

'Of course we didn't, because we both knew your wretchedly superior moral standards would blind you to reality.'

He turned on her then. '*Reality?* Really? And while we're on about reality, why were you so certain that Cara Higgins's records would not be at St Catherine's House?'

Kate hesitated, then looked straight at him. 'You told me.'

Sebby frowned. 'How's that?'

449

'The night we watched the videos. We were talking about poverty, remember, and you told me that the Higginses were surviving on eighty pounds sixty-five a week with housing benefit, hardship payments and twenty-four pounds child benefit. If they had really had three kids, they would have been claiming thirty-three pounds fifty benefit, and I couldn't understand why a family like that would miss out on any extra. There had to be a pretty good reason.'

Sebby looked at her blankly. She wasn't normally so au fait with the problems of the poor. 'You probably don't remember,' she said. 'It was ages ago, the last time we went to dinner with Mummy and Daddy, and we had that silly argument over who should be paid child benefit. I said I'd find out the facts, and I did. I probably told you at the time, but you didn't listen.'

Sebby said quietly, 'If we're going to be honest with each other at last, was it then that you went to Leo? He'd already approached you, hadn't he? He'd already told you he wanted me to come to Marigold with him, and given you some idea of what was going on?'

Kate looked down and pulled at each individual finger before deciding which angle to take. When she raised her head, her long hair fell back and her colour was high. 'Yes, I did go to Leo. I knew this information was important to the project, and he and Sarah and Jennie and Alan all felt we should use it to give the film yet another dimension, to make it that much stronger.'

Now Sebby was up and striding agitatedly about the room. 'But you led me to believe that Cheryl's baby didn't exist. You carried on about mental stress, abortion, cot death, and you even suggested they might have killed her. You sounded so caring and so positive, I went along with your bloody ideas and took them to the police. Christ!' He gritted his teeth, squeezed his eyes closed. He couldn't bear to look at her. 'You guessed what the consequences were likely to be, you knew the authorities were concerned over Cheryl's mental condition and you played on that, dragging me into the front line with you.'

'Damn you, Sebby. It's what you wanted to believe. I couldn't convince you of anything if you weren't open to the idea, that's why I knew you wouldn't join Leo, and that's why I went in instead.'

'So that's what happened.' Sebby's voice held no expression. He had always considered it odd that Kate had taken a job in a bank. She had been helping to set up Marigold Films. She was good at PR work, she was experienced with promotions and selling. She'd been coming home nights and lying. He said, 'They put Cheryl into a mental ward. They drugged her. They stripped her. They humiliated her and abused her. And you were perfectly happy with that, if it gave the project another dimension?'

'Shit, shit, why must you be so bloody high-minded?' Kate's voice was equally controlled. 'Don't you see where the future lies? It lies in challenging the tired old traditions. Television of the future must be forthright and brave. Don't you see that Griffin are old news, stuck in a rut, no new ideas, carrying on with the same boring formats?'

451

Sebby couldn't tolerate this. Kate was a ventriloquist's doll spouting Leo's words, the weight of all his fanaticism behind them. 'But there're humanitarian issues involved here, immoral practices, and the public's right to understand what sort of misery this voyeurism can cause.'

'Precisely,' Kate told him cuttingly. 'And that's what this project is all about.'

Sebby had not understood her then, and they ended the conversation there. But now he is watching the finished product, so brilliantly done, such a pioneering piece of work. And, reluctantly, he begins to see a great deal more even than that.

Cheryl squirms when she hears herself spilling everything out to Leo in the terrifying confines of that closed hospital ward. He has carefully edited out of the film all his questions, all his responses. It looks as if Cheryl is talking directly to the audience, with no prompter in sight. If these film-makers are brought to book, which Art thinks is unlikely, there is no way the TV regulators would be able to identify any one individual apart from the narrator who might or might not be Alan Beam. The interviews are done on the lines of a personal video, as if Cheryl and Barry have set it all up by themselves.

But as the film rolls on towards its terrifying conclusion – the chase through the streets outside St Hugh's, when both Cheryl and Barry had felt their lives were in danger – one thing is made glaringly obvious: they are the victims of the most appalling exploitation. As far as their personal lives are concerned, and their hopes for the future, nothing more positive could have been said. No-one is left in any doubt that a grave wrong has been done.

'Well I'm blowed. This is unbelievable,' is all Art can manage. 'These bastards are going to end up making the rules for everyone else!'

'If only they knew . . .' moans Sarah, weakly.

It has to be stopped, said the voice-over grimly, ending on a message aimed at elevating this documentary's motives in the eyes of the industry. 'Only a determined regulator can reintroduce the unfashionable public service broadcasting standards which might help commissioning editors limit the combined pressures of the ratings barons, and change the legislative framework within which factual production has been casualized, and news and current affairs slip ever further into the abyss.'

'What a scam. And it's worked. It is what they have always been after,' says Art. 'Power and influence. They have the resources, they don't need anything more, and this documentary is going to bring them nothing but admiration from the powers that be, for their sincerity and their integrity.'

The flat feels empty and cold without Kate. There was no way they could survive the split, and, heartbroken as he is, Sebby is coming to terms with the fact that they had never really been soulmates; that what they had could never have lasted.

Two weeks ago he had gone, on a whim, to Leo's house in Putney. Originally he had intended to ring the bell and confront his old colleague, to air some of his grievances, to get some questions answered.

He hadn't needed to ring the bell to realize that there was nobody home. The house was large and expensive, perfectly maintained, with a drive going in one gate and out the other. A Porsche was parked in front of the garage. Leo himself drove a Jeep. This young family lacked nothing, not in any material sense. In these circumstances it was, Sebby supposed, understandable that their aims might be different: for prestige, or power, or professional excellence. Leo had achieved excellence: the acclaim of his peers had come early for him.

'Looking for someone?' a gardener called, raking leaves from the neighbours' front lawn.

Sebby shook himself out of his reverie.

'I was going to call, but there's nobody home.'

The gnarled man looked this way and that, well aware of being thought indiscreet, but torn by the chance of a natter. 'Know them well?' He jerked his head towards the Tarbucks' house.

Sebby considered his answer. 'Not really. I thought I did, once.'

'Nobody talks around here, of course, so I can't be sure, but I'd say all was not well over there.'

'Really?' Sebby endeavoured to show polite interest.

The gardener closed one rheumy eye. 'She never speaks. They don't, round here. Hoity-toity, like. Of course, I saw her with them in the car, strapping them into their baby seats, and of course I assumed she had twins. Two little champions they were, one so dark, one so fair . . . and a pretty, blonde-haired au pair, or a nanny, properly trained most likely, to give her a hand. Then suddenly there was just one. The nanny left, and you don't like to talk about it, do you, what with those dreadful cot deaths and meningitis.'

454

Sebby drove home in his Morgan deep in thought.

He recalled a scene in the fifth-floor flat when they were making *The Dark End*. He vaguely remembered a sentence of Cheryl's, as she stood at the window before all this hell began. 'If I wanted to get away from it all, I know where I'd go.' Leo was with her at the time, and Sebby remembered him looking out, following her finger. Had she been pointing at the railway sidings? Sebby was busy with something else. It was just a desultory conversation. One of thousands. He hadn't taken much notice. He had forgotten all about it till now.

Leo must have guessed all along where the Higgins kids had been hidden.

It was then that he must have taken control.

That child had not been kidnapped for money, but for dramatic effect.

And Donny? How had Leo got around Donny?

Not hard to fathom. Both he and Sebby knew Donny well by the time the filming was finished. It was Annie who had confided to them Donny's problem with booze all that time ago. 'But she's as right as rain now,' she'd said, or something like that. 'Doesn't touch a drop.'

How much pressure would it have taken from the charming, the handsome, the charismatic Leo, with a couple of bottles of Gordon's in tow, to persuade Donny to allow him into the wrecked train, to come to trust him, to believe what he said and to confide in him the day and the manner in which the children were to be returned? So if Leo told her he'd come for Cara, and Cheryl wasn't around to ask, how long would Donny hold out? Would it take one

455

visit, two, or three? The bag lady couldn't know she was part of a plot. She hadn't asked any questions. She'd just been pathetically grateful to be trusted with the Higginses' babies, to be around kiddies again and to have a safe roof over her head, however briefly.

But no, no – Leo would never resort to murder. Alan? Jennie? No. That could never have been part of the scheme. Although some insurance must have been taken against Donny's explanations when Cara was found missing . . .

After a short investigation, the old woman's death was put down to natural causes. But were they natural?

Like hell they were.

How could they have been, when everything else was so carefully planned?

Dear God. Had Kate known this when, every morning, she'd set out for that house in Putney? To play the au pair? The nanny?

And what was Sebby to do with this knowledge, half guessed at, half proven? At the end of the day the harm had been mended, apart from the murder of poor Donny, and there was never proof of that. Since then the train had been destroyed and all the evidence with it.

The last visit he had made to Tring came vividly to his mind. A struggling couple with little hope, three kids with not much of a future, had transformed themselves so magically it was almost a fairy tale. The last thing they needed was more publicity. Maybe they would consider their journey to hell and back well worth the trauma, now that they had all they'd ever desired. How much easier for the

Higginses to achieve satisfaction, than for someone so talented and driven as Leo and his new unscrupulous partners.

If Sebby went to the law with his unfounded suspicions, what would be the result? Would even Art believe his story? Sebby doubted he would.

Donny was dead – but she had been ill. Her heart could have carried her off at any time, easy to make a blow on the head seem like the fall of a grossly inebriated woman, and the likes of Leo would not consider her life to be worth that much. In his eyes, she would be dispensable. The Higginses were happy. Their children were safe. The victimization had turned into caring. Exploitative docusoaps and media houndings were, for the moment, toned down as a nation licked its wounds for shame.

Kate had gone, but she would have gone anyway. In time he would get over that; they say people do. Sebby's career with Griffin was promising, and if Marigold had not broken away and needed a convenient lever to pull, how many more victims would there have been? How many more lives destroyed for the entertainment of a vacuous public?

Round and round went his thoughts.

But Donny was dead. *Maybe murdered.*

Marigold Films should be brought to justice.

But Sebby should not have tortured himself; he should have concentrated on the business of getting over his broken heart. There were other people, apart from him, who had a good idea of what was what, and forces far more able to wreak the kind of revenge Sebby felt was all they deserved.

And worse . . . much worse.

As soon as the child is born, the mother or the midwife carries it out of the room on the pretext of warming it, raises it up and offers it to the Prince of Devils. And this is done by the kitchen fire.

The Malleus Maleficarum

'Xilka, Xilka, Besa, Besa.'

She calls the names of the demons eleven times, then pauses.

There is now a solemn period of waiting.

It's an autumn day of blue mists and distant bonfires of leaves. Silver trunks and ashy branches stretch into the sky like straining arms, with all the power of upthrusting life.

In the kitchen of the cottage in Tring, with its brown oblong of vegetable garden directly outside the back door, and its straight spiral of smoke crayoning from the chimney, two women sit at the table. It looks as if they might be making models for some church fête, or gingerbread men for the PTA fair, or corn dollies for the Christmas appeal. Two children are having their lunchtime naps, one wrapped in a pram in the garden, the other upstairs in her little bed with the gingham curtains drawn. The three-year-old is at nursery school, doing finger-painting and singing.

The man of the house is at work.

Their concentration is so intense that the young woman with the fierce sprout of hair has her tongue halfway to her nose while the large, dishevelled one with the fag drops ash indiscriminately onto the clean kitchen floor.

'It worked on Dill, that evil gossip who came to my door with odious tales about Fred. It worked on

458

the Smiths – that Marge and the others. On the hard shoulder of the M25 the lorry ran straight into them. Their heads were sliced off, they said. And on countless other occasions that you never heard about.'

Chilled, the younger woman stays silent, thinking, and then: 'But when Dill died I got hurt, too, and Fred went to prison and then disappeared.'

'You were meant to have been in bed. Didn't I tell you to stay in bed that night when Dill came babysitting? What d'you think I bloody well felt like when I knew what had happened to you? D'you wonder I lost my mind? And that bugger Fred got his just desserts.'

Incense burns in the background, but the odour will soon turn noxious.

'Bagahi laca Bachable.'

There are no shortages of demons to call on – these delinquents of the astral dark exist in their millions.

The daughter asks no more questions. She has lived with her mother's diabolical leanings all her life. She accepts them; they were passed down by a grandmother she never knew, but this is the first time she has summoned malefic forces to work on her own behalf.

This is the first time she's felt such pure hatred.

They work within the confines of a crude green pentagram, drawn in washable felt pen on the kitchen table. The five dolls look like an acupuncturist's display, with the pins stuck carefully in selected places; the heart, the brain, one eye, the genitals and the stomach. On the table there are two men and three women, the differences grotesquely

459

emphasized in wax, the substance from which the effigies are made.

'*Effusus labor. Defuncta vita.*'

Neither woman doubts that one day this magic will work on Jennie St Hill, Alan Beam, Leo and Sophie Tarbuck and Kate Spearman, Sebby's former girlfriend.

None of the five has a future.

But how, and in what maleficent way this is done, remains for the demons themselves to decide.

THE END

VEIL OF DARKNESS
by Gillian White

'He, who killed me with his smile, had to die . . .'

It was only a book, after all. A fat, old-fashioned looking book, tucked away in the library of the Cornish hotel where Kirsty was hiding from her husband and all the violence and horror of her old life. The book seemed to offer her an escape, a new start, a different life for her and her children. For surely Kirsty deserved better – money, a decent house, security and friendship – and the book suddenly, miraculously, promised to give her all these things.

But slowly, insidiously, things started to go horribly wrong. The book seemed to take over her life and those of her friends, influencing their behaviour and leading them down bleak and terrible roads. Kirsty's past began to catch up with her, until she had to confront the worst of her fears in the darkness.

'Simply spine-tingling'
Woman and Home

0 552 14564 5

UNHALLOWED GROUND
by Gillian White

Once upon a time, it is said, the devil walked in this valley . . .

On a snowbound February day, when Georgina first saw Furze Pen – a picturesque thatched cottage in a peaceful valley on Dartmoor – she thought it just the place to recover from the recent nightmare of her job in London. True, the cottage was cold and isolated, and the neighbours weird and strangely threatening. But Georgie needed to work out her life, and Furze Pen seemed as good a place as any – until the terrors started.

There was the lone watcher on the hill – at first she thought it was a scarecrow, so stark and still was it standing – and then the unexplained fire, with the remains of a child's doll smouldering in the ashes. But there had never been a child at Furze Pen. And as the seasons turned and snow once again blocked off the remote valley, the frightening began in earnest . . .

In this truly terrifying novel Gillian White has created a world of dark secrets which hide behind the seemingly ordinary lives of her characters. It is a world which is scarier than most people's worst imaginings.

'A complex psychological thriller which will fire your imagination and fuel your fears'
Western Morning News

0 552 14563 7

THE SLEEPER
by Gillian White

*'Peace on earth and mercy mild . . .' But there's no mercy
here. There is no telling how long the body has been down
in the cellar, rising as the water level rises . . .*

In a wintry seaside resort an old woman goes missing
from her residential hotel for the elderly, the
inappropriately named Happy Haven. And in a remote
farmhouse not far away, the Moon family gathers
for Christmas. Clover Moon, the farmer's wife,
looks forward to the forthcoming festivities with quiet
desperation and dread.

What terrible secrets from the past are coming back to
haunt them? As gales and blizzards cut off the power
and maroon the Christmas gathering, where did the
body come from which is swept into the farmhouse
cellar by the rising flood water? In Gillian White's dark
and disturbing world, where nothing is quite as it seems,
a mystery from the past becomes a terrifying ordeal in
the present, and a traditional family Christmas turns
into nightmare.

'A dark, disturbing tale'
Sunday Telegraph

'A first-rate psychological thriller – perceptive, witty and
full of suspense'
Good Housekeeping

0 552 14561 0

PAYBACK TIME!

As good as Barbara Vine or your money back!

If you don't agree, we'll refund your money!

Simply return your copy of this book with your till receipt, stating where and when you bought it and the reasons for your dissatisfaction, and we will give you your money back.